Faithful Unto Death

Enjoy the mystery!

Becky Thacker

Faithful Unto Death

A NOVEL, BASED ON TRUE EVENTS

Becky Thacker

THE UNIVERSITY OF MICHIGAN PRESS

ANN ARBOR

Published in the United States of America by
The University of Michigan Press
Manufactured in the United States of America
♾ Printed on acid-free paper

2014   2013   2012   2011   4   3   2   1

A CIP catalog record for this book is available from the British Library.

Library of Congress Cataloging-in-Publication Data

Thacker, Becky.
    Faithful unto death : a novel, based on true events / Becky
Thacker.
        p.   cm.
    ISBN 978-0-472-11788-8 (cloth : acid-free paper) — ISBN 978-0-
472-03469-7 (pbk. : acid-free paper) — ISBN 978-0-472-02764-4 (e-book)
        1. Murder—Investigation—Fiction.   2. Missionaries—Fiction.
3. Small cities—Fiction.   4. Benzonia (Mich.)—Fiction.
5. Michigan—History—1837—Fiction.   I. Title.
PS3620.H326F35   2011
813'.6—dc22   2011003382

Acknowledgments

This book required the assistance of several folks who cheerfully gave their time to the project. I want to thank Debbie Eckhout, former director of the Benzonia Historical Society, who shared her insights about the culture of the town of Benzonia. Thanks to the Benzonia Library and its staff; they provided a wealth of old newspapers and other documents.

Special appreciation to Charlotte Parfitt for her many recollections and theories about the main players in this drama, and to Francis and Ingrid Thacker, who shared our interest and enthusiasm, drove us around the Betsy County area, and helped us find things we'd never have discovered on our own.

My father, Thomas Thacker, and my uncle Gale Thacker also contributed their recollections, as did my grandparents Ralph and Harriet Thacker, now deceased. These many relatives never failed to surprise us with the wealth of detail they'd been quietly carrying around with them; it was as though they were just waiting for someone to ask.

Additional thanks to my brother Brian Thacker, who takes such joy in ferreting out obscure facts, names, and dates.

Much, much, much appreciation to Ellen McCarthy of the University of Michigan Press for giving *Faithful* a fighting chance, and to Eric Miller of Miller Trade Books for believing in it and helping things along.

Many thanks also to the University of Michigan Press editorial staff for their many suggestions, corrections, and helpful comments.

Thanks to Dr. Judith Richter, specialist in toxicology, for her information about arsenic and its effects on the human body.

And of course thanks to Harriet Clare, my nearest and dearest, who can spot a typo quicker than anybody I know and who shares my pleasure in plundering the secrets of the dictionary.

Contents

Prologue

SHORTLY AFTER 4:30, Ralph, aged seventeen, awoke in the dark. The sun would not rise for another four hours. He slid silently from beneath the heavy layers of worn quilts and shivered into his overalls, then pulled another pair of wool socks over the thinner ones he'd worn to sleep in. He decided not to use the pot beneath the bed; though Lottie would see to it later, he'd be out in the barn in a few minutes. He went downstairs to the kitchen where his sister Lottie, now fifteen years old, had stirred up the fire. She had warmed some water in a basin for his hasty ablutions and set a plate of cookies on the table. He nodded to her, slid two handfuls of the cookies into the pockets of his overalls, and stepped into his father's oversized boots.

He pulled a thick cap, knitted by his mother, down as far as it would go on his head, put on a heavily patched and stained jacket, and then, after some thought, wrapped a knitted scarf around his neck and lower face so that only his eyes showed. A year ago he'd have put on the scarf only under duress and pulled it down as soon as he was out of sight from the house, but now he felt his mother would have wanted him to wear it. Skin froze quickly in the sixteen-degree Michigan winter air, especially when the wind blew hard across the frozen lake. He put on the woolen mittens knitted by his sister, and added two leather mitts without thumbs.

Thus dressed as well as their means allowed against the wind, Ralph stepped outside carrying the broken-off spade they kept inside the kitchen door during the winter. He fought his way through the drifts, some of them navel-deep, in the dark, toward the barn he knew to be awaiting him.

The day was starting out well; the door swung open on the first hard shove. Other days, the door was either half buried in snowdrifts or frozen into a sill of ice that required several minutes' chipping with the edge of the shovel to clear it away.

Ralph stepped into the warm smells of hay, grain, and cow flatulence. Leaning the spade against the now-closed door, he stripped off the leather mitts and shoved them inside the pocket of his overalls, careful not to damage the cookies. They were the only breakfast he'd have until morning chores were done.

He fished one of the last "Lucifer matches" out of the box on the windowsill. An eerie light came through that small, dirty-paned window with its load of cobwebs and fly husks; sometimes Ralph wondered whether the snow didn't produce its own light at night. He lit the lantern that hung from a bent nail on one of the low rafters and turned the knob to set the flame at its lowest. Lamp oil was costly. He began to fork hay through the trap door, down to the level where the two family cows stood mooing with impatience.

As each cow munched on her carefully allotted ration of hay, Ralph warmed his hands under his armpits. This was an oft-debated topic among Northern dairy farmers, but Ralph believed that cows hated icy hands on their teats. He remembered, with a small smile, the many times his older brother, Roy, had been kicked, Ralph believed, because he was in too much of a hurry to warm his hands properly. Made a mess of the milking and refused to even help with the chickens, yup, that was Roy, all right.

"You always want the quick and easy way," their father would admonish, as Roy cursed and got to his feet, righting the milk pail and, often as not, knocking a chunk of cow manure into the pail from his shirtsleeve. Still, his father rarely sounded angry with Roy as he sometimes did with Ralph, but then Roy was the oldest and according to his mother, being the oldest made him especially blessed by God.

Ralph leaned his head against the cow's warm side and began pulling, one-two, one-two, the thin metallic splashing sounds rising to his ears from the bucket. He reflected, not for the first time, that God wasn't entirely angry and vengeful as their mother had so often claimed. God had had the mercy to wait until Ralph was old enough to do a man's work before He'd allowed Mother to be poisoned with arsenic, and Father to be arrested for her murder.

Death in the North Woods

CHARLOTTE LAY GASPING in the small upstairs room. It felt to her that the warm close air was a hot woolen blanket that would not go through the tiny opening that was her throat.

"I thought we might ask Ruth to help," Nelia had tentatively suggested to her husband. Ruth was an elderly Ojibwa healer who had attended the missionary church once to try to discover the magic that lay behind the strength of the white people, and then stayed because she found them so entertaining.

She, like others in her community, was intrigued by these whites who had come to the area, so inept in so many ways but also so single-minded. One could envision them following their demons to the four points of the earth if the demon captured their imaginations, as the one they called "God" seemed to have done.

And their arrogance! Ruth had to admire it. Nothing they did seemed to have any connection with reality, but this never deterred them in their quest to subjugate everything in their paths. Their ceremonies, too, intrigued her, devoid as they were of color, pattern, or the cycles of the earth, but accompanied by grotesque grimaces and bizarre utterances.

"Why do you say," Ruth asked David Spencer one Sunday, "'take, eat, for this is my body' and then eat only pieces of bread? Is your god so easily fooled that you can say you eat its flesh without bothering to hunt and kill it?"

"I've explained many times," answered David wearily. "It's something called 'symbolism.' The Bible is full of it. It's like saying that something like, well, like that cardinal," and he pointed to the small crimson bird that perched nearby and watched them warily, turning its tiny crowned head this way and that. "I might say 'there was a single ruby shining in that tree.' Of course it's not really a ruby, but anyone who had ever seen a cardinal would know what I intended."

Ruth understood symbolism very well, and indeed carried many

3

symbolic articles in her medicine pouch; she nodded, though she hadn't the slightest idea what a "ruby" was. Still, she knew the whites were fooling themselves in the matter of this "communion" ceremony. "When our ancestors used to eat the hearts of a respected enemy or drink the blood of an especially strong bear they had stalked and killed," she explained, "they did it so that the courage or strength of the adversary would enter into them. It seems an especially weak sort of ceremony when you want the spirits of this god to enter you, but only eat the lumps of dry bread and drink some juice you squeezed from berries."

David shook his head sadly, despairing of ever teaching wisdom to these foolish heathens. He would have been more discouraged had he realized how similar Ruth's feelings were to his own.

Now he felt some annoyance at his wife's suggestion that they turn to this old backsliding woman's nostrums for help with their sick child. "Ruth," replied David with some asperity, "is an illiterate savage. How could she help? And you know what the Bible says about witches."

"Are you suggesting we go to her house and murder her?" responded Cornelia tartly.

"Well, no," admitted David. "But you understand the sentiment. If American medicines aren't good enough, then, well, it's just the Lord's will if Charlotte takes a little longer to mend," he concluded, aware even as he said it how lame and futile this sounded.

Neither realized the extent of Ruth's pharmacy, which contained such items as a willow bark extraction that would have eased the child's aches and fever, a form of horseradish that, in a poultice, loosened mucus in bronchial tubes, blackberry leaves and bark whose tea, sweetened with wild honey, soothed raspy throats, and many other helpful remedies.

David sighed and sat down, leaving Nelia to return to the bedside of their wheezing, choking child, armed with nothing more than a bottle of sweetened alcoholic "patent medicine" and a basin of cool water.

Nelia sat in the dim light of the lantern and read, pausing now and then to exchange the warm damp cloths on Charlotte's forehead for cool ones from the basin. Charlotte, dazed with the fever and the tonic her teetotaling parents had dosed her with, watched her mother's shadow on the drawn curtain, the shadow now a sharp silhouette as she read, then a looming shapeless mass whenever she leaned toward Charlotte. Charlotte drifted between vague terror and vague peacefulness.

Outside, the night noises were gradually eclipsed by a whining mumble. To Charlotte, it gave a monster's voice to the monster's shape on the curtain, and her eyes grew wide. To Nelia, it was "another of those poor souls from the Indian village," staggering home from an evening's drinking at the tiny trading post down the road that doubled as a saloon in the evenings. As the sound grew louder, Cornelia frowned. In a muzzy voice, the words floated up toward the window, "Rock of aaages, cleft for me . . ." Charlotte relaxed. It was only an Indian, after all—maybe more than one. She suppressed a wheezy giggle; the Indians sounded so funny. Still, she realized with a three-year-old's perceptiveness that her mother disapproved of the Indian's funny song.

The curtain moved; Charlotte heard the sound of a small rock tapping against the window. She frowned slightly, trying to understand how a rock outside the window could move the curtain indoors. Her mother fell across her; there was an odd messiness below her breast. As Cornelia sprawled across the bed, Charlotte could see a small round red spot on her dress in the back. She realized that there was blood spattered across the coverlet, and suddenly the blockage in her throat was gone. Charlotte screamed and screamed again, until her father threw open the door. "Nelia! Lord have mercy!" he shouted and rushed to the bed, where his dead wife lay across his shrieking youngest child.

Behind him, five-year-old Anna wrung her hands, not understanding what had happened but terrified by the panic in her father's voice. She whimpered, "Please, dear Jesus, make my mama be all right and I promise I'll never disobey again. I'll let Lottie wear my hair ribbon whenever she wants, please, please." If God heard these promises, He was unmoved.

The funeral for Cornelia Leonard Spencer was small. In the hot wind that blew from the prairie into the woods that provided the missionary homes, David stood holding the year-old Brainard in his arms, and Anna stood beside him, holding his coat in one hand and Charlotte's hand in the other, the children's small faces pale and bewildered. A few families of whites attended, and one of the men read some scriptures from the Bible.

Ruth stood hidden in the protection of a willow thicket and silently watched the box being buried. She worried about the children, left to the care of that stubborn, intense man.

The other remnants of her tribe, many of them members of David's small missionary church, stayed away because of a sensitivity that David

5

would never have recognized or understood. So did the store and tavern keeper, because it was only too evident where the drunken sniper had gotten the liquor that inspired his spontaneous act.

David Spencer, in a letter to Cornelia's mother, concluded, "I have no murmuring or repining thoughts; the terrible stroke has touched the apple of my eye and torn from me the dear companion of my life, her upon whom I leaned for counsel, my interpreter, the instructor of our mission boys, and the faithful mother of our children. Toward the wretched murderers I have no feelings but those of pity and compassion. I bless God that another saint has gotten safe home to glory; and that the blow has fallen upon one of the very few in this region who we have reason to believe are prepared as yet for aft exchange of worlds.

"In regard to the future, I have no plans; nor do I conjecture what designs the Lord may have in respect to me and mine. Until brother Barnard returns, my duty is plain: to stay on the ground, secure the crop, and take care of the mission premises. Then if the season not be too far advanced, it is possible that it may be thought best to go back to the State this fall with my two eldest children, and I know of no one other than yourself with whom I would be willing to entrust them. They are with me yet; but the babe is being cared for by friends in the village."

He returned with Mr. Kittson (a merchant), with several hundred carts of furs and skins, bringing the Indian woman who had been entrusted with the care of the young babe. The two little girls were seated with the nurse in the cart, while for infant Brainard, a swing was suspended from the high axle under the body of the cart. It was carried all the way across the plains to St. Paul, a distance of about four hundred miles.

Though the Spencer tribe moved away soon after, Cornelia was never completely forgotten by the small settlement, which later became part of North Dakota. Nelia's headstone stood with several others in an area of the Walhalla cemetery, later marked as "Walhalla Martyrs." The site remains today in a little tree-shaded corner of the cemetery, surrounded by a low concrete wall.

Benzonia: A Congregationalist Utopia

MICHIGANDERS WILL DEMONSTRATE locations on the Lower Peninsula by holding up a hand, fingers together, thumb extended to the right. At the tip of the little finger lies the region known as Sleeping

Bear Dunes. Much of the surrounding coastline is still diverse in plant and animal life; while the wolves, cougars, and elk have departed, the deer, raccoons, beavers, and squirrels remain.

Some shoreline is rocky, much as the glaciers left it. Other sections are sandy, and some have developed into natural harbors where a river once broke the border of the lake and then widened. Some of these were completely sealed off by the moving sand and gravel of the shoreline and became small inland lakes, ponds, and swamps.

Early Europeans came in long heavy canoes. In their own language these latter called themselves "voyageurs," and they traded with the Indians for furs. The voyageurs followed the shoreline, collecting furs and moving on, but they made note of particularly rich areas to visit on their future circuits of the lake. South of Sleeping Bear, the shoreline resembled, to them, the sawed-off beak of a bird of prey, so they named the area Point Aux-bec-Sies, meaning "sawed beak point" or "blunt beak point," later to be called Betsy Point.

The voyageurs were followed, in the early 1800s, by settlers, this time over land, from the south and east. As they did elsewhere on the continent, the white-skinned people managed, over time, to infiltrate and to appropriate the land that had formerly been shared by the red-skinned people. In 1850 the state of Michigan revised its constitution, declaring its people "of Indian descent" to be citizens.

The land, which the "new citizens" were allowed to stay on for five years, until they could be relocated, was appropriated by the government to confer on its citizens of European descent as it wished. The government generously offered to relocate its original citizens to land beyond the Mississippi River. Disgusted by the paucity of the land offered to them (much of it had been inhabited by distant relatives who'd fled West during a particularly virulent war; they became the colorful "Plains Indians"), most of the remnants of the People of the Three Fires relocated themselves to Canada, there to write their own stories.

The grantees of large tracts of the now-vacated land settled in and began to shape the land to suit their own needs and wants. Large areas of huge trees, maple, elm, oak, wild cherry, basswood, pine, and ash, all began to fall to the ax and saw, some of the trees to be floated and railroaded to southern parts of the state for building homes and furniture, much of it to be burned for industrial purposes such as the smelting of metals, and some to build homes for the settlers, who proceeded to raise livestock, plant some crops, and clear more land.

South of Sleeping Bear Dunes and inland from Betsy Point is tiny Crystal Lake, fed by springs and runoff from melting winter snows. It is bordered to the south by the unassuming Betsie River. Land between Crystal Lake and the river, inland from the town of Frankfort, was granted by the U.S. government to a small group of families that called themselves Congregationalists, so they could start a college.

This group of settlers established a colony that they intended to be modeled after that of the Congregationalists at Oberlin, Ohio. Their principles included temperance, antislavery, and opportunities for education for all, regardless of sex, color, or station in life. They had a high regard for hard work and self-improvement. They named the tiny town Benzonia.

The land grants allowed Charles Bailey, his family, and four other families to settle, build their houses, and establish Grand Traverse College. The college began modestly enough with thirteen students, who attended classes in Mrs. Carrier's house.

Like other land grantees, it disturbed these pious folk not a whit to be the recipients of stolen property. To their credit, at least they began their endeavor with good intentions; the offspring of the families that settled in Northern Michigan had nowhere to go in pursuit of higher learning unless it was to leave the area entirely. Furthermore, any young persons, black, red, or white, male or female, were welcome to come and partake of knowledge as long as they promised to abide by the community's requirements of chastity, temperance, and certain other selected characteristics of Christianity, and were willing to work to pay their way.

David Brainard Spencer, reft of his young wife in the Minnesota territories, keenly felt the need for a new wife, not only to care for his three young children but also because the Bible told him that every man should have a helpmeet. With the assistance of his former mentor in Oberlin, he was soon supplied with the necessary article and married Elvira Ferry. The re-formed Spencer family came to Benzonia to help continue the noble work of educating the next generation of hardworking Christians.

"A Little Dolly"

THAT THE SPENCERS' ARRIVAL at Benzonia caused a stir among the villagers wasn't surprising. The town was so tiny that any addition of five breathing bodies was enough to inspire a round of welcoming dinners, hymn-sings, and a picnic at which young Brainard became ill from too many bread-and-butter pickles.

Anna and Charlotte were more cautious than Brainard about testing the waters, and both shrank from entering, for their first time, the room where Sunday school was held for the girls. The teacher led them to the front of the room. "These are your new classmates, Anna and Charlotte Spencer. Mr. Spencer comes to Benzonia as our new postmaster. I hope you'll be good to them and make them feel at home." The children nodded in unison, their heads bobbing like marionettes; after the briefest glance Anna and Charlotte kept their eyes stolidly on the toes of their best shoes. As class ended, they hurried to join their father and stepmother in the makeshift chapel for the two-hour service.

Charlotte was cooed and exclaimed over by many of the women and a few of the men. "Cunning!" was the pronouncement, and "Why, she's a little dolly." The crowd of little girls shyly clustered around her, causing Charlotte to shrink back and clutch Anna's hand more tightly.

"The elder, too, is a fine, good girl." Elvira sometimes wearied of the attentions so often paid to timid, dainty Charlotte to the neglect of good, plain Anna. Anna paid no heed to the fluttering little girls around them. Her brown pigtails swung forward against her lowered face as she whispered reassurance to Charlotte. "They're just being friendly, Lottie, they don't mean any harm."

Brainard reluctantly parted from his new friends and trailed after his family into the church.

"ANNA, I DECLARE!" exclaimed an exasperated Elvira. "If you bring Charlotte home early from school one more time, I shall have to take a switch to both of you!"

"We had to come home," earnestly explained Anna. "Charlotte was feeling peckish, and Teacher said she didn't know what to do with her. So I said I'd take care of her." Charlotte nodded miserably, eyes cast down.

"Well, you're here now. Put Charlotte up in bed and read to her for a while. Then you may come down and shell these peas for me. Here, take this pot upstairs along with you; I just rinsed them out a while ago and they're still damp." Grumbling, Elvira turned back to her mending.

"CHARLOTTE, DEAR, YOU KNOW I like to play with you more than I do with anyone else. You're my only sister, and we'll always be the best friends in the world. You know that, don't you?"

"Are you all right, Anna? Why are you talking this way? Of course I'm your sister and we're friends."

"I just don't want your feelings to be hurt when I tell you that I want to play with some other girls sometimes. Susie Carr was quite put out when I refused to stay behind after school this afternoon. Honestly, Charlotte, must I walk home with you every afternoon?"

Stunned, Charlotte stared at her. Her lower lip began to quiver. "I thought you liked me best, Anna, you always say that you like me best," she whispered.

Torn between impatience and pity, Anna bit her lip. "Of course I like you best, but we needn't be the only friends each of us has. You could play with Rosa sometimes, you know, the girl with the pigtails tied in loops. She looks like she might be congenial, or perhaps the younger Piper girl." Charlotte continued to stare at her.

"Charlotte! Are you even listening to me? Why do you stare so?"

"Oh yes, I'm listening. You don't want to play with your own sister. Well, just never you mind, Anna Spencer, I'll go find someone else to play with, see if I don't!"

"MAY I PLAY TOO? I'll hold one end of the rope the whole time, if you want." Ruthie Hawthorne turned, surprised, to behold Charlotte Spencer. The jump rope caught on her ankle.

"I thought you were afraid to play with us. Now look, you made me miss," snapped Ruthie. "And I was nearly to 'Red Hot Pepper,' too."

"I'm sorry," said Charlotte humbly. Mattie Bailey, glad to relinquish her end, proffered the knotted rope handle to Charlotte. "I'm after Ruthie, then!" The game began again.

"You can take a turn now, Charlotte," said Ruthie when it became obvious that Charlotte had patiently turned the rope far beyond a fair share of time.

"No, that's all right," said Charlotte quickly. "Truly. I like to turn." Ruthie shrugged.

"That's fine," said Mattie, who hated the tedium of turning the rope. "She can turn if she wants."

"But it's not fair," objected Ruthie. "Go ahead, Charlotte. You can jump now."

Charlotte hung back, then, with some urging, walked to the side of the turning rope. After one or two false starts, she ran in and began to jump. Silently she jumped, one, two, three hops. "Why, this isn't so hard," she exulted to herself, then remembered that when the other girls had jumped, they had recited some piece of poetry. What was it they were saying? Something about "Mabel, Mabel set the table," how did that go? Nine, ten hops, and all the other girls are looking at me . . .

Nimbly she skipped outside of the turning rope and held out her hand to Mattie's end of the rope. "I don't mind turning. Remember, in Galatians it says, 'Bear one another's burdens, and so fulfill the law of Christ.'"

Mattie rolled her eyes at Ruthie, but she handed the rope to Charlotte.

"OH, MAMA, MUST I?" Constance Piper, soon to be nine years old, was helping her mother plan her birthday party.

"I don't see why you don't want to invite that darling little Charlotte. She's more close to your age than her sister, and yet I see Anna is on your list and Charlotte is not. Have you and she quarreled?"

Constance sighed, overwhelmed with the impossible task of explaining the unexplainable to her mother. Adults seemed so blind at times!

"No, Mama, we haven't quarreled, exactly. She's just, well, she's so everlastingly timid, but she gives out to be holy about it. One day, me and Ruthie Hawthorne and Mattie Bailey were . . ."

"Suppose you say, 'Ruthie Hawthorne, Mattie Bailey, and I'? It is better grammar."

"Yes'm. Well, anyway, we were going to take our shoes off and wade in that little stream by the lake, and Charlotte, well, she made out like it was a sin to do that." Constance finished up triumphantly, "And all the time she was just afraid of crayfish pinching her toes!"

"Did she tell you that?"

"No'm. She never did. She just made us feel like we were doing something we oughtn't, but you never minded if we waded in the stream, Mama."

"Perhaps Charlotte Spencer's father is more strict with his children than your papa and I." Then, more firmly, "I think we must have little Charlotte come to the party. It wouldn't be very friendly of you, not to."

"But Mama . . ."

"Perhaps you'd prefer to have no party at all." Constance knew that tone of voice brooked no arguments. Charlotte was added to the list.

"ANNA, WHY DO THE GIRLS like you and they don't like me?"

"What do you mean? I'm sure they like you. I've seen you play with Ruthie, Mattie, and Constance at different times."

"Yes, they do, but I don't think they like me. They look at each other like this," and Charlotte rolled her eyes exaggeratedly. "And sometimes they mimic what I say in a mincing way, like this," and then, in a falsetto, "'Judge not lest ye be judged.'"

"They're mimicking you with Bible verses? I'm not quite sure I understand."

"Well, when I say something to them out of the Bible, they say that thing to each other in a mean, ugly, sing-songy way. As though I shouldn't be quoting scripture."

"Well, do the other girls often quote scripture to one another?"

"Not nearly as often as they ought," declared Charlotte firmly.

"I think that might be the problem. Children expect grown people to quote scripture, but they don't often say it among themselves."

"We do. Anyway, we used to," said Charlotte reproachfully. "It was our best game."

Anna refrained from commenting that "scripture battles," the contest to see who could complete the most verses correctly, was Charlotte's favorite game and not Anna's. Brainard often outstripped them both, though he never suggested the game himself. They usually played it because Charlotte sulked and wouldn't play if they wanted another parlor game.

"Perhaps it's best not to do that with your friends. 'Render unto Caesar,' you know."

"But they're not Caesar, they're just mortal girls."

"Nevertheless, I think they might find it a touch condescending when a girl their own age presumes to preach to them."

"I don't feel I was preaching," said Charlotte, somewhat hurt.

"That may be how it seems to them. Perhaps you should try being a little more, well, like just another mortal girl. If they are a little mischievous, just join in the fun."

"Be sinful?"

"Well, no, don't be sinful or naughty; just take part with their harmless little doings and pranks. Your conscience will tell you what you may do."

"Well then, I'll do just that," announced Charlotte with an air of decision that tickled Anna.

"Good for you," she encouraged her sister.

"DASN'T DARE!"

"I do, too!"

Charlotte caught her lower lip in her teeth. She could feel, rather than hear, the edges of her pinafore move against her dress as her heart raced in terror. Maybe going uninvited into Mrs. Bailey's parlor wasn't exactly a sin, but it felt like one. She paused in the doorway, glanced back at Rosa.

"You mustn't watch me! Watch the door!" she hissed. The whisper, faint to Rosa, seemed to Charlotte to echo through the hallway.

One step, then another, across the turkey carpet. On the mantle, a china clock ticked busily. Charlotte had heard about this clock. "Porcelain, from Bavaria, with hand-painted pink roses picked out in genuine gold," Elvira had intoned reverently. "It came all the way from a dealer in Chicago in its own padded crate."

It had roman numerals on its face. Charlotte stuck her tongue out at the smug clock face, and then looked around. On the cherry wood table next to a forbidding horsehair sofa ("Is that a davenport?" she wondered, then, "What is a chaise? How can a carriage and a sofa both be a chaise?") lay a family Bible, more florid in cover than the Spencers' Bible, ("and edged in real gold," she could hear Elvira's voice again), and some tracts. There! Take one of those! That would prove she had done it.

Her trembling hand reached toward the top tract on the pile. "Look at what is before your eyes. If any one is confident that he is Christ's, so are we," read the large print at the top of the folded, flimsy sheet.

She clutched that one, scattering the others across the tabletop. There! What was that sound from the passageway? The board floor creaked again.

"Hurry up!" hissed Rosa. Every one of Charlotte's muscles seemed to lock. Her very tongue ached, so stiffly was it pressed against the roof of her mouth. Wasn't there a passage about "May his tongue cleave to the roof of his mouth"? What was it? Why, when she wanted so badly, needed so badly to replace the tracts in their exact spot on the table ("Why are you just standing there, foolish wicked girl? Run!" screamed her brain, which seemed to have developed several voices, "My name is Legion . . ."), why was she just standing here?

"She's coming!" hissed Rosa. "I'm going to run out the back door!" And, more urgently now, "Charlotte!" The sound of rapid steps down the passageway lent meaning to her words.

Psalm 137! That was it, "By the waters of Babylon, there we sat down, yea we wept." And, "If I ever forget you, oh Jerusalem, may my tongue cleave . . ." Yes! That was the very one!

Deft again, her hands neatly stacked the remaining tracts. She thrust the top one down the top of her pinafore, dashed to the door.

Mrs. Bailey opened her front door and paused, frowning slightly. Didn't that sound like the kitchen door had banged shut? She shook her head. "Be hearing mysterious footsteps in the fog next," she muttered.

Behind the hydrangea, two small girls clung together, their giggles like tiny, breathless screams. After a moment of fearing she would wet her drawers, Charlotte became able to turn and run down the path, Rosa close on her heels.

CHARLOTTE TOOK A DEEP BREATH, feeling the hot blood-taste in the back of her throat again. Her belly clenched; yellow bile dribbled into the ceramic pot. She sighed, reached down, careful not to overbalance and tumble out of bed, and set the pot back onto the floor. Charlotte lay back onto the pillow, warm in the comfortable feeling that her stomach must now let her rest for another hour or two.

Two more outbursts of vomiting later, Elvira came in carrying a tray. "I've brought you some nice scotch broth. Will you be able to keep it down, do you think?"

Charlotte opened her eyes drowsily. "Thank you, Elvira. I'll try to eat a little. Might I have some toast later?"

"Let us see how you do with the broth, first. My, I hope your sister and brother don't catch this. Remember, back when you all were small and came down with the measles one right after the other? I thought I'd never get a moment's rest."

Silence followed this; Charlotte had pushed the bolster behind her pillow as Elvira chattered along, and now sat quietly waiting for Elvira to set the tray down.

"I'll just give you this and get back to shelling those beans, shall I?"

"Thank you, Elvira."

Elvira went back downstairs and returned to her chores. Five minutes later the sound of retching echoed down the stairway. She sighed and continued picking over the basin of beans in her lap.

That Charlotte! One moment she seemed as fragile and dainty (and holy!) as a china angel, and the next minute she controlled the house with her demands. Recently, she seemed to overlay these traits with a harum-scarum daring, challenging her other little girlfriends with fool-hardy pointless dares. Anna was a joy and a pleasure to have around, and a good thing it was, with that other one on her hands, thought Elvira, plinking a discolored bean into the bowl for rejects with more vehemence than was necessary. She felt ashamed for a moment. Charlotte was only a little girl who had lost her mother early, and it was Elvira's job to teach and lead by example. She sighed again and shook her head, then stood up to put the beans on the stove.

"ROSA AND CHARLOTTE, I can't think what possessed you girls. Whose idea was it, to run over and knock on the boy's outhouse door? The very idea!"

Rosa twitched her eyes toward Charlotte and then looked back at her shoes.

"Very well, then, if neither of you will admit to it, you may both stay here until I have finished grading these papers. Then I expect you to both tell your mothers and fathers why it is you are late."

"We're sorry, Mrs. Carr."

ROSA'S MOTHER, after spanking her daughter, sought an immediate interview with Mrs. Carr. "I'm sure my Rosa wouldn't have thought of such a thing on her own. She has always been a very docile child, but every time she and that little Charlotte Spencer play together, some sort of dickens ensues."

"That surprises me. She appears so timid and demure when I've seen her. Little Charlotte, I mean. I know that her health is delicate; Mrs. Spencer has explained that she misses so much school time because of her attacks."

"I don't wish to speak uncharitably of anyone, especially not a child, but I wonder if I oughtn't to forbid Rosa her company when un-supervised."

"That seems a bit extreme, certainly, for a child so young?"

Rosa's mother sighed. "I suppose you're right. Rosa will simply have to practice greater self-control when in her company." She turned to Rosa. "If I let you continue to play with Charlotte Spencer, do you think you can resist her temptations?"

"Truly, Mama, sometimes I think Charlotte is two different girls in the same body. Some days she will seem afraid of her own shadow, and then she is very holy and preaching to the rest of us. We just feel so aggravated with her sometimes. Then, not a day later, she's so wild and unrestrained that I simply get caught up in her ideas."

"Even when you know that her ideas are naughty ones?"

Rosa looked ashamed. "Especially then, Mama. She makes them sound so daring and exciting that one would feel cowardly to refuse."

"Then I shan't forbid you the company of Charlotte; I have decided that this is harsh, especially since you two are of an age and such great friends. Suppose my girl tries harder, in the future, to look to her conscience before she embarks on these adventures."

"Yes, Mama."

"ANNA, RUN UPSTAIRS and see why Charlotte hasn't come down to breakfast yet. She mustn't be late again today; Mrs. Carr will wonder what sort of household I'm running when your sister is constantly late for school." Brainard had finished his mush and dashed out the door, his books done up in a strap. Elvira clattered his bowl and spoon into the basin.

Anna returned. "She says she can't go to school today, Elvira, she feels dauncy again."

"Dauncy? What in the world does she mean by that?" Exasperation rang in Elvira's voice. "You just take yourself back upstairs and tell her I want her down here in five minutes, or I'll know the reason why. What was that you said? Come back here, young woman, and repeat what you just said!"

"I only said that you know what Charlotte will do, if you make her go to school. She'll start to make throwing-up motions and Mrs. Carr will just send her back home. And likely there'll be a mess to clean up. You know how she is."

Elvira sighed gustily. "So I must interrupt myself every hour and go up to wait on her all day, with all that I have to do." Anna stood irresolutely in the passageway, eyes on Elvira. "Oh, go along and get to school. You are right, of course you are right. I'll take her up some mush later."

Anna left for school without another word.

As the Twig Is Bent

TRAVERSE CITY, 1860

DUST SPURTED UP from Henry's bare feet as he tried to match strides with his father.

"Papa, why are we going to help Mr. McNair mend his chicken coop? I thought you said he was a mean old—"

"Hush, Henry," John Thacker tried to look stern. "I shouldn't have said that about poor old Mr. McNair and you shouldn't have been listening."

"But it was funny how you said it," giggled Henry, remembering it. "You said he was so tight he squeaked when he walked."

"When I said that, I didn't realize how he was ailing. Mr. McNair can't get his crop in unless we all help out, and in the meantime his wife can't keep losing hens to that fox."

"Can we find that old fox and shoot it?"

"Let's fix that chicken coop first."

At least one day every couple of weeks, John Thacker would walk or drive to the aid of a neighbor who was ailing, who'd run short of hired help, who'd had everything break down at once. His own farmstead was as prosperous as industry could make it; John didn't see why his own duties should keep him from "doing a turn for the fellow down the road."

TRAVERSE CITY, JULY 1861

HENRY, NOW EIGHT YEARS OLD and too big to cry, tightened his lip to stop its quivering. Too big to call his father "Papa" too, he thought, so he thrust his hand out and said shakily, "Goodbye, Father. I'll do all the chores until you come back."

John Thacker still felt foolish in his crisp new Union blues. Everything seemed off-kilter to him, and his own son's speech sounded odd and stilted. "Henry feels as at sea about all this as I do," he decided. John, a peaceful farmer, had never gone to war before. His son had never seen his father go to war before. Gravely, he took the small sturdy hand and gave it a manly shake.

"I know you will, Henry. You're a good worker and a good son," and here he had to stop and take a breath. "And I know you'll make us all proud."

THOUGH ALVIN, the somewhat simple hired man, handled the plowing and other heavy labor, Henry performed his own chores conscientiously for the next four years.

Now and then, a neighbor would answer a knock at the door to greet a young boy. The boy would have his father's toolbox in his hand and would say, "Afternoon, Mrs. Atkinson. I hear you're needing someone to help mend your pasture fence, and I was just happening by . . ."

Sunday-School Teacher

ANNA, FIFTEEN AND mature-looking in her long navy blue poplin suit, burst through the door. Her cheeks were flushed a lively pink, and her dark eyes shone.

"Elvira! Can you guess!"

"Anna! You nearly scared the life out of me! Now sit down here and catch your breath. What in the world is it?"

"You're looking at the new teacher of the Wednesday-morning Little Friends Bible class!"

"Oh, Anna, how wonderful! You've studied so hard; nobody deserves the position more than you do. Your father will be especially proud."

"Charlotte! You'll be the second person to know, after Elvira. I got the position!"

"The Bible class? Truly? Oh, I am so pleased for you!" Charlotte threw her arms around her sister and gave her an extravagant hug. "This just makes me determined to study harder than ever, so I can follow in my big sister's footsteps."

"Oh, you have no need to follow in my footsteps. You'll do great things in your own way, I'm sure."

"Perhaps I shall. But this is your triumph. We must have a special reading tonight, to celebrate. I'll go right now and pick out the verses for it, shall I?"

"Suppose you let your father decide on the readings, Charlotte?" Charlotte stopped, her hand on the knob, her face wooden. Elvira could have bitten her tongue once the words were out. Charlotte clearly meant well by her sister; she always did. Why did that always result in the attentions being trained on Charlotte instead?

"Of course I will, Elvira, if you think that's best," said Charlotte.

The Hired Boy

"MR. SPENCER, this is John Thacker, the fellow I spoke of the other day. His boy William thinks he'd like to partake of higher education, and needs a place to board. John, I'd like to introduce you to David Spencer. He and his good wife Elvira have kindly offered to open their home to a young man of good character."

"That's good of you, Mr. Spencer. My boy, Henry we call him, is a real fine young man, hard worker, and I think you'll like him."

David smiled. "I'm sure we shall manage with the young man, ah, Henry or William, did you say? No matter, we shall make him welcome. I have a son who is just beginning at the college this year as well. Brainard is studying for the ministry. Henry shall room with our Brainard. Bring him along any time in the last week of August, and we'll see that he gets settled in."

"We'll still be haying that week," mused John, "but I expect we can spare him that Saturday."

"Your Henry will be in good hands at the Spencers'," confided Horace Burr after David had taken his leave. "Come of missionary stock. The older Mr. Spencer was a Harvard man, and David Spencer ministered to the Indians in Minnesota for a time before they moved here. He has two daughters who teach at the Sunday school, nice young ladies. Anna's very popular with the older ladies, always willing to lend a helping hand. Charlotte's the younger of the two." He looked as though he'd begun to say more, John noted, but then didn't. "I'm not sure if young Brainard's as likely to follow in the Spencer ministerial footsteps as his father assumes, but he's well liked among the younger fellows. Elvira Spencer sets a very good table, I've found."

WILLIAM HENRY STOOD on the doorstep of the Spencer house, uncomfortably aware of the rivulets of sweat running down his sides, soaking his best shirt under the arms. His feet were encased in his good boots, worn but newly polished, heavy and hot for an August afternoon. His Sunday straw hat had a new band to it, his trousers were neatly pressed, but Henry felt in his heart that he looked like a bumpkin as he stood in his heavy boots, the worn carpetbag's handle sticky in his grasp.

Several hours ago, with what imaginings had he packed this bag: He was the scion of landed gentry, packing silk shirts and ties into a slim leather valise, preparing to depart for University on the afternoon train. He sat at the head of the Spencer table toying with a glass of something sinful and red, mesmerizing the young ladies Spencer with his urbane wit and cleverness. In these glorious envisionings, the ministerial

Brainard, effete and villainly, had looked on gloomily from his place at the foot of the table, next to the kitchen maid.

The reality, of course, was that he, William Henry Thacker, had ridden into town on the back of the Steeles' farm wagon and then walked the dusty road south to the Spencer house. His father would have been only too happy to bring him, but his stepmother made a point to occupy John Thacker's weekends with visits to her widely spread kinfolk around the Traverse City area. Henry tried not to be bitter about this.

His "slim leather valise" was actually a carpet satchel containing four shirts, two of flannel, two of cotton, a clean pair of overalls, some well-worn underclothes and much-darned socks, a snaggle-toothed comb, a Testament that had belonged to his grandmother, and a notebook with a cover of battered cardboard. Four bits jingled in his pocket.

The reality was that he, William Henry, was to receive "room, board, and washing" with the Spencers in exchange for performing whatever chores Brainard now performed by himself. Likely he'd be the one sitting at the lower end of the table, if indeed he'd be allowed to sit at that table with the family at all.

The further reality was that Squire William Henry was developing a blister on the big toe of his right foot, caused by friction between his sweaty foot and a poorly aligned patch of darning.

He sighed and knocked again on the door. Brainard—it had to be Brainard, Henry knew, not effete and villainly at all, but a perfectly ordinary fellow—Brainard leaned around the corner of the house and yelled, somewhat inelegantly, Henry thought, "Here! What're you banging on the front door for, on a Saturday afternoon? Around to the back!" His head disappeared around the corner again. Henry, ears red, picked up his bag and followed.

Elvira Spencer, hair limp with steam and heat, was supervising the canning of several bushels of green beans. She looked up wearily at the youth who presented himself. "I don't have time to show you to your room," she said flatly, and Henry's ears glowed yet more brightly. In the inferno of the kitchen nobody noticed. "Brainard, show him where to put his things, and then you can show him around the place. He can start by bringing in some more wood for the fire." The budding university grandee followed Brainard up to the room he was to share with the son of the house, to change into his overalls.

The sun had begun to set when the family gathered at the kitchen table to dine on yet more of those green beans, now enlivened with boiled new potatoes. By the time David Spencer had concluded a lengthy and all-inclusive blessing and everyone had sat with much scraping of chairs against the bare wood floor, Henry had begun to feel more like himself. Clad in his accustomed overalls and sun-bleached cotton shirt, feet freed from the confinement of boots, he was comfortably aware that he had contributed more than his expected share of labor.

The condescending looks from the Misses Spencer had softened to nods of appreciation as he untiringly brought in armload after armload of stove wood throughout the afternoon, pausing to feed the fire every time the rolling boil in the great boilers began to die back to a simmer. As the last jar was wiped and set on the board to cool, he continued working. He brought in enough wood to fill the entire wood box and then went, unasked, to the barn, to feed and haul water for the livestock.

As he strode back toward the house, he was joined by Charlotte as she returned from shutting the hens into the henhouse for the night. They walked side by side in a silence that was not uncomfortable, a fact that surprised him; Charlie Burr had already informed him that Charlotte was known about town as "the pretty one."

That appellation, however, had been applied by young men who had never spent a hot August afternoon in the kitchen with her as she dripped sweat from the end of her nose and was unable to wipe it away, consumed as she was by the need to wrestle another bucket of water to the stove.

"—In Jesus' name we pray, amen," concluded David Spencer. Henry raised his head but made no move toward the bowls in the center of the table, instead waiting until Elvira, seated at the end nearest the stove, had served herself and passed the bowl to him with an approving nod. "I'm glad to see that you were raised in a mannerly home," she said to Henry.

Brainard paused in loading his own plate with potatoes and stared briefly, then, shrugging, went on shoveling. Elvira continued, "We rise somewhat early on Sunday. We feel it unseemly to rush through morning chores and prayers so as to arrive at church on time. I trust Brainard will see that you are awakened in time."

"Waking up won't be a problem for me," responded Henry, assaying a small joke. "Staying awake through some of those windy sermons has always been a bigger problem." Silence fell in the kitchen. Hands holding forks wavered; the forks sank back to plates again. Lips thinned disapprovingly. Henry looked from face to face, his smile fading. Brainard looked down. The sisters stared at him, Henry thought, "as though I'd spoken the D-word." "Mr. Spencer," Elvira said stiffly, "has often assisted Dr. Waters in selecting material for his sermons."

"I'm sorry, ma'am," said Henry meekly. "Of course I didn't mean those sermons . . ." forks again rose ". . . particularly," he finished. Anna's mouth twitched. Charlotte pressed her napkin to her mouth and coughed.

The dinner continued, and gradually Henry's ears ceased glowing at the tips. After the family finished their berries and cream, everyone bowed their heads for another blessing. The men retired to the cooler porch to fan themselves, while the women washed up and scraped the leavings into a pail for the chickens.

Anna, in the room she shared with Charlotte, sat on the bed and unbuttoned her dress. "He seems like a nice young man, don't you think?"

Charlotte paused in unpinning her hair. "Nice enough, I suppose, but somewhat frivolous, didn't you think?"

"Oh, maybe he felt nervous. Well, no matter, if he doesn't suit Father, we'll only see him during mealtimes and at prayers, and he'll be gone at the end of the term."

At the end of this very long day, Henry and Brainard retired to their still-hot room. "You put your washing in this bag here," mumbled Brainard. "Basin and jug are there, soap's gotta last us until next Friday. You want the inside or the outside? Don't snore, do you?"

Henry shook his head, and, at Brainard's look of impatience, added, "Outside, I guess." Of course he and Brainard were expected to live in the same room, sharing the double bed, the wash basin, the dingy cake of soap, bristling with tiny whisker shavings. Henry had never thought of himself as "fastidious"; he'd have scoffed at the idea as somehow effeminate. Still, he resolved to purchase his own bar of soap as soon as he was able. As it was a Saturday night, though, he did enjoy the luxury of dropping his once-worn underclothes and shirt into the wash bag with Brainard's dirty clothes, knowing that Monday was washday.

Henry awoke shortly after the first birds began to mutter drowsily to each other. He lurched up, reached over, and gave Brainard's shoulder a shake. "Whuzzit? Wha?" mumbled Brainard, and he burrowed more deeply into his pillow. "Wake up, Brainard, we've overslept!" hissed Henry urgently. "We're supposed to get up early today, it's Sunday, remember? It's nearly sunrise!"

Brainard shook his head blearily, pushing himself up on one elbow. "It's dark out, you muggins," he grumbled. "We don't get up for another couple of hours." He squeezed his eyes shut, then squinted at Henry in the half light of predawn. "Did you think we had to plow a couple of acres before Sabbath prayers or something?" Shaking his head, he turned over and was immediately asleep again.

Henry, wide awake, pulled on his overalls and tiptoed downstairs. Going barefoot across the dewy grass, he breathed deeply in the cool morning air before going into the barn to pitch some hay down to the sleepy and astonished city cows that were unaccustomed to breakfasting before dawn.

SCHOOL BEGAN ON Monday. The school, then called Grand Traverse College, educated the young people who desired to advance beyond the few years of one-room school then available in rural communities for those who lived close enough to walk or ride to Benzonia.

"I'm not rightly sure what I plan to study for. Just now all I know much about is farming. I'm not sure that I'm smart enough to be a teacher or holy enough to be a minister. And sick folks make me fidgety, so I wouldn't be much hand as a doctor," Henry told the headmaster frankly. "Maybe I'll become postmaster like Mr. Spencer, or even be a selectman."

"Suppose you start out in General Studies," suggested the headmaster gently, amused by the young man's ambitions. Henry therefore enrolled in math, science, and history, as well as practicing such niceties as perfecting a good, legible script and learning to sing in tune at morning chapel.

He was fortunately possessed of a pleasant light tenor and was accustomed, as were most young people of his time, to community singing in school, in Sunday school, and at church services. Now, however, the singing was done "in parts," sometimes with written scores in which the sections intertwined, the notes rubbing against each other in seemingly promiscuous confusion.

A Student of the Fairer Sex

HENRY RETURNED HOME that first afternoon proudly carrying his three "new" (secondhand) textbooks. He paused, thunderstruck, in his walk around to the back of the dooryard. There were the results of Monday's washing, displayed for all to see. His simple faded three-button cotton undershorts and his shirts, fluttering lewdly on the clothes-line near the underpinnings of the women, gave him a complicated inward writhe. Benzonia women, apparently, wore a lot of lacings, petticoats, stockings, and other fussy things under their outer garments, even in the hottest part of the summer.

Living closely with women was no novelty to Henry; though his own mother had died when he was young, John Thacker had remarried not long after that. Henry had been too young to notice or think about what women wore at the time, and his stepmother had come from a family more modest, evidently, than the Spencers.

Henry could imagine his Germanic stepmother pursing her mouth prior to saying, "I see no need for the rest of the town to know what the Thackers wear next to their skins. Nor, for that matter, for any of the Thackers to study what the other Thackers wear next to their skins." The more intimate laundry on her lines had been discreetly walled behind the sheets and towels.

In all his imaginings about living in proximity to the Spencer daughters, somehow he'd not imagined this sort of intimacy, and there it hung, there they hung, where anyone who stopped by might see them. Did he want to know this much about what the Spencers were wearing, right now, against their skin?

"What ails you, Henry? You've just pecked at your supper this evening," frowned David.

"Maybe his first day of school upset his stomach," Brainard suggested.

"Don't be indelicate at table, please, Brainard. Henry, are you ailing? You may be excused if you are."

"Nothing, sir. Just preoccupied, maybe." He kept his eyes on his plate and tried helplessly to not imagine which of the sisters was now wearing one of those pink cotton garments like he'd seen dancing on the line.

He escaped as soon as he decently could, and carried his books out back. He sat under the elm tree and tried to focus on his lessons.

THE DAYS AND WEEKS, then months, had fallen into a pattern of work and study for Henry. Up with the sun, and as the days grew shorter, up before the sun, he forked hay to the two milk cows and to Arabelle, the brindle heifer, and forked manure into barrows that he wheeled to the pile outside. He milked the cows, carried the milk to the springhouse or into the house depending on need, rinsed and wiped the pails and strainers, and let the cows out of the barn to graze for the day. He cut wood and carried armloads of it into the kitchen and, as the weather cooled, into the parlor, where a small cast-iron stove did its best to heat the rest of the house.

Then he washed, changed into clean clothes, and left for school. Brainard, whose studies at the college led him toward studies for the ministry, usually left home well before Henry returned to their room to change.

Henry lay on his stomach near Charles and Tom on the grassy area under the oaks along West Field. They were supposed, by their chemistry instructor, to be quizzing one another on the elements.

"Honestly, fellows, I think they live in a different world from men. They seem to work alongside of us, but they don't talk the same when we're around as when we're not," insisted Henry to a scoffing Charles.

It was true; the Spencer women seemed to exist in a sphere apart from the men of the household, treading a limited circuit from the kitchen to the hen yard, around the rooms of the house, to the yard and garden, and rarely into the town except for Sunday school or church functions or to the general store. Two Saturdays a month they would exchange eggs, butter, produce, and sometimes even cash for the staples they needed.

Elvira, nearing fifty years of age, was already a faded woman whose meager store of energy went into growing, preserving, preparing, and serving food, washing and mending clothes, and praying. With two grown stepdaughters to "help out," she was considered a woman as well-off as any and better off than most.

Anna, a grave and stately figure despite her youth, assisted her stepmother in her many tasks. Silently she worked and prayed through her days and prepared elaborate lesson plans for the Sunday-school classes she taught, singing in the ten-person church choir as her only form of recreation.

Charlotte, "the pretty one," was now nineteen; her features were generally more round than Anna's, and her high cheekbones and slightly tilted eyes gave her a slightly exotic look. Anna vaguely recalled that her mother had these same eyes, and David Spencer tended to treat Charlotte with a tender regard missing from his other dealings with women.

"I don't see that ladies have it so hard, nice ladies, that is," argued Charlie. "Man must toil unto the end of his span, after all. A young lady can just marry a man of prosperity and have hired help, and sit on a cushion and embroider all day."

"There's that in what you say, Charlie. When I look at my own step-mother, it doesn't seem like she does so much, just spends her days driving 'round visiting her kin, but then I have to stop and think. Who cooked the supper that's on the table every evening? I surely didn't. Unless they're rich or stay old maids, and teach school or something, they all have to do the same jobs."

"Jobs!" Tom jeered at the very idea. "Jobs? Sitting on the front porch gabbing with a bunch of other old ladies, shelling the peas, or sitting by the fire of an evening sipping tea," here Tom stuck out his little finger mincingly, "and moaning about having to darn all those big heavy socks."

"In general, I think ladies everywhere do the same tasks, just some make more of a muchness about it than others," insisted Henry. This was true of the ladies of his acquaintance, anyway. They had to marry and produce and then mind their young children, keeping them from wandering unattended into the outhouse to ignobly drown, an occurrence he'd heard of more than once, or climbing on the pigpen fence and falling into the pen to be trampled and partially eaten. The tiny creatures had to be fed and kept clean until they were old enough to do it for themselves or be turned over to an older sister who would see to it.

The ladies had to prepare the meals and clean up afterward, and keep the house as clean as circumstances and health demanded. They also manufactured much of the family's clothing and cared for all of its cleaning, mending, folding, and putting away.

All of the women in Henry's limited experience also produced at least some of the family's food, tending kitchen gardens, fruit trees, some chickens, and sometimes ducks and geese. Even in the town, most women seemed to have a small plot of land to care for, and most kitchens simmered and steamed during the summer months as whatever was in season was pickled, stewed, jellied, candied, and put up in jars.

His attempts to explain this to his friends brought more heated denial. "Well, maybe some of the poorer farmers' wives in the country need to do all that, but look at the ladies right here in town. Mrs. Case hardly needs to lift her little finger, she has the girls that board there doing all the chores, peeling the potatoes and scrubbing the pots."

"Well, that's as may be, but Mrs. Spencer always looks tired, and most times so do the young ladies Spencer."

"It's true!" he insisted against a chorus of hoots. "Anna's up as early as Mrs. Spencer, and her hands are always red and sore looking from one messy job or another. And even so she's always as neat as a pin, and so's her sister and Mrs. Spencer, and so's the house. It's a mystery to me how they manage, everything's so everlastingly finicky in town."

In town, these chores seemed to be needlessly complicated by some need to keep up appearances. A country woman visiting another wouldn't notice tracks of manure through the kitchen when the woman of the house was busy with three small children and a box of orphaned chicks behind the cookstove. Town women seemed endlessly preoccupied with sweeping, dusting, wiping, and scrubbing, along with the other chores.

Both men's and women's clothes seemed more elaborate and finicking as well. Elvira and the girls were constantly steaming, pressing, and brushing David's two "everyday" sets of coats and trousers and doing the same for Henry's and Brainard's Sunday finery. They would give their own dresses and the men's Sunday shirts an extra soaking in some cloudy liquid, then carefully press each interleaved tuck and joint before the fabric had time to dry completely. As the shirtwaists and shirtfronts gained a neat, crisp appearance, Anna and Elvira wilted proportionately in the hot kitchen as they pressed with sizzling, hissing wrought-iron flatirons, alternating the ones they used with the ones recharging on the woodstove.

"In the springtime, for an instance," Henry recalled, "my father always takes an extra few minutes on his way to the fields to disc the kitchen garden area for my stepmother. I can't imagine Mr. Spencer does that." Henry's stepmother would then be left with the "easy" task of breaking up the clods and turning in some seasoned manure that Henry or John fetched from the "old" side of the pile, pulling out the stones that had worked their way to the surface during the winter, and raking the seedbed smooth before putting in her seeds.

"The Reverend," as Henry thought of David in his own mind, never seemed to give a thought to any of the women's work at his home. Sure enough, when spring came, Henry saw Elvira and Anna struggling in their garden plot, breaking the crust of earth and early weeds, turning it over and over by hand before beginning the actual preparation for planting. Had the Spencers possessed a plow, Henry would have offered to break the ground for them, but for some reason he was embarrassed to offer to do this by hand, so he kept his ideas to himself.

AS LONG AS THE LIGHT HELD in the evenings, Henry would read or work on his lessons outdoors under the elm tree at the back of the yard, waving mosquitoes away absentmindedly with one hand. As he wrote or worked algebra problems, he would hear the sounds of Elvira, Anna, and Charlotte finishing up the dishes, scraping the plates into the slop bucket for the chickens, clinking forks against crockery, the whistle of the kettle as they heated the wash water; all were overlaid, like the low murmur of contented bees, with the women's easy, quiet conversation. Sometimes he would strain to overhear the conversations of the women in the kitchen, ashamed of himself for the impulse but unable to prevent himself from it.

"And that's another thing I've noticed about ladies," he advanced to his classmates during a "study session." "They have different ways of talking than we do."

"They sure do," agreed Charles, thinking of too many ignominious routs by his own sisters. "They don't argue fair, and if they think you're on the winning side, they'll go crying to your pa and he'll take their side."

"No, that's not what I mean. They talk differently when men are around than when they're alone."

"If they talk when they're alone they're likely addled," Tom volunteered wittily.

"When they're just with other ladies, I mean," clarified Henry. "They use a different tone of voice, and I think they talk about different things."

At the table, the Reverend's talk dominated, echoed by Brainard's, answered by Henry's. Men, he noted, had much the same things to say no matter who was around, saving some earthiness of expression they edited when ladies were present. The "ladies," meanwhile, worked together at their appointed tasks, and except for the chattering of little girls, remained silent in mixed groups except for such homely phrases as "I'll fetch more butter" or "Has that cream gone sour already? My land!"

Apparently, when they worked together without the subduing presence of males, all their bottled-up words poured out like butter from a crock in a warm kitchen.

As the days shortened and the elm tree's hospitality faded, Henry moved indoors. From sensitivity none suspected him of having, or perhaps from simply being too embarrassed to sit uselessly so near the women as they worked, he often stayed in the parlor and tried to look interested in the Reverend's conversation for an extra hour before returning to the kitchen table, where Brainard eventually joined him. This allowed the women to tidy up the kitchen at their leisure and eased the pressure of their daily allotment of conversation. They generally then retired to their individual pursuits, he noticed, or sat in the parlor and worked on the endless mending that lay piled in the workbasket.

One evening Henry found himself alone at the clean kitchen table as he opened his copybook; Brainard had left for a meeting with his friends. Elvira startled him by sitting down in her seat at the end, sighing as the pressure on her tired soles eased. She looked frankly across at him, and he shyly looked back. It occurred to him that Elvira Ferry must have, before work and weather took its toll, been a handsome woman. Now, lines went upward from the bridge of her nose into her forehead, and downward from the sides of her nostrils to the corners of her mouth. It made him think, for a moment, of her face as a soft bun with a dried pear pressed down into its crust before the bun was entirely cooked. Still, her eyes, though tired, seemed kind.

"It does seem as though you put a good many more hours into those books than Brainard ever does," she observed. "And he studying for the ministry."

"I s'pose some people just have to study harder than others," Henry answered diplomatically.

"I expect it seems to you that we carry Brainard around on a silk cushion somewhat," she said. "He's the only boy and the youngest besides." Henry saw no reason to respond to this.

"Not that pampering ever did much for any child, that I've observed. I expect you'll go a lot further in your own life, having to put in a good day's work for your board." She glanced toward the parlor, though she needn't have, Henry knew; her words would be indistinguishable to the others.

She'd kept her voice low and smooth, not unlike, he realized with surprise and inward pleasure, the way she spoke with her stepdaughters as they shared their work. The Reverend wouldn't pay a bit of attention to talk in that tone of voice, any more than he did when she spoke with the girls.

As though he'd mentioned them aloud, Elvira went on, "The girls, now, they're both good hardworking girls, though Charlotte isn't the worker her sister is. Left to her own devices I fear she'd be flighty and filled with notions. Anna's more like a real daughter to me, kind, and tries to spare me trouble. Charlotte, now, she's never seemed able to warm up to me too much. You'd think, being the younger, she'd remember less of her own mother, but somehow it's as though she feels like it's her biggest job in life, to carry that memory around and decorate it like it was a fancy wedding cake." She spoke with no bitterness, but with a certain wry amusement.

"I expect it's hard, being a step-ma," Henry observed. "You'd want to take an interest in the children, but if you understood them too well, they'd rightly resent that as if you'd stolen it from their real ma."

Elvira smiled at that insight, as if she'd been given a gift.

Theology

"MY BOYS, LOOK UPON the works of the Lord and marvel," intoned Professor Cottrell, as he led his botany class along the through the woods to the west of campus. "This maple tree has labored through the summer, storing up all that it needs to survive through the winter. Now it paints itself in glorious raiment to delight our eyes in this season of harvest. Then, during the long, bleak days of winter, it produces syrup with which to delight our taste in spring. Yes, Mr. Thacker?" This last, wearily.

"Doesn't the tree really produce the sap for itself, though, and not us?"

"Yes, but God has given Man dominion over all, and it is because of Man's own wisdom and labor, given by God, that the tree produces its sap, its wood, its color, for Man's use. The tree provides for itself in order that it may provide for our wants."

Henry had hoped that higher education would answer some of the questions that constantly roiled in his mind. Somehow, this wasn't exactly what he had in mind, though Henry wasn't sure what was lacking.

"But what about the plants and animals that aren't here to provide for us? Why do they do the things they do, then? Why, for instance, do some of the woodpeckers always walk up the trees and some of them always walk down, and some go around in a spiral?" And the answer from the science and mathematics teacher would be an annoyed "Because God made them that way, Mr. Thacker. Your assignment for Wednesday is to observe and write an essay on the habits of one of the useful animals on this list."

How things worked, why they looked and sounded as they did, was always interesting to Henry. The way the milk splashed into the pail, and how the same milk poured from pail into jug or churn or bowl. The way waters spun and eddied through the little streamlets along the Betsie River.

His father and other men who farmed were surprisingly astute in reading the predictions to be found in the patterns of wind and water. They needed these for their livelihood, but Henry had hoped that college would explain more of the why of these phenomena.

Why the weather came in little cycles, through a pattern of warm and warmer, then damp and heavier, until the wind changed and a storm resulted. How cool and light the air was afterward, then gradually warming and growing heavy again. And the little cycles fell into the larger ones of the seasons, the storms themselves becoming cooler, now producing some sleet, now some snow that became rain, now returning to cold crisp days, now returning to heavy gray skies that could dump two feet of snow in as many hours.

"But when you look at the waves out on the lake," he wondered aloud to some of the other young men, "they just keep rolling in the same direction like the water is going somewhere. Why doesn't all that water pile up higher and higher, and end up on the shore?"

"You're very queer sometimes, Henry," observed Lot Nevius.

But in fact, they all knew that in the winter that's just what happened. The waves didn't exactly march on to land in neat, orderly rows like soldiers, as Henry had envisioned, but crept up in a stealthy way, the layer on top freezing and the powerful winter waves sneaking beneath the frozen layer, shoving it shoreward and freezing in their turn, building fanciful turrets and fumaroles on the shoreline.

Sensible folks didn't have much use for the Lake Michigan shoreline in the winter, even when they were able to approach it. Low temperatures and high winds made it bleak and uninhabitable for most. Elaborate ice sculptures were treacherous, thick and solid in one place, and thin as a crystal goblet two feet away, and all of them looking alike from the surface. One minute you might be shivering gloriously atop your castle wall, looking out at the charging gray and white waters, and the next you'd plunge straight down into those icy waters. Likely you'd freeze or drown before anyone could fetch a rope to haul you out. So sensible people stayed in town and left the bleak shoreline to foxes and fools. Henry had few reasons to visit the Lake Michigan shore in winter, but the otherworldly beauty of the winter shoreline still fascinated and stirred him.

School, however, rarely seemed to unlock those mysteries. The students learned what was useful for young men to know in those times, things like measurements and mathematics, history and social studies, how to speak and write clearly and decently, and such literature and music as a reasonably cultured man of small-town America was expected to know in those times. Oh, and they learned about the Bible, and why God expected them to be sober, clean, and honorable citizens, to work hard and prosper.

All of this was useful in its way, but it never really addressed the mysteries that confronted a truly inquiring mind. "Lot," said Henry, exasperated, one day, "am I the only one in this school who gets into trouble for asking all these questions? Doesn't anybody else wonder about the why of things?"

"Why should they?" asked Lot reasonably. "What good does knowing that do anyone? Seems like a fellow just has so much room in his mind to hold things, like you do in a cold cellar. Fill up the cellar with all those hows and whys, like pretty stones, and you won't have any room for, well, eggs and potatoes."

Lot was pleased with his metaphor, and Henry was impressed by it as well. "Lot, you got the makings of a poet in there somewhere. But maybe those shiny stones have a purpose too." It troubled him that he couldn't fathom just what that purpose might be.

"HENRY, DO YOU HAVE ANYTHING special to do today after class?" inquired David Spencer at the breakfast table.

"I thought I'd work on my theme for history," Henry answered cautiously.

"We don't need to turn those in until Friday," volunteered Brainard as he refilled his bowl with whole wheat mush from the bowl in the center of the table. This concoction, known as "graham mush," was a staple item for breakfast; dried wheat grains were coarsely ground and then boiled in the manner of oatmeal. It could be enlivened with sugar, butter, milk, or chunks of dried fruit.

Henry glanced at Brainard, then turned his eyes back as David continued, "I'd like for you to turn out all that old straw in the cow barn and put down fresh from those bales from last summer."

"Yessir," mumbled Henry.

"And Brainard," continued David, "it wouldn't hurt for you to get out there and help with the job."

"Yes, sir," mumbled Brainard. They finished their breakfasts and mumbled the after-meal grace, then left for school.

After school, Henry changed into his overalls and headed toward the barn. Brainard was just strolling into the dooryard.

"Where've you been? I want to get this done so I have some time before chores to work on that theme."

"You go ahead," was the casual response. "I thought I'd go into town on some business." He continued strolling toward the house to drop off his books.

"Hang it all, Brainard! Your pap said you were to help with this job, too!"

"He didn't say I had to. He just said it wouldn't hurt if I did. That's not the same thing at all. And don't call him my 'pap'; he's Mr. Spencer to you." Henry glared at his retreating back for a moment, then turned and stomped into the barn. "Dang him," he muttered and looked guiltily around as a shadow darkened the doorway to the yard; the Spencers had all, in their turns, admonished him for "swearing"; this term seemed to encompass any expressions of frustration that he uttered. The barn lightened again, and he lifted the hay fork.

More daring now, Henry again grumbled, "That danged Brainard!" as he lifted the first forkful of smelly straw. A shadow fell on the wall before him. He yelped and spun around. Arabelle the heifer poked her head around the doorway in hopes that the sun had lied and it was indeed feeding time. "I didn't say anything to you," growled Henry. Disappointed, Arabelle lowered her head, one ear back, and backed away. Henry chuckled, his annoyance forgotten. He fell into an easy rhythm. Scoop, lift, turn, and toss. Scoop, lift, turn, and toss. Henry began again to rehearse how he would frame the opening paragraphs of his history theme.

David Spencer stopped at the barn on his way in and inspected the work. While the odor of cow was permanently embedded in the timbers and the floors, it was noticeably fresher, overlain with the smell of clean straw and lye soap. The mangers had been scraped clean, the stanchions wiped down. Both cows stood contentedly hock deep in their new bedding, crunching on grain. Pleased, David was expansive at the supper table. "Bet it took you fellows a while to clean up after that job, didn't it?"

"Yes, sir," said Henry.

"Yes, sir," echoed Brainard, and Henry stared at him incredulously. Anna, eyes demurely on her plate as usual, didn't appear to notice. Charlotte did, but simply flicked her eyes to Brainard and back to Henry, and said nothing. Henry shook his head, then shrugged and helped himself to another potato.

HENRY FOUND CHEMISTRY particularly interesting. He'd known that different substances had different properties, of course. Something in manure, when folded into a field, made the green things grow, but not flower or seed. Boron made the beets taste sweet if you put it on the developing plants. Something in "washing soda" made the clothes cleaner with less scrubbing. "Baking soda" made cakes rise. The commonly used mouse and rat poison known as "Rough on Rats" contained arsenic, which was also poisonous to humans, and in fact a cat that ate a poisoned mouse often sickened and died as well. Farmers stored the poison in their outhouses, sheds, and on porch shelves, well away from the livestock feed.

Housewives might keep it in the house, but at the back of high shelves out of the reach of small children.

In chemistry class, they discussed the various properties of such commonplace substances, and so now they became something more, in Henry's eyes. They were chemicals! He now knew that ordinary table salt was actually "sodium chloride." Its crystals were of a different size and shape than sugar crystals. He was thrilled to examine each of them through a microscope, eagerly lining up with the other students to take his turn to squint through the eyepiece, adjusting the mirror that sent light through "the objective."

Best of all, the chemistry professor rarely felt it necessary to intone something about "God's Great Plan" at every lecture, but instead waxed enthusiastic about the metallic elements, esters and oxides. Henry found this more refreshing than he dared admit at the Spencer table.

Brainard and "the Benzie Boys"

"BRAINARD? BRAINARD! Are you out there?" called David, irritation plain in his every lineament. He scanned the yard one more time and turned back. "I don't know where he's gone this time." He shook his head in weary disgust, and looked at Anna, who looked back, no expression on her face.

Charlotte made no attempt to hide her annoyance. "We've been looking forward to this lecture for a long time, Papa, and I for one don't care to miss it."

"Charlotte and I can escort ourselves to the lecture," said Anna.

Henry cleared his throat diffidently. "I could escort them to the lecture," he volunteered, and inwardly cursed his ears as he felt them redden. "That is, if you don't mind."

"That's a capital idea." David rubbed his hands briskly, pleased to have this minor difficulty removed from his plate. "Elvira and I will proceed to dinner with the Waterses, then, and we'll see you at the lecture directly afterward. Thank you, Henry, for your generous offer." He went upstairs to change into his second-best shirt.

Henry, aghast at what he'd brought upon himself, went outdoors and began to chop kindling. Anna and Charlotte, their evening restored, went to the kitchen and began to heat the skillet for the potatoes.

Brainard, meanwhile, was hotly trying to keep order among his compatriots, "the Benzie Boys." This trio, all sons of the village founders, had just found out about a scheme their elders had concocted to bring prosperity to the backwaters of northwestern Michigan.

"By opening a canal between Crystal Lake and Betsie River, a channel might be made following the course of the outlet that would permit the passage of a small-sized steam craft from Lake Michigan and Frankfort, by way of Betsie River and the outlet, up and into Crystal Lake. If we dig a navigable canal between Crystal Lake and the Betsie, the loggers can drop those trees right into the Betsie, then float them through the canal and right out to the boats on Lake Michigan." This had been Archibald Jones's suggestion, eagerly seized upon by Sam Jaqueth and others.

"Not only will the loggers spend their money right here in Benzonia," was John Osterhout's contribution, "but we might have a steamer built to ferry passengers and freight between the lakes." The Betsie River Improvement Company was organized.

Brainard, Alden Case, and Albert Adams intended to make a grand show as soon as the canal became navigable. "We'll build a raft and pole it through the canal. That will make us the first sailors through it. We might even get our names in the paper."

"Shouldn't take much work," commented Brainard. "We could use some raft pieces that the children leave around the lakeshore, and just add some more pine logs."

Albert scoffed. "Children's rafts, nothing. We're going to build a new one, high and dry, that won't fall apart if the current's strong at first. Stands to reason, at first, there'll be a rush."

"Certainly," agreed Alden, warming to the image, "we should build something narrow but stable. Put the platform high enough above the waterline to keep our feet dry."

Reluctantly, Brainard agreed, and added, "We should start poling from the river. That way the river current will push us partway into the canal."

Albert agreed. "Better to float grandly by than to sweat and labor into view of everyone at the ceremony. We'll smile and wave as though it was all planned, and old Mr. Jones will have to accept it or look foolish."

They bent to their work again.

Henry awoke an hour or two after he'd drifted off to sleep. Brainard, creeping into their shared room, had shaken the bed as he sat down to pull off his stockings.

"Where've you been, Brainard?" mumbled Henry. "Your pap's about as mad as a scalded cat at you, for disappearing and staying out so late."

"What's it to you?" hissed Brainard crossly. "And don't call him my 'pap.'" He fell into bed with a groan. His back hurt, and his feet twitched irritably—he was sure they'd wake him up in the night with a Charley horse. But Henry was already asleep again, and Brainard soon joined him in slumber.

After afternoon classes Henry returned to the Spencers' to do chores, and Brainard disappeared to the woods with Alden and Albert. As the canal digging proceeded, the raft grew apace and was secreted on a soggy spit of ground above the river.

Shall We Gather at the River?

"A NEW DAY OF PROSPERITY for all the good citizens of Benzonia" was the theme of Archibald Jones's speech to be delivered on the final day of the canal project. The remaining shovelfuls of sodden dirt between the flowing Betsie and the lake were to be removed ceremoniously in a presentation after church on Sunday.

"Anna? Have you seen Brainard? It's time to leave for church."

"No, Elvira. Perhaps he and Henry have gone ahead. No, here's Henry. Was Brainard with you?"

Henry, just coming downstairs, shook his head. When had Brainard voluntarily gone anywhere with him? "He was still in bed when I got up to milk, and was gone when I went up to change for church. Perhaps he's just gone ahead." The three of them contemplated the likelihood of this. Without comment they joined Charlotte and David and proceeded on to church.

"There're the Cases."

"Alden's not there, either."

"Do you see Albert's family?"

"Are those boys up to something?" This last from Charlotte.

"Never mind," grumbled David. "I'll speak to Brainard later." He couldn't refrain from adding, "And he reading for the ministry."

Brainard grunted as the Benzie Boys pushed their craft into position in the eddying waters at the lower end of the new canal bed and hopped aboard. Poles in hand, they braced for the surge and lift of the water beneath their feet.

"It won't be for another hour at least," said Albert. He sat down to dangle his feet in the stream and stretched his back luxuriously in the warming sun. "Church will have to finish and everyone come to the canal. Mr. Jones will have to make his speech, and then the children's choir will sing. Alden? What's wrong with—" He spun half around to face the direction Brainard and Alden were now staring, jaws agape, then scrambled to his knees and clutched the edge of the raft. It would be many hours before he became aware of the large splinter jammed under the middle finger of his left hand.

Rosa Jones, seated next to her husband in the Congregational Church, raised her head before the "amen." "Archibald?" she hissed. "Do you hear that?" Adjacent heads were raised, noses pointed toward the west windows with the alertness of setters in hunting season. "Sounds like a flood," muttered someone behind Rosa.

"The river!" exclaimed someone else.

Sam Jaqueth leaped to his feet, ignoring the affronted gaze of Reverend Waters. "The canal!"

He rushed for the door, closely followed by the Joneses. A bevy of youngsters, overwhelmed by the roar of water, leaped to their feet and followed, convinced that whatever they found would be well worth the whippings that would follow on the morrow. (The Sabbath was deemed too holy for administration of corporal punishment.)

"GraceofGodtheloveandfellowshipoftheholyspiritrestandabidewithyounowandforevermoreamen," speedily intoned the Reverend, and he stepped down from his pew. The remaining congregation parted to let him pass, and then closed together and followed him out the door.

Well read in matters biblical, mercantile, and administrative, the canal builders hadn't thought to consult an engineer before embarking on the project. Neither they nor the young adventurers had reckoned with the force of water flowing from a higher level to a lower one. The water, concentrated into a narrow channel, had tired of awaiting the attendance of the good people of Benzonia. It completed the ceremonial joining of the two ends on its own.

In a reversal of the famous Red Sea's contortions, the waters met, with violence, embraced, and jointly gushed into the Betsie River. They shot across the slower flow of the river, and, cutting through the opposite bank, continued into the sodden adjoining low areas. The waters raised the level of the marsh several inches and. when the hydrological enthusiasm finally subsided, permanently dropped the level of the lake several feet.

"Jehosephat!" gasped Brainard from his center of the raft as it spun in a lively eddy. Two other shoulders pressed against his. The poles had gone, they knew not where.

"Where are we?" muttered Albert dazedly. "In the river or in the swamp?"

"Both, I think." Alden watched the saplings and shrubs travel laterally past him. These plants, though well designed for their marshy environment, were doomed to eventual death by immersion. "I think I see some dry ground over there. No, it's the top of a bunch of sumac."

"Where'd that sun go? It was warm a minute ago."

"What time is it?"

"My watch is wet," said Alden miserably. His father had given it to him for his nineteenth birthday, accompanied by a speech about man's estate and wisdom. "I think we've been sloshing around for more than a minute, though. More like several minutes. Maybe almost an hour, now."

"I'm ready for some lunch," volunteered Albert.

"I have some cookies in my pocket," offered Brainard, pulling a soggy mass from his jacket. Albert grimaced and shook his head. Their progress slowed, and they sat silently for several more hours, trying to get their bearings and decide whether the water was shallow enough to wade to higher ground, now surely more than a mile from where they now floated.

"You're too big to whip, Brainard. One might argue that at the age of twenty, you ought to have had better sense," said his father with weary disgust as Brainard, early next morning, dripped before him on the study carpet. "Now wipe that mud off yourself, and after you get something to eat I expect you to mop up any mud you've tracked into the house."

Brainard wearily turned toward the door, and his father added, "And don't find a way to make your sisters or Henry clean up for you, either." Brainard nodded and went to his room. Henry, as soon as it was determined that Brainard hadn't drowned in the flood, had prudently left for school.

A Mormon Husband

"HENRY? ARE YOU PLANNING to attend the magic lantern show tonight?"

Henry looked up from pushing his peas onto his fork. He and David were the only ones still at the table. "I thought I might. Is there something you'd rather I do?"

"No, no, that's excellent," said David Spencer. "I was wondering whether you might consider escorting my daughters to the show as well. Brainard said he couldn't, he had a meeting. If it's an inconvenience, of course, I could . . ."

"No, no, that's fine, I don't mind. I'm going there anyway." Henry realized that this sounded rather ungallant. "That is, it would be much pleasanter with the company. It's a fine night tonight for a walk into town. With company."

After the show, the three young people strolled down the road. "That was very interesting, the part about how the Indians might be related to folk from the Japans, wasn't it?"

"That seems quite unlikely," contradicted Charlotte, somewhat rudely, Henry thought.

"I don't see why," he countered. "Folks move from place to place all the time, and if we're all descended from the original Adam and Eve, the ancestors of the Japaners and our Indians might well have been related. Maybe our own Indians used to have civilizations and temples just like in the Orient." He stopped, turned around. Charlotte had stopped walking several paces back and stood in the road. Her features, as far as he could make out, seemed set and severe.

"Charlotte? Is something wrong?" He stepped toward her.

"What do you know about Indians, Henry Thacker? Nothing at all, that's what!" Her tone was wrathful.

"Whatever in the world are you talking about?" Henry, all at sea, asked her. "Weren't we just talking about the magic lantern show and lecture? Whatever has you so riled up?"

"'Our' Indians, as you call them, have never been civilized. No better than animals, all of them. They should be driven away to the farthest wilderness, or exterminated completely!"

He was shocked. "Well, I don't know if I'd go that far."

"Well, I would, and it's not for you to say!" She stepped past him and flounced toward home. Frowning, he began to follow but stopped when he felt Anna's hand rest on his arm.

"Let her go, Henry; she'll come to herself in a bit and then act as if nothing happened."

"What was that all about?" He scuffed his shoes against the dirt clods as they walked. He knew it wore the leather, but for the moment he didn't care. He might just be the "hired boy," but she needn't treat him like a disobedient servant!

"She's just touchy about some subjects, is all. Our mother was killed by an Indian, you know," Anna told him gently.

"I'm sorry." Henry was shocked anew. "I never knew that."

"It's not something we care to discuss. It was a terrible time, and Charlotte was present in the room when it occurred."

They walked the rest of the way in silence.

"SAY, LOT, DID YOU KNOW that Henry here has decided to break off from the church?" Shocked, Lot stared at Henry, who stared at Tom, equally flabbergasted. Tom was a round-faced young fellow with a large Adam's apple and hands and feet to match. He styled himself, often unsuccessfully, as a wit.

"Suppose you explain yourself!" demanded Henry.

"Nothin', only I heard you were planning to go out west and settle with the Mormons, that's what I heard, you and your two wives."

His ear tips warmed. Henry knew that eyes had followed him as he, in company with both Spencer sisters, entered the church for the missionary's lecture on the Holy Lands. Days had passed with no comment, however, so he thought that nobody had noticed their joint attendance at the magic lantern show either.

"There was nothing wrong with my going to that lecture with the Misses Spencer. I was just helping the Spencers a bit, that's all."

"Helping? Escorting two ladies at once, that's how you earn your board with the Spencers, hey? Wish I had employment like that."

"Which one did you try to kiss first when you took them home?" This was racy stuff indeed; Henry and Charles were shocked by this boldness from Tom. Nice young ladies, they knew, didn't kiss until they were engaged, and then reluctantly.

"You oughtn't to talk that way about them, Tom. Both of them are nice young ladies, and Mr. Spencer trusted me to walk them to the lecture when Brainard was, well, you know where Brainard was that evening." The four chuckled, back on safer ground.

"HENRY, WAIT FOR ME!" Lot, a stout young man, hurried to catch up. "Are you going to the band concert on Saturday? Want to sit together?"

"Course I'm going. If you get there first, save three seats for me, will you?"

"For Tom and Charlie?"

"Well, no, for the Spencer sisters."

"You're escorting both of them? Mercy, I'd be afraid to escort one of them."

"Oh, well, it's not as serious-like since I live there anyway. It's almost like I'm a brother. Well, not quite a brother, maybe a cousin. Or more likely . . ." He cursed himself mentally, aware that he was explaining far too much.

"Well, anyway, Henry, maybe I'll just sit with some of the other fellows."

"What's the matter? Afraid someone will think one of the young ladies is your company for the evening?"

Lot did a complicated squirm with his shoulders. "Well, that, maybe, and I wouldn't know a thing to say to either of them. There's something about those Spencer girls, I don't know, a body just doesn't know what to say to them."

"Oh, I used to feel that way too, but now they're just, you know, Anna and Charlotte. But that's all right, I understand if you'd rather not sit with us." Henry was surprised to realize that this was practically the truth.

As the long days shortened again toward fall and the trees ran riot in their baroque finery, Henry continued to squire the Spencer sisters to

Benzonia events. They walked to the bazaar one crisp Saturday afternoon, Henry carrying a basketful of Anna's jams and Charlotte's stitchery.

A month later, Henry drove the sisters to a concert in David's buggy one rainy evening. Another month passed; Anna, Charlotte, and Henry rode early to the church in the Spencers' sleigh the evening of the Christmas pageant.

Anna coached the children as they stumbled through their parts at the manger and as "the shepherds that watched their flocks by night." Charlotte rehearsed the older children, who were to sing, and Henry led the young men in decoration of the sanctuary. He balanced precariously from a rickety wooden ladder as they hung the star, arguing boisterously about whether it should actually be hung on the east side, requiring a complete rearrangement of the manger, until Charlotte shushed them.

The young men draped an incongruous string of paper "Japanese lanterns" left over from a summer gala across the rear of the church, and then Henry left them to their devices and went to watch Anna with the children. Gently she guided them, bringing out the shy ones and suppressing the boisterous ones with such tact that they hardly noticed.

ONE FRIDAY IN LATE APRIL, Henry drove the horse off to the side of the road. You had to be careful where you pulled off once the roadside weeds began to grow tall in the spring; drop-offs and holes lurked behind tufts of grass and weedlings. You could break an axle, lose part of your load, or a startled horse could bolt. The wagon rolled neatly to a stop in the sandy soil.

Silence fell, a pregnant pause, as the birds, disturbed in their important business of seeking territory and mates, assessed the dangers inherent in the arrival of three humans, two matronly horses, and a well-used farm wagon. An early bee, scouting for flowers for her matriarchal village, buzzed audibly. For a moment, a breeze stirred. Then the tiny mint green leaves so bravely unfurling in the nearest trees, deepening to a darker olive in the forest depths, hung still. Henry marveled at how the sun's rays, so pale and watery only a week ago, had now grown thicker, warmer, more yellow, hinting at impending summer scorchers.

Henry, Anna, and Charlotte had taken a half holiday from studies and chores so they might look for fiddleheads in the marshy woods bordering the river just to the south of town. Tiny streamlets led to the Betsie River, creating isolated glades, treacherous to boot and ankle in the early spring but bewitching to the eye.

Trilliums blanketed the ground under the trees like light snow, tinged palest pink. Dainty mushrooms, gills blushing pink and sometimes bright orange, clustered at the bases of trees that had succumbed in recent years to wind, parasites, or disease. A few lady slippers had begun to take advantage of the brief interval between winter's cold and the entire blockage of light by the now-leafing trees.

Elfin fern shoots, called fiddleheads for their curled resemblance to the carved scroll of a violin, had just begun to thrust their pale tentative fingers above the boggy ground. Later, lacy tips of mint would appear, providing rich harvests for the bees. For now, the three young people were the only harvesters of the crop around them. The townspeople, like the Three Fires People before them, desperately craved the taste of fresh greens in the springtime. They had lived through most of the winter on dried and canned produce from last summer's fields and gardens.

Anna and Charlotte smiled as they nimbly began to fill their baskets, oblivious to the dampness that gradually soaked through their skirts and petticoats as they knelt on tussocks. "Just when we think we can't bear another dinner of boiled potatoes and pickled eggs, up come the fiddleheads! And when these are finished, we'll be picking dandelion greens and asparagus."

"And then strawberries," added Anna. "First the wild ones and then those in the kitchen garden."

"And you can make jam for me," added Henry gaily. "The kind where you boil the strawberries with honey to thicken it."

"Honey has no place in the making of jam," corrected Charlotte brusquely.

Henry's ears reddened. "My grandmother made it that way and said it was the best," he retorted.

"You must not have paid attention. Nobody would use honey."

"You can't be sure of that!" snapped Henry.

"And just who made you the expert on the making of jam?" demanded Charlotte.

Anna looked sharply at Charlotte, who'd drawn herself up haughtily. Too many times she had found herself in the middle of pointless arguments like this with Charlotte. A minor disagreement over something trivial, and then suddenly they seemed to be reenacting the Battle of Shiloh. She never knew what might set Charlotte off. Then, as abruptly as it began, Charlotte would become her usual sisterly self as though she didn't remember a thing.

Now the storm was brewing with someone else as the hapless target. Anna tried to catch Henry's eye; she wanted to shake her head, forestall him and ward off the gathering clouds.

Henry, oblivious, was continuing the debate. "You don't need to be an 'expert' on jam-making to know there are lots of ways of doing it."

"I don't believe I've seen you in the kitchen, checking ingredients, washing bottles, hulling berries, standing over the pots, and stirring the jam, have I? Have I?" she demanded.

Henry, realizing at last that the discussion had moved into some other mysterious realm than that of jam, stood and stared at her. "What's gotten into you, Charlotte? Weren't we just talking about jam? Why are you so mad?"

"I don't think I'm the one who's mad. You're the one who seems obsessed with the subject. In fact, I'd say you're becoming fairly ridiculous about it."

Anna finally caught Henry's eye, shook her head. He clamped his lips shut and moved away, feeling something damp against his pant leg. He looked down; in his clenched hand an uprooted fern dripped, its pale roots looking naked and bruised. Ashamed, he knelt down and tenderly tucked its poor feet back into their nest.

By silent but mutual agreement, they returned to the wagon soon after. Charlotte ignored Henry on the return trip but chattered happily with Anna. After a day of this cold-shoulder treatment, Charlotte, to Henry's mystification, greeted him cheerfully at the breakfast table as though they were the best of friends.

TERM'S END APPROACHED more rapidly than any of the students would have preferred. Henry often studied with Charlie and Lot, but on this particular day Charlie had been detained after class, an unfortunate circumstance that ambushed good-natured, easygoing Charlie far too often.

"You know," said Lot diffidently as they chuckled about poor Charlie's difficulties, "Charlie used to walk out with Miss Spencer, for a little time anyway. The younger one, that is. I wouldn't have mentioned it, but someone mentioned it the other day, and I thought sooner or later you'd hear it anyway. I thought, as a friend, that you'd want to know about it from me."

"That's all right, Lot, truly. I don't mind. I'm not walking out with either of them, not really. We're just companions, as it were."

"Well, then, that's all right." And neither of them brought the subject up again.

But soon after that conversation, Henry managed to get Charlie off by himself. "Say, Charlie, somebody happened to mention, just in passing, you understand, that you used to walk out with Charlotte Spencer."

Seeing Charlie blush, he hastened to say, "It's all right, really, I don't mind; it's just that I thought you could help me get my mind clear about something."

"It wasn't for very long, Henry, honestly, and it was a while back, before you ever came to school. It's that sneak Lot who told you, wasn't it?"

Henry waved this aside without bothering to disagree. "What I wondered was this: I hope you won't take this the wrong way, Charlie, but did you ever find yourself having, well, disagreements with her, just about minor things?"

"What did she tell you? I call that hard, to gossip about one fellow with another one!"

"Steady, old chap. She never said a word. I'm just, well, I'm concerned about something. About Miss Spencer, I mean."

"I don't feel right, telling you anything about her. It's a bit like, oh, like, gossiping about a lady."

It was Henry's turn to blush. "I know, and I feel pretty low-down even asking a thing like this. But it's something I'm trying to understand, and you see, I can't ask her sister or her brother, or anyone else. But I really need to know if it's me or, maybe, well, maybe there's something a bit, well, queer about her."

He'd said it, and he felt like a heel for having said it. But he also felt some relief in seeing Charlie's knowing look.

"You have, haven't you?"

"If you must know, yes. It's why I stopped calling on her. If you tell anyone else I said this, Henry Thacker, I'll never trust you again."

"I won't tell another soul, I promise."

"This happened three times. We were just walking along, talking of this and that, when she said something, it wasn't anything important but it was inaccurate, and I, well, I disagreed with her. I didn't feel like I'd been rude about it. I just said something along the order of, 'Are you sure that's so? I always thought it was the other way.' And she stopped, right there in her tracks, and drew herself up just like a duchess. 'I suppose you claim to be an expert, is that it?' and I felt a bit heated. She made me feel as though I was a child who'd contradicted his mother, and so I said, 'No, I'm not an expert, but neither are you so you needn't take on so, Miss,' and she said, 'I? Take on? You're the one who's all red in the face.' And she was right, so I was, it made me that angry, so I just said something like, 'Forget I said anything.' She was pretty cool after that, and I left her at her door and went on home, figuring that was the end of that friendship."

He paused and Henry finished for him. "And a day or two later she came up to you just as nice and friendly, as if nothing had happened, is that it?"

Charlie stared. "That's just right! And so I decided she'd just been having some troubles of her own, or wasn't feeling good, so I said no more about it."

"Until it happened again?"

"Just so! And then the same thing happened another time yet, so that decided me, that I just wasn't able to keep from annoying her, so I've been polite, of course, but I didn't call on her anymore."

Henry said no more, immersed in his own thoughts.

"But you know, Henry, that a couple of weeks after that, she came up to me as I was leaving church, and she scolded me for what she called 'turning against an old friend.'"

"What did you do?"

I just told her I was sorry, my Pa'd kept me pretty busy at home and I wasn't getting out much at all."

After another pause: "Look here, Henry! You wouldn't tell her any of this, would you?"

"'Course not, Charlie. You've taken a big worry off my mind, that's all."

Understanding dawned. "She's done the same thing to you, hasn't she?"

Embarrassed, Henry nodded.

Curious now, Charlie asked, "Her sister doesn't do any of that, does she?"

"Of course not! Anna Spencer's as nice a lady as any I ever met!" Henry assured him.

"HENRY? A word with you, please. In my study."

"Is there something wrong, sir?" Henry couldn't think of anything he had done recently to upset David Spencer.

Henry could tell that David was deeply agitated; his beard wobbled. As men matured, they let their beards grow. It was supposed to show their wisdom, according to the Bible, but secretly Henry rebelled against the idea of himself in a beard, no matter how venerable he became.

There was something pompous about those untidy straggles of hair dangling from their sagging jowls, emphasizing rather than obscuring their weak chins, and too many of the old men seemed to have difficulty keeping them tidy. Henry felt sorry for the many wives who struggled all their lives to keep home and children neat and clean, and then had to deal with a bossy old man with food in his facial hair.

But just now, Henry felt an unexpected pang of pity for David Spencer. Whatever his concern, the wobbling beard bespoke, rather than hid, the face behind it, and it made him seem naked. Normally, Henry would have averted his mind from such an image, but just now he felt a warm sympathy for the man's humanity.

David sat down behind his desk. He moved his inkwell from one side of the desk to the other, then moved it back again. He moved it to the middle, then picked up a nib and began to fiddle with it.

"Sir?" said Henry. "Are you all right?"

David sighed. "Mrs. Spencer has prevailed upon me to speak to you."

"Have I done something to offend Mrs. Spencer?" Mentally he reviewed all his activities that crossed her sphere of influence. Wood box was full, chickens were fed, milk had been strained and brought in, and slops from earlier in the day carried out for the pig, which resided in state at the east edge of the property. Kindling? Had he split enough kindling?

David affected a negligent laugh. The attempt fell flat. "Oh, no, this is nothing like that."

Silence fell between them. Henry studied a spot on the worn carpet. Ink? Part of the pattern? No, because then there would be other spots of the same color elsewhere on the carpet.

David cleared his throat. He pushed the inkwell to the left, then back to the center of the desk, and carefully arranged a pile of papers so that the upper edge was an inch below the inkwell. With his ink-spotted left forefinger, he poked the top sheet in line with its subordinates. Henry finally looked at him with concern.

"Are you all right, Mr. Spencer?"

"Of course I'm all right. You asked me that once already. I'm just organizing my thoughts, that's all. Don't hurry me."

Henry was relieved; this sounded more like the man he'd worked for and shared meals with for the last three years. He waited.

"Henry, how old are you now?"

"I'll be twenty-one next year; you remember, I was seventeen when I first came here."

"Hmmm, so you were, so you were. Henry, are you planning to return to your father's farm when you finish at the college?"

Cautiously, "I'd thought about it."

"What if you had something to interest you here in Benzonia? A job offer, perhaps, or something of a more, hmm, tender aspect?"

Henry tried not to stare. The man appeared to be blushing!

"Thank you, sir, but I'm not sure I care to be involved with the postal service."

David Spencer glowed redder still, and coughed again. "I wasn't, hmmm, wasn't offering you a position in the post office. You should know that by now, those are government jobs."

"Oh. Then, you meant, th . . . oh. No sir, there is no young lady. None in particular, that is."

"Ye gods and little fishes, man, are you as dense as you seem?" David, in his extremity, seemed not to notice that he had sworn. "I mean my daughters. Those young ladies you've been escorting to every social function in Benzonia for the last year and a half."

"Oh," said Henry, again.

"David Piper asked me last week which of my daughters was being courted and which was the duenna. I was embarrassed not to know the answer to that."

Henry's curiosity got the better of him. "What did you tell him?" David shot him a glare from which icicles flashed. He saw that something was expected from him, so he fumbled for the right words.

"I think Anna and Charlotte would tell you that there is no courtship involved, sir. We just fell into the habit of going together to things. It kept them from worrying about what young man was to ask them" (or who would stay home alone if no young man was forthcoming, he did not say) "and kept me from having to find a young lady to escort, and we seemed, well, congenial, so we just continued that way."

"Precisely. And during this time, no eligible young men have had the temerity to ask either of my daughters to accompany them to functions at the church or the college. Might this be because they assume that one of them is your intended?"

"Might be. Hard to say, sir."

"Let us cut directly to the point, Henry. Do you harbor feelings of particular affection for either of my daughters?"

Henry thought carefully before framing his reply. "My feelings are friendly, but not for either one more than the other, sir."

"Let us leave it at this, then. A man in my position is able to help the right young man to get a respectable start in life. If you should wish to become that young man, you may continue to escort either of my daughters to social functions. If you cease to keep company with them both, I will assume that your interests lie elsewhere."

David felt put out with himself. To have suffered through this humiliating conversation and have so little of consequence to show for it! Still, it was preferable to having had the same conversation with Anna or Charlotte.

Henry Makes Up His Mind

ANNA GATHERED HER TRACTS and checked the contents of the basket again. The Little Friends Bible class picnic would begin at 11:00, and the wagons that were to carry children and provisions needed to be loaded half an hour before that. Henry came in through the back door, his mind clearly on other matters than the Little Friends picnic.

"Henry, aren't you dressed yet? Can you carry this jug of lemonade to the wagon for me?"

Henry stopped in his tracks, surprised. "Dressed for what?"

"Don't you remember? The picnic! My class! We have twenty minutes to get to the church."

"Oh, the picnic. Of course, the Little Friends. Why, certainly, I can carry the lemonade for you. I'd better go and hitch up the horses, hadn't I?"

"Hurry! And then change your clothes, you can't go like that."

Henry looked down at his work clothes, streaks of dirt on the pant legs and a greenish glob of chicken manure sticking out from the sole of the left shoe. "I suppose not," he agreed, and went back out.

The sun began to dip down behind the trees by the time the last of the Little Friends had been delivered safely back to the church. To

Anna's surprise, Henry turned the horses to the left out of the church lot, back toward the Frankfort road.

"I thought we'd go home the long way around," he explained.

"That's a pleasant notion," agreed Anna, and they jogged along in companionable silence for a while.

Or so Anna thought, not realizing that Henry's thoughts raced, trying out one phrase and then another, seeking just the right way to begin. He finally took a breath and plunged in. "Anna, I'd say you and I are pretty good friends, wouldn't you?"

Her eyebrows drew together in perplexity. "Henry, are you all right? Of course we're friends! Why, is that a problem?"

"Oh, no, nothing like that, nothing at all. No, that's not what I meant to say. No." He realized that Anna had turned to stare at him as though he'd grown another nose. He drew another breath that was like a gasp and plunged in again. "I meant that, well, we get along pretty well, don't we?"

"Yes, I'd say so. Henry, what on earth is the matter?"

"Anna, have you ever thought about, about, thought about who you'd marry? Someday, I mean?"

"I suppose every young woman thinks about that at one time or another," she said seriously. "I hope someday to marry a good Christian man."

"I'm a good Christian man, I hope," said Henry, his ears glowing like coals now.

"Henry Thacker, are you asking me to marry you?"

"That's what I said, wasn't it?"

"No, it isn't. But I think you were, weren't you?"

"Anna, stop this foolery. Let's get married, shall we? We work together well, we enjoy each other's company, so why not?"

"Why not, indeed?"

Henry stopped the horses and turned to her. Tentatively, he reached for Anna's hand. She allowed him to lift it, enfold it in both hands. Confusion overtook him again; what was he to do with the hand, now that it was in his? He gave it a quick pat and returned it to Anna. He lifted the reins and sent the horses homeward with a glow of satisfaction; he was now an engaged man.

"OH!!" Charlotte stopped at the porch doorway, startled at the sight of Henry, holding the hand of her sister and whispering something into her ear. Anna's eyes were cast down shyly; she smiled in a manner Charlotte had never, to her memory, ever seen. They both turned at her entrance, but Henry didn't drop Anna's hand.

"Charlotte, I asked Anna to let me be the first to tell you. You'll be the first person we've told, after your father. I've asked her to be my wife, and she has agreed."

Except for a flicker of eyelids, Charlotte's face didn't change. She looked at him for a long moment and then turned to Anna. Her lips tightened.

"Aren't you going to give us your blessing? I know this must seem rather sudden."

"Congratulations, Henry. I hope you'll be very happy with my sister, who never used to keep secrets from me."

"Oh, Charlotte, I know this is unexpected. I didn't expect it either; really, it was such a surprise when Henry asked me. I always thought you would be the first to be married."

Charlotte forced a laugh, a painful attempt at carefree gaiety. "I don't ever intend to marry."

"Oh, Charlotte, you don't mean that! You're far too pretty to remain an old maid!"

"Have you looked at the married women in this town, Anna? Is there anything about them that any girl with any intelligence would want to emulate? I mean to do, well, something better with my life. Something besides rearing up a collection of barefoot children and putting dishes of boiled potatoes on the table for some, some *man* to wolf down without so much as a 'thank you.'" She said "man" so witheringly that Henry felt ashamed for being one.

"You mean to be a schoolteacher or such? Charlotte, Anna's right, you are too pretty to be an old maid."

"Or a missionary, like that nice Mrs. Coffing," she said. "I might travel, and see the world, and do good in the world." Mrs. Coffing, of the Central Turkey Mission, had arrived in Benzonia while visiting relatives on furlough from Marash, Turkey. She and Charlotte, to the family's surprise, had struck up a close friendship.

"A missionary? You?" He shook his head disbelievingly.

"Yes, and why not, I'd like to know? Mrs. Coffing is a wonderful woman, and she is a missionary. Our father was a missionary, of course, and so was our mother. Or the wife of one, anyway." Feeling that her argument had fallen short, she quickly went on. "Our mother died in the service of the Lord. Anyway, she was more than just a *wife*." She said the last with such scathing contempt that Henry winced.

"Charlotte, dear, I see that you're upset. Please don't be angry with us, Sister. You'll soon grow used to the idea of it." Charlotte walked past them into the house, and shut the door behind her.

CHARLOTTE LINGERED in the large empty upstairs bedroom. She was supposed to be sweeping up the dust, using a damp cloth tied over the end of her broom, and being "particularly attentive to the corners," per Elvira's directions. As if she didn't know how to dust a floor by now! She wasn't sure which she resented more, the necessity of polishing every room in this enormous house (entirely too grandiose, to her mind, for a brief ceremony that would occur in two rooms downstairs, well, three if you counted the kitchen) or Elvira's constant and unnecessary chivvying.

"Charlotte Spencer, I declare! This is your only sister's special day, and it's the least you can do . . ." And her especially nasty gibe, "If I didn't know better, I'd think you were jealous of your sister!"

Jealous! The very idea made her shake her head in disgust. She did, however, have to admit to slight feelings of hurt, hurt at her sister's thoughtlessness. They had always shared all their news and secrets; Charlotte knew she'd always been there for Anna, anyway, though sometimes out of pity, truth be told, because she, Charlotte, was the pretty one and she'd always known there was something special about herself.

As girls they'd shared a book of fairy tales, a magical volume with quaint pictures of giants, witches, and diminutive folks in gauzy draperies; her favorite stories had been of princesses in hiding, tucked away in "hamlets" or poor woodcutter's cottages until the truth became known and the beautiful princess came into her own and married the prince.

Charlotte at age seven knew better than to risk ridicule by suggesting point-blank that she, also, was royalty in disguise. Still, guided by the story about the princess on a bed with twelve thick mattresses and a pea beneath the bottom one, so extreme was her delicacy that she'd been unable to sleep a wink, Charlotte made the experiment.

"I don't know why, but I tossed and turned all night long," announced Charlotte at the breakfast table. "There seemed to be something hard under the mattress."

Brainard snorted.

Anna volunteered, "I slept just fine," and added, unnecessarily, it seemed to Charlotte, "I always sleep just fine."

Elvira, skimming cream at the counter, added (even more unnecessarily), "Hard work and a good conscience are the best sleep medicine there is."

"Cast not your pearls before swine," thought Charlotte contemptuously, though she buttered her bread as daintily as she could despite their denseness.

Soon Charlotte had put away the book, deeming it sinful since it lured the mind to sorcery and witchcraft. Even so, the belief stayed with her throughout her young years that she was somehow different from her fellows.

When Henry Thacker first joined the household, her imaginings had imbued him with a rosy aura, colored by that childhood story about the handsome young swineherd who'd turned out to be the youngest son of a king. It became quickly obvious that Henry, though quite nice-looking, was no prince, being rather arrogant and argumentative, to her mind.

Anna, of a more plebeian outlook, seemed to think otherwise, and after all, what sort of future could the poor girl have, except married to a commonplace man, producing commonplace children? Charlotte, as befitted a superior person, had graciously allowed Anna the field. Still, Anna might have told her in advance about the courtship, perhaps asked for Charlotte's counsel, before accepting his suit.

So, jealous? Certainly not. Hurt, slightly hurt, but that was all. Well, no, she was also ever so slightly annoyed by all the hubbub. You'd think nobody had ever been married before. Every young girl flocked around Anna, asking what she planned to wear, wasn't she excited, emitting meaningless chitchat that was echoed by all the older women, who looked syrupy and gushed idiotic sentiments like, "Weddings make me feel as giddy as a schoolgirl!"

She'd had to go shopping all the way to Traverse City with Elvira and Anna to help pick out "things a bride might need," as Elvira said, with Anna nodding in a shy blushy way that made Charlotte itch to slap her.

Even so, she'd gone along with all the nonsense in a most agreeable way. Here she was, the day before the wedding, dusting rooms where nobody would even be going, in a whole house rented for its stairway so that plain, scrawny Anna could make an entrance sweeping down it on Papa's arm.

"We'll hope she doesn't trip and roll all the way down and land at Henry's feet," she thought, suppressing a giggle.

Too, it was annoying to catch the glances of their friends—did they pity her, because Anna was marrying the hired man? Ridiculous! Still, it made her long to escape the dismal little town.

More and more she'd been giving thought to the comment she'd tossed at Anna, and Henry's response. "A missionary?" "You?" And why not! No, not to go and live in the north woods in a shanty and minister to the savages, who were nothing more than wild beasts, to her mind. No, the American Missionary Board had gone much farther afield, to the East, as far as China and the Japans, but most of all, to Turkey.

In the last year, two different visiting lecturers had spoken of the need to bring religion and its civilizing influences to the Mohammedans. Several schools had opened up to educate the children of the Armenians, those stalwart souls who'd converted to the True Faith at the time of the Crusades and established their Christian communities along the routes where the Crusaders had passed.

The Sultan of Turkey hated all Christians, it was said, and today's missionaries would be the new crusaders, bringing religion to the infidels once again.

Charlotte couldn't help feeling a tingle of excitement. While the stories of Ali Baba and other such tales were of pagans and Saracens and not appropriate for Christian children to dwell upon too deeply, they left an exotic odor behind in her mind. It smelled of desert nights, camels, flying carpets, and evil sultans, in close proximity to the lands where Jesus had walked, and it was far more compelling than getting married and raising a pack of mewling babies, no matter how handsome the swineherd.

She'd written to the Missionary Board and awaited the reply, and she had not mentioned it to Anna at all.

Riding One and Leading the Other

"HENRY, I'VE TAKEN A STEP without consulting you, and I hope you'll forgive me. I want you to go to Traverse City this Friday, and fetch back two horses from Cooper's livery."

"But Mr. Spencer, have you forgotten? Saturday's the big day! I'd planned to spend some time with my family and just, well, get ready."

"Oh, rubbish, Henry, a young man doesn't need to do anything special to prepare for his wedding; he's not the one people look at. Well, perhaps he needs to place his faith in the Lord and be sure to bathe well. I need these horses, and I promised Mrs. Spencer I would be at her disposal all of Friday. She has already worn herself to a frazzle cleaning the Bailey house for the wedding, with only Anna to help her." Neither man saw fit to comment on Charlotte's reluctant assistance in the wedding preparations.

Henry left, somewhat crankily, on his errand early on Friday morning. Saturday noon, he reported to David Spencer. He'd ridden back on one handsome bay gelding and led its match, by a rope tied to its halter.

"These are certainly fine horses, Mr. Spencer. I can understand why you wanted to make sure of them. Two other men were admiring them at Cooper's when I arrived."

"Do you like them, Henry? Then I am pleased. They are for you and Anna."

Henry stared at him, momentarily speechless. David looked at his feet, embarrassed. Henry turned to the nearest horse and stroked its soft nose. "A wonderful gift, Mr. Spencer, thank you very much. Anna will be touched, as I am, by your thoughtfulness."

"Don't thank me, Henry; I just want to give my daughter and her husband a good start in life."

Half an hour later, Henry ran a dandy brush briskly along Squire's flank. He had renamed his horses (his horses!); it seemed in keeping with his new status. One day he was a boarding student, the "hired boy," and then he was a graduate, and now he was a property owner, with two fine horses, "broken to ride or drive." Soon he was to become a husband and a family man!

Squire and Star were a handsome pair, as well matched as twins. Henry already knew them apart; Squire's blaze ran from beneath his forelock all the way to his nose. Star's blaze stopped a good two inches above his nose. He also seemed the more affectionate of the two; Henry's dark hair was sticky with bits of chewed grass and Star saliva. When Henry had felt his hair tugged, he'd whirled around and witnessed the horse's toothy open-mouthed laugh. Well, maybe it was a yawn. But it seemed the horse had twinkled at him, and it felt affectionate. He slapped the rumps of his horses and sighed happily, and then Elvira's peremptory voice demanded that he put those horses up, now, and get changed for the wedding.

THE WEDDING WAS EVERYTHING Anna might have wished; the early May weather cooperated, and as she came down the wide staircase of the Charles E. Bailey house, she felt the warm breeze as it softly stirred through the windows. The dress she wore was plain, an ecru that would take a good dark dye for later use; she had embellished it with early violets. "She looks almost pretty," whispered a neighbor kindly, and it was true.

For the moment, it mattered not a bit that her eyes were somewhat small, her nose long and narrow, and her lips just a little too thin. Anna had worn her hair loose, and it waved around her face, softening her sharp features. Her usually pale cheeks were pink with excitement, and her dark eyes shone.

She stood tall and straight, holding her white Bible in hands that trembled only slightly, and spoke her responses clearly. More clearly, it must be admitted, than those of her new husband. Henry's hands shook as though with palsy, though he finally managed to thread the ring onto Anna's thin finger.

Once, during Anna's responses, for no apparent reason he pushed his hair back from his forehead and gave a sickly laugh, drawing Anna's and Reverend Waters's startled eyes to him. He awarded a silly grin to each of them, and the ceremony concluded. He leaned forward to kiss Anna's lips and nearly lost his balance; Anna steadied him with a wry smile. He took her arm gratefully, and they turned to face the assembled guests.

"Oh, Elvira, how can we begin to thank you? It was so clever of you to rent this beautiful house for us for the wedding!" Anna hugged Elvira again, warmly. Henry shyly followed suit.

Elvira and David glanced at one another. "I suppose we needn't keep it a secret any longer, Anna. The house is our gift to you. See that you keep it well and make it a godly home. Fill those other three rooms with children!" he laughed with some embarrassment.

Speechless, Anna gazed at them both. Her thin lips trembled momentarily, and then firmed. "You've been too good to us both. We can't begin to thank you, either of us."

Henry grasped David's hand and pumped it heartily. "We're, that is, I'm, we, oh thank you sir! Thank you both! You're both too kind, much too kind . . ." He laughed shakily and then turned to Charlotte, next in the line. "Well, Charlotte . . ."

Charlotte primly turned her cheek for him to kiss. "Let me be the first to congratulate you, brother. I know Anna will be a good wife to you." She coolly accepted Anna's warm hug. After a moment's uncomfortable pause, Henry turned to Brainard, who took his offered hand cordially.

"Wish you both the best," muttered Brainard, and allowed Anna to kiss his cheek.

"Congratulations, son," muttered John Thacker huskily; he pounded Henry warmly on the back before bussing Anna enthusiastically. The couple proceeded down the line.

"I wouldn't have believed it," muttered one matron to another below the general din of festivity. "When David Spencer announced an engagement after church that evening, I was sure that it would be Charlotte's engagement, not Anna's."

"Look at Charlotte," hissed a younger girl maliciously to her companion. "Doesn't she look green?"

"I knew he'd never ask her," was the response. "He's lived with the Spencers long enough to know what she's really like under that pretty exterior. Handsome is as handsome does, my mother always says, and so say I, as well."

To Be a Missionary

JULY 1875

"CHARLOTTE, YOU HAVE A LETTER. It appears to be from the Congregational Near East Board of Missions." David frowned as he handed the letter to his daughter. "Why is it addressed directly to you and not the Christian Endeavor Society, I wonder?"

Elvira paused, her hands buried in the dough on the breadboard. She and her husband looked curiously at Charlotte, who slit the thin paper and unfolded the single page.

"Dear Miss Spencer," she read aloud. "Allow me to congratulate you on your acceptance by this board to serve as a missionary. The Congregational Church has assigned you to carry the Good News of Jesus Christ to the Armenians, at Biltis station, in Turkey. A letter will follow within the next two weeks, containing further details about your posting and the necessary preparations."

"Why, Charlotte, you're never serious!"

"I certainly am. The American Missionary Board has accepted me, and I intend to go."

"Ridiculous! Your health would never allow it! Why, Charlotte, you know that you can't even face a new Sunday-school class without coming home ill one day out of ten."

"Oh, pshaw, Elvira, you do exaggerate things sometimes. I haven't had a spell in ages. Oh, this is so exciting! Papa, will you take me to Traverse City? There are so many things I shall need."

David Spencer wiped his spectacles with his handkerchief. "Charlotte, we may never see you again if you go so far away. Of course I'm proud of you, my dear, but Turkey is so very far away. So very far . . ."

"HOW LOW THE MIGHTY HAVE FALLEN!" thought Charlotte, although she supposed it wasn't a very Christian way to feel about her only sister's One Big Day. It had been very tiresome, though, to stand by and watch the whole town carry on as though a queen were being enthroned, when it was really only skinny, pointy-nosed Anna marrying the somewhat pleasant-looking hired hand.

Now, however, the silly townspeople had an event worthy of note to celebrate. It wasn't every day that one of Their Own was called directly to the service of the Lord, to a place practically in the Holy Lands. In a way, it surpassed Brainard's accomplishments; true, he was ordained, but even he hadn't followed in Papa's footsteps and become a missionary.

She tried not to be puffed up and proud. Hadn't Jesus taken to task those hypocrites who stood on the streets praying so as to be observed by men? So she remained outwardly demure and humble, trying not to seem proud when Reverend Waters made the announcement from the pulpit on Sunday and a gasp ran through the crowd, and now young girls, their eyes alight, asked, "Charlotte! Aren't you afraid, going that long way?"

She felt eyes upon her when she stood at the grocery counter buying cream of tartar, felt those eyes following her as she went about the streets, looking solemn and uplifted. Now it was Anna's turn to accompany Elvira and Charlotte to Traverse City to shop. Papa came along also; while wedding shopping was merely "women's business," preparing for missionary duty overseas was the Lord's business.

Charlotte had to admit, humbly of course, that this was highly gratifying.

David helped Elvira down from the buggy and turned to Charlotte as she stepped down. "I'll need to help myself from now on, Father."

"Nonsense, daughter, the day hasn't come yet that I'd fail in manners, especially to a daughter that I may never see again." His wispy beard trembled slightly as he realized the import of his own words. Elvira, at his side, wept openly.

Anna stepped forward sobbing and drew Charlotte to her. Henry blew his nose loudly, but kept his distance.

"All aboard!" called the conductor, and Charlotte extricated herself from her sister's grasp, fished her handkerchief from her sleeve, and blew her nose. She took a step backward and nearly tripped over her valise. Henry sprang forward and righted her.

"Oh, Henry, brother . . ." Charlotte sagged against him momentarily and then turned away with a light laugh. She mounted the steps to her car and turned, stark against the dark interior of the railway car, exhilarated for a moment by awareness of the great adventure before her. But as she fell into her seat and turned, her stomach did so also. Her family, always so large in her personal sphere, suddenly looked tiny and distant on the platform. "God in heaven, what am I doing?" she murmured, and put her handkerchief to her mouth. The train rolled south.

"ANNA! We have a letter from Charlotte! Open it up, where does she write from? What does she say? Where has . . ."

"Don't jostle me, Henry; do give me a moment to open this properly. Now see, the stamp is torn."

"Biltis, Turkey, August 30, 1875.

"My Dear Sister Anna, and Brother Henry,

"I hope this letter finds you well, and that Papa, Elvira, and Brainard are likewise. I am told that my letters will be a long time on the road back to you and yours, which I now understand. I have been three days on the train to New York City, ten days on the freighter to Gibraltar and five more through the Dardanelles and the Sea of Marmora to Constantinople. There I met two other missionaries, Miss Jacobson with whom I will room, and Mrs. Campbell who is joining her husband. We stayed at Bible House for three days, then traveled by a much smaller steamship to the coastal town of Trezibod.

"That was only the beginning! We have been on the journey from Trezibod to Biltis for nearly four weeks, my dear family, with the heat nearly unbearable during the day. Temperatures moderate at night, and in the mountainous areas, which encompass most of the approach to Biltis, I am told the cold may become extreme in the mountains from September through April.

"I have begun to learn some Turkish and some Armenian words. We stayed in khans, which are inns, on the road, and we rode in arabas, which are heavy horse-drawn carts. I shall begin teaching girls in mangaran, which is grammar school, with assistance from an English-speaking Armenian woman named Rakel.

"The dirt and poverty would horrify you, Sister, as it continues to do me. Wherever we stopped, I attempted to sanitize our table and cooking surfaces, only to awaken in the morning covered with bites from fleas and other insects. We sleep in our own bedding, in our folding beds, so I cannot imagine where these nasty things come from. I despair sometimes, but of course much of our work involves educating these ignorant people, so I must have more patience.

"This will be the last letter I will be able to send for quite some time, for I shall be very busy. Please promise me something, Sister. When I realize how fervent my sisters and brothers in Christ are here, and with what devotion they dedicate their waking hours, I am ashamed at the laxity that so often abounded in our own home and in my own heart. Please, dear sister, remember us especially during your Sabbath observances.

"My love to all, your sister, Charlotte."

"I don't know as we're all that lax, here in Benzonia," protested Henry.

"Oh, you know what Charlotte means. We involve ourselves in mundane pursuits, forgetting the purpose for which we're put on this earth. The missionaries' daily tasks are all dedicated to bringing the heathen to Christ, while we worry about whether we have enough canning jars for the cherries."

Henry assayed a joke. "Cherries are important too, Anna. They are God's gift to us, after all."

"Don't be frivolous, Henry, you know exactly what I mean. We must rededicate our lives to the Lord's purposes. We must share this letter with Papa and Elvira and Brainard. I know they've been terribly worried, as we have. Imagine, my own sister, all alone in a tiny ship on the great Atlantic. We should never have let her go."

"Now Anna, we couldn't hold her back if she wanted to go. Charlotte's always done pretty much what she wanted, far as I can see."

Henry and Anna

"ANNA!" Henry burst through the screen door.

"Henry, you nearly scared me out of two years' growth!" Anna set down the paring knife that had come close to removing her thumbnail. "And look at that screen door; you nearly put your elbow clear through it!"

Henry absently turned and popped the bulge in the screen outward with the tented fingers of his hand. When he pulled his hand back, the screen popped inward again. He shrugged and turned back to Anna. "What would you think about my becoming a deputy sheriff?"

"It all depends, doesn't it?" asked Anna mildly, taking up the bowl of lima beans and sitting back down again.

"Don't you think it'd be a great opportunity?"

"How much would it pay you? How often would you need to be away nights?" (Here a faint blush colored her cheek.) "And would it put you in the way of danger?"

"Not much to start with, it's true, but the job will grow, in time. The college has nearly 150 students now, and Sheriff Chandler says they'll get up to all kinds of harum-scarum behavior, sure as, well, sure as anything, and he'll need an assistant. Would you miss me if I had to be away?"

Anna made an "away with you" gesture, and pared the stem end off another gray-green bean pod, inserted a thumb into the resultant aperture, and deftly rubbed the interior beans into her bowl. "You didn't answer the question. Is it a dangerous sort of position? Will it make me a widow at an early age?"

"Oh, not likely. Often I'd be handing out summonses, testifying in court, what Sheriff Chandler calls 'routine duties.' It'll be some money coming in during the winter, which we sorely need."

"You needn't tell me about that, Henry Thacker. I'm the one that must make the pennies stretch at the market, and that's just for the two of us."

"You didn't answer my question. Would you miss me if I had to be away?"

"I might, if I didn't have company."

"Well, but you can't expect the other ladies to stay with you every time I'm away, you know."

"I didn't mean that company. I was thinking of someone, well, smaller." Anna rarely looked diffident.

"Why Anna, what do you mean? Oh. Oh! Truly?"

"Yes, Henry, I didn't want to say anything until I was sure. Elvira assures me my surmise was correct. Henry! Put me down!"

"When? Should we have the doctor in today? What shall we call him? Or her?"

"Don't be foolish, Henry, it won't be until spring. Now go back to work and let me be."

"Don't scold me, Anna, but give me a bean. I'll tell the sheriff yes, then, shall I?"

"As you will, Henry. Now away with you, I must finish these beans. I'm taking a stew to the social tonight, and I've only begun this batch."

MARIETTA WATERS STOOD at the counter of Stockton's store, picking through a basket of early strawberries suspiciously. "I've never heard of hothouse strawberries," she muttered as Elvira stepped up. "I'd bet a cookie they're sour as can be. I'd wait another month for proper ones, but Father heard about these and has his heart set on shortcake with whipped cream. But I'm forgetting my manners, Elvira. How have you been keeping?"

"We're all well at home, thank you. We're terribly worried about Charlotte, what with the cholera epidemic over there and all."

"I'm sure you must be. It's a terrible thing; and she somewhat frail anyway. A pint of these berries for me, Dora, please, and put them on Father's account. Rest assured Charlotte is in our prayers, of course, as are all of you, and dear Anna, of course. Don't tell her, but I'm making a special baby quilt for her."

"Marietta, your secret's as safe as houses," Elvira assured her, and she picked up her shopping basket again. "Oh, and if you'll add a few drops of vanilla extract to the berries when you crush them with the sugar, that should cut any sourness."

The ladies nodded pleasantly to one another, and Elvira, basket laden, stepped out into the brisk spring sunshine.

Leroy Ferry Arrives

HENRY, GRAY IN THE FACE, paced in the parlor. Another groan floated down the staircase. "Dang," he muttered and then looked around guiltily. David, in the kitchen, clanked dishes busily.

"This tea's just the thing you need to set you up."

"David, you're much too cheerful about this. That's your own daughter upstairs on her bed of agony."

"I know, son, but just remember, I've had three of my own. Women just have to endure the pain the Lord sends, in hopes of greater joy in the child to come. We've prayed enough, and it's in Christ's hands now. Anna's tough, she'll be fine."

"Sure doesn't sound fine. And what do you mean, you've had three? You and I can't begin to imagine it, can we?"

"Henry, it's not like you to be irascible. Calm down. It might be some time . . ."

"Oh! What was that?"

David smiled beatifically. "Sounds like your son is here. Or your daughter."

Nasal wails rang faintly down the staircase. After a few moments, Elvira called down, "Henry, would you come up here, please?"

Henry's knees sagged, and David pulled him up. "Up you go, son. Until you're up there, I won't know a thing. I know Elvira."

Henry stepped through the door. His head buzzed, and the floor seemed to rise up darkly.

"Henry, take a deep breath," commanded Elvira. He complied.

"Better?" Henry nodded gratefully. "Good. Don't drop him now." Elvira handed Henry a wrapped, bleating bundle. Henry took it and looked doubtfully at the red, wrinkled face. The face glared mistily back at him.

"Him? Well, hello, Leroy."

"Leroy?"

"Yes. His middle name is Ferry."

Anna, ignored on the bed, nodded. "For you, Elvira."

Elvira's eyes misted as she looked down at the squeaking bundle. "Bless you, Leroy Ferry." Then she briskly took him from Henry's arms and returned him to Anna. She glared at Henry and nodded toward Anna.

Henry cleared his throat. "How are you, Anna?"

Anna smiled wearily at Henry. "I'm well, husband. Isn't he a fine boy?"

"If you say so, Anna." At her affronted stare, he tried again. "I mean, well, he's very small and rather rumpled . . . but I'm sure he'll fill out just fine, won't he?"

At Elvira's look, he backed out of the room and made his escape.

David chuckled. "They always look puny like that at first. Well, guess I'd better pay my respects. Boy, is it? What's the name? Leroy Ferry? That's nice. Elvira must be very pleased with that."

"BILTIS, TURKEY, September 10, 1875

"Dear Sister, I take pen in hand to tell you that I have risen from my sickbed and feel able to resume my duties. Despite our efforts to educate the women in sanitary cooking practices, many of their children and the weak die of dysentery. I have been fortunate in having good care.

"I'm very pleased to hear of the arrival of your first child, and I pray that you and he remain in good health. I have already sent a box with some embroidered dresses for him. The older girls are being taught this craft and some of their work is quite nice. . . ."

ANNA SET DOWN the vegetable bowl and backed away from the table. Ordinarily she loved cabbage, but there was something about this batch that had gone sour. Or no, maybe the cabbage wasn't the problem. She hurried out to the privy and retched.

Henry returned from the barn, two pails of milk in his hands, and looked around the kitchen. Dinner was partly on the table, Leroy playing happily on the floor, but Anna was nowhere to be seen. A moment later she came in the back door.

"I hope I'm done with feeling like this in time for Thanksgiving," she commented wanly to Henry.

He patted her on the hand. "Leroy's a handful, isn't he? Why don't you stay home from service tonight, and I'll keep an eye on him for you."

"No, Henry, it's not that I'm tired. It's just that I've begun feeling sick in the mornings again."

"Oh? Oh, Anna, that's wonderful news!" He picked up Leroy. "Hear that, Roy? You're going to have a playmate!"

"That's as the Lord wills. Sit down before the potatoes get cold now." She bowed her head and waited for Henry's hasty blessing.

"CONGRATULATIONS, HENRY! You have another son. Anna says you agreed on Ralph for the name?"

"Ralph Leonard. Leonard for Anna's mother Cornelia Leonard, that is. He looks a little better than Roy did at the start, doesn't he?"

"BILTIS, TURKEY, September 15, 1877

"Dear Anna and Henry,

"By now you must surely have your new daughter or son. I have sent a small gift of knitted items for her or him, and hope they fit.

"Tensions continue to grow with the Turks. Several of the men of the Gregorian church were arrested last week. We continue to await word of them. Of course, although we disapprove of their form of worship, we are also aware that the government disapproves of any form of Christianity and turns the same hostile eye to the rest of us.

"As I mentioned in my last letter, the British consulate has asked that Protestantism be recognized as a separate religious community from the many Gregorian churches that abound both here and elsewhere, but so far that has not transpired. We are very much aware that we remain here at Sultan Abdul Hamid's pleasure, and that he could evict us, or worse, at a moment's notice. Pray for us, dear sister."

Leroy amongst the Angels

LEROY, AGE THREE, danced with excitement as his mother helped him dress. She had promised him that if he was very good in church the day before, neither squirming nor rustling during the two-hour homily, he might go to the chicken yard with her today and help feed the hens. He had often admired the chickens from a distance. He clasped his chubby hands behind his back to keep them in check; too often had they flown out in excitement and knocked things over, earning those hands a brisk slap.

The chickens ran about on legs so quick and nimble, thought Leroy. Their heads stretched out on their limber, softly feathered necks, enabling them to stare at a choice tidbit on the ground with now one eye, then with the other, before with a lightning-quick strike they snatched up the object. It disappeared like magic! He thought these chickens must be something like the angels that Dr. Waters described, winged beings that could do magical things.

He had once watched one especially canny speckled hen dance over to a pile of discarded cabbage greens his mother had dropped over the fence. In the huge green pile, she alone had sighted the fat green caterpillar and pounced on it, impaling it on her yellow beak. She did a solitary dance with her prize, shaking it, dropping it, stepping daintily in a sideways circle, and again lifting, shaking, dropping it, dancing, crooning to her treasure. Her tiny round eyes seemed to shine with joy. Then as a special hen's sense warned her of another's interest in the plump morsel, she pounced a final time, tossed it into the air, caught it neatly, and swallowed it.

Today, at last, he was to be allowed to approach those marvelous beings on their own ground, mingling intimately with them the way that only his mother was allowed to do, strewing offerings in their path. Face and hands washed, hair combed, mush eaten, and face wiped again, Leroy trotted along behind her. He carried the smaller bucket containing cracked grains; Anna led the way carrying a pailful of water in one hand, the bucket of parings, shells, and plate scrapings in the other.

Anna's chickens were unused to assaults from small creatures; dogs that attacked poultry in that struggling farm community were summarily dispatched, as were marauding foxes and hawks and egg-stealing raccoons or skunks. Until this day, the most excitement most of these fowls had experienced was the occasional too-close approach by a visiting farm wagon.

Anna set down her load, unlatched the opening, and waved Leroy through. As she stooped to pick up her buckets again, Leroy, with a crow of joy, dashed toward his speckled favorite, intending to offer her the first of the grain. He flapped his hands; the bucket flew and then bounced, grain showering in every direction.

Henry stepped out of the barn with a barrowful of manure in time to see the terrified hens exploding in all directions, squawking and shrieking. Leroy halted, amazed at the birds' reaction. A hard hand grasped his roundabout and jerked him back; his foot kicked his mother's pail, spilling orts all over the ground. For one confused moment he thought one of the hens had grabbed him, and he cowered, arms above his head. He looked up into the terrifying face of his mother; a wail escaped him.

Henry hurried over, forgetting momentarily that he pushed a large smelly barrow, further disconcerting the hens. Anna jerked Leroy out through the gate, latched it, and dragged the howling child over to the lilac bush, from which she began to twist a limb. Henry frowned.

"Anna, surely that's not warranted? He didn't really hurt the chickens, did he?"

"He has to learn some time. Some of these hens will be off their feed for days."

Giving the lie to this, most of the hens were already serenely picking over the scattered grain, at least until she led the wailing Leroy over to the scene of his transgressions and began to switch his legs.

Anna led him to the house, where he was to stand in the corner in disgrace for an hour. "Those nasty old hens. They told Mother to switch me," he brooded.

"BENZONIA, 1878

"Dear Sister,

"The retirement party for Father was quite lovely, and nearly every one of his friends was able to attend. As he has told you, the office of Postmaster has long since been taken over by Jesse Packard. Can you believe it? The man has immediately opened up a small general store in the post office!

"Elvira was completely worn out after the party, poor thing, although I made the utmost attempt to handle most of the cooking and cleanup. I think she is constitutionally unable to sit still and allow anyone else to 'do' for her in any way, even when the event is actually a family affair. Father looks more tired than he ought for a man of only sixty-seven years, I feel. Perhaps I worry more than I should; you know how he hates to be fussed over, so I keep my thoughts to myself.

"How are you feeling? Every time I hear about another outbreak of cholera, at home or on foreign shores, I think of you, dear sister, and utter a silent prayer on your behalf . . ."

They Just Keep On Coming

ANNA SUPPRESSED A SIGH as she sank into the rocker, her hands full of mending. She noted that her workbasket had begun to look frayed, the green and white cane cracking near the top. Anna cared not a whit about the basket's appearance, but too many perfectly good stockings had been torn by clutching basket splinters. The basket had been Elvira's. Its green canes were fading by the time Anna was old enough to help with darning, her patches neat and even enough to please Elvira's exacting perusal. You could tell, by squinting sideways, how bright the green had once been, a neat clean contrast to the pale white splines that crossed it. Now it was nearly past its usefulness, and she'd never find a basket as neat and handy as this one. It was just small enough to tuck under one arm if you had a squirming baby under the other, yet large enough to hold holey stockings for a growing family.

Again not sighing, Anna pulled out the first stocking, a long black one belonging to Leroy, she thought. She frowned, looked at it again. Ralph's? Maybe. And with a great hole at the heel. What did that boy do, to make the heels wear out before the toes so consistently?

Another Saturday evening. Children washed and in bed, dishes washed and put away, cream skimmed and set on the back of the stove to sour for the potatoes. Kitchen floor washed, breakfast set up and ready for morning. Anna had decreed that on the Sabbath no actual cooking was to be done, but that leftovers could be warmed. Her final tasks included gathering up the children's toys and books and putting them away for tomorrow, frivolous games and pursuits deemed unsuitable for Sabbath. Only the Bible and other religious writings could be read, though Charlotte's letters were acceptable for reading over.

She sighed. The Lord sent his strength to those who needed it, she knew, but sometimes it seemed to waver. She stretched her back. This child seemed more restless, and seemed to delight in kicking her squarely in the back. She knelt on the floor, folded her hands on the seat of the chair she had vacated, and tried to focus on her many blessings. The baby kicked her again.

"BILTIS, TURKEY, December 1879

"My dear sister and family,

"I am so pleased that you saw fit to name your daughter after her Aunt Charlotte. We asked a special blessing for dear little Charlotte Spencer Thacker at our service on Wednesday, and some of our orphans asked me to send their sincere greetings and wishes for her health and good fortune.

"My health is improving. The Campbells have been very kind, sharing many of their delicacies with me when I have felt unable to eat the coarser fare that is available in the wintertime in these mountains. Miss Jacobson has cared for me as tenderly as a sister might, so you see I am in good hands.

"Conditions continue to be tense. Our nerves are often on edge, as we now know we have reason to fear the worst . . ."

"BILTIS, TURKEY, March 1882

"My dear sister and family,

"My health continues to improve, thanks in part to the tonic you sent, for which many thanks. Thank you also for the gloves; they have already served me well. I shared the box of 'ribbon candy' with Miss Jacobson, who enjoyed it greatly.

"I share your concerns about this new president, Chester Arthur. I pray, however, that the son of a Baptist preacher will have an appreciation for the importance of Christian education both at home and abroad.

"Although I don't remember Amelia Brace very well, I, too, am happy that Brainard has found a good girl of good family on whom to affix his affections. When is the wedding to be?

"I'm sure you will share with me in rejoicing about this good news. The sultan has granted the Missionary Board permission to open the girls' school in Smyrna. Rather than awaiting the permits to build anew, they will modify several homes for this purpose. While my experience might have been of value in this endeavor, I feel that my place is here for as long as the Lord sees fit to keep me here . . ."

A Full House

BENZONIA, MARCH 1883

HENRY STOMPED the wet leaves from his boots. The rain had eased off, but the brightness of the lamps and the warmth of the stove were welcome nonetheless. Roy and Ralph sat at the kitchen table with their books.

"Papa!" Lottie ran to him and threw her arms blissfully around his legs. He laughed and tried to fend her off.

"You'll get all wet," he scolded her playfully, as he peeled his coat off.

"Grandpa's sick," she informed him solemnly. Henry frowned, turned to Anna, who glowered at Lottie. "Miss Big-Britches needs to mind her own business." Lottie, abashed, backed against the wall.

"Anna? Whose father is sick, please?"

"My father. He's had another bad spell. Dr. Steward fears he may have had a shock. His left arm is numb, he says, and he seems a little confused."

"Oh, that poor man," said Henry. "Shall I go over there now?"

"No, Henry, don't, it would only disturb Elvira. The poor thing is quite worn down as it is, what with nursing and worry. Were it not for you and the children, I'd stay over there with her for a few days."

"Now, Anna, you know full well that we can look after ourselves, for a day or two. We'll decide what to do if he isn't back on his feet by then."

"WELL, DAVID, how are you feeling today?" David's face quivered as he attempted to form words.

"Shouldn't you be on your way to Frankfort to carry that summons?" asked Anna while she dabbed at the saliva that dribbled from the left corner of David's mouth, runneling into his beard.

"Oh, we're fine," Elvira answered Henry's question. Her worn face seemed to have developed more lines in the last few days.

David pushed impatiently at Anna's hand, the one with the washcloth. "Drewring rike a wayby," he slurred, his chin quivering with the effort to speak plainly.

"Henry, you must convince Anna to return home. We feel so mortified that you and the children must shift for yourselves in her absence."

Henry had already made a decision; he hoped Anna wouldn't mind his unilateral high-handedness. "Elvira, David, why don't you both come and stay with us, just until David's feeling better? We have plenty of room, you know."

"Oh, Elvira, do," urged Anna. "We can move a lounge into the downstairs room for you, and David can have the bed."

"We couldn't possibly!" Elvira was indignant, and David shook his head.

Two days later, without understanding exactly how it had happened, the Spencers were installed in the east room of the Thackers' downstairs. A row of lilacs shaded the room from the bright morning sun; for the first two weeks of David's installation the fragrance of their blossoms drifted into his room on the warm air.

"BENZONIA, July 3, 1883

"Dear Charlotte,

"Please, dear sister, do reconsider your refusal to come home, at least for a few months. We continue to be concerned for Father's health. Dr. Steward feels he may have had another shock. His speech is very difficult to understand now, and Elvira tells us he complains of a coldness in the legs that worries her greatly, as it does us.

"We fear for your safety as well, dear sister. We have read accounts in the newspapers about the murders of the Armenian Christians, and assaults on the missionary compounds in many of the areas. You are rather in the thick of these, we find from a close examination of the atlas, although you have not seen fit to share much of the news with your own family. Your father yearns for a sight of your face while he is able to view it on this earthly plane, as do we all.

"I know that you feel your place is there, with your orphans and those poor beleaguered women, but we who are bound to you by stronger ties need you as well. Please come home. If the Missionary Board is unable to provide the fares, we will certainly provide them. Potatoes did especially well this year, and Henry has just received a slight increase in salary."

BENZONIA, JANUARY 1884

CHARLOTTE ACCEPTED THE HAND of the porter to steady herself as she stepped from the train. She paused, bewildered, and looked around. The midday sun shone on her cheekbones; her face appeared to consist of little more than eye sockets and teeth. Anna stepped forward, hesitantly.

"Charlotte? Is it you?" Tears clung to her lower lids as she reached for her sister. She blinked them back, laughed shakily. "When you said you'd been ill, I just didn't realize! Oh, of course, I should have thought."

"Well, none of us are quite the same as we used to be, are we? And brother Henry, how are you keeping? Are these the children?"

Roy shyly stepped forward and offered a limp hand to the gaunt woman, Ralph nervously at his heel. Charlotte missed the proffered hand and stepped over to Lottie, who sturdily stood her ground by her father.

"I am your auntie Charlotte. I'm told they call you Lottie, and not Charlotte, is that correct?"

"Yes, Auntie Charlotte. Thank you so much for the many beautiful things you've sent to us. These are my brothers, Roy and Ralph."

"How do you do, boys?" They mumbled their greetings, and Henry gave her a peck on the cheek before picking up her bag for her. He led the way to the sleigh.

"I had thought that after we had a bite of lunch and you had a chance to settle in for a slight rest, you might like for some of the ladies from our Christian Endeavor Society to come in for tea."

Charlotte's color brightened slightly at this prospect. Arm in arm, the sisters walked slowly away from the station. The children followed, and Henry stayed to help the porter with Charlotte's trunk.

BENZONIA, AUGUST 1884

THE COFFIN STOOD OPEN at the front of the church, Elvira at its head, tremulously greeting each person in the long line of mourners. Young Mrs. Barnes pressed Elvira's hand tremulously, her eyes brimming with heartfelt tears. "Elvira, my dear, be comforted. Your David is in the arms of our Savior, and I know he is smiling down upon us this very moment."

Elvira, supported by Anna and Henry on her right and Brainard on her left, moved her lips soundlessly and patted Mrs. Barnes's hand in return. "Thank you for being here," whispered Anna.

Charlotte sat on a chair near Brainard's elbow, handkerchief to her face. Periodically she fanned herself with the handkerchief; it was cruelly hot that August day, and Charlotte's pallor matched Elvira's. Several women hovered around Charlotte's chair.

Lottie edged up to Henry's side. He smiled down at her and pulled her against his side. His red eyes matched hers. David's stiffness had, over the years, unbent most with this young granddaughter. "I'll miss him too," he whispered to Lottie.

The organist began the first chords of "There Is a Green Hill Far Away," and the mourners drifted to their pews, Elvira helped to her place by Brainard and Henry.

Arcadian Interlude

ARCADIA, DECEMBER 1884

TEN MILES SOUTH of Frankfort, at about the second knuckle of the little finger in the Michigan "mitten," is a lake once called Bar Lake because of a sandbar that separated it from Lake Michigan, later renamed to Arcadia Lake. The village of Arcadia, founded in 1870, sits on the shore of this small lake. A lumber mill is its central feature, but the community supports itself by farming as well. It boasts two churches, and in one of these, on a cold December morning, a wedding was in progress. Jesse and Virginia Bunker, parents of the groom, were not important in the Arcadia hierarchy, but days were long in December in Northern Michigan, and the church was nearly filled.

"And do you, Forrest Bunker, take this woman Minnie May, to have and to hold . . ."

Orah, conscious of all eyes upon her, stood up straighter and held her basket of dried flower petals closer to her. Few nine-year-old girls got to be flower girls at a wedding, but her brother's intended was a reader of novels and, as Virginia Bunker snorted, "had her fancies." Orah knew very well that had it been her other brother Torrence who stood now at the altar, Orah would be in pews between her parents and sternly enjoined to "keep her trap shut."

". . . I now pronounce you man and wife." The harmonium did its best to burst into peals of exultation, and the wedding participants turned to walk up the aisle, Orah thinking that when she married, there'd be a pipe organ or she'd know the reason why.

Elvira Rejoins David

BENZONIA, AUGUST 1885

A ROBIN STOOD on the peak of the Thacker home, tweedling chirpily to the westering sun. Sad, how cheerful the rest of the world seemed, when in this darkened room Elvira struggled for each breath. Anna knew it was sinful of her to wish that the struggle might simply, well, stop. She told herself that Jesus would understand how this feeling of sad pity just wore a body out after a while. Elvira's features had a way of tightening between each exhalation and the beginning of the inhalation, as though a small animal were biting her, deep inside her lungs, and her gaunt frame dreaded to provoke it again.

Henry tiptoed into the bedroom where Anna nodded drowsily in her chair. "Go and lie down, Anna. I'll sit with her for a bit." Elvira slept on, only occasionally stirring faintly when the animal bit too deeply.

Anna rose sleepily. "I thought she might be growing stronger again, but now I think not. I wonder if we should send for the Reverend yet?"

"Rest now, Anna. If she seems to slip deeper, I'll come in and waken you. How is Charlotte feeling? Is she able, do you think, to sit with Elvira for a while?"

"I sent her to bed some hours ago. Poor thing, she's quite worn out with grief and worry. Perhaps I should go and look in on her for a bit."

"No, Anna, you must get some rest also. Charlotte can sleep and I'll stay here. Go and lie down."

Elvira died quietly two days later and was buried next to David.

Charlotte, the Belle of the Ball

"RALPH! SHAME ON YOU!" whispered Lottie, scandalized. Ralph, his worn brown boots in one hand, stood in his stockings in the passageway outside the front parlor, eavesdropping on the ladies. Ralph flapped a hand at her impatiently. "Shhh! Auntie's telling stories about the Turkish soldiers." Lottie edged in behind Ralph and cocked an ear toward the doorway.

". . . and then those Turkish soldiers went through each and every one of our buildings, even our own personal quarters! Some of the men protested, but after the soldiers pointed their guns at us, we felt it better to let them do as they please. Of course, we were terrified, not only for ourselves but for the men of the village."

"Well, I should say so! And you say some of the men disappeared afterward anyway?"

"Before AND afterward. These last two years have been utterly hair-raising, I can assure you. Whenever we stepped outside of our compound, crowds of men and young boys would dog our footsteps, chanting 'Prote, Prote' at us."

A chorus of "tsk tsk" arose from the women, before Mrs. Bailey was emboldened to ask, "Dare we ask the translation of that imprecation?"

"That is their word for 'leper.' When they heard that we called ourselves 'Protestants,' they immediately seized upon the opportunity to make the connection. Of course there are a good many lepers there, and so we immediately realized how much they loathed us for not being Mohammedans."

"Lottie, you may bring us more tea, please," called Anna from the parlor. Lottie jumped guiltily and tiptoed to the kitchen. Ralph nearly dropped his boots as he followed after her. Lottie pushed the door shut behind them, and they giggled guiltily. Ralph sat on Anna's spindle-backed chair by the back door and pulled on his boots, then stepped outdoors. Brother-like, he left Lottie to wrestle with the heavy tea things on her own.

"BUT MOTHER, I didn't mean to make a racket, the pot just slipped!" Lottie knew that she was making excuses and only babies did that. Still, it seemed unfair that they now had to stay quiet during the day, even on Saturdays!

"Your auntie had just gotten to sleep, Lottie, and I call it careless of you to waken her so rudely. Now you just go in there and apologize, Miss! And if she asks you to do anything, I expect you'll obey more prettily than you did the last time."

"Yes, Mother." Lottie pushed the door open into the darkened downstairs room where her aunt now resided.

"Anna? What was that terrible noise? I feared something terrible had happened . . . oh, it's you, Lottie."

"I came to apologize, Auntie, for disturbing you. I accidentally dropped a pot as I was putting it away. Is there anything I can bring you?"

"Now that I'm awake, I could certainly do with something soothing. Go ask your mother if there's any of that boiled chicken left from yesterday's dinner. And maybe some boiled potatoes if it's not too much trouble."

Half an hour later, Lottie slipped out the back door. "Is dinner on the table yet? I'm hungry as a bear! Hey, what's wrong with you?" Roy and Ralph, carrying their books in a strap, usually came home for the midday meal.

"I dropped a pot and woke Auntie up," explained Lottie. "So Mother made me go in and take care of her all morning. I had to bring her some chicken and potatoes and then more water, and make her special tea, and rub her head. The ladies from the Endeavor Society are coming this afternoon, and Auntie says she fears she'll be too poorly to do her part, so I must stay in the kitchen while Mother helps her entertain the ladies."

"Why doesn't Auntie just go back to Turkey where they appreciate her?" whispered Ralph, after looking carefully around. "She sure doesn't like living in a house with children."

"I do wish I could have gone to school this year. I'd lots rather sit in a schoolroom with a book than stand in the kitchen with a dishcloth."

"I'd hate to be a Turkish orphan at Auntie's school, wouldn't you?" giggled Roy. Ralph elbowed him, and they straightened their faces before presenting themselves in the kitchen.

FALL 1887

CHARLOTTE LEANED on the handrail of the back steps. She could vomit into the basin under her bed, and Anna would empty it for her, but this dreadful flux of the bowels was another story altogether. She had been to the privy three times since lunchtime, and her lower belly felt sanded. Yes, that's how it felt, scrubbed with sand and then lemon juice poured onto the raw places. She groaned, and turned back toward the privy. Not again! Then, she knew, when this bout finally ended she would be costive for the next several days.

"Maybe if you took more exercise," Emily Case had ventured timidly during one of their Endeavor Society meetings.

Charlotte smiled faintly and shook her head at the foolishness of the notion, but said, "I'll ask Dr. Powers when he comes to visit me on Friday."

Dr. Powers set his black leather bag onto a chair and opened it, the nested divided trays spread to either side in stair-steps. His stethoscope resided in its cavernous depths, and he pulled this out to listen to the busy rumblings in Charlotte's abdomen.

"Don't you think it might help me if I took a little Pluto Water each day?" suggested Charlotte.

Dr. Powers snapped his medicine bag shut. "There's nothing special about Pluto Water that can't be gotten from Frankfort Water, which is much cheaper and easier got. I can write an order for them to send it regularly by the afternoon train, if you will send someone to fetch it. That, and be sure that your diet includes plenty of bulk. Oh, and a brisk walk each day might do you a world of good, when weather permits."

Charlotte fell back against the pillows. "Oh, I couldn't possibly manage that. What if I should faint and nobody was there to assist?"

"Perhaps you could do some of the marketing for your sister. Plenty of people there, and Anna could do with the help, I expect."

"Very well, Doctor, I shall certainly consider that. Don't you think I should take a pill of some sort?"

Dr. Powers accordioned the shelves of the bag inside and snapped the catch decisively. "Rest, exercise, more bulk, and Frankfort Water.

That should pick you up if anything will." With no further farewell, he clicked the door shut behind him, and she heard his footsteps march away down the passage.

"SISTER, DO YOU THINK Henry would very much mind fetching my Frankfort Water from the train?"

"I'm sure he'd be happy to, Charlotte. He's back and forth from Beulah several times a day. Do you think you could eat an egg if I boiled it soft, the way you like it?"

"You're good to me, Anna, better than anybody deserves. Yes, I think I could keep it down."

Henry stepped into the kitchen and hung his hat from one of the nails in the wall at shoulder height. It kept company with Anna's straw shade hat, two worn calico aprons, and two miniature oilcloths, shared among the three children as, on rainy days, they came and went on their outdoor chores.

Anna stood at the sink, rinsing out Charlotte's dishes. A bucket of potato peelings stood on the floor at her ankle. She accepted Henry's kiss on her cheek with a perfunctory smile. "Set that bucket out on the back porch for me, will you, Henry? Oh, and Charlotte's having Frankfort Water delivered on the train Tuesdays and Fridays, would you bring it along home those afternoons?"

"For pity sakes, Anna, why does she want that water? It's a purgative! She spends more time in the privy than any three women as it is."

"Hush, now, Henry, she'll hear you. Please try to remember that my sister has destroyed her health, working herself sick in the service of the Lord in the land of the heathen, facing dangers that you and I only imagine, and coming home to watch her father and mother die one right after another. Her health is broken, and she's nowhere to go until she recovers."

With an effort, Henry lowered his voice. "I know, I know. I only wish Brainard had room for her sometimes. I'm sure it's hard on the children to have a sick woman living in their house, and I see that it's made more work for you as well."

"We'd be failing in our duty to our children if we didn't raise them with a Christian regard for their elders, Henry. And please remember that she is your sister as well as mine."

"Yes, Anna, I'm trying hard to remember that." He reached for his hat.

"Where are you going? Supper is nearly ready!"

"Sheriff Chandler asked if I would drive out past the mill and look for that whiskey still. Make me up a dinner pail, will you?"

Anna set her lips and went in to pack her husband's dinner for him. Henry went across the yard to saddle his horse. She handed him the pail without another word, and he leaned down to peck her cheek. Pity moved within him, and he said more gently, "I'll fetch the water for Charlotte, Anna. Go in now, and have yourself a good dinner. You're getting much too thin."

Anna looked at him bleakly. "I couldn't keep it down anyway, Henry. You remember how it was with Lottie? It's just that way again this time, everything I cook seems to smell just awful. Only tea will stay with me any amount of time. Oh, don't look at me that way, what do you expect, when you don't give me a moment's peace, even on the Sabbath?"

"Anna, call Dr. Powers if you feel that poorly. We can afford it this year."

Anna's chin trembled. "I wish Elvira could be with me again, she was so restful and such a help."

"I know, Anna, I miss her too. Both of them." Henry put his arm around Anna, who stood still and endured his embrace. He kissed her cheek again and turned away to tie his dinner bucket onto the ring on the back of Hanna's saddle. He was half a mile down the road before he remembered that he hadn't taken the bucket of potato peels to the porch for her.

Those Dreadful Sundays

BENZONIA, FEBRUARY 1888

RALPH LOOKED OUT the window again. Try as he might to focus on his verses, those thin cries insistently blew up the hill and into the kitchen with him. Archie, Neal, and Charlie were sledding on the hill across the road. This hill dropped down all the way to the meadow below, and Saturday's snow was packed down hard. A crackling frost in the night had turned the walks and roads to ice slicks, treacherous to the step of this morning's churchgoers. Even Old Balky, his heavy sled with the wooden runners, would fly on packed snow such as this.

He turned again to his book. "Can the prey be taken from the mighty, or the captives of a tyrant set free? Surely, thus saith the Lord . . ."

"Your turn to guide it!" came a gay call, faint on the western wind. Dinner was long over, dishes piled in the sink waiting for the morrow to be washed. Aunt Charlotte was out visiting. Mother sat in the parlor, Bible at her elbow, letter paper stacked neatly at hand. Ralph had written a dutiful page to his grandmother Thacker, thanking her for the new wool scarf. It would be tucked into his mother's much longer letter, along with notes from his brothers and sister. Roy and Lottie sat in the dining room, listlessly reading over their lessons, but Ralph hadn't been able to sit for a moment longer. Papa was away; often Sheriff Chandler told him he must help out, Sabbath or no Sabbath. That's what Papa said, anyway, but Ralph couldn't think that it was very much of a privation. Certainly he himself would have much rather been out in the weather, doing almost anything besides sitting at a table studying a tract.

"Whoops! Made you—" he couldn't hear the rest of Charlie's shout, but saw Nealie dancing at the top of the hill and gesticulating angrily at Charlie. What game were they playing? Old Balky leaned against the outhouse wall; probably the wax on the runners was worn completely away. His mind lingered on the yellowed block of beeswax that sat on the ledge inside the shed behind the outhouse. The outhouse! Mother might think he was going to the outhouse!

Action followed swiftly on thought. He pulled on his wool cap, his jacket, and the heavy boots. Ralph was a small, neat, nimble boy; his activities were nearly silent. He eased the kitchen door open, slipped out, eased the latch into place, carefully closed the screen door. He hurried to his sled and grabbed its frayed rope, then darted behind the shed and to the road, keeping to the lee of the bushes and hoping Mother wouldn't finish her letter and come looking for him yet.

Moments later he belly-flopped onto his usually balky sled, which responded magnificently. He had known it would.

"You're going to get the dickens when your mother finds out, aren't you?" asked Charlie anxiously as they hauled their sleds back up the hill.

"Oh, maybe," replied Ralph. "And you know what? It'll be worth it!" He whooped as he turned Old Balky around and belly-flopped onto her again.

Works and Days

"HEAR THE RAIN! My land, it sounds fit to blow straight through the window panes!"

"Mother, isn't Papa coming home again tonight?" Ralph shivered to think of his father out in the driving rain, patrolling the empty country roads. The lanterns' flames seemed to quiver in sympathy with him. Lottie paused in rinsing her paintbrush in a cupful of water and looked mournfully at the weeping window with Ralph.

Anna wrung her dishcloth out impatiently. "Your father has his work to do, sir, and you have yours. Finish your composition and then bring some more stove wood in from the porch for tomorrow. You didn't fill the box completely."

As Ralph came in with the load of sticks, Roy spoke up around a mouthful of biscuit. "Ralph, it's your turn to get the Frankfort Water tomorrow afternoon."

"Is not! I got it on Tuesday, when you had your music lesson."

"Yes and your day is Friday, and today's Thursday, so it's your day."

"But you have your Tuesday lesson twice a month. That's not fair!"

"Oh, come on, Ralph, be a sport. I'll do my share every other week, anyway."

He went upstairs to practice his music, and soon the wavering strains of "Alas, Those Chimes" drifted down the stairway.

Ralph sighed. Next afternoon he went "down the hill and up the hill" again, fetching the heavy glass jug of cloudy, foul-smelling water. "If he wasn't my brother, I'd hit him in the snoot," he muttered to himself as he trudged uphill from the train stop with his burden.

LOTTIE WORKED HER WAY down the row behind Mother. The spinach had just emerged, two tiny grasslike leaves on each fragile stem. Irish green, that was the color of them, bright in the late April sunshine against the dirt, soil rich and brown as to be nearly black, but lightened with sand. Lottie closed her eyes for a moment, printing these colors against the insides of her eyelids. She wanted to remember them for her next picture, perhaps rows and rows of these tiny plants reaching back to the horizon, the brown/black earth softened like velvet with the sprinkles of white quartz sand, the sky color like the knees of her brothers' denim overalls when they were nearly worn through.

"Lottie!" Anna's voice was sharp. "Look alive! You've fallen a whole row behind me, girl, where is your attention?"

"I'm sorry, Mother; I was just looking at the garden. Isn't it lovely this year?"

Anna softened. "That it is, child. But then, I think we say this every year when the seedlings first push their heads above the dirt. It's the earth renewing itself, I do believe. Land! Look at this purslane; it's nearly as big as the lettuces. Step lively, now, we have three more rows to finish before lunch."

Anna hastened her work with the hoe, chopping away the weeds peeking up between the rows. Lottie's task was to follow behind, pulling those weeds close in to the plants where a hoe mustn't go. She watched Anna's easy rhythmic swing, the blade sharp and unerringly singling out dandelion and thistle from pea and beet.

It seemed to Lottie that you crossed the line out of childhood when you were allowed to use grownup tools. She'd know when she was truly a big girl: when she had the garden hoe, its handle polished by years of use, in her own hands. Often Mother sent her to the shed to fetch spade, garden fork, or hoe. Under her bare feet the dirt changed from sun-warm to shivery-damp coolness; in her nose the dusty smell of old soil dried and fallen from the tools. She would hand over the tools with a sigh, resigned to stooping along the rows behind Anna, to grub in the dirt with her bare hands, feeling babyish.

When she was allowed to fold a dishtowel into a pad for the handle of the boiling kettle, and the ladle to dish the stew, she'd no longer be a little girl. It would be soon, she knew, because Mother was going to have a baby. Papa had told Roy and Ralph, and Ralph had told her. She, Lottie, would be a big sister.

Imagine, through no activity of her own, she would graduate from being the baby of the family to being a big sister! Lottie gazed affectionately at Mother's back, grateful for this favor soon to be bestowed. Mother would be busy with the baby, and she, Lottie, might carelessly walk out to the shed and get the hoe for herself, to weed the garden.

How They Grew

HENRY CAME DOWNSTAIRS smiling gently. Lottie ran to meet him and tugged at his hand. "Papa! How is mother? Is the baby well?"

"Children," began Henry, and then included Charlotte in his smile, "and Sister, I'm pleased to announce that William Henry Jr. has deigned to join us."

"A baby brother! I'm a big sister now!" Lottie hopped up and down in her joy, and Roy and Ralph grinned at their father.

"Little Willie, in the best of sashes . . ." began Roy.

"Fell in the fire, and was burned to ashes," wickedly added Ralph.

"That's not funny! And anyway, his name's not Willie, it's William!" retorted Lottie. But as William grew, somehow his name shrank to Will, and Will it remained.

THE TAX ASSESSOR APOLOGIZED to Anna when she came to the door. "I know you have your hands full, what with the baby and your sister feeling poorly, Anna, but this was the only day I have to make these twenty calls. I know Henry's gone to Traverse City for the day."

"He has indeed, but come in, Mr. Steele. Lottie can watch Will while we go over the forms. Ralph shall show you around the barn when he gets home for lunch."

Ralph showed Mr. Steele around the property with a proprietary air that quite tickled the assessor. With pride he introduced Minta and Bessie, the two cows. "Minta's the better milker, but Bessie's thrown twin calves twice, now. Those are hers, the bull calf and the brindle. The little one's Minta's, of course. Likely we'll sell that one. Come on out the back way here; watch your step and now I'll show you the potato field. We're thinking of trying out that new strain of Idaho this season, it's said to be a good keeper and very resistant . . ."

When the assessor and Ralph came back in, Anna was bathing a squirming Will in a basin wedged into the kitchen sink; a woven dish-cloth kept it from sliding about.

"I see you have your hands full, Anna, so I'll read the property list to you, and if you think of anything I've missed, Ralph or Henry can come by and add them on. Here's what we have: forty acres with barn, twenty of these acres improved, two six-acre lots in Benzonia village, one with a house on it, and twenty more acres all improved. Also four horses, two cows, three calves, and fifteen sheep, plus two wagons, a carriage, and two sleighs, plus mechanical and agricultural implements and tools. I put the value of those last at one hundred dollars."

Ralph spoke up, "I'd say not more than seventy-five dollars, sir. Some of those tools have seen hard use, and we're going to need a new harrow next year."

"Ralph, hush," Anna told him sternly. "Don't contradict your elders."

"Let's say ninety dollars, then."

"Eighty-five dollars, then," countered Ralph gravely.

"Young man, you are going to get a licking," Anna informed him.

"Eighty-five dollars it is," agreed Mr. Steele. "Try not to be too hard on the boy, Anna. He already knows his business about as well as several of the men I've talked to this week."

LOTTIE STEPPED ONTO the back porch with a bowl of plate-scrapings for the hens, and paused when she heard Roy, his back to her, recite in a falsetto, ". . . some of the men protested, of course, but after the soldiers pointed their guns at us . . ."

Ralph felt himself unable to resist the invitation to join the performance: ". . . of course, we were terrified, not only for ourselves but for the men and women of our village . . ." He spun around guiltily at Lottie's helpless giggle. "Oh! Lottie, don't sneak up on a fellow like that!"

"You mustn't make fun of poor Auntie that way. You know she's had a very hard time of it. No, I mean it; it's really true. Why does it sound so foolish when I say it?"

"Because everyone says it, and you never do what everyone else does, Puss," said Ralph.

"Well, at least don't do that where anyone else can hear you. You know that it would hurt Mother very much."

"You're right," agreed Roy reluctantly, "and I know that you're tired of these everlasting stories about the danger and the hardship these saintly people have endured." His voice rose to a cooing falsetto again, and he fanned himself with an imaginary palm-leaf fan.

"Terrible boy," giggled Lottie, and dumping her leftovers into the slop pail, she returned to the kitchen to finish washing the dishes.

BENZONIA, 1889

LOTTIE LOOKED UP at the clock. The big hand had moved only five minutes. She sighed, shifted in her chair, and looked down at her book. "These are the chiefs of the sons of Esau. The sons of Eliphaz the first born of Esau; the chiefs Tehman, Omar, Zepho, Kenaz, Korah, Gatam and Amalek; these are the chiefs of Eliphaz in the land of Edom; they are the sons of Adah."

She clamped her teeth shut on a yawn. Outside, an oriole called; the high singsong notes spoke of joy and freedom in the highest branches. A jay responded raucously. A soft breeze stirred the poplin curtains at the window. The big hand was nearly to the "II." Willie, her baby brother, cooed happily in his crib. Mother moved quietly about in the parlor. What did she do in there, when she wasn't praying?

"If I hold my breath and count to sixty, then breathe out really fast, then hold my breath for another sixty—" Her eyes went out of focus, and her ears collected a hum, a fuzzy gray nonsound. With a jerk she snapped her head back up, blinked. The outdoor sounds brightened again. "These are the sons of Reu'el, Esau's son . . ."

Her half-finished picture of daisies in a vase, started just last evening, whimpered to her in the darkness of its prison. "By tomorrow the daisies will be all wilted and I'll never get new ones arranged the same way," she thought, and felt the slight pang that an indulgent mother feels who is prevented from making another batch of Tibby's favorite cookies. The big hand had moved another grudging three minutes. Its face looked smug, its ticks busy and self-important. "Fresh thing," Lottie thought, and looked at her book again.

BENZONIA, MARCH 1890

"CONGRATULATIONS, HENRY, you have another daughter. Anna says you both favored Josephine for a name?"

"Yes, Josephine. Shall I come up and see them now?"

"A girl! Goody!" Lottie had served as Will's second mother whenever Anna deemed her behavior worthy of reward, but she soon proved so helpful that Anna gave her free rein. She could warm a dish of runny cereal on the stove, feeding it neatly to Will with a tiny spoon. She could tidily mop up messes from either of the baby's leaky ends, dress him in his little gowns, and coax up a bubble as well as any experienced mother. Will would nearly always smile for her, even during his rare bouts of colic, and his baby face twice daily glowed with joy when he heard her steps come in from school.

As Will learned to pull himself up upon the furniture and to toddle about the rooms, Lottie followed him about, smacking his hand when he reached for forbidden items, rocking him in her arms when he wailed, kissing his scrapes and bruises. Now she looked forward to dressing baby Josie like a little dolly and teaching her to play cat's cradle when she grew a bit older.

The Massacre

"WHO CAN OPEN the doors of his face? Round about his teeth is terror . . ." Charlotte rocked as she read aloud, tears streaming down her face. Anna ushered their longtime friend Mary E. C. Bailey into the room.

"Charlotte, my dear, I came as soon as I heard. How dreadful!"

"Mariam, Rakel, Yeva, Lishbet, all of them, all dead. Sweet Vartuhi, who always started the hymns for the choir, carried off by the Kurds; nobody knows her fate. Avedis, Bedros, and Aram, lined up against a wall in front of their families and shot. 'His heart is as hard as a stone, hard as the nether millstone . . .'"

"What is our government doing about the massacre? There's no mention of any action in today's piece; what does your letter say?"

"I can tell you right now that President Harrison has no intention of taking any meaningful action. Oh, he'll make a statement, but the Turks won't be the least bit intimidated. I should be there with them. Here I lie, in idleness. Oh, Zion . . ."

Little by little the details became known to the American populace. The Turkish government had become increasingly incensed by obstinacy of the Armenian people, who insisted on clinging to their Christianity. Some remained Orthodox, or Gregorian, as the Protestant missionaries termed it, and some followed the imported Western variety.

It was all one to the Islamic Turks. With the wholehearted encouragement of their sultan and his army, petty Turkish officials harassed and threatened the occupants of villages and missionary compounds. Here a church was burned, the worshippers shot, stabbed, or beaten as they tried to escape from the flames. There a village was attacked in the night, men shot in their beds and their wives dragged away shrieking, never to return, their children snatched away with them, or left to wander until taken in by a nearby farmer, or handed casually to the nearest mission school, or left to die of hunger and exposure.

British and American diplomats remonstrated with Sultan Hamid, who had no liking for either of these unbelieving nations. In response, he would declare a temporary lull in the hostilities and allow the renegade Kurds to do his work for him. "What can we do against these mountain bandits?" he would protest. "We are helpless even to protect our own citizens."

After a suitable time, his specious grip on the troops would loosen, and the ferocity of attacks again increased. Five hundred Armenians would die this month, twenty-five the next, and nobody knew how many the next; Armenians who disappeared seldom returned, and those few who did reported systematic massacres that, we now know, served as dress rehearsal for events in Europe fifty years hence.

Overwhelmed

"ANNA, AREN'T YOU READY YET?" Henry, spruce and neat in his new broadcloth suit, paced impatiently in the passageway. Lottie, in her new gingham dress with a tiny velvet ribbon at the neck, held his hand. Henry had recently been elected as a trustee of the church, and tonight was his first public appearance as an elder of the community. Grand Traverse College would dedicate the new Barber Hall, and Henry was to speak at the dedication.

"Not yet, Henry." Anna sounded harassed. "Why don't you go on ahead and leave me Lottie to help with the children?"

"Lottie, I think I could eat some of those peas you had for dinner," came Charlotte's querulous voice from her downstairs room. Lottie stood indecisively; a slap sounded from upstairs, followed by a thin wail. Lottie started toward the stair.

"You go and see to your aunt," said Henry in a low voice. "I'll go up and help get the children dressed."

He went upstairs and stopped in the doorway. Anna, tears in her eyes, held a sobbing Josie. On Josie's tiny cheek, red fingerprints glowed. Her nose ran, unnoticed, down the front of Anna's good slate taffeta. Will, his roundabout partially buttoned, stood mutely behind her, fingers in his mouth.

"Anna, what in the world?"

"I had Will nearly dressed and Josie's gown on her, then she was naughty and wouldn't hold still and tore the buttonhole . . ."

"Anna, she's a baby, how could she tear a buttonhole?"

"Oh, Henry, what could you possibly know about it? Now she'll have to wear her second-best." Anna abruptly set Josie back on the bed and began to ruffle through a jumble of indistinguishable odds and ends of children's clothing in the press.

Henry finished with Will's buttons. "Take him downstairs, please, Anna, and I'll finish dressing Josie."

"Oh, that won't do, you'll dress her in one of her old gowns and not even know the difference."

"That's as may be, Anna. Please take Will and go downstairs. Please."

Anna paused, then bowed her head and reached for Will's hand. Henry buttoned Josie into a pinafore that looked clean and presentable and picked her up.

"Anna," said Henry the next morning as he sat at the breakfast table, "let me advertise for help from the college. The children are too much for you, now that Lottie's at her art classes." He tactfully omitted mentioning the burden Charlotte had become to all of them.

Anna sank onto her chair by the stove. "I can't say I'd mind having a capable pair of hands around the house," she admitted reluctantly. "Where would she sleep?"

"I hadn't thought that far," confessed Henry.

"She could stay in my room with me," offered Lottie, excited at the idea of having a college girl as a roommate.

"I think we could clear out the west room downstairs," suggested Anna. "The boys can help me."

Roy looked up from his plate. "I have band practice this afternoon, Mother. Maybe Ralph . . ."

"Your practice isn't until midafternoon, Roy, and it won't hurt you to help move some boxes around this morning."

It was decided. Anna stood at the door of the small room at the end of the hall and surveyed the chaos. Odds and ends of furniture, boxes of broken household items awaiting mending, winter woolens and boots, some of David Spencer's textbooks from Harvard; everything that wasn't in daily use tended to end up in this room.

"Why don't we just saw this room off and let it drift away?" suggested Ralph. Roy stifled a snigger.

"You hush, sir, and fetch us some rags from under the kitchen sink," Anna demanded. Ralph complied. By the end of the morning, the catchall room was transformed into a tidy alcove. A cot stood against the south wall, neatly made up and covered with a crocheted throw. A small table served as a washstand, next to the old wardrobe, softly agloss with fresh beeswax. The faded curtains drained in a wash pan on the porch, ready to be starched and ironed. The floor shone. A pile of discards on the porch awaited a trip to the shed.

"I guess the girl will be satisfied with it," allowed Anna. Ralph, who'd shared a room with his older brother all his life, nodded, thinking that the girl was lucky to have a room of her own.

Henry stopped at the college that afternoon. In the office, there were two lists, one of boys and one of girls seeking situations: room and board in exchange for help around the house, garden, nursery, barn, or woodpile.

"There are two girls available," reported Henry. "I've talked to Professor Stewart, who knows a bit about both. One of them, Kathleen, I think the name was, has little sisters and brothers. The other one has little experience with children but seems a more sensible, capable young woman in Professor Stewart's opinion. Her name is Alma or Olga or something. From Arcadia, I believe."

"Either one sounds fine, Henry."

"Well, but don't you want to interview them both?" To Henry, the selection of a live-in girl seemed an important matter, one that required tact and deliberation. He also knew that he didn't want to make the choice.

"I haven't time to interview anyone. Can't you stop up at the college and meet them both, and decide for us?"

"Well, I think I'll be busy the rest of today . . ."

Anna, her eyes on peeling the carrots and watching the stew, said with some asperity, "Oh, for mercy's sake! The sensible, capable one, then. That Olga. Is she a Swede?"

"Anna, I don't know. Shall I ask Professor Stewart to send her around tomorrow?"

"That's fine," said Anna absently, giving the stew pan another stir before setting it on the back burner.

Orah Bunker Comes to Stay

"ORAH BUNKER, MA'AM," Orah held out her hand. Anna wiped hers on her apron and gave it a tentative squeeze.

"Oh, we needn't stand on ceremony. I'm Anna. Lottie and the boys are off at school, of course. Roy's about your age; likely he'll be in some of your classes. This is Will." Will, owl-eyed, hung behind Anna, clinging to her skirt. "And the baby, Josie, is having her nap upstairs. Come this way and I'll show you your room."

As they started down the hallway, Charlotte's voice rose sleepily behind them. "Anna? Is someone there with you?"

"It's all right, Charlotte. The new girl has come today." They backtracked across the parlor to Charlotte's door. "Her name's Orah. Orah Bunker, from Arcadia."

Charlotte eyed Orah critically. A handsome, somewhat sharp face, neat, trim figure, clean and sprucely dressed. "What church do you belong to, young woman? I'm not familiar with anyone from Arcadia."

"Church of Christ, ma'am," answered Orah, crisply, eying Charlotte in her turn. The woman looked like a cadaver, she thought, lying back among her pillows, an open Bible on the bed next to her. The room smelled musty and stale. "Have to give this room a good airing," she thought.

ROY HELD OUT his hand to Orah, embarrassed, and mumbled a greeting.

"I saw you on the west field today," Lottie said shyly when her turn came. "You were with two other ladies."

"Those were my classmates," responded Orah kindly. "I'll introduce you to them some time."

"Sit down and I'll dish up," said Anna. "Tomorrow you can start working." Ralph nodded politely, pulled out his chair, and stood behind it. Everything felt odd and formal, as though they were having company. And this girl was going to live here with them!

"My husband is often away at mealtimes," Anna chattered on to Orah.

Orah sat with Sadie Bedell and Mattie Wilson, under the oaks that bordered West Field. She opened her satchel and took out her lunch. She offered a handful of carrot sticks to Mattie, in exchange for a boiled egg. Sarah traded half of her cheese sandwich for another boiled egg; Mattie's family raised more poultry than any other family in the area, and Mattie couldn't abide the smell of the boiled eggs that had graced her school lunches since she was a tot.

"I heard that young Mr. Keelor's putting an addition onto the new house he's building so other students can board there. I wouldn't mind moving into town, if Papa could afford the board."

"You could get a job like the rest of us poor working students," observed Orah wryly.

"Speaking of working for board, I sat next to Roy Thacker this morning in chemistry. Professor Clark will assign lab groups tomorrow, and I want him to get into the habit of seeing us together," said Sadie.

"Piffle," said Orah. "Roy's a conceited young sprig. If you had to sit at breakfast with him every morning, you'd tire of him soon enough."

"Oh, I think he's awfully handsome," gushed Sadie. Orah took another bite of her egg and looked bored.

"Earnest Judson is handsome too, I think," offered Mattie.

"They're both children, as far as I'm concerned," said Orah, "When I'm ready to look for a beau, I'll look for an older man. It's too bad that Orville Pike's leaving for Lansing at the end of the year. And it's too bad Professor Harney's already married; I could definitely go for him."

Mattie giggled, scandalized. "Orah, you're terrible!" she squeaked.

Sadie said nothing; Orah, after only one full term at Grand Traverse College, already had the reputation of being, if not "fast," entirely too worldly for a young lady not yet "walking out" with anyone. Still, you could always find the young men buzzing around wherever Orah was. Orah, who could lace her waist to eighteen inches, who always made her limited wardrobe appear more stylish than anyone else's, was a girl who never lacked for a following.

A Much-Needed Rest

"ANNA! Lottie! Ohhhh . . ." Charlotte's voice, quavering, drifted into the kitchen. Lottie pushed her chair back, jumped up, and hurried across to Charlotte's room.

"Auntie! What's the matter? Papa, come quick! Auntie's dying!"

Henry hurried into the room behind Lottie. Charlotte's eyes had rolled back so that only the whites were visible. Half of her lay off her bed, one bare foot on the braided rug, the other leg folded back under the bed. Her nightgown had rucked up above her knees. Her hair spread, tangled, over the pillow.

Henry averted his eyes. "Lottie, what's wrong with her? Has she ever been like this before?"

"Never like this," said Lottie, clinging to Henry's hand. "I wish Mother were home."

Orah strode past both of them into the room. She gripped Charlotte under the arms and hoisted her heartily back onto the bed. Charlotte's head bumped against the headboard; she grunted. Orah lifted Charlotte's legs back onto the bed and yanked her nightgown down. "Send one of the boys for her doctor," she ordered.

Anna returned home just as Dr. Powers was putting his bag to rights. Charlotte, breathing heavily, slept the sleep of the heavily sedated. "Good evening, Mrs. Thacker. Your sister has had another of her spells."

Anna rushed to Charlotte's bedside. She lifted Charlotte's hand, patted it gently, set it down. She followed Dr. Powers into the hallway.

"What's wrong with her, Dr. Powers? I can't seem to make hide nor hair of her ailments. One day I think she's just malingering, and another day I think she's truly at death's door. I haven't wanted to interfere between Charlotte and her doctor . . ."

"Frankly, Mrs. Thacker, I'm at a loss as well. It's possible that she's still carrying a flux from her time in Turkey. Sometimes I think that if she would get up from her bed and find something more to do with her time than entertain the Mission Society with stories, she would be well in a jiffy. Then again, she may simply be too weak to sustain any effort, as appears to be the case just now."

"Will she ever be better again?" Anna realized she was clutching Dr. Powers's arm, and pulled her hands away.

"I'd like to admit her to the clinic in Traverse City for a few weeks. We could observe her more constantly and perhaps determine a better course of treatment."

Henry helped Charlotte to the buggy. Roy walked on Charlotte's other side, ready in case the walk proved too much exertion. Anna followed, carrying a bag of Charlotte's things. She climbed into the buggy after Charlotte and leaned out for Henry's kiss.

"I should be home late this evening, Dr. Powers says. Orah will see to supper and putting the children to bed." The buggy drove away, Anna's eyes on her sister, who lay against the seat back with her eyes closed.

HENRY AND RALPH came through the back door after carefully wiping the mud from their boots. "One more day should see the finish of the oats," Henry announced to Orah, who nodded absently and gave Josie another spoonful of mush.

"Supper won't be for another half hour," she informed them both, wiping the overflow from Josie's lower lip.

Ralph nodded and went upstairs, glad to have some time to work on his composition, due on Wednesday. With the wraithlike figure gone from the downstairs room, the house felt lighter, somehow freed of an unpleasant aura. While he had no wish for harm to come to poor Aunt Charlotte, Ralph wished she would get better and, well, go somewhere else and live a life of her own.

He fiddled with a corner of his composition paper, curling it between his fingers and then smoothing it out flat again, considering the fate of an old maid with no family of her own. Auntie had "a little money of her own," he'd heard, but clearly not enough to set up her own household. What, indeed, could she do? Teach school, perhaps, or find an old widower to marry. For a moment he felt a strong pang of pity for his aunt. True, she was a bother, but he supposed, given the same circumstances, he'd be a bother, too.

He sighed and bent to his composition. One might think that Aunt Charlotte had been enjoying the life of a Turkish pasha, being waited on hand and foot and telling stories all day to whoever came by to visit. Better to be Ralph, he realized now, with cows to milk and a composition due Wednesday.

After supper Henry sat at his desk with the ledger open before him. If the lower field did as well as last year for hay, he'd be able to pay off the cultivator at summer's end. There was still the quarterly fee for Lottie's art teacher; otherwise everything was up to date.

He set his pen down, filled with a sense of well-being. If only Anna weren't so exhausted all the time! Even with Orah to help out, it seemed as if Anna had no vitality at all. His eyes fell on Orah, seated on the divan with her book open in her lap.

The first week of Orah's stay she had adjourned to her room immediately after her chores were finished. "Ridiculous!" Anna had scoffed. "She can sit out here with the rest of the family in the evening." So Orah sat in the "back parlor" with Anna and the children, reading her assignments or doing her needlework. Henry liked to come home in the evenings and see Orah with his family, all cozily about their respective tasks.

They all sat there now, all except for Anna, away at Traverse City. Will had been fretful at bedtime, asking over and over again when "Muvver was coming home," but Orah was patient and finally had gotten him to sleep.

"You're very good with the children," admired Henry. "For one not used to small children, that is."

"Oh, I'm used to them," Orah told him. "I taught Sunday school for the baby class for many years."

"Many years?" Henry smiled. "You're not much older than Roy, are you?"

"I'll be nineteen in August. Roy's only seventeen, isn't he?"

"An infant compared to you," smiled Henry. Roy scowled and flipped a page in his American history book.

"Girlie"

ONE AT A TIME, the older children excused themselves and went to bed. "Orah, there's no need for you to sit up any later. I can let Mrs. Thacker in when she gets home."

Orah, stifling a yawn, rose stiffly. "I can stay up a while longer, I don't mind," she said, her step toward the door belying her words.

"Oh, go to bed, Girlie, you're asleep on your feet," joked Henry. Orah smiled wearily and retired.

An hour later a buggy pulled up in front of the house. Henry hastened out to meet Anna and help her down.

"How were the children for Orah?" she asked.

"Good as gold. Come in, and I'll put the kettle on. Are you hungry?"

"I couldn't eat a bite, I'm that worn out. Oh, Henry, if you could have seen poor Charlotte when I left her, it would have broken your heart. She looked completely at sea in that strange place."

"Orah says she's going to turn that room completely out in Charlotte's absence. If you don't mind, that is," he added hastily.

"Why would I mind? Henry, thank you for waiting up for me. We'll talk tomorrow. I'm going to bed now, good night." Anna grasped the handrail high up and pulled herself up the stairs as though she were climbing a mountainside.

"ANNA THACKER, my dear, it's been weeks since I've seen you!" Reverend Waters greeted her warmly.

"It has, indeed. You were down with the ague, I hear. I trust you're much better."

"Oh, pshaw, that was ages ago. You haven't been to church since I got back on my feet. Have you been unwell?"

"No, not so much unwell as just plain tired. Everything seems to take more effort than I'm able to generate. I do my chores and then just sit. Maybe I'm just getting old." Anna laughed shakily, surprised to feel tears sting her eyes.

"You could never be old," retorted Reverend Waters. "You'll always be the sedate young lady I taught in the young adults class. Come over here and sit down, Anna, and tell me all about it." He led her to the bench in front of Stockton's store.

"I'm so ashamed," confessed Anna. "I have everything to be thankful for: a good husband, healthy children, peace and prosperity. My troubles are nothing like those of the poor farmers who are losing their homes willy-nilly to the banks, or those poor starving Armenians, or even my sister, without health or a home of her own."

"I didn't ask about the Armenians, Anna, but about you. What's troubling you?"

"Nothing, Reverend Waters. I just feel so, well, so tired all the time. Tired for no reason, just tired. It's all I can do to take care of the younger children. I leave everything else to the girl, and stay home as much as possible."

Reverend Waters had been more than a minister to the Spencer family, a family friend who came to counsel and stayed to dinner. Elvira used to say that Reverend Waters could polish off more of her baking-powder and sour-milk biscuits than the rest of the family combined. Today, as always, his thick gray hair curled neatly back along the crown of his head, but two stubborn wisps protruded, like the feathers of a disheveled bird, out behind his ears. Anna, Charlotte, and Brainard used to nudge each other and giggle when Reverend Waters became voluble and those tufts waggled at the back of his head. Anna smiled fondly at him, tears misting her eyes.

"Have you had the doctor? Perhaps you're really ill?" He studied her face anxiously.

"I'm not ill, just tired. I'm sure I'll be back to church in another week or two."

"But surely you're coming to the installation of Reverend Shaw? Having served on the committee, you couldn't bear to miss seeing your hard work come to fruition, surely?"

"Oh yes, I intend to try. If Josie's sniffles aren't better, of course, I shall have to stay home. Henry and the girl can bring Lottie and the boys, at any rate." She pressed his arm warmly and set off toward home. Otis Waters shook his head with concern as he watched her walk away.

THE WIND HOWLED around the corners of the porch; Henry paced and peered out of the parlor window again. Right out of the northwest, he could tell by the way the leaves swirled and eddied, always working their way toward the corner of the porch to his right. It was only a matter of hours before the snow began to fly. Henry was to accompany the Shaws and the top students from the adult Sunday school class to the annual convention. While snow wouldn't prevent the train from going to Lansing, it surely would put a damper on the excursion.

He heard Orah moving to and fro in the kitchen, with the rustles and clinks common to women in kitchens. "I've left two pies in the pantry, Anna," he heard her say. "And Will's clean shirts are put away in the drawer."

"Don't worry about us, Orah, we'll be fine," replied Anna. "It's only for two days, for mercy's sake."

Orah said something else that he couldn't hear; her voice disappeared down the passageway, and then she returned moments later carrying the small bag that she had moved in with. Henry took it from her with a smile. "Excited, Girlie?" he asked her.

She smiled noncommittally. "Hadn't you better say goodbye to your family now? We should be leaving for the train no later than 4:30."

Henry set down the bag, his ears pink at the tips, and stepped back to the kitchen to bid his wife goodbye. "You'll manage all right for a couple of days, won't you? Lottie's a big girl now, she'll help you."

"Oh, Henry, don't fret. I take care of things here perfectly well when you're away; it's not like I'm an invalid." Henry brushed her cheek with his lips and turned to go.

After the door clicked shut behind Henry and Orah, Anna turned back to her stove. The soup was ready; she ladled a portion into a bowl, which she placed on a wooden tray. A heel of bread, Charlotte's favorite part of the loaf, lay on a saucer. She added a spoon and linen napkin to the tray and carried it to Charlotte's room.

Charlotte sat up in her bed, swung her feet over the side, and slid them into a pair of carpet slippers. Anna set the tray in her lap and sat down on the lounge, by the door.

"They've left, have they?" inquired Charlotte.

"Oh yes; Henry was anxious to get the young folks gathered at the train before the weather broke."

"Anna." Charlotte's voice was hesitant. "Do you think there's anything, well, odd about Henry these days?"

"I'm sure I don't know what you mean. Odd in what way?"

"He rarely comes in to talk to me, of course, so I must base my judgments on very few observations. But he does sometimes seem rather fatuous about young Miss Bunker, don't you think?"

"Of course he is, Charlotte, just as he is about all of the young ladies in the church. I believe he feels himself personally responsible for every one of them in some sense. Don't you remember when he went with them to the skating party and wouldn't leave until he had skated around the edge of Crystal Lake with every one of the young ladies? I thought my toes would turn gangrenous and fall off before he would allow us all to go home."

"Do you really think that's all it is?" Charlotte was unable to keep the skepticism from her voice.

"Of course I do. What else could it be?"

"What else, indeed?" agreed Charlotte, her eyes on her soup spoon again.

HENRY STOOD at the horses' heads, gloomily waiting for Orah to come out. It was term's end, and she was to return to Arcadia for the summer.

"I don't suppose your parents would let you stay on with us for the summer?" he had suggested one evening a week before. Anna looked up from the bowl of cereal she was feeding to Josie. "We've certainly been glad of your help, Orah. Henry's right, we'll miss you this summer."

"You're good to say so," responded Orah. "But Mother's been writing to say how much they're looking forward to my return, and of course I miss my family."

"Of course," agreed Anna.

"Of course," Henry had said.

Now he wondered what was wrong with himself. Indeed, this ache beneath his breastbone seemed excessive when he thought about it. Most of the young ladies from the college returned to their own homes, some in the nearby countryside, so that they continued to be active in the local social affairs, and others absent until the next fall, or for good and all. Orah was just one more of these young ladies. Of course, she had been a member of the household for these many months. He lifted his head and took a breath. It's not as though he were sending his own daughter away for the entire summer, after all

Henry drove Orah to the station. He stood and waved as her train pulled away to the west.

"YES?" said Virginia Bunker.

"Mrs. Bunker? I see that you don't remember me. My name is Henry Thacker. Your daughter boarded with us this year. We briefly met at Parents' Day, but then I had to leave for work."

"Oh yes, Orah has spoken of you. Won't you come in?"

Henry removed his hat and stepped into the front room, pulling a folded sheaf of papers from his vest. "I happened upon Mr. Case yesterday, and he told me that he had these insurance forms ready for you. Since I needed to come this way for business, I offered to stop by and drop them off."

Virginia Bunker took the offered forms and looked at Henry curiously. What ailed the man? He didn't seem to want to meet her eyes, just kept peering around at the room behind her. Was there a mouse? Finally she could stand it no longer; she turned and looked behind herself. Nothing, so far as she could see. She turned back to him, noting the sunset hue of his ear tips.

"Have a seat, Mr. Thacker. Can I fix you some lemonade?"

"Oh no, no thank you." Belying his words, Henry sat in the proffered "best chair." Mrs. Bunker looked at him expectantly for a long, embarrassing moment, before Henry asked, tentatively, "Is Orah in, Mrs. Bunker? Might I speak to her for a moment?"

"Oh, she's gone into town with her brother. You recall our son Torrence, I'm sure?"

"Oh, oh yes, Torrence, Orah's brother. Certainly."

She sat in the straight-backed chair opposite Henry, hands lying loosely in her lap, trying to think of a way to put the man at his ease. He was a sheriff in Benzonia, she knew, and prominent in the church. Odd that such a man would be so lacking in social graces!

"You have five children, I understand, Mr. Thacker?"

"Yes, oh yes." He paused, collected his thoughts. "Three boys and two girls. You have two boys, I understand."

"Yes. Forrest, the elder, is married. Torrence appears to be in no hurry to 'leave the nest,' as they say. He has been a great help to his father."

"Orah, too, has been a great help to us."

Virginia smiled appreciatively. "I'm glad to hear of that." Her right hand had begun to pat her left hand.

After a long pause, Henry arose. "Do give her my regards, Mrs. Bunker. Our regards, I mean, mine and my wife's."

"Of course." she stood in the door and looked at him as he stood, holding his hat. "Do come back another time, Mr. Thacker, and be sure to tell your wife we'd love to see her as well."

"Of course," said Henry, as he retreated to his wagon.

A Man of Your Position

BENZONIA, WINTER 1892

HENRY STOOD at the door of Reverend Shaw's office, rotating his hat brim slowly through his fingers. The hat was two years old, but weather and much handling had worn the felt shiny in spots; the band was spotted with rain.

"Come in, Mr. Thacker. Have a seat."

"Oh, just call me Henry. All my friends do, and I'd be a pretty poor fellow if my own minister wasn't my friend, wouldn't I?" He sat and fidgeted some more with the brim of his hat, running a finger across one of the shinier spots.

"Henry, I'm sure you know why I asked you to stop by."

"Can't say as I do, Reverend. Of course you'd want to get to know everyone in town eventually, and sooner or later you'd have to get to the Ts." He smiled at this attempt at wit. Reverend Shaw pursed his lips.

"Well, certainly that." Reverend Shaw shifted uncomfortably in his chair. These conversations were so much easier when the sinners confessed straight out, so they could get to the contrition part. "But also, I wanted to talk to you about a problem that's come to my attention. A problem concerning you and, uh, Oma Bunker."

"Problem? Orah's a perfectly nice girl, Reverend. She's a great help to my wife, and her school reports have been excellent. We consider her a welcome addition to the family, my children and I."

"And does your wife, also, consider her a welcome addition?"

"Orah's a great help. I'm sure she does. A great help." He stopped, thinking that he'd said "a great help" too many times. But that's just what Orah was, wasn't she? Why did that sound so feeble?

"Mr., uh, Henry, I'm sure your motives are pure," interrupted Dr. Shaw. "But you surely must understand that in the eyes of your neighbors you spend entirely too much time squiring Miss Bunker around town in the absence of your wife. And when you are together in a group, you and she have an unfortunate, uh, tendency to move away from everyone else and talk exclusively to each other. Surely you must understand how the thing looks. A man of your position especially, a man of law, and a trustee of the church, such a man must be above reproach in the eyes of the community."

"Of course, of course, Reverend. Truthfully, I don't really know how this sort of talk got started around. You ask anyone, they'll tell you that I've always tried to be good to the young people, give them a help up the ladder, so to speak, and this thing with Orah, why, it's no different."

"But it's the look of the thing, don't you see. A man comes to church week after week with a hired girl young enough to be his own daughter, the girl walking close beside him, holding onto his arm, and his own young daughter trailing along behind. I hear Miss Bunker has refused to keep company with boys and girls her own age. Now, I've tried to talk to your wife about her absences from church and other public events, and I must say I've had little success. I'm told she used to be in the thick of everything, but she puts me off and tells me she's just tired, or that her sister needs her."

"That's just it, don't you see? Anna and I, well, we used to be such great friends. She'd smile in a special little way when I said something she disapproved of and didn't want to laugh at . . ." He stopped, his voice thickening in his throat. He took a breath and went on. "Nowadays, she's just like a ghost around the house. Charlotte's the sickly one, but

Anna, why, she's just not there any more for me or for the children. Do you see? It's so lonely. Like coming home to a ghost. Or else she's locked away in Charlotte's room, nursing her, or else they're reading scriptures together."

Dr. Shaw frowned. "Mr. Thacker, you say that almost bitterly, as though you disapproved of your wife reading scripture together with her sister." "Henry" had slipped from his vocabulary again, Henry noted.

"It's not that they read scripture, it's the way they read scripture," Henry tried to explain, feeling the hopelessness of making himself clear to this frowning man across the desk. Why had Dr. Waters gotten old and retired! "It's just, well, it's just lonesome. I come home to the children like a widower, but Orah's there in the kitchen, making a homely rattle with the pans, and it makes the house warm again. A man needs a little warmth in the house when he comes home . . ." There was that little pursing of the lips again. The man seemed determined to misunderstand his every word!

"Let me say this as plainly as I am able. Let this girl move to another household. Stop keeping any sort of company with her, in any way whatsoever. If you feel the need for a little warmth," he said somewhat dryly, "then just come home early and start the fire in the stove for your wife. Or take your children out for a brisk walk."

Henry laughed shortly at the hat brim in his hands, imagining himself marching briskly down the road with his children strung out like ducklings behind him. He could envision Roy muttering beneath his breath about having to march around the streets after he'd already put a long day in at school and in the fields, Ralph quietly but doggedly striding along behind him, Lottie asking whatever in the world they were doing, and the little ones round-eyed in confusion. They'd think he was insane! And maybe they'd be right. He looked up from his hat, and Dr. Shaw did that thing with his lips again.

"I fail to see the levity in this situation, I must say."

"Oh, it wasn't the situation, Reverend, it was something else entirely. You're right, it's best that she go. I'm not guilty of what it looks like, but anyway, I suppose it's best she go." He heaved a great sigh, rose to his feet, and started to turn toward the door.

"Let us pray," said Reverend Shaw, stopping Henry in his tracks. Henry turned back around, looked unblinkingly at his feet, and mumbled along with the minister: ". . . have mercy upon us, most merciful father, for our manifold sins and wickedness . . ."

"I'm not sure I understand, Orah." Anna's hands tightened on the sock she had been darning. "If the Shaws need help as badly as all that, why don't they go to the college and find a student for themselves? Why must it be you?"

"I'm sure I don't know, Anna. Reverend Shaw was very insistent that I come to work for them, and Reverend Harney told me that I must move my things to the Shaws' by the end of the month. I daren't go against Reverend Harney. You know that he's very influential with the dean of women students."

Anna sighed. "I have no idea how we'll get along without you, Orah, indeed I haven't. And the children will be very distressed."

The children, truth to tell, were divided in their responses.

"I'm glad she's going," said Roy to Ralph as they prepared for bed. "It's mortifying to hear my own father talk to the hired girl in that fond way he does."

Secretly Ralph agreed, but was milder in his judgments. "I suppose he considers her like another daughter. But she's not our sister, so it sounds peculiar to us. Still, this leaves Mother in a pickle. We'll have to do our best to save her work and worry."

Roy agreed that was so. They went to bed filled with a virtuous resolve.

"We'll miss you, Orah," said Lottie. She spoke truthfully; Orah had lifted a burden from her young shoulders. Orah was always ready to wipe up a spill, remove a boiling kettle from the flames when Mother was busy with Josie or Will, pick up Josie when she tumbled from the sofa and wailed, peel the potatoes or help with the dusting. Orah sometimes chatted with Lottie almost as though she was one of the young ladies, and paused in washing up the dishes to admire one of Lottie's drawings.

Orah, whom Papa loved nearly as much as he loved Lottie. Lottie could tell this by the way his eyes warmed when he came through the door and saw Orah at the kitchen table, feeding mush to Will, a textbook open before her on the table. "Girlie," he called her. It annoyed Auntie to hear it, Lottie could tell.

Auntie was glad that Orah was going; Lottie could tell that too, though why that was she didn't know. Orah freed Mother's hands ever so much, gave Mother more time to spare for Auntie. Now she, Lottie, would have to step in again. She sighed and set her drawing tablet aside.

The dishes sat on the table still, and Orah was in her room, packing her things. Someone had to clear the table, and Mother was upstairs putting Josie to bed.

"I guess I ought to say goodbye now, Anna." Orah stood in the doorway of the small room that served as the nursery. "I'll stop by now and then to see how you're all doing, of course."

Anna lifted Josie to her hip and walked to the door. "Goodbye, Orah. Thank you for all of your help. We shall miss you very much." She brushed Orah's cheek with her lips, which quivered slightly. Orah patted Anna's bony shoulder, then turned and left.

Henry delivered Orah to the Shaw household. After a terse "hello" to Mrs. Shaw, he set her bag down inside the door. "Goodbye, Girlie," he told her. "If you need anything, you know where we are."

Without another word, he made his departure. The door closed behind him. Mrs. Shaw, startled by the abruptness of his exit, blinked after him for a moment. Orah stood in the entryway by her bag, patiently awaiting her notice.

"I SUPPOSE HENRY's been moping," observed Charlotte. Anna thought she said this with some satisfaction.

Anna paused in running a feather duster across the mantelpiece, the lantern held up in her other hand. "Moping? I don't understand. Why should Henry mope?"

"Oh, for mercy's sake. Why do you think?"

Anna set the lantern down and began work on a spindle-legged end table, setting books and a lace doily onto the couch arm. She paused, duster in hand, and looked inquiringly at her sister, who glowered at her.

"I'm sure I don't know. Charlotte, you know how provoking it can be when people talk in riddles. Is there something you're trying to tell me?"

"Oh, some people are just determined to ignore troubles that are right under their noses."

"Charlotte! Whatever in the world is the matter with you? You're not making a bit of sense."

"That's just like you, Anna. I suppose you'll just continue to ignore the truth that's right under your nose, no matter how it affects your own family."

"What truth would this be?"

"About Orah's leaving."

"Are you trying to tell me that Henry caused her to leave? I think you're mistaken, Charlotte. Orah tells me that the Shaws insisted on her coming to them."

She replaced the doily and the books on the table and looked around the neat parlor, nodded approvingly.

"Never mind. You're determined to ignore the facts, I see. Never mind me; I'll just let you go your own blind way." Charlotte slapped her hand down on the arm of the couch, rose, and stalked from the room.

Anna looked after her, shaking her head.

"MAY I ASK what you wish to see Miss Bunker about, Mr. Thacker?"

He shifted uncomfortably on the hard cushion, fumbled about in his vest pocket, and pulled out a small parcel, which he thrust at Mrs. Shaw.

"I came to give her this," he explained. Silence fell for a moment, as she eyed the package suspiciously.

"Is this something of Orah's? Some possession she forgot to bring with her?" She looked at Henry, oddly, he thought.

"Oh, no, not at all. It's, ah, the medal she received from Bible class. I was coming this way on business, and I thought that since I was coming this way, I thought I'd drop it off. For Orah, that is. Since I was coming this way."

"Oh. I see. How kind. I'll see she gets it immediately she gets back." Package in hand, she continued to look at him expressionlessly. After a long moment of this, he made his farewell and departed.

"OH!" Mr. Pettit, a trustee, was closing up the church. Noticing an open door at the top of the second floor, he had gone up to close it. In the dark, a figure stood at the window. Mr. Pettit stood, his hand on his chest, and took a deep wheezing breath. "Mr. Thacker! I had no idea you were up here."

"Oh!" He jumped again, right hand joining the left at his chest. "Miss Bunker!"

Henry shuffled his feet sheepishly. "I'm watching Mott's store, Mr. Pettit. You know we've long suspected him of selling spirits."

Benzonia had been founded as a "dry" community. In fact, deeds to many of the properties, especially the ones erected by Benzonia's founders, included the clause, "In consideration that no tobacco shall ever be sold, and intoxicating drinks ever sold, manufactured or given, except strictly for mechanical or medicinal purposes on above land."

"I see that this window provides an excellent vantage," agreed Mr. Pettit, standing next to Henry and peering out the window with him. He then turned to leave. "Miss Bunker?" She looked inquiringly at him. "I'm closing up now, Miss Bunker. You may leave with me now." She bowed her head and followed him.

"Stop by and see us soon, Girlie," Henry called after her. "Lottie has been pining for a sight of you."

"GOOD EVENING, MRS. SHAW." Henry stood on her doorstep clutching a packet of paper. "May I speak to Orah for a moment?"

She eyed him suspiciously. "She's in the kitchen. Step into the parlor, please."

He carefully wiped his feet and stepped in to the passageway. Several coats hung from pegs on the wall of this hallway, partially blocking the door. He sidled past them. Pine floors shone with beeswax; he hoped his feet were completely dry. Clarence and Edward, the Shaws' two small boys, paused in their game with lead soldiers and goggled silently at Henry.

"Evening, young fellows," said Henry. Both small heads quickly turned away from Henry and toward one another. Both small boys giggled, and then forgot him as the War Between the States was resumed. Henry waited, ignoring the military carnage on the floor.

Orah stepped into the parlor, wiping her hands on a dish towel. "Good evening, Hen—Mr. Thacker," she said.

"Well, hello, Girlie," he said. "I brought your letters to you. Looks like one from your folks."

"Thank you," she said and took the bundle primly. Mrs. Shaw stood stolidly and watched them both.

"You be sure to remember us to your parents when you write them, won't you?" said Henry, backing toward the entryway. Orah followed him. Behind her, Mrs. Shaw's lips tightened.

"Here comes Old Stonewall!" called Edward, moving a mounted figure across the floor toward Clarence's front lines, consisting of three likewise mounted figures, one of them missing an arm, another leaning drunkenly due to his mount's absent foreleg.

Orah had nearly disappeared into the shadowed passageway after Henry. Mrs. Shaw heard whispers. She stepped forward. The outside door opened quickly; another muttered word, and the door closed again. Orah returned to the parlor, her face impassive. She walked past Mrs. Shaw without another word and returned to the kitchen.

Charlotte Changes Her Will

"ANNA! COME RUNNING!" Charlotte's wail drifted into the hallway. Anna snatched up a towel and used it to move her skillet to the cool side of the stovetop. She hurried to Charlotte's room and paused at the door, gasping at the stench; the basin beside the bed reeked of feces and some other smell. Something medicinal, perhaps, but Anna wasn't sure of the source. Charlotte groaned again.

"Lie still, Sister. I'll send one of the boys for Dr. Powers."

"No, don't call Dr. Powers! I don't want to see him ever again! It's all I can do to be civil to that man when I see him in church."

"Why, Charlotte! Dr. Powers has always cared for you as kindly as he has for the rest of us!"

"Yes, he has, until recently. He said something I can't forgive him for. It's too bad, but there it is. Dr. Powers is no longer my physician, I discharged him after that. He can't be depended on."

"But this is an emergency! Let me send for him, Charlotte!"

Charlotte straightened. "No, please, have them go for that new Dr. Dean. He's stopping at Mary Bailey's." She gritted her teeth and curled around the fists she'd jammed against her abdomen. Anna's footsteps tapped briskly away.

"Ralph? Are you out there?" Charlotte heard her call. The wind whisked away Ralph's reply from somewhere out in the yard. "Oh, not again," moaned Charlotte, placing a shaky hand on the bed to steady herself to rise.

Shadows from the west window had faded; Lottie had lit the lamps in the kitchen and the parlor, and was setting the table for dinner. Henry came in, splashed with mud.

"Papa." She ran to him and wrapped her arms around his waist.

"Careful," he warned. "I'm all mud. Had a little ruckus and got pretty wet. Why, what's wrong?" He tilted her face back and looked down at her.

"Oh, Papa, Auntie's dying."

"Dying! Surely not."

Anna, hearing his voice, stepped into the passageway. "Henry, can you step in here? Charlotte must speak to you, she says, while she's able to."

He came to Charlotte's doorway and stopped, his face working. "Good G—" he choked the words off, tried to erase the strangled look from his face. "Charlotte, what is it?"

Charlotte straightened up, clammy sweat dripping from her face. "Henry, brother, I must speak to you. I feel I shan't live until morning."

"Oh, Charlotte, surely not." What in the world was the source of that smell? Could she truly be so ill? She reached a hand weakly toward him. Pityingly, Henry took the hand. It felt limp and clammy; he fought an urge to wipe it off.

"I've spoken to Anna," whispered Charlotte. "About my will, you know that I've made a change to it, a change in your favor."

Henry looked out the window, desperately wishing himself back outside on the muddy roads. He met her eyes, looked away. "Charlotte, you don't need to change your will. It's all right."

"Henry, I did it for you. Brainard disapproved, but I did it anyway."

Henry squirmed. "That's all right." He looked out the window again. The black pane reflected his uncomfortable face and his hand holding the soggy right hand of Charlotte. He set the hand back down, patted it nervously, and backed away a step. "Charlotte, that's all right." He turned and fled. Charlotte doubled over again.

Long past midnight, Anna came to bed, her face pale with weariness. Henry rolled over, came awake. "How is she?" he whispered.

"I think she'll be all right in a day or two. Dr. Dean tells me her condition is more painful than dangerous. It was just one of her 'episodes,' but somewhat worse than usual."

"DR POWERS, I'm afraid I've come here under false pretenses. I'm not really ill at all."

He laughed dryly. "I suppose you mean that it's not something you can bring yourself to tell me."

"No, not at all! Its that I , I . . . oh, it's about my sister."

"Anna, you know I can't discuss Miss Spencer's case with anyone unless she gives me her permission to do so."

"I understand that. But this isn't exactly about her case, it's something more personal than that."

"More personal than the state of your sister's health?"

"I know that Charlotte doesn't want to entrust her care to you any longer, that she insists on seeing Dr. Dean. She seems to feel that you've insulted her in some way."

He waited, patience evident in every line of his posture.

"I know you wouldn't insult anyone on purpose, of course. I know that Charlotte can be, well, difficult at times."

"Did she tell you what I said?"

"No, she just said you'd insulted her. I'm sure that Dr. Dean is perfectly competent, but he hasn't your years of experience with her condition."

"I can deliver her records to Dr. Dean, if that is what Miss Spencer wishes. She need only tell me so herself."

"She won't, Doctor! You know how she is!"

"Yes, indeed I do. So perhaps, given that, you can infer something of what I said to her. And nothing I said was untrue, in my opinion. Unpleasant, perhaps, but true. I can do nothing more for your sister. Perhaps she will fare better with Dr. Dean. I sympathize with you, Anna, I really do, but I can do nothing more. Nor, I admit, do I care to any longer. I don't know . . ." He seemed to think better of completing his thought.

Anna bowed her head sadly. "Thank you for seeing me, Dr. Powers."

"CHARLOTTE, DEAR, you needn't have Dr. Powers any more if you no longer wish to. But I cannot agree to forbid him the house, not unless you can convince me that he has actually behaved," and here Anna laughed nervously, "inappropriately. Can't you tell me what he said, at least?"

Charlotte drew herself up, eyes ablaze. "I can't believe you would turn against your own family in prejudice for that rude old man. Just because you think anything in pants is preferable to your own sister . . ."

"She's off again," thought Anna sadly, and knew better than to pursue the question further until she had soothed Charlotte's fury again.

"I DON'T KNOW WHY she doesn't have Dr. Powers." Henry's voice was annoyed.

"She feels that Dr. Dean is more sympathetic to her particular problems." At Henry's skeptical look she added, exasperated, "She says he insulted her in a way that she cannot forgive."

"You can't make me believe that Dr. Powers deliberately insulted her.

Had the temerity to disagree with her, more likely." He sat on the edge of the bed, wrestling his boot off. Anna's back was to him, her hands busy at the back of her head as she undid the complicated knot that held her hair up.

Her hands froze; back rigid, she turned to face him. She pulled several hairpins from between her lips to say, "Henry, I didn't say it was deliberate. I'm perfectly aware that Charlotte can, sometimes, provoke a person. Even so, to call her 'crazy,' well, I can't think what possessed him."

"I can't imagine." Henry forced himself not to grin, but even so, Anna's steely look skewered him. Gently he lowered the boot to the floor.

"It's not the least bit funny, Henry. This has upset me, and I could tell that Dr. Powers was upset as well. What if one of the children should fall ill?"

"Well, but it's not for her to forbid Dr. Powers the house, is it? She needn't see him if she doesn't want to, but after all, Anna, it is our house." At Anna's look he amended his words. "It's our house too, I meant to say."

"I call that cruel of you, Henry Thacker, to be so unsympathetic to your sister-in-law after all she's suffered."

Henry forbore to say the uncharitable thing in his mind and said instead, "Do you know, the evening she was so sick, she told me she's changed her will, though I don't know why."

"Perhaps she hopes you will dislike her less."

"Anna! I don't dislike your sister."

"She believes you do."

"She's mistaken." Henry was fully awake now, annoyed by the direction the conversation had taken.

"She says you avoid her. She couldn't help noticing that you showed more affection to Orah than you ever do toward her."

"Anna, you know why I stay away from Charlotte. She begins by being sweet, entirely too much so, and then gradually she begins to, oh, you know, she tries as hard as she can to provoke a quarrel. If ever I do contradict her in the slightest, all that sweetness turns to vitriol. It's like a cat that rubs against your legs, and when you reach down to stroke it, it leaves scratches on the back of your hand and then runs away."

Henry realized that he had said too much; Anna's spine had stiffened, and she would not look at him. Unwisely, he blundered on; surely, if he could make her understand, she, Anna, could drop the matter from her mind. He simply couldn't warm up to Charlotte, and that was that.

"Maybe Dr. Powers wasn't being insulting when he said what he said. Perhaps he tried to suggest to her, sympathetically, you know, that she really is . . ." his voice trailed off at the look on his wife's face, but he took a breath and finished, ". . . what he said. That she couldn't be held responsible for her actions, that is."

Anna had finished with her hair and was now pacing back and forth. It was too dark to see her face, but Henry saw clearly that she was very annoyed with him.

"I've tried to be patient with her, Anna, tried my best, but Charlotte is simply beyond me. I think I get along pretty well with my fellow man, but Charlotte won't be satisfied with getting along. Sick or well, we seem doomed to this dance of cross-purposes. It's best I keep my distance, so that's what I do. Come to bed, Anna. You're exhausted." He reached for her hand, and she allowed him to take it and pull her toward him. She sat down on the bed, then raised the covers and slid in to lie, back to him. Eventually they fell asleep.

Charlotte did not die. By daylight, her pains had eased, and the "attacks" grew more infrequent. Henry went to bed that evening without waiting for Anna, who seemed determined to busy herself around Charlotte's room without joining the family in the parlor at all.

Henry awoke in an empty bed the next morning; Anna had stayed on the lounge in Charlotte's room all night. She stayed there the following night, and the nights afterward. Neither Henry nor Anna remarked on this, nor did the children.

THE OFFICERS OF the Christian Endeavor Society smiled at Anna as they left. They'd been to tea with Charlotte. Lottie was away at her art class, so Anna had shuttled between Josie and kitchen duty, catching snatches of conversation, prayer, and Bible quotations. Now she was gathering up plates and cups, piling them carefully on a lacquered tray.

"Sister, I simply must speak to you. I've been avoiding the subject, but hearing it spoken of again today makes it imperative that I bring it up."

Anna sighed, set the tray back onto the table. "Bring up what?"

"Henry. And his behavior with that girl."

"Whatever are you talking about? What girl?" Anna looked blandly at Charlotte.

"Oh, don't pretend to be so stupid, Anna! You know very well what girl! She moved to the Shaws', so suddenly he began to visit at the Shaws'. You never said a word to him about it. She moved to the Pettits', so suddenly he began to visit at the Pettits'. Not a word from you then, either, even though the whole town was talking about it! Now she's at the Judsons', and he's visiting at the Judsons', and his wife goes serenely on about her business. I can't stand it!"

"I'm not sure that this is something for you to stand, or not stand," said Anna, mildly. "This is my husband we're talking about, isn't it?"

"It affects the whole family, and you know it! How do you think I feel when the ladies look at me in that pitying way?"

"Perhaps they sympathize with your ill health," suggested Anna.

"That's just like you, Anna, acting like everyone's your best friend and letting them walk all over you." Charlotte was flushed, her hands opening and closing.

"What gets into you, Charlotte? One moment you were saying goodbye to your group and now here you are, in a rage at me because of some silly town gossip. Why does this make you so angry?"

"Angry? I'm not angry, you're the one who seems bent on making a major issue out of this!"

Anna, forgetting her good intentions, rounded on her sister. "Sister, Henry's right, sometimes you simply make it impossible to get along with you."

Charlotte stared at her; her face had paled except for two red dots of color, one on each cheek. Her eyes had dilated alarmingly.

"Charlotte? Are you all right? What's wrong?" Anna reached for Charlotte's hand; she snatched it away, glaring. Anna shrugged and picked up the tray, and left the room.

ORAH STOPPED at the threshold of West Hall and squinted in the bright sunshine. It was the first really warm day of spring, the ground dry enough to sit on and eat her lunch. She was alone; Sadie and Mattie had gotten terribly busy lately and seemed to have had no time to visit, just the three of them, for a long time.

She espied Cinda Woodruff across the lawn, just opening what looked like a parcel of sandwiches. Cinda was poor company, and Orah's set generally avoided her. It wasn't just that she was "homely as a hedge fence," though she certainly was. Flat fore and aft, her eyes a muddy green that put Orah in mind of mucus, hair a rusty brown, large lips like a bass, and large feet that turned out and gave her an awkward walk, no, Cinda certainly wasn't much to look at. Even so, a girl with sparkle in her personality, a keen mind, or a clever wit could overcome the handicap of a dismal appearance. Cinda had a dull average mind; she parroted whatever beliefs prevailed at the moment, whenever she managed to speak up at all. No, none of Orah's set cared to seek out Cinda's company, though of course she was welcome at church events and those parties to which all the girls were invited.

Still, it was such a pleasant day, and nobody she chummed with seemed to be available just now. Orah walked over to Cinda. "It's a nice day for a picnic, isn't it?" she asked pleasantly.

Cinda jumped; her cheeks flushed a mottled red when she saw who had greeted her. "Oh, yes, oh yes, it certainly is," she babbled, her eyes shifting guiltily around as if, thought Orah, amusedly, she had been caught daydreaming about her favorite stage actor.

"Shall I join you?" asked Orah.

Cinda's blush faded, but she still looked nervous, almost panicky. Whatever was wrong with the foolish thing?

"I was, ah, just finishing my lunch. I have an appointment, yes, with one of the professors." As Cinda said this, she'd begun to wrap up a sandwich that had only one bite taken from it, a parcel of dried apples, and a cookie, untouched.

"Which one?" asked Orah.

"Which what?" Cinda struggled to her feet, her lunch packet clutched in both hands to her flat chest like she was a miser with a bag of gold.

"Which professor?"

"Oh. Yes, I have an appointment. Good day to you, Orah," and Cinda waddled away quickly.

Thoughtfully, Orah sat in the place vacated by Cinda. It occurred to her that it wasn't only the girls in her set who had been busy and preoccupied lately. From being reasonably popular, she had recently become, she now realized, a pariah in much the same way Cinda had always been. And now Cinda, lowest of the low, didn't care to be seen with her. What in the world?

"Sadie! Stop a minute, please, and talk to me," commanded Orah. Sadie stopped, but in a way that reminded Orah of a hummingbird, ready to dart away at any second. Her eyes darted from side to side as well, as though she were planning her escape.

"What is it? Orah, I have to rush, really, I'll be late."

"That's fine," replied Orah, smoothly. "I'll walk with you wherever you're going." She noted the panicky look on Sadie's face, then stopped in front of her, bringing Sadie up short. "You don't want to be seen with me, isn't that it?"

Sadie flushed. "Really, Orah, I don't have time for this right now."

"Yes you do, you minx!" snapped Orah, not budging. "I want to know why you and Mattie, yes, and half the school, are avoiding me. Have I done anything to deserve it?"

"You know." This was barely audible.

"No, I do not! What terrible thing am I supposed to have done?"

The words came out in a rush. "Everyone knows, everyone at school and at church and in the town has been talking about it, what you and, and, Mr. Thacker are doing!"

"I see," Orah replied quietly. "And what, exactly, do they suppose we are doing?" Sadie stared at her, lips compressed, her face red. "What has Mr. Thacker done with me that he doesn't do with half the girls in the Sunday school class, taken their arms when walking in the snow or lifting them down from the buggy? Mr. Thacker is just naturally friendly and jolly, and I'm a friend of the whole family. Is that a crime?"

"It's different with you, Orah, everyone sees that. It just is." And defiantly, "So of course no nice girl wants to be too friendly with you— what would people think, if not that we were that way too? Now you've gone and made me say things I didn't like to say. I'm sorry for you, Orah, and that's the truth." Her dignity restored, Sadie stepped around Orah and continued down the walk.

Orah stood rooted to the spot and watched her go.

And Anna in the Middle

ANNA PAUSED at the parlor door, adjusting her light spring coat. She had lost more weight since Josie's birth, and the sleeves hung low on her wrists. Take up the cuffs? Or wait another year and see if she filled out again? Lost in contemplation, she studied the way the material draped over her upper hands.

Childish wails started up from the kitchen, then died down again as Lottie's voice spoke placatingly. Anna seemed not to notice.

"Anna? Are you going out?"

Anna spun around, looking, Charlotte thought, sheepish. "Whatever ails you, Sister?"

"I didn't know you were in here," laughed Anna nervously. "I thought you were resting in your room."

"Well, I'm not. Why did you jump so? You looked like a cat caught in the cream pitcher!"

Anna took a deep breath, let it out again. "I'm expecting some company in a few minutes. I had planned for us to take a walk before coming back for tea."

"Who's to watch the children while you're gone?" Charlotte sounded peevish now.

"Lottie has them. She's in the kitchen, studying."

Charlotte, relieved of the threatened task of child care, relaxed again. "Perhaps I'll join you in here when you return from your walk. Who is coming?"

Anna fiddled with her sleeve again and looked away guiltily, like a child. "It's Orah Bunker."

Charlotte stiffened. "With everything the town is saying, you've invited her to tea? In our house?"

Anna, hearing footsteps on the path outside, lifted her head. Charlotte had heard them too. "Don't let her in, Anna. Go to the door and tell her what-for!"

Anna looked at her sister. Charlotte looked feverish, excited. Did she enjoy the idea of a common row on their own doorstep? My own doorstep, she corrected herself.

"Certainly not, Charlotte, what an idea!" She strove for a tone of lightness. "You'd have me believe that Dr. Powers was right about you!" At Charlotte's outraged look, she tried again. "Forgive me, dear. It's only that I met Orah by chance at the market yesterday and invited her for tea and a walk outdoors. It's just that simple. The weather has been lovely lately, hasn't it?"

She turned her back on Charlotte and hurried to the door, where Orah awaited. "I'm just ready, Orah."

Excited voices rang from the kitchen, "Orah! Orah! She's here!" Will ran out, followed closely by Josie, and embraced Orah's legs. Lottie trailed them, her grammar text in one hand, finger marking the place.

"Where are you going? Can we go too?" demanded Will.

"Only for a walk with your mother, and then I'm coming back here for tea," said Orah.

Lottie grasped Will's roundabout and kept him from following his mother and Orah out the door. "You and Josie stay here with me," persuaded Lottie, "and help me make the tea ready."

But it was no use. Five minutes later Charlotte stood at the window and watched as Anna and Orah walked across the yard, trailed, as if by chicks, by Will, Josie, and Lottie. Two red spots burned on her cheeks. Her stomach clenched; she stifled a sour belch.

"I CALL THAT HARD, SISTER. You know that I'm in poor health and unable to see to anything. With all that you have to do, Henry could stay home and help us instead of whoring after that Jezebel. Yet you never say a word to keep him home. After all I've sacrificed, the very least you could do . . ."

"Sacrificed?" Anna seemed honestly amazed by this.

"Certainly, sacrificed! I left my post in Biltis, and came back here because you and Elvira needed my help. Then, when I needed help in return, what did you and Henry do but produce two helpless babes to distract you, leaving everyone else to struggle along as best they could, and me with only a heedless girl to see to me."

Anna looked at her quizzically. "That is possibly the oddest thing I've ever heard you say, Charlotte. You seem to think that we had Will and Josie just to make your life more difficult!"

"Well, perhaps I worded that poorly," conceded Charlotte. "But you must admit they've been very inconvenient for everyone. But that's not the point at all." Her brow furrowed; Anna assumed she'd forgotten where she wanted to lead the conversation.

"The point is," Charlotte seemed to have found her train of thought again, ". . . the point is, that you're married to Henry Thacker because I let you have him all those years ago. He gave you those two babies to distract you from his philandering, and you allowed it to happen. And now you're just throwing him away to that woman of the streets."

Anna barked a hard, incredulous laugh. "You let me have Henry? How could you possibly let yourself believe that?"

"What do you mean, how can I believe that? Have you forgotten that he used to escort me everywhere and we allowed you to come along? Don't you know it's because we felt sorry for you? And so, when Henry made his interest toward me plain, why, I told him that I wasn't interested, that I had a higher calling. I did it for you!"

"Charlotte, you're being ridiculous. I cannot allow you to continue to think this way, I'm afraid. We've taken wonderfully good care of you for a long time, and gotten precious little thanks, I must say."

Charlotte drew herself up, lips pressed into a line, eyebrows up, eyes starting from their sockets. Anna could feel her sister's rage welling up, fuel for another eruption of vitriol.

Anna was tired. Her sleep was interrupted frequently by Charlotte's many nocturnal needs, and all day long the children seemed to require this or that little thing. Henry, it's true, was little help, mooning about sighing when home from work, or abruptly going out on this or that errand.

Anna had no doubt that he met Orah on many of these trips. While it made her sad, it was also a relief that he too wasn't forever asking things like, "Anna, where's the book I left here?" or "Anna, do I have any more clean handkerchiefs?" Too, whenever he went out he could run the errands to town that used to take so much of her time, fetching this or that item that Charlotte or the children always seemed to require.

She knew that she herself had become snappish and ill-tempered, even to the friends who came less and less often to visit, and especially to the children and to Henry. This, too, made her sad.

She supposed that Henry's foolish infatuation with a pretty young woman was a small price to pay for the comparative peace of mind; she no longer felt reproached for her neglect of him.

It now occurred to her, for the first time ("Why didn't I notice before now?"), that the main cause of her exhaustion and sadness now sat before her, glaring like a gorgon. When had Charlotte lost her prettiness and become this ill-favored, scrawny, draggle-haired woman? Anna had felt such pity for her younger sister all these years, but was now shocked to feel it curdle into something like weary contempt.

Charlotte, she knew, was now rehearsing her next verbal attack. Anna had long suspected, but not consciously let herself know, how much Charlotte controlled everyone around her with her too-ready rages. Charlotte had always seemed to be as much a victim of her own fury as her targets were, but recently Anna had begun to think that Charlotte was in perfect control of her "fits" of ire. They were more useful than physical blows for enforcing obedience to her every whim, from friend and relative alike. Nobody argued with Charlotte if they could help it; it was just too much work and not really worth the trouble.

So Charlotte, once-pretty almond-eyed Charlotte with the dark glossy hair, high cheekbones, and twinkling eyes, now sour-breathed, too-thin Charlotte with the eyes that only shone when she was angry, had ruled everyone around her, and somehow had knocked the whole center of the Thacker home awry.

Startled, Anna voiced this before she thought better of it.

"It's not really Orah who's the problem in the family, it's Charlotte. All along, it's been Charlotte!"

"What!"

Anna smiled at her sister. "Yes, it's been you. Oh, yes, I know that Henry's quite taken with Orah, and probably I should worry about that. But you're the reason we needed Orah in the first place, and the reason Henry, and the children for that matter, have made her the center of this family, where a wife and mother belong. Why, Charlotte, all this time we've been so wrapped up in dancing attendance on you that we've hardly said 'How-de-do' to each other! How foolish we've all been!"

And astoundingly, Anna laughed. It wasn't the tired laugh of a woman made sad by overwork, not the angry laugh of a woman arguing with her sister. It was a gay, happy laugh, the free and joyous sound a little girl made when she'd finally mastered ice-skating backward or a difficult jump-rope maneuver.

"Poor Charlotte, look at you! I'm so sorry we've let you become this way, dear. I think it's time we all had a change, don't you? Charlotte, how would you like to go and visit Brainard for a while? It's been several years since you had an outing, and I'm sure they'd all be delighted to have you. Or, what about this? We could move you to Mrs. Bailey's boardinghouse; I'm sure we can help with the expense . . ."

Anna felt younger than she had in years. She knew Charlotte was furious and about to explode into poisonous words, but, for a wonder, she found that she didn't care.

Poisonous Words

BENZONIA, MAY 4, 1894

HENRY AWOKE, confused, to a silent house. Normally he awoke to morning kitchen sounds: rustles and clatters, metallic tones of spoon on bowl and mellower ones of dish on plate, and heavy thumps of firewood into stove box. Today it felt later than usual, and the house was still. He heard the rooster crow, a muffled crow that meant he faced away toward the woods. It *was* later than usual, and nobody was stirring. Was the house stricken with the sleeping sickness?

He arose, pulled on his trousers, and rapped on the doorframe of the girls' room. "Lottie? Time to get up."

Lottie, bless her, was instantly awake. "What's the matter? Where's Mother?"

"I don't know. I haven't heard a sound from downstairs. See to Will and Josie, would you?" He pattered down the stairs barefoot. Contrary to her habit, Anna was not in the kitchen, nor was she out in the yard. He didn't bother checking the outhouse; the fire in the kitchen was not even lit. Anna always did that first thing, only omitting that task when Orah had been there to do it for her.

Charlotte's door remained closed; he hesitated a long moment, then tapped. "Anna?" A soft moan answered him. He sighed. Charlotte must be having another one of her attacks. He heard a soft retching.

Bracing himself, he opened the door. "Anna? Do you need any . . . ?" His mouth dropped open. Charlotte lay in peaceful slumber in her bed. It was Anna who bent over the chamber pot, her sides pumping like those of a Clydesdale pulling a heavy load.

Nothing came up. She looked dolefully at him; her face had a greenish cast that alarmed him.

"Henry, would you mind very much if I didn't make breakfast this morning? I'm feeling rather poorly."

Charlotte stirred, opened her eyes, saw Henry, and blinked. "Is something wrong?"

"Anna seems to be ill this morning. Can you look after her while I prepare the breakfast? We're all sixes and sevens, it seems."

"Certainly I will. Anna, lie down; that often helps me when I feel nauseated. Let me pour you some water." She took the glass from the nightstand and refilled it from the pitcher that stood there.

Henry, in the kitchen, began to prepare graham mush for eight people. This wasn't a difficult recipe; over the years he'd watched Elvira, then Anna, then Orah make it. Make up the fire and as the stove heated, set the table. Pour the milk, set out the sugar bowl. Fill the pot to the proper level with water, set the pan on the stove to boil. Measure out graham meal to the proper level in the cup, and as the water boiled heartily, stir the coarse flour into the water. Let it bubble for five minutes, move the pot to a cooler part of the stove.

By this time Ralph was up. He filled his bowl, added milk and sugar, and began to eat. Roy wandered in, buttoning his shirt. "I'm going to need some help this morning, boys," Henry told them. "That disker's due to arrive right after lunch, and I want to get those potatoes dug up before then."

Ralph brightened; missing morning classes to work around the land was always a pleasure. Roy was less pleased but said nothing.

Lottie came in. "Where's Mother?"

"She's feeling sick this morning. Go in and ask her if she feels like eating anything."

"I'll take Auntie's mush to her now, too," said Lottie.

Anna, looking less green, followed Lottie back to the kitchen. "I think I could eat a little of that mush, now." She sank into the chair beside the stove and leaned her head back against the wall.

Henry ladled a bowlful for her. "Milk and sugar, the way you like it?" At her weak nod, he doctored the mush and handed the dish to Anna. She fumbled it, but recovered herself. Slowly she began to eat.

Lottie looked at her with some alarm, until Will, in an excess of youthful spirits, popped Josie on the head with his spoon. "Stop that, Will, you bad boy!" scolded Lottie.

"Bad boy," repeated Josie, happily.

The family finished their breakfast, and rose to begin their day. "Anna?" called Charlotte from her room.

"You just sit," said Henry to Anna as she wearily set her bowl aside and began to rise. He went to Charlotte's door. "Anna's still a little weak, Charlotte. What was it you wanted?"

"Would you have one of your boys bring me another pitcher of water? And this glass is soiled. Will you bring me a fresh one?" Henry accepted pitcher and glass; Ralph went onto the porch where the Frankfort Water jug reposed and refilled the pitcher. He silently delivered it to his aunt, who silently nodded her thanks.

"If you need anything else," he told her, "Lottie's in the kitchen with the children. Roy and I will be out with Father, but she can fetch us."

After Anna finished her breakfast, she felt a bit better. The weather had been fine for several days; she had been looking forward to starting her flowers. Nearly a dozen paper packets of seeds, carefully collected the previous fall and folded into brown parcels, sat on the back of a pantry shelf; she imagined that they were becoming impatient for her to plant them. One of the simple joys of her life was to see the first tiny leaves pop out of the nearly black soil. She hated to think that illness would prevent her from this beloved spring ritual.

She rose carefully and, avoiding any sudden moves, collected the packets into a basket. Delphinium, nasturtium, marigold, a riot of color contained in these tiny grains. Anna stifled another wave of nausea and stepped outside, pausing to draw a long breath. The shed where the garden tools resided seemed a long way away.

Two hours later she felt wonderfully better. The air was clear and soft, the sun warm. She had planted row upon row along the front of the house, curving around the sides, and had begun a row of nasturtiums along the border of the kitchen vegetable garden. The robin (was it the same one every spring?) stood in the lilac that shaded the kitchen window and warbled his spring greeting.

Henry came in from the field, followed by Roy and Ralph. "Feeling better, I see," said Henry.

Anna looked up from the pot she was stirring. "Wash up and sit down—it's nearly ready. Lottie? Bring the children in and see their hands are clean, will you?"

Lottie complied. Anna set the steaming bowl of stew on the table, added a bowl of potatoes and another of canned beans. They fell to; Anna retreated to her chair by the stove. Sweat rolled down her face.

"Mother?" said Ralph. Worriedly, the children looked at her. With a tiny smile she shook her head. "You go ahead and eat. I'm not very hungry, all of a sudden."

Lottie finished her lunch and began to clear the table. "Shall I do the dishes for you, Mother?" she asked.

"No, you go and take Auntie her tray, please." Anna set the kettle to boil, and then sat down again.

Henry looked searchingly at her. "Do you need anything from me, before we go back out?" Anna shook her head. Doubtfully, they left, Ralph looking back once. "Auntie says she only wants some of her prunes," said Lottie. She went to the pantry where the glass jar of Charlotte's prunes sat, filled a dish of these, and took them to her.

Anna did the dishes and went to the flower garden again, working until teatime. During that time she had two more "spells"; the first time she was able to make it to the outhouse. The second time she was overwhelmed so suddenly that she spattered the row she had been hoeing. She sat down on the back step and leaned against the door.

The afternoon sun which had seemed so warm and welcoming before now seemed to burn into the top of her head. Her head felt swollen, and throbbed; her tongue tingled, and the nausea seemed to spread from her stomach to all of her limbs.

Lottie found her there and helped her to come indoors. Between attacks of vomiting, Anna lay on the lounge in the sitting room through dinner, which Henry and Lottie prepared.

"I think I'd better go to bed," said Anna. It sounded as though she spoke through a throat full of egg whites. Leaning on the back of the sofa, she made it to the door; her legs buckled once, but she straightened and made it to the room she now shared with Charlotte.

"Sister? Don't you think you should send for someone to help?" Charlotte's voice was sharp with worry.

"Perhaps so," agreed Anna. "Would Mrs. Waters come, do you think?"

"Send your boy for Mary Bailey is my suggestion; she's had more experience with nursing than anybody."

"That's so," agreed Anna. She scribbled a note, and handed it to Lottie with a hand that shook.

"Mercy sakes, Anna!" exclaimed Mary Bailey when she saw Anna, now bent wretchedly over a tin basin. Anna had returned to her spot in the kitchen, seemingly unable to lie still. She had never been a heavy woman, and a single day of vomiting and diarrhea seemed to have reduced her to a mummified version of herself.

"Let's get you to bed," Mrs. Bailey ordered. Anna obediently rose and started toward Charlotte's room.

"That's no good," objected Mary Bailey. "You, boy," she snapped to Roy, "help me move that lounge from your aunt's room. We'll set her up in the parlor and hang a curtain over the door."

In a few minutes Anna was installed in the parlor, with a blanket hung on a line across the doorway, clean sheets under her, and a freshly rinsed pot within easy reach. In a few minutes more, the sheets were no longer clean.

"I'm so sorry," whispered Anna. "I don't seem able to have any control." Mrs. Bailey pursed her lips. "I think we need to send for the doctor. Boy, will you carry a message to Dr. Dean?" She had snagged Ralph by his sleeve as he passed by her with an armload of wood; May evenings were cold, and the parlor fire hadn't been lit yet.

"Roy can go," offered Henry, who'd been standing in the doorway of the parlor, a handful of blankets bunched in one hand, staring helplessly at his wife.

Within the hour, Dr. Dean strode in, crumbs from his dinner spice cake sticking to his vest. After an examination of Anna and a glance at the contents of the basin, he pulled some bottles from his multitrayed bag. "I'm going to leave you some powders of subnitrate of bismuth and some exolate of peptide. If those don't make a difference by Sunday, we'll try some carbolic acid." He measured the powders into papers and wrote a note on each folded packet.

Prayers to No Avail

HOW LONG HAD SHE been lying here in a puddle of something wet? Days? Hours? She moved her head; neck muscles creaked. The inside of her head buzzed, the echoes crescendoing at times to a shriek, much like the din when the cicadas come out in August. From behind her eyes, over her crown, and down the back of her head there seemed to be something hugely swollen, pulsing like the heart of a living thing. She tried to avert her mind from this thought; it seemed that if she allowed the image room in her mind the thing would grow yet more, a great leech filled with her own blood, growing and filling the space between brain and skull. When she vomited, the pressure seemed to threaten the very bones of her skull. How long, O Lord, must I endure this? she thought, and again her diaphragm clenched, sending the pain upward like a throbbing heart, and downward like a swarm of rats eating their way out through her bowels.

She tried to pray and realized that her tongue, rather than shaping words, poked like a wooden thing from her mouth and flickered right, left, right, left from her mouth. She must look grotesque; certainly she felt repulsive, filthy, sweaty, smelling of vomit and excrement. The whole room was permeated with the stink; if this were one of the children, she would busily put things to rights, bathing the child, scrubbing the pots, laundering the sheets. Instead, she was the child, helpless to even pour a glass of water without her shaking hand spilling it. Oh, if Elvira were only here, how gladly she would look into those warm eyes!

Or Dr. Powers, who had been the family's doctor since Anna was a young woman. Why had Mrs. Bailey sent for Dr. Dean instead? Was it because Charlotte preferred him? Oh, but who was she to judge the merits of one doctor over another, she who couldn't even turn over without a flood of nausea washing over her?

Another hot flash of fever flooded her and she lay, panting, wishing that someone would bring in another dish of ice water and bathe her face.

ANNA LOOKED UP at her sister, her yellow face a picture of woe. "I thought, yesterday, that I was slightly better. I had so hoped . . ."

Charlotte examined Anna's face critically. "It doesn't seem as though you've been well since breakfast that first morning."

"If I only knew what was causing this! At first I feared for the rest of you, that I had some sort of contagion." She lay back on her pillows, took a deep breath. Her tongue, seemingly of its own volition, poked out and darted from one corner of her liverish lips to the other.

"Lottie? Would you go out and see what is the matter with Will?" called Charlotte. She listened and, when she heard the back screen door slam, leaned to Anna's ear. "Anna, have you considered the possibility that you have been poisoned?"

Anna didn't open her eyes. "Oh, Charlotte, what an idea."

"I'm serious. Maybe something was put into your food."

"What, deliberately? Who would do such a thing? Nobody has been here except for the family and Mary Bailey."

"Who do you think?" Charlotte leaned forward, her eyes on Anna's face. "Who has become the talk of the town because he wants another woman? Who fixed your breakfast for you that morning?" Her eyes glittered. "He's trying to poison me, Anna, and he's poisoned you as well."

Green haze floated behind Anna's eyelids, and the hissed word "poison" slithered through the haze, matching its color. The lounge rolled unsteadily beneath her. Her mouth tingled, tasted green and metallic. At the same time, her sister's preposterous words seemed unimportant.

"You're being foolish," the words blurted out unthinkingly. "The idea is perfectly crazy." Charlotte drew herself up, outraged. A silent moment lengthened, and then Anna reached for the basin again. It nearly dropped to the floor, but she managed to drag it to the edge of her pillow before the green fluid dribbled from her lips. Anna didn't notice when Charlotte stood up and left the room.

"He's Trying to Poison Me as Well"

LOTTIE STOOD at the kitchen table, kneading biscuit dough. Twice she had needed to turn her head to the side and sniffle, to keep her nose from dripping into the dough. How had everything gone from normal to terrible, so quickly? It wasn't just that Mother was so ill, though that was bad enough. Mother had, she realized, been the quiet center of the home, and she'd never known how steady that center was until the center had dropped out and everything wobbled.

Now everything was wrong. Well, when she thought about it, things had felt wrong for a while now. The Shaws and several of her teachers had begun to treat her as though there was something wrong with her; their voices were solicitous, faces falsely smiling. She knew that nobody, least of all Auntie, approved of the family's friendship with Orah Bunker, though nobody would say quite why that was, and why that should make the ladies of the town pity her, she didn't know.

When Mrs. Bailey came to help with Mother, she always stopped in Auntie's room. There the two would whisper, sibilant angry hisses that stopped if they heard Lottie's footsteps. The adult world seemed, at times, to be a dark and secretive place, with hidden sins at every doorstep and disapproval attending the most innocent of acts. Lottie felt dirty, as though she were at fault for Mother's sickness and the ladies' disapproval. If she could just understand what the nature of her failings was, she could correct them or at least pray for forgiveness.

And Mother! Oh, poor Mother; Lottie yearned to comfort and heal her. When she thought about her mother lying in pain and sickness, she wanted to put her arms around her, to whisper endearments that were never said out loud between family members once they grew too old for such things.

But when she stood at the door of the parlor, when she could see (and smell!) the gaunt, retching body, its skin an oddly orange color, its tongue darting around the grayish-brown lips, she wanted to run the other way. Perhaps this was why Auntie and Mrs. Bailey whispered, but Lottie didn't think so. They seemed most upset with Papa, though he seemed barely aware of them.

"Henry," Mrs. Bailey had said last evening, "you simply must have a nurse. Your wife is in a pitiable state, and needs the care of a woman."

"I don't think she wants anybody else," Henry had replied dully. Mary Bailey had clucked her tongue disparagingly and shaken her head. The man behaved as if in a stupor, while his wife lay helpless. Even a child Lottie's age seemed more able and alert than this husband. At least she could cook and look after the two young ones.

Meanwhile, Mr. Thacker floated around the house, fetching and carrying and cleaning up as well as a man was able, it was true, and those boys of his, well, the idea of having them as nurses, the idea!

Charlotte Spencer, poor woman, was now at their mercies. If she needed anything of a personal nature, her only recourse was to wait until she, Mary, came by, or to call vainly for young Lottie.

Now here was this other matter. "He's poisoning my sister and now he's trying to poison me as well," Charlotte had told her.

Charlotte had always been flighty and emotional, that was accepted. Mary had been skeptical about some of her stories from Turkey, they seemed so far-flung and fanciful, filled with blood, dirt, and danger. Yet the news from abroad bore out a good many of the things Charlotte had narrated. True, also, were some of the insinuations Charlotte had made against Henry, in the matter of the hired girl. There were many witnesses to his excessive fondness toward Orah.

Still and all, accusing a man (and an assistant sheriff, at that!) of trying to poison his own wife and sister-in-law seemed too far-fetched even for dramatic Charlotte to have invented.

More to placate Charlotte than anything else, Mary had accepted the dish of "poisoned" pudding and promised to deliver it to Dr. Dean, who boarded with her. She had done so with some embarrassment; Dr. Dean had shaken his head smilingly and set the dish on his wardrobe, promising to inspect it "when he had a little more time."

This had not placated Charlotte, however, but only encouraged her to continue her fanciful accusations. A dish of prunes on Sunday, one of them hollowed out and filled with gray powder, a piece of blotting paper with a dusting of the same powder, followed the pudding.

On Saturday, Charlotte had told her, she'd found some white powder in her water, so she'd poured the water off and collected the powder on a piece of paper. After the paper dried, she had carefully written on it where she found it, the date, and her signature because, she said, "I thought it possible that I might have to give testimony." Mary Bailey had smiled when she told this to Dr. Dean. He smiled also, but added these to the collection on his wardrobe.

Now here it was, a week later, and poor Anna was no better than before. Charlotte was as nervous as a scalded cat; only yesterday Mrs. Barnes and Mrs. Barnard had stopped by the Thackers, and they reported that their appearance at the doorway had sent Charlotte into a panic. "Oh, don't come in, we are not ready!" Charlotte had cried, and the ladies retired to the porch in great confusion. A moment later, calm again, she had ushered them into the parlor. Anna had been able to greet them, but faintly.

Exeunt Charlotte

MAY 12, 1894

ON SATURDAY, Ralph stood at the grocery counter and doled out $2.73 for his items. It was odd how your outlook could change so quickly in the face of misfortune. Among his purchases was a pile of pads, white soft cotton pieces welded together by some arcane process that Ralph didn't understand. They were nearly always purchased by girls or women; they served as diapers for infants, but also, he knew, they were used by women during their "ladies' times."

A week ago he'd have died rather than stand here in view of anybody who might walk in, a bundle of these pads on the counter before him. Now, though, it didn't seem to matter. His own mother needed these, and she was so ill that she might die. Who cared about some pieces of cloth in the devastating face of that?

The fact that his aunt seemed to be having a personal crisis of her own was a minor consideration. She had, Ralph thought, never really liked any of them except for Mother and, perhaps, Lottie. Ralph had often wondered if she only stayed with them because she had nowhere else to go. While he continued to pity her, he wished she had simply stayed in Turkey.

The next evening he was amazed to find that his wish had, in a way, come true. There was Auntie, her old carpet valise packed, supervising Roy in the packing of her trunk, which she had loaded with rocks, or so Roy later insisted. Mrs. Bailey waited on the porch, her buggy tied up to the tree that served them as a hitching post.

"I'll come back to see you as often as I'm able," Charlotte assured Anna, who seemed too drained to comprehend that her sister was leaving. "When this terrible illness has passed, you can come to visit me at Mary Bailey's." She kissed her sister, who smiled vaguely and whispered a weak "Good night." She then left the house, leaning on Mrs. Bailey's arm.

"I'm to deliver her trunk before Monday," grumbled Roy to Ralph, "and you can help me load it onto the wagon."

Lottie stood in the kitchen doorway looking mournful.

"What's wrong?" asked Ralph, "Do you miss her already?"

"She didn't even say goodbye to us. After all the time she's lived with us, and the only person she said goodbye to was Mother!"

"Oh, that's just Auntie," comforted Ralph, patting her shoulder. "You'll see her later on and she'll make it up to you. You know she always liked you best anyway."

The house seemed unusually quiet. Henry had disappeared to the barn, and Anna slept, quiet and at ease for the moment. Lottie brightened. "Let's have cookies in the kitchen."

Ralph felt a pang at this; how long had it been since any of them had smiled the way Lottie was now?

The five of them gathered around the table, Will and Josie swinging their chubby legs from their tall chairs, and munched molasses cookies. Outdoors, a robin chortled his evensong. Perhaps Mother would start to get better and all would be right again.

MAY 15, 1894

THOUGH THE SUN had come up four hours ago, Anna's lounge lay in deep shadow, as did Henry's spirits. Yesterday Dr. Dean had told him that the blood he had thought was part of the diarrhea had actually been bloody hemorrhagic discharges from her uterus. Dr. Dean, not knowing that Anna had been spending all her nights in Charlotte's room, had said, "Mrs. Thacker thinks it possible she might have aborted from her retching."

Henry had simply replied that it was only five or six days before that she had had her monthly sickness and that he did not think it was possible for her to have aborted, but confusion battled with his grief. When had they last slept in the same bed, how long ago had it been? Days? Weeks? Months?

He now sagged in the chair, his head against the wall. He had lounged this way overnight, halfway between sleep and wakening, oblivious to the cramp that developed in his neck. At some point Anna had lapsed from spasmodic vomiting into a lethargy, broken periodically by a gush of greenish-yellow fluid from the corner of her mouth onto the pad Henry had tucked under her face. This bitter liquid was now drying on her lips; an early fly buzzed around her, landed, tasted, and found it good. Neither Anna nor Henry noticed it at first, but eventually the tickle roused Anna.

She moaned and moved her head feebly; the fly rose, circled, landed again. Henry opened his half-lidded eyes and sat up, wincing at the sharp pain in his neck. His head didn't seem to want to straighten. He waved the fly away, dampened a cloth in the basin of lukewarm water that sat on the stand, and wiped Anna's cracked lips.

"Henry." The word was little more than a sigh. Wearily Anna took a breath and spoke again. "Henry, I'm worried for the children. If I don't get better . . ."

Henry shushed her. "You'll be fine Anna, it just takes a while to get over—whatever this is."

She took a deeper breath and seemed to gain strength from it. "I'm not afraid to die. I've done my best and put my faith in the Lord. I know that sometimes you've thought me harsh with the children, but I did what I thought was best for them. See that you try to do the same, Henry, if it should so happen that I die of this illness. No, let me speak." She paused, panting slightly. "I want you and the children to have the house, Henry, I want to sign it over to you."

Henry patted her hand, which, he noted reluctantly, resembled the claw of a chicken, all bone and orange scales, with yellow keratin at the tips.

"We'll see to it, someday soon, when you feel better," he tried to soothe her.

"Now," she insisted. "You can fill in the deed and I'll sign it." Almost petulantly she pushed his hand away and made a limp shooing motion.

Henry went to the alcove where the rolltop desk stood, and after some rummaging through farm machinery orders, seed invoices, and several loose postage stamps, he found the document, now yellowed at the edges, in a pasteboard folder labeled "Important Papers." On the back of the deed, he wrote the date. He wrote his name on the appropriate line and brought the document, pen, and ink bottle to Anna.

"Shouldn't there be a witness to your signature?" he asked her. "Mrs. Bailey will stop by later, if you'd rather wait."

With an effort that hurt Henry to watch, Anna raised herself onto her elbow. A low rasping sound rose from under the blanket; neither of them paid attention to it or to the attendant smell, except for Henry's mental note to change the pad.

Henry drew the low table closer to the lounge and moved the pitcher, glass, bottles, and folded medicine papers aside. Anna took the pen in her palsied hand, dipped it into the ink as Henry steadied it, and signed the deed in a wavering script.

"I don't want Brainard or Charlotte trying to take anything from the children," she told Henry. It was the clearest speech she had spoken for two days.

"Make Mother Better if It Be Thy Will"

MAY 15, 1894

ON TUESDAY, Dr. Dean brought Dr. Kinnie, from Frankfort, to examine Anna. At that time they noted that her pulse was between 140 and 160 beats per minute, so they gave her some digitalis "to strengthen the heart." The news meant little to Lottie, so she resolved that when her chores were done she would look up "digitalis" in *Home Physician,* the family medical book. Perhaps it would give her a clue about how sick Mother actually was.

At first, Lottie thought, taking care of Mother wasn't so bad; it made her feel rather proud, in fact, as though she were returning some of the care that Mother must have given to her when she was very small. Mother's illness seemed not so different from Auntie's spells.

As the days passed, however, she became frightened. Her mother had never been ill for so long, not even after she had given birth to Josie, which, she'd said several times, had "just about worn her out."

Lottie could pinpoint almost to the hour when Mother had gone from being an invalid to something else, a body that still moved and spoke, yet was breaking down like a dead groundhog in the sun. The sickroom smell of chamber pot and vomit changed to something more sour and somehow metallic. Mother's skin looked stretched over the bones of her face and hands and body, and it shone an odd bronze color with green underneath.

Oh, and the sounds she made, when sleep conquered her usually stoic will! Low, racking groans that changed to whimpers. Then this morning, just before she awoke, Mother lay curled on the lounge, crying "Oh! Oh! Oh! Oh! Oh!" Lottie shuddered to remember it—she didn't want to think of it, but those little breathless yelps kept coming back to her like a snatch of song sometimes did, as she mindlessly moved from task to task.

Then, a day or two ago, Lottie couldn't remember when, the blood had come. Bright red blood in the pot, soaking through the bedclothes, and then the pads, more blood than Lottie imagined could fit into one thin body.

"Please, God, make Mother better," she prayed repeatedly, and nearly always remembered to add, conscientiously, "If it be Thy will, amen."

She had learned in school about the democratic process, and Papa had described how the candidates rode in carriages in torchlight processions and handed out cigars to prospective voters, and how, after a candidate was elected, the voters could write and demand that he consider their wishes during his governance. Feeling slightly guilty that she might be lobbying God in this same way, she nonetheless enlisted the support of Will and Josie, who now went about the house likewise muttering, "Please, God, make Mother better if it be Thy will, amen." She didn't ask Roy or Ralph to join the campaign, fearing they would think she was being foolish.

Dr. Dean, she knew, had tried every remedy he could think of. She had learned to recite some of these to herself, and had only found a couple of them in the *Home Physician*. Bismuth, for indigestion, was there. Cardamom and ginger, she knew. William Davis, Brooks & Co.'s elixir of calisaya iron, that was one to keep in the mind, it would have been poetic were it not so terrifying, and strychnine, that was in the book, another powerful remedy that could act like a poison if not handled carefully. None of these things seemed to make much difference to Mother's condition, unless they made her sicker.

Today, Dr. Dean had brought another doctor with him. Mother had said, "My condition does not seem so very serious, why don't I get any better?" and she said it so pathetically that Lottie could no longer control herself. She set the basin carefully down on the floor in the hallway and fled to her room, to throw herself onto the bed and sob quietly into her pillow. When her sobs finally changed to hiccups, she rose, wiped her eyes and nose neatly on a handkerchief from her bureau, and came downstairs again.

Nobody had tripped over the basin, she was glad to see. It still stood in its same place, tidily bisected by the shadow of the doorway. The cobalt flowers and vines around the rim looked crisp and clean against the creamy white background, except where a smear of some reddish-brown slime defaced it. Lottie grabbed up the basin and hurried to the rear of the house with it.

Reverend Shaw was to come to see Mother again this afternoon. While the family was always glad to have a visit from a minister, Lottie knew that Papa and Mother preferred the visits of Reverend and Mrs. Waters. Papa, especially, never seemed to warm up to Reverend Shaw very much. This was unusual for her easygoing father, who seemed otherwise to view every man as his friend.

MAY 16, 1894

RALPH CAME IN from the yard. During Mother's illness, he, like Lottie and Roy, had stayed around the house and outbuildings, seeing to the animals and helping Father with any of Mother's care that required lifting and moving her. This morning, Mrs. Waters was due. Mother had asked for her especially. Mrs. Bailey, of course, came frequently without being asked, bringing broth and news about Auntie, who now convalesced at the boardinghouse.

Ralph tried to feel charitable toward Aunt Charlotte, but it was difficult. Mother had never been seriously ill, and now that she was, it seemed heartless of her only sister to leave, as though resentful of anyone else getting all the attentions. Then, it had been unpleasant every time Mrs. Bailey came. When Auntie was here, it seemed the two of them whispered together as though conspiring, though in what regard he couldn't imagine.

After Auntie had gone, Mrs. Bailey looked at Father as if she were biting into raw cranberries. She had told Father that they should have a woman in to help with Mother's nursing, and Father had shut her up sharp. Ralph thought he knew why; if they weren't free to have Orah come to help, as Mother would have wished (as they all would have preferred, all but Roy, anyway), then the family would look after its own, thank you very much.

Since then Mrs. Bailey had contented herself with sullen looks and cold politeness, especially toward Father and the two older boys. Yet she came every day to see Mother.

Mrs. Bailey had had a hard life, he knew, one child after another dying tragically, and then finally her husband, Mr. Lorenzo Bailey, one of Benzonia's founding fathers, had died. All the wealth he was said to have had evaporated. Mrs. Bailey was left with the enormous house on Orchard Hill, and now kept herself by taking in boarders. Dr. Dean was one of her boarders; Ralph thought with some amusement that Auntie, now installed in a large room on the first floor of Bailey's, would likely make Dr. Dean step lively.

Mother seemed to be sinking despite the best efforts of Dr. Dean and Dr. Kinney, the "specialist" he had called in. This specialist had merely annoyed Mother, asking the same pointless questions that seemed irrelevant to them all. Did she think she could have been poisoned, indeed! When they all ate the same food, and none of the rest of them were sick. "We don't keep it in the house," she had said, in a decidedly caustic manner.

For a moment she had sounded like her old self; Mother had never suffered fools gladly. But no, that bit of spirit seemed to have been the last bit left in her.

Now she just wanted the family and old friends nearby. He watched for Mrs. Waters's friendly face. She might not be able to help Mother's poor sick body, but the presence of this beloved old lady who'd brought them all arrowroot biscuits when they were babies and laughed at the dinner table with them was the best medicine Mother could have.

And so it had proven. Mother's vomiting and purging had finally ceased, and she lay in lethargy, occasionally rousing to talk briefly with Father or the rest of them. Dr. Dean was there, but he merely sat quietly at Mother's head.

Will had been afraid to come in to her until yesterday. The odd smells and noises, and that decidedly odd thing she kept doing with her tongue, kept Will, despite their combined urging, rooted to the doorway, his eyes huge.

Josie had frequently whimpered at the doorway the first few days of Mother's illness, but did allow herself to be led up to Mother; now she came and went readily, and often patted Mother encouragingly with her little hands. "Will and Lottie and I are praying to make you all better," she'd said to Mother, who smiled in a manner so sweet that it brought tears to Ralph's eyes for a moment. He'd blinked them back, and nobody had noticed.

Now Mrs. Waters had scooped Will up, though the effort had cost her a grunt of pain (Will was a big boy now, for five), and carried him in with no fuss, to Mother. He sat now on Mrs. Waters's lap and goggled at Mother, who lay propped on two pillows.

Ralph thought secretly that Mother now looked a bit like the outlandish pictures from the geography books, of those Egyptian kings, mummified and buried in pyramids to be discovered thousands of years later by English explorers. Unwrapped for the world to see, they also were mostly skin and teeth and hollow eye sockets and discolored like sheets that had been sweated on and allowed to dry with the yellow-brown stains on. Mother had never been vain, but Ralph was glad nonetheless that no mirrors hung in the parlor.

"I'm not afraid to die," Mother was saying now in a whisper like the early morning breeze. "I've made my peace with the Lord and I trust in his goodness." At Mrs. Waters's request, Roy opened the Bible and began to read from Psalm 86: "Incline Thy ear, O Lord, and answer me . . ."

When he finished he passed the book to Ralph, who continued, "Teach me Thy way, O Lord, that I may walk in Thy truth . . ." And then Lottie took her turn, followed by Henry, whose voice shook as he read. He handed the book to Mrs. Waters, who rested it on Will's chubby legs and allowed him to follow the words with his finger as she read.

Anna lay with her eyes closed during these readings. At the last "amen," the family sat and gazed at her still, sleeping form. "Mother be better soon," volunteered Josie. Henry trembled all over at that, and Mrs. Waters peered at him. "Henry, when have you last eaten? You are shaking like a leaf. Why don't I go out and make some tea?" She began to set Will down, but Henry, with a ghastly smile, shook his head. "I couldn't drink a drop of it," he whispered, and pulling out a handkerchief that had seen hard use, wiped his eyes and nose.

Time passed; Josie fell asleep curled beside Anna's legs, and Will drowsed against Mrs. Waters's well-padded bosom and belly which, over the years, had joined together into a warm billowy cushion that every small child in town found comforting. Numbly the older children sat and stared at Anna. Henry shook and was still, shook and was still again. When Anna breathed her last breath away in a sigh, Henry sighed with her.

Gone Home

AFTER DR. DEAN had snapped his bag shut and left, it was Mrs. Waters who first spoke of practical matters. "I suppose Mary Bailey should come and do what's necessary for Anna?"

Henry was aware of several pairs of eyes on him; clearly, this suggestion was no more welcome to the older children than to him.

"Lottie, take the children outdoors, will you?" Lottie wiped her eyes and nodded. Will slipped from Mrs. Waters's lap and started toward the door.

"Josie? Wake up, we're going outside and look for flowers, for Mother." Lottie's voice broke slightly on the word "Mother," but she took Josie's hand firmly enough and helped her down from the lounge.

"Mother's asleepin' now?" asked Josie uncertainly, peering at the still form. Normally she spoke much more clearly, but this midmorning nap in the parlor had disoriented her.

"Mother's gone to be with Jesus," Mrs. Waters told her. "You go outdoors with Sister now."

"I, that is, we, can do what's necessary." Henry brought Mrs. Waters back to the concern at hand.

"Oh, but I thought certainly, since Mary Bailey is such a friend of the family . . ."

"Mrs. Bailey is an old busybody," stated Roy suddenly.

"Roy!" Mrs. Waters was shocked.

"What Roy means is, Mary Bailey has been very high-handed and interfering in the family business, involving herself in my sister-in-law's personal affairs. I don't like to speak ill of her . . ." He stopped, realizing how priggish that sounded, knowing what Anna would have said to that.

Mrs. Waters seemed to understand, however. "Of course, people often prefer to do for their own. I've often felt that way myself," she said, and sent Ralph to the kitchen for a basin of cool water.

As she and Henry prepared Anna's body, they discussed plans for the funeral. "Will you ask Reverend Waters if he could be ready by tomorrow afternoon?"

"Wouldn't you prefer Dr. Shaw? Oh, and what about Anna's brother? Surely it will take more than a day for him to arrive, and of course you will want the notice in the paper first."

But Henry was adamant. "Brainard won't be able to come in time. For the children's sake, I don't want this to drag on. And I don't want Shaw, I want your husband. Anna would have wanted that."

"Well, I'll ask Mr. Waters, but I'm sure he'll think it terribly hurried."

MAY 17, 1894

THE THACKERS STOOD in a row to one side of Reverend Waters, next to the open coffin. Outside, a soft wind rustled the just-opening leaves on the trees around them. Henry looked about him, as though he had mislaid something important. Roy and Ralph, themselves dazed, flanked Henry as though to prop him up should he require it.

Lottie felt a moment's confusion—if it was true that people went to be with Jesus when they died, why was the family standing there looking down at the wooden box, a box soon to go into that deep hole out in the cemetery? She scolded herself—of course she knew about leaving behind one's earthly remains; that's probably why they called them "remains." She knew about ascending to Heaven in incorruptible bodies. But it still felt as though Mother was in that pitiful, smelly ruin that lay in the box. She had been in the ruined body for so long, corrupted though it had been for the last two weeks, how could she leave it so quickly?

When did the soul leave, and how fast did it travel? And if the "remains" weren't Mother, who were they? That was her unruly mind again, circling around things that she'd prefer not to think about, just like remembering those sad little "Oh! Oh! Oh!" cries when Mother lay asleep the other day; would she never stop hearing those? And thinking about Mother's "remains" in that box, in that hole? Oh, terrible thought, what if Mother weren't dead yet at all? What if she woke up later and was . . .

Her knees trembled. Will squinted up at her curiously. "Lottie?" he whispered.

Ralph looked at Lottie with some concern. She looked as bad as Father just now. Probably none of them looked too lively, come to that, he thought; then when Lottie smiled weakly at him, he turned his attention back to Dr. Waters, who, despite the tears on his own cheeks, had begun to raise his voice. "Death, where is thy sting?"

"Gone Home" was the title of Anna's obituary in the *Benzie Banner*. It read, "Mrs. Anna Spencer Thacker, wife of W. H. Thacker of this place, died quite suddenly of nervous prostration Wednesday forenoon. Although she has been quite sick the past few days, yet the end came more suddenly than was expected. The funeral occurred this (Thursday) afternoon at the residence, Rev. O. B. Waters conducting the services. Mrs. Thacker was an earnest and conscientious Christian and always took an active part in church matters. A more complete article will appear next week."

The following week a lengthier obituary was given for Anna: "In Memoriam. Died at Benzonia, May 16th, 1894, Mrs. Anna Spencer Thacker, a few days short of 45 years old. She was born at an Indian mission in Minnesota, near the head waters of the Mississippi, May 24, 1845. Her father, Rev. David Brainard Spencer, a descendant of David Brainard, the famous Indian missionary of early New England times, went in 1847 or thereabouts far beyond the white settlements of the day to Leech Lake, Minn., where his daughter Anna was born. In 1862 occurred the great Indian uprising and massacre in that region, at which time the missionaries were driven out. Mr. Spencer came then to Grand Traverse County and settled first in Homestead, from which place he removed a few years later to Benzonia. Here Miss Spencer attended college several years. In May 1874 she was married to W. H. Thacker; her last sickness began just twenty years from the date of her marriage. She leaves five children.

"From early childhood Mrs. Thacker was an earnest follower of Christ, and from young womanhood an active Christian, interested in missions and in all good causes. She had an earnest and self-sacrificing spirit despite the burdens of her home, by reason especially of the long illness of her second mother, and an invalid sister, Miss Charlotte Spencer, who survives her; but she bore these burdens with steadfastness and unfailing cheerfulness. She gave distinct testimony to the presence of her Savior with her last hours."

The Widower

HENRY BROODED at the dressing table. Anna's things were still here, the plain comb, the wooden-backed hairbrush, handle polished from years of use. Elvira had left her good tortoiseshell set, comb, brush, and hand mirror, to Charlotte. "It's right that she do so," Anna had said gently. "Charlotte's always been the pretty one."

Henry recalled saying, "You're pretty enough for me," meaning it as a compliment at the time; now he was not sure it had sounded all that flattering.

Anna hadn't been a beauty, and somehow that hadn't seemed to matter. They'd been a team; privately he had thought of them as a pair of good working horses, neat but not fancy, doing the day's work without fuss or bother. Then the children had come; what matter if Sam or Sarah's parents were plain or pretty? He sighed, finished dressing, and left the room, nearly tripping on Will's wooden pony that lay on its side in the hallway.

"Have to get someone in now, to help with the little ones," he thought.

Brainard Capitulates

CHARLOTTE WAS LIVID. "I cannot believe it. I will not believe it. Even our brother-in-law would never do such a disgusting thing, with our sister not yet cold in the ground!"

Brainard made no attempt to hide his impatience. "Henry Thacker never had a bit of sense, Charlotte, we both know that. Anyway, I suppose he'll just say that he needed someone to keep house while he's away, and of course he's right about that. I don't suppose the daughter knows much about housekeeping at her age."

"Having a housekeeper and having *that* housekeeper are two entirely different things. You've been away too long, Brainard, you can't know the extent of the talk about Orah Bunker. And the way Henry behaved around her, it was the most sickening thing I've ever observed. Brainard, I'm absolutely certain that he had something to do with our sister's death."

"I know, I know, he's been trying to poison you," Brainard shook his head. Why, if one of his sisters had to die, did it have to be the one that wasn't unstable?

"I want you to go and talk to the sheriff. Tell him everything I've told you; take Dr. Dean with you and tell him everything. I know you don't believe me, but it's true. Henry Thacker poisoned our sister and he tried to poison me."

Brainard shifted uncomfortably. "Why don't you go and tell him? For that matter, if Dr. Dean suspects anything, why doesn't he go?"

"You know I can't go, I've been too ill even to go to Anna's funeral." Her voice trembled slightly. "I pretty nearly can't go to meals, and some-one has to help me back to my room."

Charlotte had been appalled when she realized that Mary Bailey not only expected her to pay for her room and board (five dollars a week!), but said she hadn't the time to carry Charlotte's meals in to her; she'd have to charge fifty cents a day for that service.

"I'm doing you a favor as it is, giving you that good room overlook-ing the hill, on the ground floor. Usually I charge seven dollars a week for that one." Mary Bailey's mouth had clicked shut firmly, just like her coin purse, thought Charlotte.

Now she began to weep. "Brainard, I'm all alone in the world now. You're all I have left."

Awkwardly, he patted her shoulder. She'd gotten bonier than ever! "I'd invite you to come and live with us, but you know how nervous the children make you."

Charlotte shuddered at the thought. She had visited Brainard and his family in Illinois one time, a few years ago, considering whether she mightn't wish to relocate there. The visit, for some reason, hadn't gone as pleasantly as she'd envisioned.

First thing, Amelia, Brainard's wife, had taken her shopping, and she had looked at too many pretty things she couldn't afford, returning to the house empty-handed and feeling, unaccountably, embarrassed.

Then, Amelia had invited some of the women from their church for a luncheon at which Charlotte had tried to entertain them with some of her stories from her time in Turkey. She could tell by the way they kept drawing the conversation off to their own frivolous lives that their in-terests lay not in God's work, but in what colleges to send their sons to, and how becoming Mrs. McKendrick's bonnet was.

Amelia herself hadn't seemed terribly interested in the stories either. Oh, she pretended interest, interjecting, "You don't say so!" and "My land!" or "Mercy on us!" at all the correct places, but as soon as Char-lotte had concluded the story about the time the Kurds burst in and threatened the young girls at their sewing class, Amelia wasted no time in popping to her feet, saying that she had to go and check on her own girls, who were squalling like two cats in their upstairs room.

In fact, May and Margaret seemed to shriek and whine constantly. Then there was the dreadful time she'd heard young Paul, right outside her door, saying to Brainard, "—don't see why we should have to, and neither does Mother. Mother says surely to goodness Aunt can go back to her sister's if she doesn't like it here, or find some old widower to marry her, or go back to that Turkey if she likes it so much and—ow!"

She'd smiled grimly at the time, picturing young Paul being removed down the hall by one twisted ear, but she'd gone home from that visit much sooner than she'd originally planned to, and she'd not gone again.

Charlotte sobbed harder, remembering that horrible time, and Brainard patted her again. At least she had gotten off of the subject of poisoning!

"See here, Charlotte, what if I turned over those notes to you, the ones from the sale of Mother's house? With those you could easily afford to stay here if you lived sparingly."

Her sobs quieted. "And you'll go and talk to the sheriff?"

"Oh, Charlotte, must we discuss that again?"

"Dr. Dean is upstairs in his room now, I heard him when he came in a while back! Just go up there now and ask him about it, will you do that at least?"

Reluctantly, Brainard did so.

Sheriff Chandler Pays a Call

MAY 22, 1894

"DID ROY COME IN YET?" Clutching the bushel of potatoes before him, Henry held the door ajar with a foot. Ralph, his arms full of wood, elbowed in behind him. Lottie, pouring milk into glasses on the table, shook her head. "I thought he was with you."

"He's not in the barn. Hang it all, have I got to do the milking too?" growled Henry. He plunked the basket onto the ladder-backed chair beside the door, the one they called "Mother's chair" even now, turned to go back out, and paused, hand on the knob.

"Chandler's just pulled up. I wonder what he wants?"

"Oh, Papa, will he want you to go to work tonight?" cried Lottie. The house felt so empty now, when Papa worked at night. During the day there was plenty to occupy her; while they missed Mother terribly, the only time desolation swept over her strongly was in the evenings, when they were "orphaned," as she secretly called it, by Papa's going out.

"What the dickens? He's gone around to the front!" muttered Henry.

His footsteps echoed in the hallway as he strode to the front door.

"Whyn't you come in the back?" was his brusque greeting to his boss. Sheriff Chandler stepped into the entryway and stood, twiddling his hat embarrassedly. Nonplussed, Henry stared at him. A long silent moment passed, broken only by Lottie's quiet footsteps to the parlor doorway.

"William Henry Thacker? I have a summons here; it says . . . aw, thunder, Henry, I have come to arrest you."

The long silence was broken by a wail on the landing. "You can't have that, it's mine!" came Will's aggrieved voice, answered by Josie's uncowed, "Mine!" Since Orah had left again (right after she'd come to help out!), the children had reverted to younger versions of themselves, squabbling and whining incessantly, or so it seemed to Lottie. Roy had begun to call them "the brats," which only made them act worse; and besides, Roy had been fairly bratty himself lately, she thought.

"Hush, children," called Lottie mechanically, then turned back to the surreal tableau in the entryway.

"In the death of Anna Spencer Thacker . . ." Sheriff Chandler was saying.

"If this is a joke, it's not very funny," muttered Henry, but something in his face told Lottie that Papa didn't believe it was a joke, not really, and now Papa was telling them not to worry, to look after things, there had been a mistake but he'd be home soon.

Then they were gone! Just like that, after a quick hug; Papa and the sheriff were gone, and she and Ralph were alone in the gloomy parlor, long shadows on the opposite walls, alone, except for Josie and Will squabbling on the landing, alone in the house that had suddenly grown too large for them.

"INCREDIBLE!" read an idler to his friend, from the *Benzie Banner*. His voice seemed to echo down the street. "Last Monday about three o'-

clock this community was startled and shocked beyond the power of expression by the announcement that W. H. Thacker had been arrested on the charge of causing the death of his wife by poisoning."

Ralph stopped in his tracks and stared incredulously at the ragged fellow, who scowled. "What're you staring at, Sonny? Hey! Give that paper back! Come back with that, you little scoundrel!"

Ralph stopped at a corner where no passersby could see and continued reading the ghastly report: ". . . the body was exhumed Monday evening, and the stomach, parts of the brain, liver, one kidney, and portions of the intestines were sent to Ann Arbor for chemical analysis, in charge of Sheriff Chandler. Not only is it true that a man must be considered innocent until he is proven guilty, but Mr. Thacker has spent most of his mature years in this community. . . . He has always been ready to help those who were in need and would go farther to do a favor than anyone we know. We sincerely hope Mr. Thacker will be able to clear himself of this grave charge. . . ."

Ralph could think of no way to keep this revolting thing from Lottie, who regularly read the paper as avidly as he and Roy did, so he simply folded it and tucked it under his arm. Head down, he plodded home.

The Children

RALPH PULLED OFF his straw hat and wiped his forehead. He'd do six more rows and then stop for a drink, for himself as well as for the horses. Star, the off gelding, was starting to wheeze again. Ralph was never sure whether the old horse's wind was starting to fail or he'd just learned a way to get more rest periods. It was pretty hot today, so Ralph would take no chances. Star could stand in the shade of the drooping sugar maples and get his wind back before they finished up the last acre.

As he worked, facts and figures swam around in his head. It felt a little like when a difficult examination was coming in school. He'd study hard, fill his head to overflowing with everything he thought he'd need to know, and then every time he had a moment to himself those facts would just swim around in there. It wasn't like you could hear an actual voice saying the things, but they'd just sort of say themselves, that was the best way he could think of it. And then even after the examination, they'd swirl around for a day or two more, just to be cantankerous.

And now, just like those faraway school facts, there were new details, more important and importunate, behaving in that same annoying way. The autopsy had indeed provided sufficient assurance of poisoning, so there was to be a trial. Where to get the seventy dollars that Mr. Covell said they'd need for "circuit court charges." Where to get two hundred dollars more for Mr. Covell's fee. Whether to put oats back in the southwest field; bad for that field, he knew, but the horses had to be fed if the trial dragged on and father's sheriff pay wasn't to be counted on. More potatoes in the near field. Keep the new filly and begin training her in the spring, or sell her for ready cash? When would the jury be chosen, and how would those men selected influence the decision? Was it better if they knew Father already, or were complete strangers?

He had asked Father, several times, what they should do about the debts that continued to collect in the rolltop desk. The day-to-day expenses could be managed; sometimes, even now, money dribbled in. Some of it, surprisingly, came from outlying farmers who had let slide their payments on this or that piece of farm machinery, but suddenly remembered their debts. Ralph wasn't sure if this was out of kindness for Father, or whether they simply wanted to wash their hands of anything to do with the Thackers.

Mr. Avery had stood on the porch Tuesday evening, worn hat in one hand, a wad of tattered bills in the other. "I was looking over the accounts on Sat'day," he explained shamefacedly, "and noticed we were still owing your pa for that harrow." Ralph, somewhat embarrassed himself (though why, he wasn't sure), had taken the bills and scribbled a receipt, "Pd in Full," not even sure whether that was indeed the case. The bills had immediately gone toward their account at the grocery.

Father, when asked about the debt owing to Mr. Covell, had just looked at Ralph, his eyes damp. Sheriff Chandler had freed Father on a twenty-five-dollar bond, but except for when he worked in the fields, Father was seldom at home. When he was, he drifted around the house in a fog, like a dog that had misplaced his bone.

Ralph wasn't sure where he went in the evenings—sometimes he harnessed up Star to the buggy and disappeared, coming home long after everyone else was in bed. It annoyed Ralph to have the horses used in this manner, kept out until all hours. There was plenty of fieldwork to be done, and a critter only had so much get-up-and-go, particularly these hot July days.

How could he present his testimony to make it clear to the jury that

Father simply could not have done this thing? And how in the name of goodness would they get along if Star really was breaking down?

Was there a better lawyer from someplace else who might defend them more effectively? What kind of devilment was Roy up to, these days? Was Lottie just unhappy? Or sickening with something? And what were "circuit court charges" anyway? Five more rows, and then they'd rest . . .

LOTTIE STOOD at the sink and stared down into the basin of soapy water. After the dishes were dried and put away, it would be time to go up and change the bed linens; the used top sheets would move to the bottom, and the used bottom sheets and pillow slips removed for washing. Josie was in the other room, giving "tea" to her dolls. She could help Lottie with the pillows.

Will was outdoors, unsupervised, true, but at five he was old enough to avoid any obvious dangers. Both of them could help her with the garden, and then she'd think about what to fix everyone for lunch.

She realized that as she'd stood there, staring down, the water in the basin had cooled considerably, and the morning shadows on the porch were no longer visible. The tips of her fingers, hanging limply over the basin edge, had turned pale and pruny. A bead of snot ran down her upper lip, raced by a tear on her cheek. She armed them both away and sighed, and began to scrub dried egg yolk from the top plate in the lukewarm scummy water. Probably she should reheat the water in the basin, but starting the fire under the kettle again would just take too much energy.

How had things gotten so wrong? Her life had become like the stories about rich girls whose parents were tragically killed by cruel viziers or swept away by wars, throwing the girl upon the mercies of cruel duchesses or boarding school teachers. She would have to become a governess to somebody's children, or have to scrub fireplaces! Now she knew she was being ridiculous. Her self-pity leaked away, the fantasy punctured by the reminder that the stove ashes needed to be cleared out today as well.

Oh, they'd manage all right, people always did. But they would have to be very saving, if they were to get through the winter and next year. Ralph said they would need to sell the buggy and some of the farm equipment, and let that fertile field outside of town go, if they were to pay the lawyers.

When Papa came home for good he'd probably have to find another job; Sheriff Chandler was already looking for a replacement for Papa. Meanwhile, Ralph was trying to keep the farm work up while asking around for extra work.

Odd, when she thought about it. Ralph was the head of the house now, and not Papa, and certainly not Roy, the eldest. Roy was rarely at home. Roy, their mother's pride, with his music lessons and good school ratings, Roy had left school and was seen, too often, with that dreadful Lannon boy and Joe Beals.

Lottie didn't know what they did together, but she noticed that Roy's clothes, in the laundry basket, often had a skunky, burnt-toast smell. She suspected, but didn't like to say to Ralph, that they smoked when they were away together.

None of the family went to church now. She and Ralph had taken the children twice, after the arrest. She didn't know which was worse, the smirks or embarrassed looks from her friends or the pitying ones of the teachers. The second time there, in the Little Friends Sunday-school class, Will had struck his little friend Geordie "for saying something nasty about Papa" and had had to stand in the corner. The Sunday after that, they had all just stayed home.

Ralph had tried to put a good face on it. "At least we don't have to sit still and read the Bible all afternoon, eh?" Oh, but if Mother could only be alive again, and Papa properly at home with them, how happily she would sit still on Sundays! And besides, painting lacked joy for her just now, somehow. After the children were in bed, there were always more chores awaiting her, and if there weren't obvious ones, her mind would scurry in little circles, like a one-eyed mouse, looking for things that she probably should be doing. Her paints lay untouched on the bureau top in her room, the cakes of bright color cracked and dry.

She willed her lip to stop trembling, took a deep breath, and began to scrub the next plate.

Henry's Trial

HENRY'S TRIAL BEGAN at the Benzie County Circuit Court on July 12, 1894.

"Why does it take so long to select a jury?" sighed Lottie. "When do they start the important part of the trial, so Papa can come back home?"

Ralph's mind had often wandered during civics class, and now he wished he'd paid more attention. "It's important to get people who will be fair," he recalled. "If everyone in a town thinks the person is guilty," he noticed Lottie's frown and added, "or everyone thinks he's innocent, they have to go out of town to find people whose minds aren't already made up. That's something called 'change of venue.'"

Lottie looked doubtful, and Ralph sighed. "We'll ask Mr. Covell when he's not so busy."

By the time all was settled, the jury consisted of men from Elmira, Crystal Lake, Inland, Joyfield, Platte, and Weldon.

Ralph knew several of them, including Arthur J. Hamlin, George Tennant, and Mr. Paradise, because how would anybody forget a man named Paradise once he'd met him, even to deliver a load of oats to him? Lottie also thought it auspicious to have Mr. Charles C. Marrigold on the jury, because how could anybody with such a floral name think ill of Papa?

The jury was housed in the former Walter Randall house on Grand Traverse Street. By this time, the temperatures had soared into the nineties. On the first evening of the jurors' sequestration, the entire panel's complaints had become so audible that Judge Aldrich relented and allowed the twelve an excursion to the beach for an evening dip. Ralph, returning home from that same errand after sweating through the day's fieldwork, smiled to himself. They'd looked so solemn and serious, even pompous, those twelve men, but walking single file behind Sheriff Chandler they also put him in mind of a row of goslings, but panting instead of peeping.

He finished the milking, brushed a mosquito from the back of his hand, and picked up the two pails. Approaching the back door, he heard Will's angry voice: "Won't! Won't, neither!"

"Either!" corrected Lottie sharply. Ralph smiled again. They might be the children of the worst criminal in Benzonia's history, but by George, they'd speak correctly or Lottie would know why.

"What are you laughing at?" demanded Lottie. Her face dripped with heat, and her hair hung limply—these days she lacked the time to care for it properly. Ralph's smile softened.

"Nothing much, Lottie, but on my way home I saw the funniest row of goslings." He told her about the jurors, and to his relief Lottie smiled too. She was quiet as she set dinner on the table (fresh summer squash!), and pale as she cleared the dishes away. After she took Josie upstairs, Ralph was alarmed to hear the unmistakable sounds of vomiting.

"Ralph!" His sudden appearance at her elbow as she straightened up from the basin made her jump.

"What's wrong?" he demanded. "Lottie, what's wrong?"

"Oh, it's nothing, just the heat."

"You get into bed this minute. You're burning up! Drat, where's Roy when I need him? You stay right here, I'm going for the doctor!"

"No, Ralph, we can't afford a doctor." Lottie's lip began to tremble again. Furious at it, she bit it, hard.

"Don't be silly. I can't, we can't, I mean, we need you!"

"But Ralph, we had a doctor last time, and Mother still died."

"You're not going to die. Just lie still, and I'll be back."

By the time Ralph had arrived home again with Dr. Dean and shown him to Lottie's room, Roy had returned home as well. "It's about time you got here," growled Ralph.

Roy sank onto the horsehair sofa; nobody sat on Mother's lounge much, these days. "Say, my head feels like a stone. Let me alone for a while, will you, Ralph?"

Frantic, Ralph started back upstairs, to be met by Dr. Dean. "Roy's not well either, Dr. Dean. Would you, could you, he's in here . . ." Ralph sank onto the chair that had stood by his mother's lounge during her illness. With some horror he realized that his father had last sat here, the day Mother died. Now Lottie and Roy were ill; were they poisoned too? He watched, dry-mouthed, as Dr. Dean tapped and listened, looked at Roy's throat, listened to his chest, peered at his eyes.

"Measles," Dr. Dean announced. "Both of them on the same day, that doesn't usually happen. How are you feeling, boy?"

Ralph felt dizzy with the sudden relief, but took a breath and the black fog cleared. "I'm fine, Dr. Dean. I think I had measles when I was younger. How much do we owe you?"

"LOTTIE? Mr. Covell wants to ask us all questions for the trial. He says he can come here and question you, but you'd have to talk to Mr. Warner and Mr. Pratt as well. Are you strong enough for that? I can put them off, if you'd rather."

"When will he come? Look at me, Ralph, I'm all over spots!"

"Oh, they don't care in the slightest what you or Roy look like, Lottie, this is serious."

"If they must, they must," she said resignedly, and the next day Lottie, in response to questioning, delivered this testimony to Mr. Covell:

"I am fourteen years old. William H. Thacker and Anna Thacker are my parents. I was at home at the time my mother was taken sick. Mother was taken sick about seven o'clock in the morning of May 4, she was sick when I came downstairs, she acted as though she was sick at her stomach. She ate some graham pudding a little after half past seven that morning—she made the pudding and Papa put the cream and sugar on it. It was in a vegetable dish and she ate all of it; after that she helped wash the dishes, then went out of doors and planted some flower seeds. This was about ten o'clock in the morning; when I came out she was vomiting. . . . She went from there into the front yard, and stayed there until about half past eleven o'clock when she came in and got dinner. After dinner she helped do the dishes up, and then went into the flower garden. She stayed there until after tea, then wrote a note for me to take to Mrs. Bailey. . . . I was in Auntie's room a good deal of the time. Mother was not in there vomiting during the day. Papa and I did the work during the time Mother was sick."

His question was gentle: "Who carried the food to Miss Spencer while your mother was sick?"

"I did," replied Lottie. "I prepared the food that I carried in. The graham was cooked with all the rest and taken from the same dish that the family used. I never put anything in her food or her pudding."

"Did you ever carry Miss Spencer any prunes?"

"Yes, sir. I got them out of the glass can. I carried her some Saturday, Sunday, and Monday, the 5th, 6th and 7th. On Thursday the 10th of May, I carried her the glass jar in which the prunes were kept; before that they were kept in the storeroom. I never took a pit out of one of the prunes and put powder in it. My aunt left there and went to Mrs. Bailey's on Sunday, the 13th. I did not furnish Aunt pudding three times a day. At other times she ate potatoes, hot water, and crackers, and on Saturday before she went away she had a half dozen raw eggs."

It was Mr. Pratt who first asked Lottie about Orah's stay with them. She hated to admit to him that they'd had anything to do with Orah; she knew now that any mention of Orah in the same breath with the Thackers caused people to look sly and make those "not around the children" comments. This talk wouldn't do Papa's cause any good, but Lottie knew that lying in court surely would be worse. Oh why, when Mr. Covell was supposed to be defending Papa, must he let Mr. Pratt ask these questions?

Mr. Pratt began: "Before your mother's sickness, had your father been away more or less during the spring? Do you know of him going off anywhere?"

Lottie stopped to think. "He went to a convention, I don't know just when, but it was at Owassa. He went somewhere else to see about a fire in a company he had charge of. He went to the World's Fair."

Mr. Pratt now began the part she dreaded, "Do you know Orah Bunker?"

"Yes, I know Orah Bunker."

"After your mother's death, did she come here to help keep house?"

"Yes, sir. She came on Sunday after Mother died. She came down here once nearly two years ago." Mr. Pratt nodded, seemed to be satisfied with the answer, but then frowned as Lottie said in a rush, "Mother said she liked to have her come. She stayed about half an hour. She went back to Mr. Shaw's."

Mr. Warner's cross-examination was fairly brief. In response to his questions, Lottie said, "Previous to May 4, Mother had had frequent spells similar to this one; I think the last one was along in the winter sometime. From along in the winter up to the 4th of May, she had severe headaches but no vomiting with them."

By the time both men had finished their questions and left her room, Lottie thought to herself that a few more minutes of this would have given her a severe headache as well. She relaxed her clenched hands and thought pityingly of Roy, who was now being questioned by the serious men in their dark sweaty suits. She imagined that Mrs. Covell, Mrs. Wilson, Mrs. Pratt and Mrs. Warner hated having to do their laundry in the summer when their husbands were going about in weather such as this.

"RALPH? Ralph! Come in here!" Roy, in their room, sounded angry, but then, of course, he'd sounded angry ever since the whispers about Papa had started around town.

"How you present yourselves during testimony may have a profound effect on your father's defense," Mr. Wilson was explaining. His voice sounded a bit strained.

"But here, what's this bit about how none of us gave any poison to Mother? Are all of us on trial?"

"In a sense, Leroy, everyone who was near your mother during the days of her illness is on trial. Therefore, it's expected for each of you to memorize this statement and be able to give it clearly. Do you understand what I'm saying?" Roy nodded sullenly.

"Now, I'll say it again, and try to remember this. You will give your name, and state that William Henry Thacker is your father, and that Anna Thacker was your mother. You will tell the court whether you had furnished any food or drink to your mother during her illness, and then state that you have never put anything poisonous in her food. Then state that you do not know of anyone who did."

Roy wrinkled his forehead, whether in annoyance or in confusion Ralph couldn't tell. "Does this show that nobody poisoned Mother, or just that we didn't? Doesn't that make it more seem likely that Father did? Seems a pretty poor sort of defense to me!"

Ralph looked anxiously at Mr. Wilson. They were counting on him and Mr. Covell to free their father; it seemed a bad idea to offend him. "Roy, Mr. Wilson must know what he's doing. We're not lawyers; lots of things he does may seem strange to us."

"Good fellow!" boomed Mr. Wilson. Roy glowered, the spots on his face giving him the aspect of a baleful clown.

JUDGE ALDRICH PRESIDED at the trial. The prosecution was led by Mr. Warner, assisted by E. S. Pratt. Defense was provided by George Covell of Wilson & Bailey, Dodge & Covell, of Traverse City.

Ralph sat in the third row. He wanted Father to know that he was near, but hated to be too conspicuous. He had agonized about what to wear to court. With Lottie's help, he had decided to wear his warm-weather second-best Sunday clothes. They chafed as much in the room in the town hall as they always did in First Congregational.

Mr. Warner, in his opening statement of the People's case, made the following statement: "At the time that Mrs. Thacker was sick in the house and during her illness, her sister, Miss Spencer, was also sick and in like manner, and in the food prepared for her there was poison taken from it, as was found by analysis on the food being sent to Ann Arbor for that purpose; she became suspicious of being poisoned and left the house sometime before the sister died, leaving the house on Sunday, and her sister died on the following Wednesday."

The prosecution first presented Dr. David S. Dean as a witness. Dr. Dean's testimony was followed by that of Dr. John Powers and Professor Moses Gomberg.

Professor Gomberg testified, "Professor Moses Gomberg, instructor in chemistry in University of Michigan at Ann Arbor: I found the stomach without any holes or punctures in it. I took the contents out of the stomach and put them in an ordinary glass. Near the cardiac end of the stomach it appeared inflamed, the rest was of dark green color. I scraped the inside of the stomach and added these scrapings to the contents of the stomach."

Ralph squirmed. The place between his shoulder blades felt uncomfortable, sort of a cross between an itch and a cramp. He wished he could go outdoors for a few minutes, or at least think about something else for a little while.

Gomberg ruthlessly continued: "I examined the bottom of the glass containing the contents of the stomach with a magnifying glass and found small white crystals, which proved to be crystallized arsenic. These crystals weighed one-sixth of a grain. I then proceeded with the analysis of the contents of the stomach, and found that it contained arsenic. I proceeded with the analysis of the liver, and found that the liver contained less than one-sixth of a grain. I analyzed the brain and found arsenic in small quantities. I did not analyze the kidney; when I received the brain, it seemed firm. The arsenic might be carried into the brain, the liver, and other organs by circulation during life, or by postmortem diffusion. If arsenic should have been in the stomach only, I mean that postmortem diffusion would carry it into different organs of the body. The amount of arsenic I found in the stomach, the liver, and the brain by examination carefully made will be about half a grain. Arsenic in crystallized form in the stomach could not get there by diffusion. It could get there through the mouth."

Ralph slumped with relief when Professor Gomberg completed this description of Mother's dissection. Surely things had to improve from here!

Mrs. Bailey's testimony concerning the progression of Anna's illness came next. She began by saying, "I gave Mrs. Thacker drink or food once or perhaps twice during her sickness. I never put any poison in the food or drink I gave her." The old busybody! She went on to concoct the most outrageous story about the poison that Auntie was supposed to have found in her food, as though she actually believed it herself! Ralph took a deep breath. How was he going to report all this to Lottie, as he'd promised? And to Roy; he'd be furious!

THE HOT DAYS DRAGGED ALONG. Lottie was soon up from bed, followed by Roy a few days afterward. They sat at a dinner of boiled potatoes and canned vegetables and argued.

"I'll go on Monday and Thursday," said Roy, "and Ralph can go Tuesday and Wednesday. You can go Friday, Lottie."

"That's not fair! Why should you both have two days? Papa will want to see me there, too!"

"Be reasonable," Ralph said peacefully. "We need you to watch Will and Josie most of the time."

"Lottie doesn't need to watch me! I can watch my own self!" declared Will. Lottie glared at him; he returned the look defiantly.

"I can too!" announced Josie. Lottie looked at her, and Josie applied herself to beets.

"Well, I'll go Monday, Ralph can go Tuesday, and you can go Wednesday. But Lottie, we can't get the haying done and watch the children at the same time. You have to be the woman of the house and that's all there is to it."

They sat in the seat in the third row, turn and turn alike, and listened to the progress of their father's case.

The testimony of Mrs. Bailey, red-faced in the July heat, puffing slightly from the tightness of her stays (and nerves? Ralph couldn't be sure; he wanted to be fair, but sometimes her words made him want to punch her, like Mother had punched the dough after its first rising), was followed by more expert witness testimony from Dr. Gomberg.

Gomberg's words made Ralph slightly queasy again, though by the turn of Dr. H. J. Kinnie, who had been called in as a consulting physician on Anna's penultimate day of life, the words began to be just words. Lottie, pale from her illness but gaining strength quickly, slipped into the chair next to him during this testimony.

According to Dr. Kinnie, Mother had asked, "My condition isn't so very bad. Why don't I get well?" He continued: "She recapitulated that statement two or three times. . . . Mr. Thacker and I adjourned to the dining-room. . . . I stated to him that I thought if she had proper care and good nursing that she would recover and suggested to him that he get a nurse for her. He said, 'My wife would object to that. She won't have anybody to take care of her but me.'"

Lottie nodded in agreement. She wasn't aware of this conversation when it took place, but that's just what Mother would have said and felt.

She was getting better at controlling her unruly lower lip; biting it hard whenever it began to tremble tended to distract it. Ralph's shoulder, slight but with strong bands like baling twine inside the thin cotton of his shirt, pressed comfortingly against hers. She took a deep breath and relaxed.

Dr. Kinnie's testimony was followed by that of Dr. John Powers. Powers, who had muttonchop sideburns of a chestnut color, had assisted at the postmortem. He substantiated Professor Gomberg's testimony.

This was Roy's day again. He listened attentively as Dr. Powers was followed by George Jones, the undertaker.

"I have an undertaking business. There was no embalming fluid used except what I used on the face. This is the same kind of fluid used for embalming; so far as I know it was only applied on her face."

"So far as he knows?" thought Roy indignantly. "What kind of shilly-shallying thing is that for a witness to say? Whyn't old Covell object to that? I could be a better lawyer!"

He listened again, for Mr. Pratt was asking, "Were you in Frankfort on Friday previous to Mrs. Thacker's death?"

And Mr. Covell said, "We want it understood that this is all under the same objection and exception."

Judge Aldrich said (as he had, it seemed a million times before! every time Mr. Covell objected, in fact), "I will allow the answer. Defendant excepts."

Jones continued tranquilly, "I could not swear positively it was on Friday before, but I am almost positive that it was. On the south side near the depot. I saw Mr. Thacker at Frankfort. This was about three-forty in the afternoon."

Mr. Pratt asked, "Can you tell us whether you saw any person there with him?"

Mr. Covell spoke, too mildly, in Roy's opinion: "Objected to as immaterial, incompetent, and irrelevant."

Judge Aldrich responded, "I will hear you on that matter, gentlemen."

Mr. Pratt, speaking in a tone of reasonableness, said, "We expect to show, your honor, it is a part of the theory of this case, and we think it admissible at this time to show that certain relations have existed between Mr. Thacker and a lady named Orah Bunker, that the relations between her and Mr. Thacker were not proper, to show a motive and a reason on the part of Mr. Thacker why he desired to get rid of his wife; for the purpose of showing that he was the person guilty of taking Mrs. Thacker's life by poisoning her. We expect to show at this time that Mr. Thacker and this young lady were in Frankfort during his wife's sickness, and that he was there with her on that day; and we expect to introduce testimony tending to show that he brought her home on the night of the day that Mr. Jones saw them in Frankfort."

Roy's hands itched; he wanted to curl them into fists and pound Pratt. Why didn't old Covell do something besides say "objection" in that calm, bored way? What did Frankfort have to do with anything? Father, Ralph, and he went to Frankfort pretty often, picking up or delivering machinery. What of it? If Orah was off to home that same day, so what? Roy tapped his foot impatiently. He stared at the back of his father's head. How did Father sit so impassively (though his ears, it must be admitted, were somewhat red) through such accusations? Roy seethed and could do nothing.

Ralph was on watch again as Dr. John Powers was recalled for more details of a medical nature concerning the properties of arsenic, and then the prosecution called Charlotte Spencer to the stand for the first of many sessions.

Aunt Charlotte testified, "I was a missionary for nine years in Turkey. I returned to Mr. Thacker's ten years ago. Mrs. Thacker was my sister. I lived in his house down the road less than a half mile. Mrs. Thacker was married nineteen years ago. Mrs. Thacker owned the property after my father's death."

Ralph stirred at this. Hadn't the house been a wedding present to Mother from Grandfather Spencer? They'd always been told so!

Mr. Pratt asked, "Do you know whether she was the owner of the property at the time of her death?"

Mr. Covell said, mildly as usual, "Object to as immaterial and irrelevant in this case."

"Of course," groaned Ralph to himself, as Judge Aldrich told him, "I will allow the answer."

Charlotte proceeded, "I suppose so, as far as I know."

"Was there any business relationship between you and the respondent, that is, between you and Mr. Thacker, by which you were to remain there?"

"I doubt as I quite understand the question."

"Well, was he in debt to you?"

"He was."

Well! Was that why they had put up with Aunt for all those years? Surely not. Mother always said they must count their blessings and be grateful for good health and prosperity, neither of which Aunt possessed. Did they in fact owe money to Aunt Charlotte as well? Ralph stifled a groan; they'd never get out of debt!

Mr. Covell tried again. "We ask to have that question and answer stricken out as being immaterial."

But again, Judge Aldrich said, "I will allow the answer to remain."

Auntie had lost her usual attitude of lassitude. She looked positively radiant! Ralph leaned forward, fascinated despite his distaste, as Aunt Charlotte continued.

"I last saw my sister alive on the 13th of last May. She was very sick. I was confined to my bed about a year and a half, almost two years."

Longer than that, thought Ralph. Aunt had been repining for most of his young life, or so it seemed to him.

". . . Mr. Thacker, his wife, five children, and myself constituted his family on the 4th of May. My sister was taken sick early that morning. She occupied a bed in my room that night. She has occupied a bed in my room during the winter. I next saw her between nine and ten o'clock. She came into my room, very much excited, weak and trembling, and got to the foot of my bed with difficulty. She vomited at intervals of from twenty minutes to a half hour during the day; so severe was her vomiting that she had to get down on her knees upon the floor. She remained in my room the rest of the day after she got there. Lottie, who is fifteen years old, Josie, who is three years old, and Willie, who is five years old, were in my room frequently during the day. Mr. Thacker was not in the room to look after his wife during the day. Mr. Thacker helped to get the dinner, I should judge by the sound of the steps. I know his step perfectly."

"I should think she does!" thought Ralph with some amusement. He'd often thought that Aunt had a soft spot for Father. He had his doubts about Josie and Will's being in Auntie's room that day or any other day, though. Aunt never liked having the children "racketing around in here." And poor Lottie, Auntie's "favorite"! Why, Aunt didn't even know how old her own namesake was!

Charlotte wound up with some brief remarks about Anna's illness, then stepped down from the box. During her entire performance she had not glanced once in the direction of Henry or Ralph. She swept down the aisle and out the door. "Maybe we're supposed to cry 'Bravo' and throw flowers," thought Ralph.

Roy and Lottie's statements were then read. Roy's statement, as Mr. Wilson had insisted, was prefaced by the statement, "Wm. H. Thacker is my father. Anna Thacker was my mother. I was at home during my mother's last illness. I never put anything poisonous in her food. . . . I never put anything in the way of a gray or white powder in Miss Spencer's food."

Roy had gone on to testify that Anna had been sick on the morning of May 4th before breakfast, and that he and Ralph and Father had worked all day in the fields and hauling machines from the depot.

Ralph's turn finally came. He took a deep breath and stood up, thankful that his knees shook only slightly on his walk to the front of the room. After swearing to tell the truth, he answered, as calmly as he was able, the questions put to him. By now, at least, he had an idea of what to expect. As coached, he prefaced his testimony with, "I am a son of Wm. H. Thacker and Anna Thacker. I was at home during Mother's last illness. I had very little to do with furnishing food and drink for Mother. I never put anything of a poisonous character in her food. . . . I do not know of anyone who did."

Mr. Pratt began, "Did you have anything to do with furnishing food and drink for your aunt, Miss Charlotte Spencer?"

Mr. Covell forestalled him. "Objection."

As instructed, Ralph obediently awaited the judge's response.

Judge Aldrich: "You may answer the question."

Ralph continued, his voice now stronger: "I never put anything in the food or drink that was carried and taken to Aunt Charlotte Spencer in the way of a poisonous character or a white or gray powder."

He relaxed and went on to say, "We opened a pit of potatoes that morning, Father, Roy, and I. I think Father went out to work at nearly the time we did. That was after Mother had the dish of mush. I believe she ate the mush, the empty dish was there. . . . I saw Mother that forenoon planting flower seeds. I should think the first time I saw her planting flower seeds was about nine o'clock. She was in the front yard at eleven o'clock when we started to the depot. We got back from the depot with machinery about one o'clock. Dinner was ready when we came home."

When he finally stepped down (the courtroom clock showed he had

been up there for less than twenty minutes; it had seemed like hours!),
Father smiled at him.

Later in the day, Aunt Charlotte returned to the stand. Ralph listened attentively as she went on to tell in greater detail about her own
poisoned food and Mother's illness.

His interest sharpened. Aunt had begun to relate a story about her
finances, a subject that had often mystified the children, with, "I made
my will two or three years before 1890."

"In whose favor was it?"

"We object to the question for the reason that the testimony sought
to be obtained from this witness would be evidence to prove a separate
offense than the defendant is charged with . . ."

This time, it was Mr. Wilson who spoke up, but Aunt interrupted
the judge's response serenely: "I destroyed it at once when I got to Mrs.
Bailey's."

Judge Aldrich, helpless in the flow of Charlotte's narrative, said, "I
will allow the answer."

Charlotte ignored him as she continued: "A five-hundred-dollar
note was in favor of Mr. Thacker alone. One hundred dollars of the two
remaining one hundred dollars was for Mrs. Thacker; the other one
hundred dollars was for the Women's Board of Missions. Mr. Thacker
was indebted to me for seven hundred dollars. Mr. Thacker had knowledge of the fact that I made a will. He helped me make it out. I have
some notes against Mr. Thacker."

Mr. Pratt consulted something on his notepad. "You have these
notes?"

"Mr. Warner has them."

Ralph wasn't sure what bearing this had on the case. Was it to Father's benefit, or against it? He listened to his aunt as she stated she had
turned the bonds over to Mr. Warner, prosecutor in the trial, "for value
received." When she was asked, "What was the value received?" Mr.
Warner objected, "I don't know as that is material in this case." His assistant said, "Let it go," at which point Aunt Charlotte became rather
vague, Ralph thought, about the specifics:

Mr. Pratt asked her, "What did he promise to pay?"

"The value represented in these notes. He did not take these notes
to collect as my agent. I turned them over for value received, assigned
them to him. I received his promise to pay, he did not state when he

would pay. The promise to pay is indefinite. He has not paid anything yet. I have no writing to that effect. I gave them to my brother this summer, when he was up here after Mr. Thacker's arrest. I did not tell him to give them to Mr. Warner."

Ralph smiled. "She's off!" he thought. Aunt had, at times, wandered "all over the pasture" in her conversations. Mother had listened patiently and usually could manage to follow the thread of her ramblings. Lottie had been less good at deciphering. Roy and Ralph considered themselves fortunate that they rarely had to try; Aunt didn't generally waste her breath on them.

Mr. Pratt looked befuddled, but gamely took a run at the topic again. "Who gave them to Mr. Warner?"

"He, himself."

"In your presence?"

"No, sir."

"Then how do you know that Mr. Warner has them?"

"Well, he did not give them to Mr. Warner."

Mr. Pratt shook his head in exasperation. The judge, Ralph could see, was beginning to fidget with his gavel. Mr. Pratt tried another tack: "Who gave them to Mr. Warner?"

Ralph was reminded of a game they used to play when he was a little shaver. It was called "Who Stole the Cookies," and they did a hand-clapping pattern while "It" recited, "Who stole the cookies (clap-clap) from the cook-kie jar? Lottie stole the cookies from the cook-kie jar!"

Lottie would then have to say, "Who me (clap-clap)?"

"It" would reply, "Yes, you!"

Lottie, without missing a beat, recited, "Couldn't be!"

"Then (clap), who stole the cookies from the cook-kie jar?"

And Lottie would have to pick up the pattern: "Roy stole the cookies . . ." He nearly chuckled, remembering the merriment when "It" couldn't think of a name to pass the game along to and the game broke up in giggles. He took a breath and returned his attention to his aunt, who continued to befuddle her interrogators.

"I gave them to Mr. Warner."

"Was your brother present?"

Charlotte wasn't put off by the seeming oddness of the question. "He had gone back the day before, and they were still in my possession."

"Is this not true, Miss Spencer," asked Mr. Pratt, "that when the money is collected on those notes they were to give you the money?"

"I can't say."

"No understanding about the collection of these notes?"

"That Mr. Warner was to get it as soon as he could."

"Is Mr. Warner paid for his service in looking after these notes?"

"Attorneys usually are, and I suppose he will be."

Ralph rather pitied the lawyers. Now Mr. Covell was trying to cross-examine her.

After describing, rambling actually, some more about Mother's illness, Aunt had changed the subject in midsentence. Ralph blinked, and so did Mr. Covell.

". . . he did not tell me he would write to Mr. Thacker and see if he could effect a settlement—I am sure that Mrs. Thacker said there was brown sugar on the oatmeal on May 4. I do not know of their having any brown sugar in the house during that time."

Mr. Covell shook his head as if a fly was pestering him. He took a deep breath and tried again. "Did you ever tell anyone that you were being poisoned or getting poison in your food?"

"I did say to Ralph that the water was poisoned on Sunday morning. The water that I had during the night. Lottie brought it. I told this to Ralph before his mother died."

Ralph scowled. She had never said any such thing to him! Unaware of her young kinsman's ire, she continued her disjointed testimony: "Mr. Warner was here the following day after my brother went away and talked with me about two hours about those notes. I don't think those notes had in them the word 'order' or 'bearer.'"

Aunt Charlotte, he noted, was now repeating almost verbatim Dr. Dean's testimony of several days ago. Oddly, she used it as describing her own symptoms, accurate in Mother's case, but almost certainly fantasized in her own respect. "When I kissed Anna, upon moistening my lips with my tongue immediately a strange, hard, dry, sore sensation went to my throat, and my mouth became shortly thereafter dry and parched, and my tongue hard and dry with a brown coat on it, and it was followed by a strange fever in the face, burning, while the flesh was cold and lifeless, had a lifeless feeling, but inside there was this burning all through the body especially the upper part of the body and great thirst. I kissed her when I came away the 13th of May. At that time, she (Anna) was weak and trembling, looking very wan, pale, and sick. She was sitting on the lounge. Mr. Thacker was sitting by the table or near it. I kissed her on both cheeks at this time. I experienced the same sensation from kissing her that I did when I kissed her on the 11th."

"What a lie!" Roy nearly shouted this, when Ralph related this in the kitchen that evening.

"Oh, she told so many lies I don't even know myself what's true anymore." Ralph laughed, a little sadly.

"How can she do this?" asked Lottie. "She was a missionary of the Lord!"

"She said that on the first day of Mother's illness, she next saw her that morning between nine and ten o'clock, that Mother came into her room and stayed until after supper. She said Father was around the house during the day, but he did nothing that day to help his wife except he helped Lottie get the dinner."

"Nor did we! How were any of us to know how sick she was at first?"

"What I mean is, we already testified that Mother was outdoors planting flowers until dinner, which she helped prepare, and other witnesses reported having seen Father across the road that day, digging potatoes with us. Aren't lawyers allowed to say, 'You're lying'?" They stared at the tabletop soberly, pondering the mysteries of court procedure.

The Scandal, ad Nauseum

RALPH, ROY, AND LOTTIE SAT on the hard bench in the third row back as the prosecution called fifteen assorted members of the church and both of Orah's parents to the stand, each to testify in turn what he or she knew about their father's activities in conjunction with Orah Bunker.

The minister's wife, Mrs. E. S. Shaw, seemed the most willing of all the witnesses to give Henry the benefit of the doubt. "There was nothing improper in Mr. Thacker's acts at the prayer meeting except moving up to the end of the seat and walking with her. I don't know of my own knowledge that Mr. Thacker ever showed any disposition to conceal his conduct with Miss Bunker. Mr. Thacker is of a friendly disposition and was friendly with all the young people in the church. . . . I would not think it improper for a married lady to go riding with a single man, it would be according to what they were riding for and where they were going. I saw Thacker riding in a buggy with Orah Bunker and two other girls. I may have walked home from church with J. Loyd Smith while he was stopping at our house. There was nothing improper in it."

She went on further to say, "I do not think it would be improper for me to ask a young man to go bathing. I was with a young man part of the time in the courtroom yesterday. I stopped and talked with him two or three minutes after I left the witness stand yesterday. I might have held my fan up by my mouth and whispered to him behind the fan. There was nothing wrong about that. I rode from Thompsonville recently alone with a young man all the way through the woods. Thompsonville is some miles from here, but there was nothing wrong about that. This was the same young man that I talked with yesterday. I have ridden with the young man before. I have talked with him on the street on different occasions. I do not know how many times I have been with him, I couldn't tell, but there's nothing wrong about that. He has visited my house on many occasions. Mr. Shaw was at home most of those times. I hired him two days to put down carpet this spring when Mr. Shaw was away."

As she passed by Ralph, she gave him a pleasant nod. He nodded gravely back, then turned his attention to Reverend Shaw as he was sworn in.

Reverend Shaw's testimony included several instances of "questionable" activity. He described his talk with Father which led to Orah's moving out. However, he concluded with the same disclaimers his wife had given.

"I have had young ladies while I was visiting sit down and talk with me and show me pictures. Since I have been pastor of the church here, I used to go skating with the girls, got them by the arms and hands and skated around the lake with them. There was nothing wrong about that. I skated two or three times, perhaps several occasions with Miss Bedell. I have ridden with young ladies when my wife was not along since I have been pastor of the church here, nothing wrong about that. My wife was not at home during the time the skating was done."

Roy glowered at his aunt Charlotte as she was sworn in to testify again, after Reverend Shaw. "Jealous old maid," he muttered under his breath, earning a glare from Judge Aldridge, as she testified of having spoken to Henry about his conduct.

"I said that I felt that this practice of their getting together and whispering while Mrs. Thacker was getting the children to sleep in the next room was carried on so long that their conduct was practically that of two people in love; making love to each other; that under the circumstances, Mr. Thacker being a married man, it was nothing less than wickedness and should be stopped."

John Betts, on cross-examination, said somewhat defensively, "I don't think I have been any more active in aiding the prosecution in this case than any good citizen ought to be at the untimely death of one of their neighbors. I think a good neighbor ought to have considerable feeling. I have had considerable. I don't know that I have been any great help to the prosecution. I am glad if I have. I have told the prosecuting attorney and Pratt everything I thought would be of interest to them. I didn't let much time fly after I found anything out before I told them. I should feel guilty if I had not told them everything I heard that would be material in this case. Whatever I have told them was what I had learned before this case was commenced and things that came to my knowledge soon after it was first talked up."

Jessie LaParr's statement simply told that Orah Bunker came to work between 9:00 and 10:00 P.M. on Friday, May 11, stayed a little over a week, and left on Sunday, May 20. "I don't know where she went."

Lyman P. Judson was even more terse: "Miss Bunker worked at my place. I consider Miss Bunker a good respectable girl so far as I know." At this point the prosecution rested its case.

THE DEFENSE PRESENTED a motion that much of Charlotte Spencer's testimony and much of the testimony concerning relations between Henry and Orah be struck from the record. It also, Ralph noted, made the point that whether or not Anna had been poisoned, there was no direct line of evidence connecting Henry to the poisoning.

Mr. Covell called John L. Chandler, who said, "I have known Thacker four years. He was my under-sheriff the first two years I was sheriff. His reputation for kindness and benevolence in the community in which he has lived has been good."

Charlotte testified again, this time saying, "I did not know what the powders contained at that time. I left my sister's and went to Mrs. Bailey's because I was helpless to do anything for my sister and because I believed that Mr. Thacker had been trying since the first of March to put me out of the way, and the only thing I could do was to put myself beyond his reach. I could do nothing for myself. My sister's sickness and my sickness together led me to have that feeling. At the time I left there, I had positive knowledge that the powders were poison, because I saw this powder in the bottom of a cup of water when I was taken sick on May 2."

On re-cross-examination by Mr. Covell, Charlotte said, "I had occupied that room since August. I had had these peculiar sensations before I kissed my sister on that Friday."

"Did you ever tell anyone that you pretended to be sick while you were down to Mr. Thacker's during the days of Mrs. Thacker's sickness for the purpose of leading Mr. Thacker on?"

Charlotte looked affronted. "Tell anyone that I pretended to be sick?"

Mr. Covell hastened to explain, "For the purpose of leading him on to get evidence against him?"

Understanding dawned. Charlotte did her best to look sly. It made her look, Ralph thought, like a cat caught up on the kitchen counter. Foolish, that's how she looked, as she burbled on, "Yes, sir. I told that, I don't know how many times I told it. I told Mrs. Bailey, and I may have told it several times. He expected me to be sick, and I did not dare disappoint him. I heard him ask in the kitchen if Auntie lost her breakfast, and that was what put it into my mind. I put some spoiled food or a little egg and some water in the washbowl, and when Lottie came in to inquire, she asked if I was sick, and I said you can see my breakfast in my washbowl. I was trying to deceive him. This was on the morning of Wednesday and Saturday."

The "redirect" was done by Mr. Pratt.

"How is your health since you left Mr. Thacker's?"

"Steadily improving. I have taken some medicine from Dr. Dean's hands."

She went on to say, "Prior to the 4th day of May, Mrs. Thacker and Lottie took all the care of me. The boys sometimes made fires. But Thacker never did anything. The peculiar sensations I had prior to that time was from taking hot water brought to me by Lottie and Mrs. Thacker. Mr. Thacker was in the kitchen on the 2nd of May while the water was heating. The water was heating on the dining room stove. I only know that Mr. Thacker was there by the evidence of my ears. I did not see him there. It was about eleven o'clock at night. I did hear Mr. Thacker come into the house. It was soon after that I got the warm water. It was customary for Mrs. Thacker to bring me warm water before retiring. Mrs. Thacker was in the habit of sitting up until Thacker came home when he was away in the evenings."

"He had nothing to do with what you ate and drank, did he, during that time?"

Charlotte ruffled. "I can't say what he did to the food in the other room."

"You don't know that he did anything to the food, do you, as a matter of fact?"

"I couldn't see through the wall," she shot back.

"You don't know whether he did or not?"

"I couldn't see though the wall. Steps don't tell what people do to food."

Mr. Wilson then called Mrs. Bailey for cross-examination, and queried her in greater detail about her delivery of Charlotte's poisoned prune to Dr. Dean.

Mrs. Bailey testified, "I did not ask Mr. Dean particularly what he thought about it. I was in the northwest chamber of my house when I gave it to him."

Mr. Wilson made a note on his pad, then asked, "Is that upstairs or downstairs?"

Mrs. Bailey looked disgusted. "Chambers are usually upstairs, I think."

Lottie, at her turn on the third row, nearly giggled at the look on Mr. Wilson's face.

Mr. Wilson controlled himself and tried once more. "I asked you, where is that chamber, upstairs or downstairs?"

Mrs. Bailey capitulated: "Upstairs. Dr. Dean was in the dining room before I gave it to him. I said to him, 'Come upstairs with me, I want to see you.' I don't know whether he wrapped it up again or not, I don't know what he did with it. I left it with him and went downstairs. I believe that several years ago an individual gave me poison."

With this seeming non sequitur, questioning of Mrs. Bailey ended.

Mr. Lyman P. Judson was recalled to make the statement, "I have known Thacker from twenty-two to twenty-four years. His reputation for kindness and benevolence has been good. I was familiar with the family, have lived near them ever since they came here. I never knew of any trouble between Mr. Thacker and his wife. I have heard reports around the country in regard to his conduct with Miss Bunker."

Lottie smiled at him as he walked away down the aisle.

Roy was called for cross-examination and reiterated that Henry had gotten Anna's mush, on the morning of the 4th, from the serving bowl that served the rest of the family. "He took the dish from the pile that was on the table and dipped it out of the bowl that the rest of us got ours from and put cream and sugar on it. He had served mush to the rest of the family before he served mush for Mother. I think he had served three of us before that. I was three or four feet from him when he got the mush for Mother and put the cream and sugar on it. He got the sugar out of the bowl on the table. It was white granulated sugar. He carried it immediately to Mother out by the stove in the kitchen. He did not stop anywhere as he went out to Mother. I saw Mother before breakfast. She acted as though she was very sick."

He also testified, "I never heard Father and Mother quarrel. Their relation to each other as husband and wife was devoted. I have recently seen my father kiss Mother when he was going away from the house. I was gathering blackberries last summer; Ralph, Lottie, and Miss Bunker were with us. Ma had asked us to go and get Miss Bunker to go along. So far as I know, the relations between Mother and Miss Bunker were friendly. I have heard Aunt express animosity toward Miss Bunker. Miss Spencer was not especially friendly toward Father."

The defense then called Dr. Z. H. Evans to testify that Anna had probably died of pneumonia. This defense, a rather feeble one, in Roy's opinion, was followed by Charles Case, Lot Nevius, and Seymour Wright, all of whom testified to Henry's reputation for "benevolence, love, and affection and kindness toward his fellow creatures," and here the defense closed.

Neither Father nor Orah was called by either side to testify. The testimony wandered to an end with objections and counter-objections between prosecution and defense about the propriety of certain actions by the opposing parties. Roy reflected that this was not the first such session to have derailed progress of the trial, and wondered how much it was costing them, per hour.

ROY AND RALPH STOOD side by side in front of the mirror, adjusting their ties. It was the first time in two months, Ralph realized, that they had donned their Sunday best. The final arguments, Mr. Covell had told them, were to conclude today. The jury would then retire and deliberate.

Lottie was helping Josie to dress; they would all sit in the third row until the jury went out, and then they would stay nearby, where Mr. Covell could easily find them. They knew already that a long wait was a good thing. It meant that the jury wasn't convinced "beyond a doubt" of Father's guilt.

"How could they think, for even a moment, that Papa did it?" Lottie had repeated this every time they discussed it among themselves, until Roy had finally told her to "give it a rest." By the time the trial had begun, they'd exhausted the subject, and themselves, with arguing about it.

Now they tiptoed around it. Mother's illness and death, the arrest, and the ugly way their friends and classmates had taken it, all these things lay like a porcupine in the back of their minds, benign if left alone, agony if stirred up. It served no purpose to visit what had become part of their lives anyway. Among themselves they discussed the details of existence; when to begin canning, Will's loose front tooth, the price of the hay that lay in the west twenty acres (prices were holding, so far).

Today, however, the porcupine must be prodded one final time. The jury would disappear, leaving them on tenterhooks for a long time (or so they hoped), and when they declared Father to be innocent, what would happen then? When could he come home for good? When would everyone begin talking normally to them again?

Soberly, Lottie took Josie by the hand, and they stepped out into the yard.

The Verdict

WILL WAS BEGINNING TO SQUIRM, and Josie had taken refuge in a nap with her head in Lottie's lap, when the closing arguments droned to an end.

There followed a lengthy harangue of instructions to the jury from Judge Aldrich. The jury then retired to deliberate, and the children, stiff from sitting still so long, made their way outdoors. Shadows had lengthened, and the evening mosquitoes were beginning to whine annoyingly.

"I'm hungry," announced Josie.

"Me too," added Will. Leaving Roy to find Mr. Covell, the rest of them went home to a cold supper.

Lottie came downstairs. "Shouldn't we go back to the courthouse and wait? Roy might not have time to fetch us!"

"I'll go back, and if they come back out before tomorrow, I'll come home and tell you immediately."

"No! I have every bit as much right to be there as you and Roy do!"

"Who's going to stay here with the children? You can't leave them here alone."

"Then you stay here and I'll go!" They glared at each other.

"Ralph, they're both sound asleep. They never wake up once they're asleep anyway. If we don't leave any lanterns or the stove lit, they'll be perfectly safe. Let me come too, and if we don't know anything by midnight, I promise I'll come back home."

Ralph prevailed, however, and he and Roy sat on the hard bench silently waiting, Roy growing more impatient by the minute.

"Might's well go home until morning," he growled for the third time, and Ralph hit him sharply in the ribs with his elbow.

"Owwww! What's—oh!"

The door had opened, and Mr. Penfold, the bailiff, returned and whispered something to the clerk. The clerk, looking directly at Roy and Ralph, rose slowly.

"They've decided, youngsters. They'll be coming back in shortly."

The *Benzie Banner* wrote, "The jury were taken to their meeting room over Mr. Koon's restaurant, and their supper taken to them. When the jury went to their room, there was a general feeling that disagreement would be the result. No one expected a verdict before morning. However, the verdict was reached about eleven o'clock and the judge called up to hear it. There were only a few present. A. J. Hamlin of Thompsonville, who had been chosen foreman, announced that they had reached the verdict."

Ralph's tongue went dry. He folded his hands tightly and reminded himself to breathe. After what seemed like several more hours (in fact it was fifteen minutes, he realized later), the jury filed back to their places. Father was led in, followed by Mr. Covell, and finally Judge Aldrich took his place.

Judge Aldrich paused for what seemed an unbearably long time. "Gentlemen of the jury, have you agreed upon a verdict?"

The foreman of the jury, full of his own importance, Ralph thought impatiently, announced, "We have."

"What is your verdict, guilty or not guilty?"

"Guilty of murder in the first degree."

Time stopped. Reality swirled around Ralph, who thought dumbly, "How can we tell Lottie and the little ones? This will kill her."

He heard a low sobbing. To his shame and pity, he realized it was his father. Voices kept talking; it was gibberish.

"Why can't he take it like a man?" muttered Roy, who'd pulled his handkerchief out and was scrubbing his nose and eyes.

Henry was led out, blindly, still weeping. Mr. Covell followed him to the door, speaking urgently to him, but then turned and came back to Roy and Ralph.

"You understood what was just said here?"

Of course! "Yes, sir, they've declared him guilty."

"Go home. Try and get some rest. We'll have to see how the sentencing goes tomorrow. Then we'll talk later about what to do."

Lottie had been asleep in the parlor when they tiptoed in, but she heard their stealthy entry. She sat up groggily; her look sharpened at their expressions.

"No," she whispered. "Roy, don't tease me, please. Ralph, they didn't?"

His face, grown thinner during this summer, was pale and pinched. "Guilty, Lottie. The judge will pass sentence tomorrow."

Her face crumpled. "Oh! Oh! Oh!" she wailed, rocking. She would have been further appalled to realize how much like her dying mother she sounded.

WILL AWOKE TO SOUNDS downstairs. He crept out of bed and into Josie's room. "Lottie's cryin' again," he whispered to a bewildered Josie. He crawled into bed with her, and they both went back to sleep.

Lottie, her eyes red, woke them next morning. "Hurry and get dressed. Your breakfast is on the table," she told Will. "We must be at court early."

His heart sank at the thought of sitting still for another whole day while the men talked endlessly of perplexing things. It was even worse than when Auntie had callers! "Why? We were there all day before."

"We must be there," Will had to strain close to hear the words, "to see if Papa must go away."

Will's reaction astounded her. He shrank back and grabbed his bedpost as though to anchor himself there forever. "I don't want to! I don't want to see him!"

"Will! For shame! Get dressed and go downstairs right now!"

Terror and defiance wavered in the face of Lottie's displeasure. "Papa's going to be with Jesus?" He clutched the bedpost again, remembering the evil-smelling thing on the lounge, that everyone persisted in calling Mother. Now the thing would pretend to be Papa, and he must go and be near it!

"Whatever do you mean? Of course he's not going to be with Jesus! He might go to prison!" She began to sob again. Will wasn't sure what prison was, but relieved, he edged over to Lottie and patted her consolingly. "Papa's not sick?"

"Of course not. He just might go away for a long time. Here's your jacket. Now button up your shirtwaist and go down and eat your breakfast. I must dress Josie."

JULY 24, 1894

WORD GOT AROUND TOWN quickly; the courtroom was nearly full at nine o'clock to hear the sentence.

The courtroom transcript reads, "William H. Thacker, the respondent in this case, having been by the verdict of the Jury duly convicted of the crime of murder as appears by the records thereof, and having been on motion of the Prosecuting Attorney brought to the bar of the Court for sentence and having there been asked by the Court if he had anything to say why judgment should not be pronounced against him and alleging no reason to the contrary, Therefore it is ordered and adjudged by the Court now here that the said William H. Thacker be confined in the State Prison at Jackson at hard labor for the period of his life from and including this day."

Henry, knees trembling, could only whisper hoarsely, "I am an innocent man before God. I have hoped that something would come out to show that." Sheriff Chandler led him away.

A Nestful of Orphans

THE THACKERS ALWAYS RETURNED home by the kitchen door, then up three short steps to the back porch, the boys being sternly enjoined to "wipe those dreadful feet, for merciful heaven's sake" by whatever adult was in the kitchen at the time. Feet wiped, jackets, dripping oilcloth wraps or sweaters, hats and scarves hung on pegs in a row outside the kitchen door, they would step into the kitchen, thence to the hall-way, to the stairs and the rest of the house.

This noon, however, they soberly entered the silent, waiting house through the front door. They stood uncertainly in the parlor for a moment, blinking after the blinding August sunshine.

"Well," said Roy. Expectantly, Ralph and Lottie looked at him. "Well," he said again, and sat down, staring at the floor.

Lottie fought down the impulse to wail and run down the hallway sobbing. If she began to cry, she felt she might never stop, and who would see to the children, upset as they must be, and bewildered by this sudden orphaning? She struggled to concentrate, then simply let habit take over.

"There's some brown bread left; why don't I make us some lunch?"

"I'm . . ." Ralph started to say he wasn't hungry, but then he understood, and finished, "—really hungry." It was necessary for them to go on without either parent, so they would. They had managed to do this for most of the summer, since Father had been absent in every way that mattered. Things were no different now, really, as long as you didn't think about the permanence of this bereavement. Younger people than they, of course, managed to get along without parents, so why did they all seem so paralyzed by shock now?

"I'm not hungry," muttered Roy, then looked up to see the look of hurt on Lottie's pinched face, and Ralph's disgusted little head shake. "What? You can't be hungry now, of all times? Don't you understand what's happened to us?"

Will's lips began to quiver. and Josie, as always, took her cues from Will. "Why didn't Papa come home wif us?" she whimpered.

With a look of "You see?" toward Roy, Lottie took charge again.

"Don't say 'wif,' you're a big girl now. Papa can't come home with us, not for a long time, so we'll just have to go ahead and make lunch now. Will, go out and pick us some radishes, please, some nice mild ones to dip in salt."

Chattering away, she steered the children toward the kitchen.

Ralph turned to Roy, who threw up his hands in annoyance. "I know, I know, 'Roy, why can't you at least try?' And of course you're right, I'm the oldest, I should be more responsible, but you know, lately I just don't care. We're never going to be prosperous again; I'm never going to be a musician and Lottie's never going to be an artist, and decent people will shake their heads pityingly at us. Oh, Ralph, let's just sell this place and go west! Uncle Brainard would probably take in Lottie and the children, or the little children, anyway . . ."

He trailed off at the look on Ralph's face. "Oh, what's the use! You don't care, you can just squat here and be a farmer and just go on the way you always do!" He stormed out of the room, and Ralph listened to his feet pound up the stairs. After an interval of slamming wardrobe doors and good shoes being slammed against the wall, Roy thundered down the stairs, through the hallway, and outside, not to return until dinnertime.

Shadows were long; they had picked desultorily at a slender supper and retreated to the parlor. Lottie stared moodily at one of her old schoolbooks; once it had been an exercise in tedium to memorize and recite from it, but now it held the charm of a long-ago, magical time where another girl played games with other ordinary girls and only worried about whether she'd be allowed to go on the "honor roll" sleigh ride this term.

Roy had come in halfway through dinner and taken his place as though nothing had happened. When he reflected, Ralph supposed that nothing really had—it was just Roy, sweet as the dickens when he wanted to be and things went his way, but moody and temperamental when things went against him. In a way, he was going on the same as usual, just as Lottie and Ralph were trying to do. Ralph grinned for a moment, and then the smile faded. He sighed as he felt the melancholy of the evening wash in again. Yellow afternoon light had faded to westering blue, and the robin began its evensong, all cheerful and tranquil, unaware of the miserable nestful of orphans within the house below.

Night had fully enveloped the house when the front gate opened. Through the window Lottie beheld Sheriff Chandler; joined to him by a metal cuff and a short length of chain was her father, come to say his goodbyes to them.

Papa looked like a ghost, Lottie thought, and then scolded herself for this dreadful thought. "He's not going to die; he's just going away!" she told herself sternly, then, "I must help him be brave by being brave myself."

In her mind she pictured throwing herself into his arms, sobbing, wailing, "Papa, don't leave us!" and behaving like the rather silly young girl she'd been less than a year ago. But of course there was no question of that, now, with this hollow-eyed, stoop-shouldered man who stood chained to Sheriff Chandler in their parlor. She took a deep breath and waited to hear what he would say.

But he said nothing, just reached his free hand toward her hesitantly, a trembly little smile on his lips and tears running down his cheeks. So she threw her arms around him, buried her face against his chest, and sobbed. He felt so thin, this strong hearty man who'd tossed her into the air a few short years ago. They held each other and rocked, crying. Will and Josie, she noticed belatedly, had attached themselves to her legs and were sobbing also.

When she finally extricated herself from them and stood back, Henry saw that Roy sat alone, weeping silently into his handkerchief. "My son," he choked, then saw Ralph, who stood in shadow, wiping his nose quietly, and corrected himself, "My sons—" but then he stopped, not sure what he could say to them, how he could leave these children of his, how they were to go on alone.

They stepped up and wrung his free hand, one after the other, but then Roy threw his arms around his father's neck, whispered, "Good-bye, Father," whirled and flung himself from the room.

Startled by this, Ralph looked uncertainly at Henry, who smiled rue-fully. "I think you might have to be the steady hand at the plow," he told Ralph. "Do you think you can manage it, or should we put the place up for sale? Your uncle Brainard might take in the youngsters . . ."

"Certainly not!" proclaimed Lottie indignantly. "Ralph and I, and Roy, of course, can see to the house until, until you come home again."

Henry's fragile smile faded. "That might be a long time."

Ralph thought about the robin who'd so cheerily welcomed Father home this last time. He, Roy, and Lottie would guard this fragile nest of chicks as faithfully as Mr. Robin guarded his.

"We'll manage, Father. We'll write and you can tell us how you want things planted, mightn't he?" This last to Sheriff Chandler, who rubbed his chin uncomfortably.

"I think they let prisoners write letters sometimes, if they're on good behavior. Best not to count on any visits, of course," he added hastily.

"Mayn't he come to the kitchen for some tea before he goes?" pleaded Lottie.

"Afraid not, Lottie. It's past time to go as it is."

The sheriff began to edge toward the door, pulling Henry's arm back behind him.

Ralph and Lottie in their turns hugged him again, hard; then Will, suddenly overcome by the sadness in the room, threw himself against

Henry's leg and clung, crying, "Papa! Papa! Stay here with us! I'll give you all of my soldiers, please, please pleeeeese stay home with us!" Josie wailed in sympathy, and finally Henry scooped both little ones up in his free arm and cried all over them.

Enough was enough. Lottie, ignoring the tears on her own face, peeled Josie loose, and Ralph extricated Will. They stood, a woeful little shipwrecked group, and watched Henry, sobbing loudly, follow the sheriff into the now-dark road away from them. Roy's sobs in the hallway echoed Henry's, gradually fading as Henry's faded in the distance.

Lottie felt Josie, a big girl and heavy to hold, relax. She had fallen abruptly asleep. Will, set down on his feet by Ralph, drooped exhaustedly as well. They were carried upstairs and put wordlessly to bed.

The Shipwreck

THE WAVE THAT BROKE over the Thackers' craft caused many a ripple within the Benzonia community. Like his father, Henry had been known as a good man to have around if anyone needed another hand.

Two years ago, for example, he'd learned that Daniel Keelor was short a carpenter for the addition he was putting on his house. Daniel had built the house as a dormitory for the college students, and the addition, at this rate, would never be ready by September. Henry had shown up early one Saturday morning, a tin dinner bucket in one fist, a wooden box of carpenter's tools in the other.

"I heard that Earl was still down with the grippe," he offered by way of explanation. Together they completed the framing of several windows and interior doors before darkness had sent them home to their respective families.

"Let me pay you what I would have paid Earl, will you?"

"Wouldn't hear of it," Henry had told him.

Daniel shook his head now over the headlines that shrieked, "The Benzonia Wife Murderer."

"Brought low by a woman," he muttered as he turned the page.

"Beg pardon, husband?" inquired his wife as she passed him the brown sugar.

"Oh," sighed Daniel, "this town's going to really miss Mr. Thacker. Shame he forgot himself as he did."

Mrs. Keelor nodded sadly. She, too, had liked and admired the man, and was disgusted that he'd so allowed himself to fall from grace. "And for the likes of Miss Orah Bunker, too."

Archibald Tennor, whose dealings with Henry had been limited to the purchase of some farm implements and the delivery of a deed, looked over his paper as he forked eggs into his mouth. He chewed, swallowed, then read aloud to his wife from the *Jackson Patriot*, "W. H. Thacker, the Benzonia wife poisoner, arrived at the prison last evening accompanied by Sheriff Chandler and a deputy. The trio came in on the Grand Rapids express at 9:05. The prisoner was not handcuffed and when they alighted from the train he preceded the two officers in to the depot, walking with a firm step. He gave no indication of anything out of the ordinary, and few of the bystanders recognized him as a prisoner. A hack was secured and the party drove immediately to the prison." He absently speared another rasher of bacon, dripping grease onto the tablecloth.

His wife frowned as she pushed the platter closer to his plate. "Thank goodness that's over. Now maybe we can have some peace and quiet in this town. What a dreadful example for the young people!" She clucked disapprovingly.

"Wife poisoning?"

She gave an exasperated huff. "You're not a bit funny. You know exactly what I mean. With a girl young enough to be his daughter!"

"Well, but I thought he went to prison because of murder, not because of adultery."

"One's as bad as the other, Archibald, as you very well know. Even if they never, you know," she lowered her voice to a whisper, "giving everyone the impression is just as bad."

He shook his head, frowning. "I don't know exactly what you mean, but one thing I do know. There's been a lot of bad feeling around town about all this. People taking one side of the fence or the other, arguing among themselves, and if you pay attention to some of the testimony, a lot of contradictions under oath. How can there be so much mendacity, in a righteous town like Benzonia? It doesn't give a person much hope for the rest of the country."

"Lies and acrimony!" she shook her head in agreement. "Charlotte Spencer and Mary Bailey saying one thing, the children saying another, and everyone glowering at one another on the street corners. Reverend and Mrs. Shaw appeared to be barely speaking to one another Wednesday evening, and nobody knows why but we're just sure it has to do with the trial. I don't like to be un-Christian, but I'm glad he's off to prison, and that's a fact. Everyone can find something else to talk about, now."

"Well, I'm sorry for those children, anyhow. Even their relatives seem to have washed their hands of them."

She shook her head. "That's what they get for telling lies in court."

"Sounds like you're doing a pretty good job of taking sides your own self."

She pressed her lips into a solid line and began to clear the table briskly. Archibald gloomily folded his paper and took himself off to work. Neither one said goodbye.

Joe Pettit, widower, had nobody with whom to share his morning's musings over the headlines. His children were grown and moved away. His son Johnnie was now the Reverend John Pettit, married to Anne and living in Benzonia. Joe had dined with Johnnie and his family while Orah had boarded there. He felt her an uppity young snippet, for a hired girl.

His tea cooled as he read the sordid story. Even the cat was still outdoors, probably stalking rats in the shed. He pulled his watch out for the third time. Still too early, he decided, to walk uptown. He knew that gossip was a devil's tool, but still, he set his jaw like a toothless old bulldog and thought, "If he can do it, I can talk about it."

Appealing to a Higher Court

"ROY? Roy!" Roy came down the stairs half dressed, mumbling. "Can you give me a hand today? You said you'd help put out the potatoes."

"Oh, Ralph, what's the use? We can spend the next two weeks planting those things and any money we make on them will go out the door and into Old Covell's pockets."

"Don't call him 'Old Covell' that way. He did his best."

"No, he did not do any 'best.' He showed up at the court, mumbled 'objection' a few times, and sent us the bill."

"Oh? What would you have done differently?" Ralph was surprised to find himself arguing against an opinion that, secretly, he'd held just as strongly as Roy. It's just that Roy had become so everlastingly flippant and know-it-all. It got on his nerves. Ralph, personally, had played over in his mind some of the arguments. It did look, on the surface, as though the prosecution had had the best arguments, and Mr. Covell hadn't really made any arguments at all, except to point out what a kind person Father was.

Still, Roy just had a talent for being annoying. Ralph felt the need to argue just for orneriness. "How would you have earned that handsome lawyer's fee? You heard the testimony, Mother was poisoned, the tests all showed it."

"Well, and doesn't a man have to be proven guilty 'beyond the shadow of a doubt'? How is it that Old Covell didn't even mention the fact that Auntie was with Mother just as often as Father was? Or why didn't he advance the possibility that Mother'd gotten it by accident somehow? Or even that she took it on purpose?"

"Roy!" Mother, whose life had been dedicated to serving the Lord since her earliest childhood, deliberately take her own life? Knowing the trial she would face at the seat of judgment? Ludicrous, and Roy knew that as well as anyone. Still, he and Roy both jumped guiltily when Lottie's voice broke in behind them.

"Roy!"

"I didn't say she did do it, did I? I just said that Old—that Mr. Covell could have at least suggested the possibility, as an alternative to accusing Father."

"Mother would have hated that," said Ralph. Slowly Lottie nodded her agreement. "Still, Mother would hate seeing Father in prison even more. She'd have hated this whole ruckus, Auntie away at a boardinghouse, not speaking to us nor us to her, the town all taking sides, her poor, sick body argued over in the court, and now all over town . . ."

He broke off, seeing Lottie begin to chew her lip again. She'd finally left off that dreadful habit now things had calmed down again. It pained him to see her, a thin, earnest, and it must be confessed, rather plain young girl, gnawing her lower lip until a dark red blood blister appeared.

He hated to admit it, but, "You're right, Roy. Mr. Covell should have at least suggested that idea to the jury."

"Maybe if we told him now? No, it doesn't work that way, does it?" said Lottie sadly.

Still, the following Saturday found Ralph and Roy, in their second-best, sitting across the desk from Mr. Covell. He studied their young-old faces and sighed. "In fact, I had considered that defense, and immediately discarded it. What is the likelihood, in fact, of your mother's doing a thing like that? No, don't get all riled up, but don't you see? That is the point. Everyone knows that it would be unthinkable for Anna Thacker to even consider killing herself. Why, anyone who'd suggest such a thing about a woman like your mother ought to be lynched! That's what the jury would think, and they'd have done just that to your father. Figuratively, I mean," he added hastily, seeing the twin looks of horror across the desk.

Ralph was the first to recover. "They pretty much did that anyway, didn't they?"

"That is true. I fear your father was convicted as much for his, ah, unfortunate expressions of friendliness, however innocently intended, toward Miss Bunker as for the possibility of involvement in your mother's demise." He chided himself inwardly. However prematurely aged the two young men might seem to him, these speculations of his were inappropriate in their presence.

"At any rate, he said that unless there was some concrete evidence, like a note or something, bringing up the notion would have done him more harm than good," Roy concluded to Lottie after they got home.

Absently, she placed some more beets onto Will's plate. "No, you can't have any more gooseberries unless you eat the rest of your potato," she chided Josie.

"What would happen if a person found a note like that, afterward?"

"Don't be silly, Lottie. We know there couldn't be any such thing."

"But just supposing that there was. What would happen if it didn't get found until now? Would they have to let him free?"

"Oh Lottie, don't be such a child," said Roy, wearily.

Ralph looked keenly at her. "Just supposing, where would a note like that have been, all this time? In her pocket? Under a cushion?"

Will had been listening with interest. "Is this like 'I spy'?"

Lottie took up the thread quickly. "That's just what it is. I spy, with my little eye, something that begins with 'B.'"

"Brother? Berries? Oh, I know, book! No, bread!"

"Yes! Now you take a turn!" The meal concluded with Josie and Will in high spirits, cheered with gooseberries and word games. Roy and Ralph, distracted, played poorly indeed.

A Note among the "Skellingtons"

RALPH STOOD on the back porch, muttering in annoyance. His shoes, thick-soled, with substantial leather high-top uppers, were heavy enough in normal circumstances. This afternoon they had doubled in weight.

The rain had abated early yesterday, and what with the brisk wind, the ground had already dried enough to allow the gently sloping southeast field to be worked.

Had, that is, until a woodchuck popped up near the thicket at the field's edge, and the horses had taken it into their fool heads to bolt downhill like the very devil was after them. Ralph had shouted and hauled on the reins; the shout, of course, had been stupid, it had only upset them more. By the time they'd stopped, horses, Ralph, and harrow, all four were bogged down in the clay soil near the banks of the creek.

It had taken some time to sort out traces, unhitch the horses and lead them back up to drier ground, and get back to work. He hadn't wasted the time it took to scrape all the clay off his soggy shoes. As he and the horses trudged back and forth along the rows, only some of the clay fell off; the rest, collecting a patina of gleaming black soil, had nicely thickened to a ceramic coating.

He surveyed the lumpish appendages that this morning had been perfectly ordinary work shoes. He knelt and, grimacing at the unpleasant feel on his fingers and under his nails, began to unlace them. The back door flew open. Hands covered in clay, struggling to remove the second boot, he stood like a dirty-legged stork and stared at Lottie.

"Oh, Ralph," she gasped. Her face was pale, but two red dots on her cheekbones gave her a feverish look. She held a paper out to Ralph, who helplessly showed her his hands.

"Come in here, Ralph, and wash your hands. Then look at what I found."

He obeyed. He read the note over a second time, and looked up at Lottie. "And this was in the *Home Physician*? What was it doing there?" he asked stupidly.

"I don't know! We just found it! I was showing Josie the pictures . . ."

"How is she?"

"She's upstairs asleep. Ralph, do pay attention! I was showing her the pictures, and she wanted to know if everyone had a 'skellington,' and as I turned the pages to find the plate, there was this paper. I almost didn't unfold it, thinking it was just a marker, but then I did, and saw it was Mother's writing, and here it was!"

Ralph read the note again. "Mother's writing? You think so? This doesn't sound like her, does it?"

"I—I'm not sure. She was already so sick by then."

"But look here." He pointed at a phrase. "And Mother wouldn't have said that, she knows better. And she certainly wouldn't have misspelled 'feels' that way."

"Then who did write it?" They looked at each other, then back at the paper.

"Anyway, Ralph, don't you think that Mr. Covell would want to know about this?"

"I suppose so," he agreed, reluctantly. "But it seems awfully queer, doesn't it, finding this now? Why would she have put it in the book and not somewhere we'd find it sooner?" Lottie, busying herself at the sink, didn't answer.

MR. COVELL turned the paper over and doubtfully examined the back side of the page.

"What's he looking for?" wondered Ralph, but held his silence.

"Do you think this looks like your mother's writing?" he finally asked them.

Roy shrugged. "She was pretty sick by that time. Maybe—"

"I don't think it does. Not a bit," Ralph spoke up. Mr. Covell glowered at him from behind his shaggy eyebrows. "Then how do you account for it?"

"I don't know what to make of it, sir."

"You say your sister produced this?"

"Yes, sir, she found it. She was showing the medical book to our younger sister, Josie. Josie's had a cold and an upset stomach lately, and Lottie says she was just fractious, you know how babies are when they don't feel good, and so Lottie got out the book and this note was just—in there."

"I'd like to speak directly to young Charlotte about this, if I may."

"Yes, sir. She'll be home now, if you like, she doesn't get out much these days, what with the children."

"I have no appointments just now. Wilson! I'm going out for an hour or so."

"It was around ten o'clock yesterday morning, I think." Lottie squirmed uncomfortably under Mr. Covell's scrutiny. "At least, I know it was yesterday morning. I'm not sure of the time. We'd had breakfast hours before . . ."

As Mr. Covell kept his face impassive and merely made notations on his page of foolscap, Lottie grew more confident. This began to feel like the other time she had testified. Why, she'd just have to do her best to remember the details and tell them right out! She began to form the images in her mind, Josie, small and feverish, leaning on her arm on the couch, the heavy leather-bound book with its grisly but exciting plates: ". . . so I turned the pages over, looking for the plate with the bones. It's opposite the one with the muscles . . ."

Mr. Covell nodded, an absent, "go-ahead" gesture. Encouraged, Lottie continued: ". . . as I just went on with showing Josie the pictures, I thought Ralph or Roy would know what to do, when they came home." Her brief narrative came to an end with her waving a hand at the note, which now lay on the spindle-legged table next to her.

"And what did your little sister think?"

"Sir?"

"Did you say anything to Josephine when you found the note? About its contents?"

"Certainly not! She's only three!"

"May I speak to her?"

"With Josie? Why, whatever for?"

"Even very young children are able to remember events and tell about them. I'd just like something to substantiate what you've just related." Lottie began to leave the room. "Now no prompting her . . ."

Reluctantly, Lottie went upstairs to find her little sister. She led Josie into the room. "Sit next to Mr. Covell, will you, Josie?"

"Aw right," said Josie agreeably, mindful of another occasion when this nice man with the ginger whiskers had given her peppermints when he'd come to see Papa.

"Did Charlotte show you a book yesterday?"

"Auntie show me a book?"

"He means Lottie," prompted Ralph despite Mr. Covell's head-shake. "Did Lottie show you a book yesterday?"

Josie brightened, remembering. "Skellingtons! Lottie showed me the skellington book! I threw up." Ralph rolled his eyes.

"Was there anything else in the book? Besides skellingtons, uh, skeletons, that is?"

Josie thought for a moment. "Muscles?"

"And what else?"

"Eyes! Big eyes!"

Mr. Covell suppressed a sigh. "Did anything fall out of the book?"

"Teeth! All the skellington's teeth fell out! Uh-oh!" she volunteered rapturously.

"Tell Mr. Covell about the paper," urged Ralph. Mr. Covell frowned at him, but Josie, thankfully, got back on track. "Paper! Paper from Muvver. Muvver's gone to be with Jesus."

Mr. Covell shook his head and gave up.

"I'm not sure how much credence a judge will give to this," he said sternly. "I'm not sure how much I give it myself. However, if this is added to some of the other questionable activities from the former trial, there is the slightest," he paused at the matching looks of dawning hope on the three young-old faces before him, "I said the slightest chance of success by reopening this issue. Now, I don't want you getting your hopes up. This won't be immediate, however the case proceeds, and I'm sorry to say it won't be inexpensive.

"I will, of course, need to take the note with me. I shall need to locate witnesses who are familiar with your mother's hand. However questionable this note is, it gives us enough leverage, added to the affidavit we have already been accumulating, to request a hearing. I see no reason for further delay; we will present the request today."

RALPH HAD RETURNED, quietly and alone, to Mr. Covell's office.

"I honestly don't know what to think of the letter, sir. You mentioned other points you had been accumulating. May we know what those are?" Mr. Covell tapped his lips with the corner of a piece of blotting paper and studied the thin, earnest face across from him.

"You see, Ralph, there are several irregularities in how the state conducted its case; each time I brought them up in my objections, I was surprised anew when the court refused to acknowledge them."

Ralph waited for elucidation.

"It is proper for the state to first present the body of evidence, what's called 'corpus delicti,' the facts showing connection of the defendant to the crime beyond a shadow of doubt. Then, if further circumstances affect the nature of the crime, the degree of criminality, so to speak, then that can be shown.

"This time, however, it appears that the state has put the cart before the horse. They prosecuted your father for the 'crime' of his, er, unfortunate friendship with Miss Bunker, and also for a crime that he was not accused of at all, to wit the attempted poisoning of your aunt, if in fact such an attempt actually took place."

Ralph would have found this fascinating even if it hadn't involved them so personally. He drank in these legal subtleties, so he might share them at home, which of course he did at the dinner table.

"Mr. Covell pointed out what we know is true: that most people have reasons for wanting some other person out of their lives. A man who wants to be foreman might wish his workmate would quit, or get sick, or just not exist. Or a student who's trying for a scholarship might wish another talented student would just dry up and blow away. But then, if that other student did die unexpectedly in a suspicious way, it wouldn't be proper to arrest the other student and use that competition as evidence in the trial. Not, that is, unless someone has already seen that student push the other one out the window."

Roy grinned, imagining some of his former friends in the band, pushing one another out of windows in order to win a competition.

"Mr. Covell doesn't think that Aunt's poisoned prune story should have been included as evidence either, since Father wasn't being tried for that, but for—for the other."

"I didn't believe Auntie anyway, not for a minute!" said Lottie. "Papa never touched her old prunes; I'm the one who always had to bring them to her."

"And you were the one with the most reason to be tired of her," said Roy wickedly. "Maybe you should have been the one on trial."

Lottie, to his chagrin, burst into tears. Will, still at the table, stared at her, open-mouthed. His eyes too filled with tears.

"Roy, that was a terrible thing to say!"

"Oh, Ralph, I was just fooling her. Lottie, I'm sorry. Don't be so all-fired thin-skinned. Here, I'll let you have some of my berries."

THE MORNING SUN had a September look to it, golden-orange yellow and gilding the edges of the leaves that wouldn't begin to turn for a couple more weeks, but appeared to consider their mortality. Their green had faded, Lottie noted. She paused at the corner, began to cross the street, and then faltered. Josie, holding fast to her hand, was jerked to a stop.

"Ow! Why are we stopping, Lottie? Hurted my arm!"

"Hurt my arm," murmured Lottie, absently.

Josie followed Lottie's gaze and forgot about her arm. "Auntie!"

Lottie swallowed and crossed the street toward the grocery, and toward Charlotte Spencer, who stood like an avenging angel in her black mourning dress, glaring at her nieces. "How are you, Aunt Charl . . ."

"I don't think I have anything to say to you, Charlotte Thacker. How could you sully your mother's memory that way? I was almost willing to forgive you for the lies you told in your testimony, even though you had sworn with your hand on the Bible! 'It's the father,' I told Mrs. Bailey. 'That murdering, adulterous father is influencing his own children to tell lies on his behalf.'"

"Auntie!" The pain in Lottie's voice had its effect; Josie began to whine.

". . . and now, just as he's begun to get his just desserts in this world, and I hope he's good and sorry or he'll feel worse in the next, here you and your brothers come making up worse lies, accusing your own mother of a most terrible sin . . ." She gasped in a breath.

"Aunt Charlotte, we didn't tell any lies, and Papa never influenced us to . . ."

"Oh! Then I suppose you are saying that I myself told some very bad lies, in court? Are you standing there, Charlotte Thacker, and saying that your own aunt is a liar? May you be forgiven!"

"Auntie, I never said you were a liar!"

Charlotte's face had taken on that stiff, righteous look that it had sometimes gotten when Papa had disagreed with her. Lottie had always, by a happy sort of instinct, managed to placate her aunt, to keep that basilisk glare from her own person. Auntie's sudden appearance had caught her off-guard. Miserably, she felt its malevolence.

"How do you account for the contradictions, then, Miss?"

"Maybe, oh, maybe you just forgot, or got confused!"

"I forgot nothing! I told the court exactly what I saw in that house, your father petting and flattering that young woman, calling her 'Girlie' in that syrupy way, and she no more than the hired help! I heard at the breakfast table, just this very morning, that she has been in our house recently. Who is she making sheep's eyes at now, since Henry the adulterer isn't around?"

An annoying shred of loose skin hung at the edge of Lottie's lip; she absently gnawed it free with her front teeth.

"Well? Well? Why do you stand there making that awful face at me? Do you deny that that person has been in your house again, just last week?"

Lottie looked thoughtfully at her aunt. Lottie herself had grown thinner in the past weeks; her hair, not as carefully tended, was lank, hurried into its customary braid in an absentminded way. Her hands were chapped, several cuticles ragged. The plain dark skirt and blouse were clean and pressed, but lacked their former starch. She studied her aunt. Had Auntie always wrinkled her mouth in that nasty way when she was angry? Lottie couldn't remember, but didn't really think so. Was this what the Bible meant, when it spoke of people being possessed by devils? No matter. She had to get the flour and some more salt for the dried peas and get back to the house—it was nearly time to make lunch.

"I think you're just jealous," Lottie told her aunt. "You're angry at Papa because he liked Orah better than he liked you. We have to go to the store now, Aunt."

She stepped around Charlotte and walked on, without looking back. Josie nearly stumbled again as Lottie pulled her one way while her head was turned back to stare, open-mouthed, at Auntie, who was making such a funny face.

"LEROY, I ASKED YOU to come by the office because I've heard some disturbing rumors. I'm told, by two different 'sources,' that you had a letter from your father, who reports some, ah, interesting dreams. Dreams about a suicide note from your mother."

Roy shifted slightly and frowned at his knees. The twill of his trousers was looking decidedly worn over the right knee. Why one knee more than another? Did a person have a knee they usually knelt on? He thought that was the case. Funny, he'd never considered this before. He looked up, met Mr. Covell's piercing stare, then looked away again.

"Is your father often in the habit of writing you about his dreams?"

"Sir? Oh, no sir, generally he just says that he's fine, not to worry, and to give his love to the others. Sometimes he asks after the horses," he added helpfully.

"Do you have in your possession a letter from your father, detailing a recent, ah, prophetic dream?"

"No, sir." He flushed and looked at the worn place again. The neat parallel ribs of the twill were, undeniably, worn down on that side. There, the evidence showed it; he was right-kneed. Emboldened, he added, "Maybe someone else started these rumors about the letter; I hadn't mentioned it to anybody outside the family."

"Have you ever seen such a letter? The truth, now. No, look at me. Did you receive a letter from your father, concerning a dream he had recently?"

Roy took a deep breath, looked up, and muttered, "Yes, I did," before looking down again.

"And where is that letter now?"

"It's at home, I think." At Mr. Covell's frown, he amended his response. "Yes, at home. I'm sure of it."

"How long will it take you, do you think, to return to this office with this letter?"

"Not long. I'll be back directly," he answered and left the office.

"ROY! Are you crazy? Why did you tell him that? Why did you tell such a story to anybody? What gets into you?"

"Never mind! If you can't help, at least don't preach at me!" Roy stormed out of the house, empty-handed.

"YOU LOST THE LETTER?"

"No, sir. I think it might have been taken by someone." He returned Mr. Covell's suspicious look with round-eyed innocence.

"Taken! By whom?"

"I couldn't say for sure, sir. We've had a few visitors lately. Orah Bunker, for example, was over just on Tuesday. Mrs. Waters comes to see Lottie, but I'm sure she wouldn't take anything without asking."

"So you think that Orah Bunker stole this letter?"

"I couldn't say for sure, sir."

"You do know that this odd business will add confusion and dissention to our request for a new trial, don't you?"

"I suppose it will." Roy looked down again.

"If you have any more thoughts about this letter," Mr. Covell's voice dripped with sarcasm, "you will be sure to share them with me, won't you, before you confide in, say, Joseph Beals or others of his ilk?"

"Yes, sir."

"Don't let me detain you further."

"Yes, sir." Roy made his escape.

More Than a Brother

"GOOD TO SEE YOU AGAIN, Mr. Thacker," said Mr. Dodge. He'd begun to reach his hand across the table, until he noticed the guard scowling and shaking his head. He pulled it back. Henry appeared not to notice; his smile was wistful.

"Mr. Thacker. I like that. Makes me feel like I'm somebody again."

Mr. Dodge shifted in his chair. "How are they treating you?"

Henry glanced at the guard who stood behind him, appearing to study a fly on the opposite wall. "Can't complain, no sir, indeed I can't."

After an uncomfortable pause: "Say, Roy wrote to me about the note. You must be here because of that, aren't you? Do you suppose it will help the appeal?"

"That will depend on a number of circumstances. As I explained to your older children, an appeal will take time, and, unfortunately, quite a bit of money. Now I don't wish to impoverish your family, but you must know that we in the legal profession have our obligations just like everyone else."

"Surely, surely. I've written Ralph about that, told him he was to sell off some of the stock and machinery . . ."

"Yes, yes. It's not the state of your family finances that I've come to discuss, primarily, that is, it's your appeal. Your sister-in-law's testimony was the most damaging, as you know, albeit many things she said were contradictory and rambling. I believe that we may be able to . . ."

"That addle-brained woman! She's Anna's only sister and I know I should be more forgiving, I know she's a sick woman . . ."

Mr. Dodge cut him off.

"When she took the stand, Miss Spencer mentioned some notes that she felt were owing to herself, or possibly to herself and her brother. She apparently had some business dealings with Mr. Warner, who, you know, led the prosecution of your case. What can you tell me about those notes?"

Henry thought a moment. "Mr. Spencer wasn't a rich man, but he saw to it that all three of his children were provided for. He knew that Brainard, being a minister . . ."

"You refer to David Brainard Spencer, your brother-in-law, I believe."

Henry nodded. "Brainard didn't have any interest in staying in Benzonia, and there was no question about Charlotte's getting married and keeping the Spencers' house. Mr. Spencer gave us the house we live in now, as a wedding present."

"I understood he actually gave it to your wife, is that not so?"

"Well, yes, to Anna, but really to us, don't you see, because we were getting married. I never really thought about it's not being both of ours, until she made such a much, there at the end, about signing it over to me so the children would be sure of having it. Mr. Spencer also gave us a pair of horses when we got married, you know that old gelding Star, he's outlived the other, Squire, by five years already. I bought Duchess, that's the mare that threw that nice little filly, after . . ."

The guard sighed, audibly.

"Let's move along," suggested Mr. Dodge. "Mr. Spencer gave the house to your wife and the horses to you both, and how did he provide for the other two of his children?"

"He gave Brainard some money when he married Amelia, and when he became ill and moved in with us . . ."

"Brainard Spencer lived with you?"

Henry forgot his circumstances for a moment and chuckled at the picture of Brainard and himself, under the same roof again, annoying the dickens out of one another. He shook his head, and returned to his narrative.

"I meant Mr. Spencer, Anna's father. He fell ill and he and his wife moved in with us. This was shortly before Charlotte came back from Turkey. They'd been sending some money to Charlotte right along, whenever she needed some little thing or another. The Spencers sold their house and had a little money, so when Charlotte came back and Mr. Spencer died, he left some of that money to Charlotte."

"And then what happened?" Mr. Dodge could see over Henry's shoulder that the guard was ready to call an end to the conference. "Quickly now, what about those notes?"

"When Charlotte was so sick and couldn't look after things for herself, she said, 'Why don't I sign some of my inheritance over to you, to look after for me?' I gave her a note for, oh, I forget exactly how much, we used some of it to build that cowshed, and some more to buy a good milker, I'd have to look it up . . ."

"So the money was hers, but you had the use of it while she lived there, was that it?"

"Well, it was, but you see she kept thinking she was going to die and thought she'd leave it all to us anyway."

"Us? Who do you mean by 'us'? You and your wife, or the children, or just whom?"

Henry looked sheepish. "Sometimes she said she was leaving it to me. She said she 'loved me like a brother,' but I noticed she didn't talk much about leaving anything to Brainard."

"Loved you like a brother? As though you were her brother? Were those her words?"

"Generally, I think. Sometimes I thought she made too much of it, as if she wanted me to be more than a brother to her, if you know what I mean. We used to be friends, long ago, but after Anna and I married, I wasn't quite sure how she felt, about either of us. That was a long time ago. Then she came back and moved in with us, and she began to behave more and more oddly . . ."

After a while, Henry fell silent. Mr. Dodge finished jotting his notes and folded the paper. He rose, began to reach his hand out to Henry, then remembered and contented himself with a nod. "Goodbye, Mr. Thacker. I will keep you informed of events."

"Thank you for coming to see me," said Henry simply, then turned and left the room, followed by the guard.

HENRY DIDN'T OBJECT to the strenuous prison labor; in fact, the only good part of the sentence was having a good hard job to tackle and work off the crawling feeling his spine got when he was closed in for too long. He'd been mortified the first time he'd been sent out to work on the roads, thinking that passersby would know who he was and stare, but he soon realized that nobody looked at individual convicts, dressed alike and chained together like oxen.

At first he'd felt uncomfortable with the other prisoners, crude and ignorant as they seemed, but in time he made some friends. His cellmate, Jim Hawks, was a good fellow at bottom, or so he thought.

He didn't remember how the subject had come up; "lifers" rarely spoke about the lives they'd left behind, it only made them feel bad, and what was the point? But there they were, chopping gnarled roots into stove-sized lengths under the watchful eyes of two armed guards, and Henry, though ordinarily he knew better, had begun to tell Jim all about Orah and the children.

"If the appeal works out and I ever get to go home again, I'm going to marry that girl. The children like her, and she's a great little house-keeper . . ."

Jim cleared his throat and spat on the floor. "It ain't the house-keepin', it's the bed-warmin' that you're thinking of, I'll warrant. So just shut your yap about your appeal that ain't ever going to happen, they never do, and your whore of a girl, or I'll shut it for you."

Henry had stopped, stunned, and stared at Hawks, who added a mouthful of profanity that Henry had never even heard before, but he could tell what was meant.

He dropped his ax and stalked toward Hawks. "I expect your mother didn't teach you any manners when she should have . . ." And the next thing he knew, he and Hawks were brawling like ill-mannered school-boys, and then he was alone in a tiny brick closet for many days, trying not to scream at the dark, the emptiness, and his own despair.

To keep his sanity, he thought about his dream: Mr. Covell coming to the prison and telling him it had all been a mistake, that someone else had confessed to the killing. His ride home in the family farm wagon, the children happily chattering about their chores and their lessons. The welcome home by neighbors and old friends. The ride to Arcadia, where the Bunkers had their farm, and the joy on Orah's face when he finally came to claim her as his bride. Long winter evenings, with the boys and Lottie at their lessons, Orah darning stockings, he sitting be-fore the fireplace in his rump-sprung cane rocker, basking in the simple happiness of having his family about him . . .

Conflicting Depositions

THE CLERK FOR Wilson & Bailey, Dodge & Covell, tapped his pen ab-sently against the tip of his nose. Married for less than a year, he wanted very much to file these tiresome documents away and hurry home to dinner. Alice-June, his bride, was an excellent cook; he was already de-veloping a small paunch in tribute to her skills.

He sighed and reached for the next page in a thick pile that dwindled with maddening slowness as he inventoried and ordered the contents, checking them against his list. On top of the pile, the note, written on a page of notepaper headed "Wm. H. Thacker, Agent for Deering Mowers and Binders, Agricultural Implements, Etc." He had read it a number of times already, and could nearly recite it from memory:

"Benzonia, Mich., 1894, May 15.

"Dear Husband,

"I am tired of life. I have been tempted ever since you bought that arsenic for dogs to use some myself. Have taken some three times. Will take more now. Take good care of the children and do as I told you, you remember. My head feals badly.

"Goodby,

"Anna"

This note made him sad whenever he read it. When Henry and Anna Thacker had stood before the minister, hadn't they, too, felt the shy, mysterious sweetness that he and Alice-June had felt, the joy and terror of the step they were about to take, the hope of a long and happy life together? Something had gone terribly wrong; whether murder or suicide, or something altogether different, something had happened in the lives of these two ordinary people to change that sweet mystery into something ugly.

He knew, like everyone else in the town knew, that the old maid aunt had severed relationships with her nieces and nephews (though she hadn't gone to live with her brother, the only relative she had left). The children had, in a sense, defended their father. By their testimony, there was hardly any way for Henry Thacker to have dosed his wife's cereal that fateful morning. In fact, Charlotte's testimony, garbled as it was, pointed more to her as a suspect; she had been in close contact with her sister the entire night before, and evidently Anna was sick from the time she'd awakened.

Did the children really believe in Henry Thacker's innocence? Almost worse, did they believe that their mother had chosen to take her own life? For a moment, the clerk no longer felt hungry. He shook his head to clear it of these musings, inappropriate in a law clerk, and went back to his task.

Following the letter was a number of depositions from various people. These included documents testifying to the probability that the "Dear Husband" note was or was not written by Anna. The first ones swore to the effect that the deposed had studied Anna Spencer

Thacker's final note and agreed, based on experience they had formerly had with writings of hers, that she had written the note.

In the "yes" camp were:

C. B. Doty, an acquaintance of Anna.

Charles F. Reed, postmaster, who mentioned that he had had opportunity to examine the handwriting of everyone in Benzonia.

J. W. Wilson, attorney, who added that Lottie had found the letter, that Henry had no knowledge of it, that they (Wilson & Bailey, Dodge & Covell) had the letter in their possession and would produce it in the event of a retrial. The clerk quickly flipped back through the pile of papers and made sure again of the safety of Anna's letter.

The inventory went on:

John Link, another acquaintance of Anna.

Mary W. Budlong, an acquaintance of Anna, who also said she visited Anna in March of '94 and Anna had told her that "she was discouraged and tired of this life and that she did not know what she would do."

Orin D. Morse, nephew of Wm. Henry, who said while he was visiting Henry and Anna in 1889 he wrote home to his sister and to his mother, and that Anna wrote a note to his mother on the other side of the same sheet, which he offered (as evidence) for comparison to the "Dear Husband" note.

Harris W. Cunningham, agent for Buckeye & Douglas Lumber Co and for Manistee & North-Eastern R.R. Co, who examined the "Dear Husband" note and compared it to other samples purported to be in Anna's hand.

Carlton A. Hammond, teller and cashier of First National Bank of Traverse City.

Thomas Bates, bookkeeper in the First National Bank and managing editor of the *Traverse City Herald.*

Don S. Dean, teller of the First National Bank.

He checked this pile against his list and pushed it aside, carefully setting a paperweight on it. He turned to the next pile. These concerned one Arthur J. Hamlin, of Thompsonville. Mr. Hamlin had been one of the jurors in the original trial. He had supposedly stated on or about June 8, 1894, that "Mr. Thacker's looks was enough to give him away and that they ought to hang him to the first tree they come to."

Alice-June's new husband leafed through the pile of these statements. Nathan Lucas, Frank Heath, Anthony Rouse, Richard Jones, and Elmer Northrup were either at Thompson Lumber Co. or outside it, in the busy Thompsonville depot, on that day and swore that Hamlin had made this prejudicial statement.

His stomach gurgled emptily. He set Elmer Northrup aside and picked up Russell C. Hill.

Russell C. Hill was also a juror—there was an affidavit from Cornelius Snider who said that Mr. Hill had said to him, on May 30, before the trial was even begun, "Of course Thacker is guilty, and he will go 'over the road' without a doubt and he ought not to spend any money for defense but ought to leave all his property to his children."

The clerk shook his head. "Dogged if I'd go down without a fight, guilty or not," he thought. He pulled the rest of the stack toward him. These documents, turned crosswise to the others, were copies that had come from the prosecution.

Affidavits that argued against the note's authenticity or against Arthur Hamlin's having made the prejudicial statement against Henry before his jury selection included:

Sarah J. McCreary, who swore that Arthur Hamlin was at her house the day he supposedly made the prejudicial statement.

John C. Steward, who said he saw Arthur Hamlin sitting on the steps of his house rather than at the depot where he made the statement. The clerk mused, not for the first time, that Mr. Hamlin appeared to be an amazingly versatile person. He wished that he had Hamlin's skill. He could not only be here doing his necessary job, but also at home with his feet squarely under a table laden with fresh biscuits and whipped butter, watermelon pickles, pot roast, and dumplings. He returned to the stack of documents and checked off the next one:

Arthur Hamlin, who denied making the statement.

Phoebe A. Stewart, who didn't see Arthur Hamlin at the depot.

Arthur Hamlin's son Fred.

G. C. Hopkins, acquaintance.

Charlotte Spencer, who once again had plenty to say, including that "I was well acquainted with William H. Thacker and Anna Thacker, his wife, that Anna Thacker was my sister . . . that affiant and Mrs. Thacker were more intimate and confidential in their relations than sisters usually, that neither of them had a secret that she did not entrust to the other . . ."

"The old maid sister," thought the clerk uncharitably. "Not hard to tell that she has an ax to grind. Star witness in the first trial, and wants a front-row seat for this one as well."

The People's "old maid" representative went on: "Deponent says that she knows that on account of their intimate and confidential relations that if her sister had contemplated suicide she would have told your deponent or intimated something that your deponent might have suspected the same; but she never did and on the contrary she was always very cheerful and happy and made the best of all her surroundings and was very much attached and devoted to her family.

"Your deponent further says that Anna Thacker remarked to your deponent, 'I know how you feel when you were so sick from your vomiting and retching' and compared her sickness with that of your deponent when your deponent was suffering from arsenical poison."

Charlotte Spencer had also argued against the note's validity on the basis of the contents of the note: "Deponent says she has not seen the letter purported to have been written by her sister the day before her death wherein she stated 'I have taken poison,' but has read what purported to be a copy of the same and that letter does not sound like her, for when she addressed her husband she always addressed him as Henry and when speaking of him always spoke of him as 'He or Henry' and that in said letter the word 'feels' was spelled 'feals,' besides errors in punctuation and capitalization which mistakes would not have occurred had it been written by Anna Thacker as she was a schoolteacher and a good scholar. Your deponent has examined two letters written by Anna Thacker; in each appears the word 'feels' correctly spelled."

Dr. David Dean likewise testified against the likelihood of suicide, referring to conversations with Anna in which she had said, "No, we do not keep any kind of poison in the house," and also that "Anna Thacker always appeared anxious to get well and would so express herself and wonder why she did not and why it was she continued to vomit."

Alice-June's husband had been to Dr. Dean one time for a severe case of dyspepsia; Dean had given him some pills that hadn't worked.

He brightened; only four more pages in this pile:

S. B. Harvey, the professor of Latin and German in Benzonia College, said "there had been an erasure in said letter, the date of the letter had been erased and rewritten, the word 'dogs' had also been erased and 'Anna' had been erased and rewritten, besides the word 'feels' was spelled 'feals'; the letter indicated and had appearance of being written by a person who was taking a great deal of pains to either write well or imitate some other person's handwriting; that two of the letters examined by deponent and written by Anna Thacker had the word 'feels' in them spelled correctly."

Flora E. Harvey, not surprisingly, agreed with the professor, and for the same reasons.

Mary E. C. Bailey used the same arguments Dr. Dean used, and also interjected a rehash of her testimony from the first trial, including, "I then inquired of her (Anna) the cause of her sickness; she replied she had been sick since she ate her breakfast, she said she ate graham pudding with sugar and milk, prepared by Henry, meaning her husband."

The clerk shook his head smilingly. If Dr. Dean said something, you could be sure that Mary E. C. Bailey would agree to it. While Widow Bailey intimidated most people, Dr. Dean, who boarded at her house, seemed to be the exception. The Baileys had always had a high regard for education, and a doctor ranked just below a minister in the hierarchy. Probably that was why Mrs. Bailey, who deferred to nobody else, deferred to her "star boarder."

In the final deposition, Arthur Ward had nothing to say about the note, but testified that he was present the day that Arthur J. Hamlin was said to have made his prejudicial statement, and that at no time did he see Arthur J. Hamlin in or in front of the Thompson Lumber Co., where the event was said to have happened. "How could he," thought the clerk cynically, "when he was being in two other places at the same time?"

With a grunt of satisfaction, he checked this last item against his list. He tapped this pile of papers into a neater stack and placed another paperweight on it. He pulled the final pile of affidavits before him now.

On August 9, 1894, the motion for a new trial had been presented by J. W. Wilson and G. C. Covell to Judge Aldrich "in vacation, to be heard by him at Cadillac." The affidavits outlined the points of the case, most of which existed in advance of the "Dear Husband" letter's discovery.

The first six points were based on points of order. The sixth motion referred to the prosecution of the case by D. G. F. Warner, who had personal financial involvement with Charlotte (and Brainard) Spencer, one of whom was a primary witness for the prosecution. This struck the clerk as a damning point, and one that trumped some of the lesser points of law brought up further down. He could imagine Mr. Wilson's caustic response to this "naïve" viewpoint of his; he'd quickly learned to listen and learn before opining such things, except at his own dinner table. Oh, that beckoning dinner table!

Points seven through twelve pertained to objections in the selection of jury members, some of whom were made familiar with points of the case by the prosecution before the jury was even selected.

Thirteen and fourteen pertained to objections that were overruled in the first trial, in which testimony tended to "connect the respondent with the alleged homicide in this case before the People had established the corpus delicti in the case," and that "the People tending to show or prove that the respondent had during the last illness of the said Anna Thacker, attempted to administer poison to one, Charlotte Spencer, who was living and residing at the home of respondent."

Fifteen through eighteen pertained to objections concerning the competency of the expert witnesses Drs. Dean, Kinnie, and Powers, and Professor Gomberg, who "only relied on their knowledge derived from reading books which treated on arsenical poisoning."

Nineteen pertained to the denial of the defense's motion to strike testimony from the record concerning Henry's alleged attempts to poison Charlotte Spencer. Indeed, it was a wonder the judge hadn't ruled more appropriately in the subtext of the case; if Henry Thacker were to be tried for the attempted murder of his sister-in-law, that should indeed have had its own trial.

It seemed odd to him that nobody, from prosecution or defense, had attempted to follow up on the source of this mysteriously appearing arsenic, all of which seemed to come from the bedroom of Charlotte Spencer in the form of clumsily concealed poison in her food. He had tried to ask Mr. Dodge about this, and earned only a sour look for his pains.

Twenty pertained to the testimony of Charlotte Spencer in reference to "certain promissory notes held by her and payable by the respondent in the sum of seven hundred dollars or thereabouts, which objection was made by the respondent for the reason that it was immaterial, irrelevant, and incompetent."

Twenty-one said, "Because the Court erred in overruling respondent's objection to the testimony of Mrs. Shaw and various other witnesses as to respondent's conduct with Miss Orah Bunker, which objection was made by respondent for the reason that the conduct of respondent by them testified about was too remote and indefinite and for the further reason that the People had not established the corpus delicti in this case, to which ruling of the Court the respondent then and there objected."

Twenty-two said, "Because the verdict of the Jury in this case is contrary to the evidences and to the law," and twenty-three pertained to a similar legal point of order.

Twenty-four was an interesting one; it pointed out that in the court's instructions to the jury, the jury was told that "to convict the respondent they must find that he had poison in his actual possession and that he knew the nature of the poison, and in another instruction that it was not necessary that they should find that the respondent had poison in his actual possession or that he actually knew the effects of poison."

This twenty-fourth point was, even to an untrained eye like his, an especially meaty one, finishing up with four legal pages describing irregularities that tended to prejudice the jury, including remarks made by counsel for the People and remarks made by certain members of the jury before they had even been selected. In this point, Arthur J. Hamlin, for example, was said to have said (and affidavits were produced from witnesses to this) that "His (Mr. Thacker's, meaning respondent) looks was [*sic*] enough to give him away and that he (Thacker, meaning respondent) ought to be taken to the first tree and hanged up."

Twenty-five pointed out that Edwin S. Pratt had not filed his oath of office as is required by the prosecuting attorney and his assistants as required by law, and also that Russell C. Hill "had prejudged this case as to the guilt of the respondent prior to the time at which he sat upon the Jury and prior to his examination on his voir dire," and because of this, "this respondent has not had a trial before a fair and impartial Jury as the law provides."

Exhibit G contained the statement from Cornelius Snider: "During said time of riding with said Russell C. Hill on said 30th day of May, 1894, the said Russell C. Hill said to affiant that 'Of course, he (Thacker) is guilty, and he will go 'over the road' without a doubt and he ought not to spend any money for defense but ought to leave all of his property for his children.'"

There! All the documents were present and accounted for. In the morning, Mr. Dodge would begin laying out his strategy. It was probably, the clerk thought as he rose stiffly from his desk, much like a playwright's craft, deciding when to bring in each actor to speak his lines to the best effect. He locked the documents carefully into their respective boxes and placed them into a safe closet. He pulled on his light summer coat, snatched his hat from the rack, and went out into the still-warm autumn evening. Would it be chicken tonight? Or pot roast?

Sheriff Judas

BENZONIA, DECEMBER 1894

SHERIFF CHANDLER KNOCKED at the back door. Then, without awaiting an answer, he stepped into the kitchen and removed his hat. Lottie, sitting at the kitchen table shelling dried lima beans, stared at him silently.

"Is Leroy at home?" His voice was formal, distant, the polite voice one uses with acquaintances and not at all the avuncular boom with which he normally greeted children about the town.

Should she offer him tea? There was so little left in the tin, and she was saving it for something special. He was their first caller since he had come to take Papa away. She tightened her jaw. This was no call! He was just doing his job. Like Judas, he'd been paid to take her innocent father away forever, and now he was here with more bad news, she could see it in his red face.

"I don't know where Roy is. Shall I give him a message when I see him?" she asked coolly. He blinked at her; was this poised yet hostile young woman only fourteen? A long moment passed, and then Ralph stepped into the kitchen behind him.

"Can we help you, Sheriff?"

"I'm looking for your brother . . ."

Ralph's heart sank. He looked at Lottie, then back at the sheriff. "He's not been home since yesterday. When you see him, would you ask him to come home? We could use another pair of hands for the potatoes."

"I'm sorry, Ralph. Roy's been accused of theft. If I find him . . ." He corrected himself: "When I find him, I'll have to lock him up."

Will, Josie behind him, had come to the doorway. Silently, they added their stares to those of Ralph and Lottie. Embarrassedly, Sheriff Chandler replaced his hat and backed toward the door.

"I'm sorry, youngsters, it's just my job, and Roy ought to've known better. At a time like this—look here! Can't you just sell what's left and go to your relatives? I know your uncle could afford to take you in."

"This is our home," said Ralph. "I'm sorry if Roy did something wrong. Losing our parents . . ." He spoke distantly, as though discussing the affairs of an acquaintance across town. "Losing our parents was hard on Roy. That's no excuse for stealing, but it also doesn't mean the rest of us must leave our home."

The sheriff climbed back into his buggy and fished out his handkerchief. Despite the crisp December day, sweat had collected inside his collar and on his face. Roy had taken the galoshes, bold as brass, but he was the one feeling guilty!

"ROY, HOW COULD YOU!"

"Oh, Lottie, don't you be all holier-than-thou. My old boots leaked all spring, but mother was too tired to think about anything and we all were too busy. I can't go through another winter with wet feet, and we can't afford new! And you can just stop looking at me like that, Miss! You're not too big I can't take you down a peg!"

"What Lottie means, Roy, is we need you at home to help out. Having you in jail is surely no help to the rest of us."

"You didn't object when I brought home ten dollars last week, did you? Well, did you? Where do you think that came from?"

Lottie was dumfounded. "You said you did some odd jobs!" She said again, "Roy, how could you!"

"How could I? Why shouldn't I?" Roy barked a short, bitter laugh. Lottie didn't like the sound; it was like the sound a barn cat made, just before it hurked up the remains of a half-digested mouse, all bones and scraps of fur. "I needed a new pair of boots and there they sat, right in the vestibule. After everything we've lost, why shouldn't I help myself to something I needed?"

Ralph stared at Roy. He had thought, when the judge pronounced sentence, that nothing else in life could shock him. He shook his head, incredulous. "You were Mother's favorite. Her pride and joy."

"Well, and she's dead now, isn't she? And our father's a wife murderer. And do you think that a stupid pair of galoshes matters to any of us, really?"

"Papa's not a murderer! And you know it!" Petite Lottie's fury would have amused Ralph, a year ago. "Little banty hen," he thought to himself numbly, and stifled a foolish giggle. A year ago. That was a different land, wasn't it, the land of a year ago?

"We don't know he's not," retorted Roy. "It's been pretty well proven that he's an adulterer, anyway. And I'd rather think that Father did the deed," he paused and looked from Lottie to Ralph, "than one of us. Wouldn't you?"

The kettle, cooling on the stove, ticked unnoticed in the silence. Ralph inhaled slowly—the whistle of air in his nostrils sounded loud to him. "All right, Roy. What's done is done. What will happen now? Are you going to prison now, too? Or must we . . ." the thought was bitter to him, "sell the southeast field to pay for another trial?"

"You don't need to worry your head about it. Joe Beals says that the galoshes were cheap ones so they can't lock me up for too long, anyway."

"Joe Beals! I might have known he'd be mixed up in this. What did he steal, and how did he get you to cover up for him?"

"None of your beeswax, little brother. I don't have to explain myself to you, so suppose you just never mind!"

Ralph thought Roy's tone of reckless defiance sounded brittle, but forbore to comment. He knew that he should feel more concern for Roy than for worldly goods, but somehow, just now, the southeast field, green and alive under the late summer sun or even gray and stark in the winter gloom, felt more precious to him than this blustering fool who'd been caught stealing a cheap pair of galoshes.

When all was said and done, Roy spent Christmas (and two weeks on either side of that day of hope and promise) in the Benzonia calaboose and in Grand Traverse County Jail, in lieu of a twenty-five-dollar fine. If Lottie wept when she learned of this, she did so in private. At least, thought Ralph, there was one less mouth to feed, in a month when they could best spare the extra pair of hands.

Premature Burial

JACKSON, MICHIGAN, MARCH 1895

HENRY WALKED SLOWLY down a tiled corridor, a guard on each side of him. His heart thudded like the hooves of a trick pony in the circus ring. The door at the end stood open, and the guards walked him through it without even a pause for prayer. A large figure stood near a door in the floor. The figure was dressed completely in black. Henry tried to memorize the man's features—it seemed important that he commit every open pore, every ingrown follicle on the man's cheek. It was that, or he surely would break down and shriek in terror, gibbering and begging for his life. He would need to be pried loose from the guard's knees where he groveled, and word would reach his children, reach Orah, reach Anna's brother and sister, who would smirk at his cowardice and his children's disgrace.

He took a deep breath, flinching only when the man pulled a hood snugly over his face. Blackness, all was blackness. The rope slid over his head, hemp strands prickling the tender skin under his left ear. The knot snugged cozily against his other ear, like a cat's whiskers without the purr.

Distantly, he heard measured voices speaking, meaningless syllables. He tried to focus, to direct his mind toward God and the next world. He'd see Anna. She'd know, then, that he hadn't done it. Or had he? Slow down, slow down; he had been in the kitchen, preparing the mush, hadn't he? But then so had Ralph. So had Roy, and even Lottie had entered and left once, or was it twice? And Charlotte, where had she been? She and Anna together, night after night with nobody else around. Abruptly, he dropped, fell, hurtled through blackness.

"Huh!" Henry jerked awake and lay there in the darkness, the sour sweat puddling on the musty canvas cover of the thin mattress beneath him. The death sentence didn't exist here in Michigan. Premature burial did, however, and he was experiencing it firsthand. Shivering in the cold puddle of sweat, Henry began to weep again.

A Stormy-Weather Friend

BENZONIA, JUNE 1895

THE NOISE GRADUALLY SUBSIDED. Stillness prevailed, a stillness that rang in the ears, made one afraid to take a step, to bump into a door jam, to knock over a lantern. Hesitantly the youngsters stood up, crept to the door, peered out. The sickly green of the sky had faded to the ordinary leaden tones of a rainy summer afternoon. They stepped out, Ralph first; Josie and Will, with the boldness of the very young, followed, with Lottie bringing up the rear.

The countryside remained firm and solid, yet it seemed to Ralph as though the shape of it had somehow altered. He turned in a complete circle, mouth ajar. The barn stood in its usual place; the house was intact save for the screen door, which dangled from one hinge. Down the hill all looked well, except that a wide path was ripped through the orchard and tree limbs lay scattered higgledy-piggledy in field and yard. His eye fell on the elm that had stood to the rear of the house for as long as he could remember. This elm had shaded their back stoop in the summers; it had been the first thing Ralph beheld when he looked out his window in the mornings; it had guarded the younger children as they toddled about the yard.

Slowly he walked over to the prostrate giant. Its limbs lay crumbled, shattered beneath its own weight. Its roots, denuded of their clothing of earth, sprawled promiscuously in dimensions utterly wrong for a tree's roots. Numbly, Ralph stared at the root ball.

He remembered the words of a missionary who had spoken at church some years ago, telling of the Dakota Indians he'd lived among for several years. "These savages were so ignorant," Brother Harold had declared, "they were unable, until we began our saving work, to discern between human life and the lives of animals and plants. They called the birds 'the winged people,' and trees 'the standing people.'" A lady in the row behind Ralph had clicked her tongue disapprovingly.

Unbidden, the image of his mother thrust itself into his mind. His mother, apt as not to slap a face or pull out a switch at the least infraction. His mother, believing implicitly that a woman's place was to be ruled by the man, had ruled the house with a will of iron. His mother, an avenging monolith. His mother, suddenly much smaller, her iron sinews reduced to so much yellowed skin-clad pudding, lying dead in her bed, green vomit caked at the corners of her lips, the smell of blood and excrement heavy in the air.

As he stared at the fallen tree, Ralph, who hadn't cried since he was six years old, felt tears sting his eyes. He felt a pain in his throat, wedged dryly like a bread crust he'd tried to swallow in a hurry.

"Mother," he whispered to himself, then, softly, "Mama." He tightened his jaw. Briskly he turned to his siblings. "Won't have to haul this firewood so danged far, anyway," he told them and led the way to the shed where the ax was stored. "Let's get these limbs cleared away and see how much fruit's left on those trees."

Thomas Rideout looked out the window and muttered again to himself. Elizabeth looked up from the pair of socks she was darning. "Whatever has gotten into you, Thomas? You've been looking out the window and cursing under your breath since supper. And don't think I can't hear you taking the Lord's name in vain when you think I'm rattling the dishpan."

"Those fool Thackers," growled Thomas. "Don't they have any relatives to take them in? Look at that!" he grumped, flapping his hand at the window. "That girl Lottie's out there in the rain, wearing those tatty old oilskins, trying to stack those great big logs, while that fool boy Ralph's trying to cut up that big old elm, in the dark, in the rain, without any light but a lantern hung under the eaves of that henhouse. If t'wasn't so wet out there, like as not they'd burn up all their chickens."

"It's what they deserve," retorted Elizabeth Ann. "Those Thackers have brought nothing but scandal and dissension to Benzonia, for all their mother's holier-than-thou airs." Elizabeth had been one of the young women who'd felt the sting of Anna's tongue more than once. "And don't you go getting ideas about helping them, either. We've got enough on our plate without that." She added an unnecessary stitch and scowled at it. "Here, where're you going?" she said with exasperation.

Thomas shrugged into his own oilskins, not much newer than Lottie's hand-me-downs that he'd just spoken of so contemptuously. "I don't care what that hoity-toity minister says, you can't tell me that it's Christian for me to sit here in the dry while those children are over there working so hard to keep their poor little bit of farm and family together!" He strode out, snatching up the lantern from the kitchen table as he left, leaving Elizabeth Ann to stare after him, open-mouthed.

The Retrial

AUGUST 1896

THE CASE AGAINST Henry Thacker had brought him to trial two months after the initial accusation was made; within three months of Anna's death, Henry had been escorted to prison to begin his life sentence. The retrial, officially requested on August 9, 1894, took two years to begin.

Lottie yawned and looked at the clock, remembering how the minute hand had crept so everlastingly slowly on those Sunday afternoons. Now it had unaccountably raced ahead to nearly midnight, and she hadn't finished mending Roy's shirt or even begun letting down the hem of her own best dress. Day after tomorrow they were to board the train for Lansing, and they looked, Lottie thought, like a bunch of tramps. They had stayed so busy, all of them, making sure of having enough to eat and putting extra aside for the taxes.

Butter, eggs, and cream they had sold in the town to the people who were willing to deal with them, and some of the fruit from the cherry tree. What with one thing and another, Ralph's "bank" in the cigar box had mounted to $120, and nothing short of starvation or mortal illness, she knew, would be sufficient for him to withdraw from this.

As she stitched, she mentally reviewed her list. Their train fares were already paid; Mr. Dodge had their tickets, he assured them. Mrs. Waters, infirm though she was becoming, would take Will and Josie in for the few days they would be away. Lottie knew they could never repay her for her many kindnesses to them.

Lunch on the train: Lottie planned to use the last of the flour in the barrel (have to add that to the grocery list, she thought) to make a batch of biscuits tomorrow evening.

Split open and filled with apple butter, they, along with a dozen hard-boiled eggs, would serve as lunch. They were to have their evening meals and breakfasts at the modest boardinghouse that Mr. Covell had found for them.

She wished that Roy could wear one of Papa's shirts, but Roy lacked Papa's wide shoulders. She should have thought ahead. Now there was no time to cut one down. The one she was mending would never look as neat as she'd have liked.

Her own dress, come to think of it, wasn't much to look at either. Once it had been a handsome frock, dark gray, her first "young lady dress," long enough to reach her boot tops. Mother had made it with generous seam allowances, as had been her wont, so that it could be ripped apart and "let out" as she grew. Ladies often "turned" the dress parts so that the darker material, not yet faded by the sun, would appear new and the fabric around the seams wouldn't show the contrast. Lottie knew she needn't let the dress out but must lower the hem; she'd stayed thin even as she grew taller.

Of course, once she had taken out the hem, the alteration was glaringly apparent; a darker strip around the bottom, made noticeable by a lighter line where the crease had been. Mother had been right: "haste makes waste."

Now, of course, turning the dress was no longer an option. It would have to serve. She knew she'd feel bumpkinish and slovenly in it, and she tried to find comfort in the specious notion that nobody was there to look at her hemline anyway.

In happier times, she'd liked the notion of being "an accomplished young lady," but she found as she learned each new needlework skill, the excitement of accomplishment quickly faded, and she grew bored with it. Mending, hemming, embroidery, all seemed to lack the joy that stroking a paintbrush onto paper brought her.

Darning, now, learning to do that had first given her some hope; at the beginning, it had seemed a satisfying pastime. First there was the darning egg, hard wood smoothed, polished, and oiled so that no roughness would "catch" on the fabric as it was slipped into the toe of a sock or the elbow of a shirt. The wood was maple—the grain was elaborate, the finish satiny, the feel of the egg warm and delicious to the palm.

You had to select a thread appropriate to the material, matching not only for color but for thickness and texture, so your darn would be discreet to the eye or to the touch.

You began by sliding your needle through a few threads at the edge of the hole, far enough away from the worn edge so as not to rip through but not so far as to make the patch too big for the opening. Then, draw the thread smoothly across the hole to the other side, and catch a few threads there. Draw the thread back across, neatly parallel to the first thread. Back and forth, drawing tidy, parallel lines with your thread, like the beginnings of crosshatch to shade an area of a picture.

You also had to be sure to make your lines even in tightness; uneven stitches would "bag" in the loose places, pull the fabric and weaken the patch in tight places. Then, at the farthest edge, turn your whole piece a quarter turn and begin to "weave" across your parallel lines, catching threads at the edges, threading your needle tip over and under the lines, to the opposite side, back and forth again, staying smooth and even and parallel.

She had loved darning her first sock, then the elbow of Father's work shirt. Darning seemed like a skill to master, rather than a drudgery like hemming or basting. As she grew proficient, sadly this too had begun to pall. Like hemming and edging buttonholes, the steps became so much mindless repetition, the sort of thing that made your eyes go out of focus so the work blurred, the mind to drowse, outside noises to fade and then become suddenly loud and jangling. No wonder Mother was always "just tired"!

She sighed, snipped the thread, and stuck the needle back into the red puffy pincushion. The dress, like the shirt, would have to do. At least they would be clean and neatly pressed.

LANSING, MICHIGAN AUGUST 6, 1896

THEY WALKED DOWN the corridor as directed by the bored clerk at the big front desk. "Up the stairs and to the right, down past four doors and turn to the left, second door on the right . . ." the middle-aged man with the lank hair had intoned, before Roy interrupted him.

"Wait, slow down! Which stairs?" Impatiently the man flapped a hand over his own shoulder to his left, and looked back down at whatever he had been reading. Bemused, Roy, Ralph, and Lottie went up the stairs, and eventually found their way to what, they fervently hoped, was the correct room. They stopped. Crowds of people buzzed around the door like flies in a dairy. Ralph felt a hard push from behind.

"Whyn't you move your carcass, hayseed?" growled a man as he shoved past, briefly separating Ralph from Roy and Lottie. They hurried through the door and rejoined him, squeezing to the left of the aisle to let the throngs shove rudely past.

"Roy!" Mr. Covell stood near the front of the room, waving his hat at arm's length over the crowd. Huddled together like cows in a snowstorm, they inched their way through the press. "Remember that day the circus tent fell down?" murmured Roy.

Ralph tried to smile at this, but it was difficult. Here was their own family business being aired for these crude and boisterous strangers. Women gossiped, babies wailed, and men in loud suits slapped one another on the back.

It's true that there had been a large attendance at the first trial. Ralph understood at the time that most of those present had a personal reason to be there. Mother had been popular among the women, and everyone had liked Father, until, that is, they had begun to gossip about him and Orah. While he resented those townspeople who had come to see Father "get what he deserved," at least he understood them; everyone had, at one time or another, felt the urge to see someone else taken down a peg or two.

These hordes in the Lansing courthouse, though, who were they? Hardly any of them knew Father or cared anything about Mother and how she had died. They seemed to be there, well, only because they weren't anywhere else. Like town idlers standing around watching a poor old dog die! It made him mad.

He pushed his elbow, hard, against a fat man who was talking loudly to a red-faced man, waving his cigar stuff that dribbled ashes. "Hey, watch it, Sonny!" barked the man. Ralph smiled apologetically but, for a moment, felt better.

"RALPH!" Lottie was aghast. "What have they done to him?" Roy and Ralph looked at one another over her head; the color had drained from Lottie's face, and yes, she was starting to gnaw on her lip again. Roy didn't look much better, Ralph thought. It was a shock, seeing their father for the first time in two years.

William Henry Thacker was dressed in a worn sack suit that looked a size or two too large for him. "Why didn't they get one of his old ones from us?" wondered Ralph.

His hair looked thinner, or perhaps it was the slipshod prison haircut that made it appear that way. He was pale, with a suggestion of redness around the eyes and nose that hinted of a cold or perhaps of recent tears.

These physical changes in Father's appearance were disturbing, but not unexpected. What Lottie meant, Ralph knew, was the change in Father's demeanor. He slumped; worse, he looked up from under his brows with a look half fearful, half ingratiating. It put Ralph in mind of Uriah Heep at his 'umblest. Ralph moved his shoulders uneasily, not wanting to look at Father but unable to look away. He felt ashamed, whether for Father or for himself for feeling ashamed, he wasn't sure.

Lottie turned her shocked eyes away from Father, finally, and began to pay closer attention to Judge Long as he started to speak.

The retrial was held at a session of the Supreme Court of the State of Michigan, in the Supreme Court Room of the Capitol, in the City of Lansing. Charles D. Long was the chief justice. Claudius B. Grant, Robert M. Montgomery, Frank A. Hooker, and Joseph B. Moore were the associate justices.

The *Benzie Banner* had this to say: "No case in the history of Benzie County has attracted the attention of the people as the present trial of Thacker. The courtroom was packed to suffocation in every session of court, as is usually the case in trials of this kind; the women are in a large majority, all straining every nerve to catch any piece of evidence that smacks of scandal and will give them a prominent topic for the next sewing circle; in fact on one or two days of the trial, and until the judge finally came down upon it, a stranger coming into court would have taken it for a kindergarten at first sight or a 'babe in arms show,' as every mother who had a baby brought it with her."

Ralph was annoyed by this when, days later, he read it. For some reason, it offended him that the babies in the courtroom seemed of greater importance to the reporter than the substance of the trial. While he didn't like the public's gawking and unhealthy fascination, it seemed worse for Father's trial to take second place in importance to the "babe in arms show."

When Henry was sworn in, everyone in the room craned forward to hear him. Huddled in the witness chair, he peered up from beneath his brows at Mr. Pratt, who loomed large over him. Lottie felt angry at Mr. Pratt, who now reminded her of Joe Beals.

Joe used to chase the smaller children home, pelting them with ice balls in winter, slush balls in early spring, and even tiny green apples in midsummer. They'd try to run, crying, dropping their mittens and schoolbooks, sometimes falling down and skinning knees or palms of hands. Joe, when confronted about his bullying by an older sister or brother, would give a contemptuous little laugh and say he was only acting in fun and of course he wouldn't do it anymore, if it upset the little ones so much. Then a week or two later, he'd be at it again. Lottie didn't know how many children besides herself had become conditioned to cringe, duck, and look up from beneath their eyebrows at the looming shadow of Joe Beals; she knew it was a lot.

She hated, *hated* seeing Papa look up that way at Mr. Pratt, who, she knew, was just doing his job. She tried not to hate Mr. Pratt as he boomed, "Speak up, Mr. Thacker! The court needs to hear your answers!" and Papa whispered louder, "Yes, sir, I'm trying to."

Mr. Pratt studied his notes and began again: "Is it not so, Mr. Thacker, that on or about the 8th of August, 1894, you wrote a letter to your older sons, to tell them of a dream you had repeatedly, and had indeed had for three consecutive nights, about a note from your wife?"

Henry furrowed his forehead, clearly perplexed. "I'm not sure I understand, sir."

"Did you not write to your sons during August of 1894, concerning a dream you were having?"

"What dream was that, sir?"

Lottie nearly giggled at the look on Mr. Pratt's face. It was the look of many a schoolteacher when yet another student, all owl-eyed innocence, said, to buy time, "I'm not sure I understand the question, ma'am."

"Serves him right," muttered Roy, at her elbow.

Mr. Pratt sighed. "Do you remember the month of August 1894? You were in the state prison at Jackson, I understand."

"Yes, sir. That is still my, er, residence."

"And during that time, did you or did you not have a dream about a letter from your wife?"

"I'm sorry, sir, I don't remember that. It's been so very, very long . . . ," this last came out in a sigh, ". . . and I've had so many dreams."

He looked up at Mr. Pratt, tears in his eyes. "A man dreams so much when he's in prison, dreams of what he's lost and will never hold again . . ."

"Yes, yes, I'm sure he does. This particular dream, however, prompted you to write a letter to your sons, did it not?"

"I don't remember. I wrote whenever I could. They only let you have pen and paper on certain occasions, you see, and only if you're in 'good standing.' I always wanted to tell the children everything, and it seemed I never really managed to tell them anything."

Lottie nodded. That was so. Papa's letters never mentioned how he felt, how he was being treated, the details of his day, or who his friends were, if indeed he had any. But of course he must have; Papa made friends wherever he went, with his hearty laugh and willingness to do favors with no expectation of return. But his letters were dry, dutiful-sounding things, as in, "I am well, trust you all are the same. Yes, do mortgage the west field if you think it will help. Love, Father."

"Mr. Thacker!" Clearly, Mr. Pratt was reaching the end of his patience. Papa ducked, raising his elbow as if to ward off a blow. "The letter in question refers to a crucial point in your appeal, to wit, the discovery of a letter purported to have been written by Mrs. Thacker during her illness. Why in—why are you unable to remember an important item such as this? You are a relatively young man. How can you be so forgetful?"

"Well, sir, it was like this." And Henry, to the fascination of the courtroom of listeners and the jurors in particular, and to Lottie's horror, described an incident where he had quarreled with another prisoner, had struck and been struck in return, had been beaten like an animal and thrown into a windowless cell, three by eight feet, and left there, alone, for over a month.

Mr. Pratt tried unsuccessfully to cut this pitiful narrative short, "Yes, yes, but if we can move on . . ." But Henry, ignoring him, continued to speak. His eyes were fixed on a spot on the courtroom wall opposite himself, but Lottie felt that he was finally sending his letter to her and her brothers telling them how it had been, and was still.

She wanted to cry—no, she wanted to put her hands over her ears and run from the courtroom, but it was too late, now here was this awful tale in her mind, to be added to her trove of ghastly treasures: Mother's unconscious cries as she lay dying, Papa's farewell to them all, the great windstorm that had sent them cowering to the cellar—no, in truth, that storm hadn't been all that dreadful, apart from the scare it had given them. It had taken the great elm but, almost whimsically, had spared the chicken house right near it and most of the fruit trees. And, of course, it had brought them the Rideouts as friends.

Mrs. Rideout, standoffish at first, had eventually thawed and now was a regular, and cordial, customer of their butter-and-egg business.

But now, of course, here was this new memory of Papa, alone in the damp and the dark for a month with no company but his own confused dreams. Papa, constantly and cheerfully out and about in all winds and weather, had then huddled in a three-by-eight hole, promising himself that he would do whatever he could, endure any amount of pain or humiliation, if only they would never put him in there again.

Ralph sat in horror, imagining Father thus immured. Father, who was happiest in early spring, working in the fields with his hat off and his shirt open to the still-chilly breezes as though to soak up every ounce of fresh air and sunshine. Father, enthusiastically wrapping himself up in his heavy winter coat and riding out to work late of an evening. Always outdoors, always hurrying from one task to another, helping a neighbor with a chore and then hurrying to finish his own, rarely still for a moment. Father, then, buried alive without a sight of sun, moon, evening stars, or friendly face. It made Ralph sick to think of it.

Lottie, as Father told his story of confinement, had buried her face in her hands and was sobbing as quietly as she could. Roy had elbowed her, but gently. His eyes were wet as well.

Now the sergeant-at-arms was calling for Roy to testify. Ralph and Lottie both knew that Roy dreaded this moment even more than they did their own turns on the stand. It was the story about Father's "dream" that he didn't want to talk about. It had followed him; one evening he had declared at dinner, "They'll probably put it on my tombstone! 'His father had a dream'! Why can't they forget I ever mentioned it and pay attention to the note that matters?"

Now he stood, hand on Bible, swearing to tell the truth, but his doggedness seemed to Ralph as though he swore, rather, to make somebody suffer if they mentioned Father's dream one more time.

Yet of course, Mr. Pratt did. He seemed unable to distinguish between the note that Father had supposedly sent to Roy, and the letter that Mother had left in the book.

"And do you have that letter with you today?"

"No, sir." Roy glowered up from beneath his brows.

"Where is this letter now?"

"Don't know, sir," growled Roy.

Mr. Pratt looked about him, humorously. "Have you, perhaps, lost it? Blew out the window, maybe?" Several men in the courtroom chortled.

"I set it on the table. Then, later . . ."

Mr. Pratt interrupted, quite rudely, Lottie thought. "So we have only your word that this letter in fact existed at all."

"That's correct, sir." Roy added, sarcastically, "Maybe it did blow out the window."

Ralph noticed that Mr. Pratt didn't find that so humorous. After one or two questions which didn't seem much to the point to Ralph, Mr. Dodge stepped up. He asked Roy to repeat as much of the text of Father's "dream" letter as he was able. Ralph and Lottie both squirmed uncomfortably; even to them, this discussion seemed rambling and pointless.

Henry, who had kept his eyes on the top of the table before him during the early proceedings, was now devouring Roy with his eyes. "Why, he's a young man!" he thought. While he had thought of the children daily, imagining their whereabouts and activities, he hadn't actually considered the effect of two years on their development. In his thoughts, Will was still a little boy, Josie just beginning to talk in sentences. He turned around in his seat and peered through the crowds. There sat Ralph, little changed, alertly watching his brother on the stand, and Lottie, who looked right back at him, trying to smile. She was no longer the little girl who'd hugged him around the waist and called him "Papa." She had a look of Anna about her, he saw now. "She'll never be a beauty," he realized, and wondered if she realized that. He wished he could tell her how little that really mattered. He turned back to the front. He watched Roy continue to testify as though it was the most marvelous thing in the world.

"Where was the letter the last time you saw it?"

"I'd set it on the table in the kitchen."

"And did anyone else come into the kitchen before you noticed the letter was missing?"

"Yes, sir. Orah Bunker came to visit. She came in from the back porch."

Orah, seated halfway down the aisle, flanked by her parents, scowled. Her life had been bitter, indeed, since Henry's conviction. At term's end she had packed her few belongings and said farewell to the Judsons. Though they'd allowed her to stay on, sitting at table had become uncomfortable for all of them.

She had stopped by the Thackers last. She would miss Lottie and the little ones. Ralph felt shy of her; he kept his counsel and spoke politely to her, but still she felt unaccountably guilty before him. Roy, after growling "Come in," had stayed in the kitchen and let her take herself into the parlor. When she last saw him he'd been poking moodily at the fire in the kitchen stove.

She had taken herself to the train station and, with no one to see her off, had gone home. A chilly reception had awaited her there. Torrence, still at home, had little to say to her but managed, silently, to convey his disdain for her whenever possible. Her mother escorted her to town for weekly shopping, and to church on Sundays; the rest of the time she was expected to stay inside the house, helping with the housework or sitting in her room moodily leafing through her few remaining schoolbooks. Her father, she knew, still had hopes of marrying her off. "Damaged goods" or not, she was a good worker.

Now here she was on the stand, being questioned by Mr. Pratt about a letter than she had never seen and probably never existed. That Roy!

"No, sir, I never actually saw the contents of any such letter." Mischievously she looked directly at Roy and added, "Perhaps that's what he was burning in the kitchen stove the last time I visited there."

"And can you tell us the purpose of that visit?"

"Sir?"

"Why were you at the Thackers on the day in question?"

"Oh, I'd stopped by to say goodbye. I was leaving Benzonia, to return to Arcadia."

Mr. Pratt took a deep breath, as though about to dive into chilly waters. "And would you describe for the court the nature of your relationship with the Thacker family?"

Mr. Dodge, who, Ralph noticed, had been gathering himself alertly like a cat ready to spring, jumped up to object.

"Pretty spry for a fellow of his years and girth," thought Ralph, then stifled the thought as disrespectful.

"Counselors will approach the bench, please," intoned Judge Long. They complied.

"Mr. Pratt, what is the objective of your current line of questioning?"

"If it please your honor, we wish to further examine the motives of the defendant, based on his relationship to the witness." Judge Long's heavy eyebrows drew together.

"I myself have scrutinized the transcript of this case in some detail. The witness is on the stand for one agreed-upon purpose, and that is to place the whereabouts of this much-disputed letter from the defendant. No other line of questioning will be tolerated." He fixed Mr. Pratt with the baleful eye of an old tomcat studying a rival, then turned to Mr. Dodge.

"And I fervently hope and expect that you will not take up the court's time with any discussions about the defendant's character, how many favors he has done for his neighbors and how many widows and orphans he has fed and clothed, is that understood, Mr. Dodge?"

Mr. Dodge nodded, remembered himself, and said, "Yes, your honor."

Judge Long steepled his hands and looked over them at the two lawyers. "Gentlemen, we have convened four other justices besides myself to retry a man for murder. Not adultery. Not character faults or personal virtues. Murder. I am not here to judge the defendant's fitness to be a deacon of the church. Justices Grant, Montgomery, Hooker, and Moore are not here to determine whether Mr. Thacker would be a good neighbor. Our time is as valuable as anyone else's, and we don't wish to be led astray by irrelevancies. Do I make myself clear?"

"Yes, your honor," echoed both lawyers.

Orah, released by Mr. Dodge with no cross-examination, left the stand, and, escorted by her parents, she left the courtroom without a single look at Henry.

The prosecution proceeded, as the *Benzie Banner* reported, "with no new developments different from the former trial except the testimony of Deputy Sheriff James Pettit and Herbert Balch, who testified as to statements made by Thacker during the first few days of his arrest, in which, according to the evidence of Pettit and Balch, Thacker said 'they may find poison in the stomach but the next thing is to guess how it got there.' Mr. Pettit made it much stronger in his evidence, claiming that Mr. Thacker said, 'There is no doubt they will find poison in her stomach.'"

MONDAY, AUGUST 9, 1896

MR. DODGE CALLED Henry to the stand.

"Mr. Thacker, it was my understanding, based on testimony from your first trial, that at the time of your wife's illness you were no longer on speaking terms with your sister-in-law, one Charlotte Spencer. Is that correct, sir?"

"Yes, sir. She and I rarely spoke to one another directly. Since she was bedfast quite often, it was easy to avoid her; I simply stayed away from her room. I suppose you might blame me for this, as much as . . . ."

"That will suffice, thank you. Now, Mr. Thacker, allow me to refresh your memory of the previous trial, in July of 1894. Miss Spencer, as you recall, was the primary witness for the People. We would like, if possible, to understand the basis of her complaints against you, the man whom she might well have viewed as a brother."

Henry shook his head sadly. "It's true, sir, that for quite some time Miss Spencer and I lived under the same roof in perfect amity, much as you say, as brother and sister might. Then, what with one thing and another, things changed."

"Allow me to refresh the court's memory. Miss Spencer stated at several places in her testimony . . ." And Mr. Dodge proceeded to read aloud from his notes Charlotte's damning testimony about Henry's behavior with Orah. Henry, ears red, looked at the floor.

His children, also, studied their feet and wished themselves elsewhere.

"Every time the talk dies down, something stirs it up again," thought Ralph.

Eventually the mortifying recital wound to a finish.

"Mr. Thacker, would you explain to the court the reason for your later antipathy toward Miss Spencer?" asked Mr. Dodge on the stand.

Mr. Dodge looked at Henry levelly and patiently awaited his response. He, Mr. Covell, and Henry had discussed this particular point prior to the retrial, with some heat on Covell's part. "We must make it abundantly clear to the court that your sister-in-law's testimony is flawed."

"I'd really rather not, sir," responded Henry apologetically.

"Why ever not? Your sister-in-law has no particular claim to virtue in the death of her sister, having deserted her several days prior to Mrs. Thacker's death, and is the primary cause of your first trial and conviction!"

"I haven't held that against her, especially. She's a sad, sick woman and I know she grieves for Anna as much as any of us. I couldn't stand up in a courtroom and slander her, it would be cruel and shameful."

"Your family needs you at home! It is cruel and shameful to leave two young children in the care of two boys and a girl no older than my youngest! Roy has already been in trouble once. You have a responsibility to your children, and your sister-in-law is quite old enough to face the consequences of her own actions. We don't ask for you to 'slander' her, but only to tell the truth, man! It is necessary for the court, and for us, to understand the basis of her antipathy, if we're to combat the pernicious effects of her former testimony. Now tell us, why did Miss Spencer apparently feel greater umbrage about your friendship for Miss Bunker than even your own wife?"

Reluctantly, Henry had acquiesced.

Now, in court, Henry spoke slowly. "Charlotte Spencer and I used to be friends, and I had truly thought of her as a sister. Then something happened, soon after her return from the hospital." He stopped, shifting uncomfortably in the chair, and the tips of his ears blazed red. His voice had dropped at the word "hospital," so that Mr. Dodge had to lean forward to hear him.

"Speak up, please, so that the court can hear you. What was it that happened?"

"She came to me, and she said . . ." He swallowed, took a breath, opened his mouth, closed it, and then said in a rush, "She came to me and said, 'Henry, I find I am growing to think too much of you and I think the only thing to do for the good of us is for you not to come around where I am, as every time you come into my presence I feel a thrill pass over me and I grow more and more to look for your return when you are away from me, so I think you must not come where I am.'"

"Huh!" exclaimed Roy. Ralph wasn't sure whether the sound was a laugh or simply a sound of surprise. He heard a sharp intake of breath from Lottie; it was nearly drowned in the wave of whispers and mutters from the observers.

"Well, sir, I didn't quite know how to reply to this, so I said something, maybe like 'I see' or 'all right,' and quickly retired. After that, I, well, I kept my distance. I just didn't want to be around her at all. I thought she'd be grateful for it, but she didn't seem to be."

Lottie was recalled to the stand. Once again, she told the story of Josie's illness. She told about the "skellingtons," which drew a smile from several women in the room. Henry smiled at her, the edges of his lips trembling.

MONDAY EVENING, AUGUST 9, 1896

MR. PRATT PACED the floor, breathing heavily. A lifelong teetotaler, just now he understood the need for a cigar to chomp on, enveloping everyone around him with clouds of noxious smoke. Even without aid of the "devil weed," however, he managed to accomplish his goal. In short, he fumed, and filled the air with his exhalations.

"Ridiculous! Where'd you say Judge Long got his diploma, at the Pea-Pod Junction School of Fiddle-Dee-Dee? The man's gutted our entire case, and he knows it. Without the Bunker girl's testimony, all we have is the same tired old warmed-up hash of the last trial!"

Mr. Warner lay on his bed, eyes closed. For two days he had fought unsuccessfully against a miserable case of quinsy. Though the fever had, just this morning, ebbed, his throat had grown more miserably sore. When he last examined it in the mirror, it had blazed red, the back of it clustered with dusty-looking white blisters thick as grape clusters. Speaking was agony; swallowing was worse. It felt to him as though he tried to swallow a large India-rubber ball with pins protruding all around it.

With difficulty, he turned his mind from this image to the work at hand. He too had been disappointed in the swift banishment of their witness. Pratt had wanted to return the Spencer woman to the stand, but Mr. Warner had vetoed that suggestion. "The woman's crazy as an outhouse rat; you can imagine what Judge Long would say if she veered off onto one of her tangents. Which, of course, she would do. She's known for it. I'm surprised the jury believed a word of her testimony the first time, actually."

Pratt nodded gloomily. "Our final hurrah, then, is the testimony against the suicide note. Slim hope."

"May as well not bother," croaked Mr. Warner. "Long's already read those depositions a dozen times, and he seemed unimpressed. There are as many arguments for it as against it, and the jurors will see that."

Mr. Pratt's pacing slowed. "That's pretty much all there is then, isn't it?"

"Um, hmmm," rumbled Mr. Warner, and let himself slip back into doze.

In a way, reflected Mr. Pratt, it was a relief to hand the tattered remains of the People's case back to Judge Long and let the panel of judges decide.

Obviously, he and Warner were required to do their best for the People, but secretly, he had had doubts since Thacker's conviction. Unbeknownst to Warner, he had brooded over his notes for months after Thacker was sent up. At first it had seemed open-and-shut, a classic case: philandering husband, poisoned wife, and the grieving sister leading the crusade to bring the murderer to justice.

He wasn't sure when the first doubts had crept in. Despite the defendant's womanly weeping at his conviction, Mr. Thacker otherwise had behaved well, neither overly protesting his innocence nor displaying the cynicism that a murdering philanderer might be expected to display.

Too, it was true that Mr. Thacker had had no more opportunity to do the deed than others in the household. The older children, the spinster sister (who was said to have been sweet on Thacker in her younger days), even the impeccably upright Mary E. C. Bailey had brought food and drink to the victim.

Arsenic was easily come by. In the Pratt outhouse, a box of "Rough on Rats" sat up on a high shelf, out of reach of small children but close at hand for dusting down the holes when vermin activity surpassed acceptable levels. He supposed the Thackers used theirs similarly.

The arsenic that Spencer had delivered to Mary Bailey, now, where had that originated? Had Thacker truly managed, under the very noses of his children, to sneak it into the sickroom food and drink? The older girl, Lottie, did much of the food preparation and serving. Lottie was only fourteen, and often played with his own daughter; Lottie Thacker would be able to perform murder, he knew, when pigs learned to fly. The older boys were boys, only in the kitchen long enough to inhale whatever food was put before them. It would have been mighty obvious had they suddenly begun cooking or even serving food to their aunt and mother.

Thacker had always been thought of as a kind and amiable man. Miss Spencer, on the other hand, had long had the reputation of being, well, unstable. Had she led the charge to convict Thacker because she was sure he had murdered her sister, or did she herself have something to hide?

The husband or the sister? What had seemed so obvious in those early days became less clear to him as the months passed.

He and Warner had prosecuted this case to the best of their abilities, and would see it through to the end. Still, he was glad the end was close and wiser heads than they might make the decision this second time.

TUESDAY, AUGUST 10, 1896

MR. PRATT WAS truly impressed by Warner's argument. Out of the wreckage of their case, he pieced together an edifice that, while it swayed slightly in the winds of conflicting evidence, yet held. Periodically, the man paused and, wincing, took a swallow of licorice-water to soothe his fiery throat. Despite the agony the man endured to perform this hour-and-a-half speech, as the *Benzie Banner* later wrote, "during the short recess which followed it was common talk that Warner had made the effort of his life and that the interests of Benzie County would be well looked after as long as he remained in charge of the prosecution of offences."

Pratt was also impressed by Mr. Dodge's subsequent argument for the defense. The man presented many of the possibilities that he himself had been considering, though, of course, Dodge presented them with an air of surety that, Pratt could tell, impressed Judge Long and two of his associates. Judge Hooker, it seemed, was more skeptical, often shaking his head as he made notes. Once, when Mr. Dodge advanced the possibility that Roy, that hotheaded young troublemaker, not only had as much access to his aunt's and mother's meals as Thacker had but also was a disobedient son, Hooker had begun to roll his eyes. Feeling Mr. Pratt's eyes upon him, however, he scowled and quickly resumed his judicial demeanor. He glanced quickly to where Roy Thacker sat with his brother (what was his name? Roger?) and sister. Roy sat poker-faced, as though enduring a rather boring and windy sermon.

Covell's performance, thought Mr. Pratt, was just that. The man seemed to have forgotten his responsibility to logic and the rule of law, depending on sheer emotion to carry the day. He narrowly skirted Judge Long's injunction against odes to Thacker's generosity to his fellows, brushing by with ". . . respected by his fellows at his job as deputy sheriff and at his church as a deacon." Then he laid on with the whip and sent his descriptive powers a-gallop, shamelessly describing "the little orphan children left at home, with their father in disgrace and their mother barely cold in the grave."

Pratt sneaked a surreptitious glance at the "little orphan children." Placid as cows after milking, they sat in a row looking straight ahead. The younger son's (Ralph! That was the name!) mouth twitched at the corner; Mr. Pratt couldn't tell what emotion that betrayed. Thacker's willingness to endure confinement and beatings rather than defame his infirm sister-in-law's good name was good for another ten minutes.

Judge Long endured the oration in stone-faced immobility. Many of the spectators, who'd come in to ogle a bloodthirsty convicted murderer, appeared completely won over by Covell's bathos. The other judges remained impassive.

While Dodge's defense had added fuel to Mr. Pratt's doubts, Covell's speechifying nearly quelled them again. He felt disgust for himself. "What's the matter with you, with all this shilly-shallying?" he scolded himself, but he now realized that in truth, he knew no more now than when he had first begun, with Warner, to prepare the case of the *People of the State of Michigan vs. William Henry Thacker* back there in May of 1894.

The defense rested. Warner, looking pale and exhausted, whispered, "See what you can do to offset the taste of that abominable performance," and left him to it.

Mr. Pratt gathered his scattered notes, took a breath to focus himself, and began to speak. As the *Banner* reported, "During it he followed the case from its beginning, step by step, point by point, dwelling upon telling features of the people's testimony with strong and convincing logic, backed up by his own style of eloquence which makes one feel that he would prefer to have him defending than assisting in the prosecution of a case against him."

RALPH TIED HIS TIE with hands that shook slightly. He felt, as Father used to say, "nervous as a long-tailed cat in a roomful of rockers." Father had a store of silly sayings; some of them made Mother frown and shake her head reprovingly, but this one had always made them all smile, picturing the tabby in question mincing her way thorough the dangerous room. Today they all seemed to sympathize with the cat—Roy and Lottie were jumpy as well.

He realized that none of them had eaten with their usual appetite for two days, nor slept very well. Nerves, partly, but also due to the greasy, heavy boardinghouse fare and the big city noises that never seemed to end, even at night. City people never slept, it seemed.

Their agony was to be short-lived, anyway; they'd know, for good or ill, today. Father would either come home with them or return to prison forever. Either way, they'd all manage, he concluded to himself. They went to breakfast, where all three silently pushed their watery scrambled eggs around on their plates until it was time to leave for court.

Mr. Pratt finished his summation: "Gentlemen of the court, I leave it to you to perform your duty and return William Henry Thacker to serve the remainder of his just sentence. I rest my case."

"Oh, hum!" Ralph jumped; it was Lottie who'd yawned loudly as a small child might. He looked at her in surprise; she sat, hand before her mouth, mortified. "It just slipped out," she whispered to him.

"Well maybe I'm the only long-tailed cat in the room," he thought. Roy looked a million miles away, as though Mr. Pratt's exhortations to the judges were nothing to do with them.

The judges had seemed an emotionless bunch; neither Father's attorneys nor the state's had seemed to "play" to them in the same way they had to the jurors two years ago. Ralph had rarely bothered to check their faces for possible clues as to their sympathies. Not that it mattered, he supposed, they'd all know soon enough how the judges felt. His hands began to sweat; why was it so hot in here? He watched the men file from the room.

"Want to take a turn around the hallway while we wait?"

Lottie shook her head.

"They'll be out for a little while, anyway," urged Ralph. "Myself, I feel as if I'd go crazy if I didn't move around."

This was true. As the final exhortations had droned on, he'd become aware of a tightening, almost an itch below his shoulder blades. Surreptitiously he'd tried to ease it by tensing, then relaxing the muscles along his spine. It didn't help. He had a vision of backing up to a doorjamb and slamming himself, backward, against it. It would hurt, but that maddening crawly feeling might ease. He couldn't think of a way to bring this about without drawing attention to himself, and was now suffering mightily.

Lottie, however, was determined not to budge. "You go without me, please. I'll just stay here in case—in case they come back soon."

In his haste to move about, Ralph left her there. Roy, curious despite his need to visit the privy, stayed behind. "Why not come out with us, Lottie? You must be as tired of sitting here as we are."

Her eyes filled with sudden tears. She blinked them away. "I wasn't there, the last time, remember?"

She noticed the lady in the seat in front of them, cocking an ear as though listening to her. The cherries on the lady's hat quivered slightly, as though they were antennae. Lottie's voice dropped to a whisper.

"I stayed home, and I was going to stay awake until you came home with the news, but it got late and I fell asleep."

Her lips quivered, and she bit the lower one. "I fell asleep, Roy. I wasn't there and I fell asleep and they said he was guilty. I—I know it's silly to think it would have been different if I'd been there, but it feels to me that way. If I stay here, if I'm here when they come back, maybe this time . . ." The rebellious lip quivered again. She wiped her eyes angrily in the crook of her elbow and finished, so low that Roy had to lean down to hear it, ". . . maybe this time they'll find him 'not guilty.'"

"Just as you like, Puss. I'll go take a turn or two, but don't worry, we'll come back when it's time."

After his privy visit, he and Ralph tramped up and down the long hallway outside the courtroom. Mr. Covell, as nervous as the cat himself, Ralph noted, brought them some jam sandwiches which they (though not Lottie, who shook her head decisively at the offer) hastily wolfed down. They might have taken their time, as it turned out; it was midafternoon before the judges returned.

Years later, Ralph couldn't have dredged up the names of all the judges and the clerks. Until the day of his death over eighty years later, however, he could bring one man's image up in his mind. He wore a houndstooth sack suit; his collar was starched so stiffly that it pushed his jowls up slightly. His bald head shone with a light coating of perspiration; a bead of moisture glistened in his neatly trimmed goatee. The man's eyes were small and dark, piercing, sunk deeply under his black brows, yet they appeared kindly to Ralph.

"Maybe I just want to think that," he thought to himself. "Maybe he thinks the worst of Father and will want to see him in prison forever ..."

But no, the words, in a light tenor voice, carried clearly across the room, "We find the defendant not guilty of the charges," and Father swayed slightly, as if buffeted by a strong wind, and then simply stood there, his shoulders drooping wearily.

LOTTIE HAD ALWAYS imagined how it would be if Father were to be freed, the joyous exclamations, hugs, Papa picking her up and swinging her around the way he used to when she was younger, the walk with him through town, welcoming hails from neighbors' front doors. She felt foolish now, for even thinking such a thing. Either Father had become a stranger, or they had all changed. It had started out properly; Mr. Covell and Mr. Dodge had enthusiastically shaken Father by the hand after the verdict. Father had smiled politely and returned the handshakes, but Lottie could see that he appeared dazed, like a man whose horse had run under a low-hanging branch and swept him to the ground. He blinked and shook his head, then sat back down at the table.

Roy and Ralph helped her to her own feet; she realized that her legs shook and wanted to fold beneath her. The three of them made their way to the front of the room where Mr. Covell, smiling, waved them over. They stopped in a row before the table, suddenly shy.

"Well, Father," mumbled Roy, and held out his hand. Henry stood up and looked at his children. His mouth trembled and he sat down yet again, fumbling in the pockets of his suit. Ralph pulled out his own handkerchief and offered it to his father. Henry buried his face in the cloth for a moment, then blew his nose, wiped his eyes, and composed himself.

"Covell, if you will take these young people to their lodgings to collect their things, I will purchase tickets for the evening train for them all." Mr. Dodge's voice was slightly hoarse, Ralph was surprised to note.

They were herded toward the courtroom door by Mr. Covell. Lottie whirled away and rushed back to the table, where Henry had begun to pull himself, swaying somewhat, to his feet again. He looked like a man who'd spent the day plowing and now must clean the barn. "Papa!" whispered Lottie, and threw her arms around him, trembling.

He stood rigid for a moment, then patted her on the shoulder, and then put her away from him, rather absently. "Go with Mr. Covell now, Lottie. We'll talk on the train."

Henry Comes Home

HENRY SIGHED and leaned his head against the window to block his own reflection, the better to see and focus on the world outside. For two years his eyes had hungered to see these things, the corn in tassel, leaves drooping and whispering in a hot summer breeze, a wind rippling across a wheat field like waves on a pond, a broad oak with arms winnowing the sky and bulky body shading the pasture beneath. He had felt the hunger so desperately sometimes that he'd bitten his own forearm to stifle an open-mouthed moan.

His diaphragm clenched as he thought of those times; he'd felt, it seemed, like the cows when their calves were taken from them. It was necessary, if humans were to have the milk, but for the first several days those calves, penned within hearing distance of their mothers, had wailed, bleating a sound like "Aw want my mmmmammmaaaa—" and the mothers had made the most desperate, hungry sounds in response. During those times Henry sometimes had wanted to cover his ears and leave the noisy, heartbreaking barn, but of course the milking needed to be done so he'd done it, trying not to imagine that the dumb brutes had any feelings like human mothers would have under the same circumstances. Of course they didn't, he knew that, but those deep, moaning wails smote him as he went about his tasks.

When he lay in prison at night, feeling that deep hunger to sweep his eyes across an open field of grass just once, he had to stifle his own outcries, or the guards or his fellow prisoners would surely call out, as he had to those desperate mothers, "Aaaw, hush up, whyn't you?" They might strike him, as well. He had indeed been struck a time or two, something that had never happened to him since he was an unruly child. Thank heavens he'd never struck one of his cows at such a time!

Now he fixed his eyes on the darkening land outside the windows and let them drink their fill. Would he continue to keep cows, now?

Probably, and yet the thought of the calf-weaning made tears come to his eyes again.

He sighed again, a hurt, weary sound. Lottie, choked by pity, reached a hand toward her father, but he kept his eyes turned to the window that held, as far as Lottie could see, only a reflection of his own face.

Henry felt the eyes of his children on him, and as dusk descended and the lights were lit in the train car, he could see their reflections in the window, staring at him. He wished they wouldn't do that, but could think of no way to deflect their attention. As the last light streaked the western sky, he saw a bat flitter crazily this way and that, chasing the evening insects. It disappeared from view as the train continued homeward.

Anna, of course, would not be there, to welcome him or push him away impatiently. The house was also relieved, he knew, of the heavy, sickly presence of Charlotte. Abruptly he turned to Ralph. "How is Star? Does he still wheeze?"

"Only when he's expected to work," Ralph replied, surprised. Odd, that he had thought to ask about Star, when he hadn't said a thing about Will or Josie!

THEY WALKED the hill from the station. Henry panted slightly; when Ralph looked at him curiously, he ducked his head and smiled. "Nerves, I imagine," he explained. "I dreamed about walking up this hill, oh, so many times. I thought I'd never see it again."

The house came into view. "It's so shabby! How did we let it get that way?" thought Lottie, and she and Ralph exchanged a look of culpability. Henry appeared not to notice. He sprang up the steps eagerly and strode to the door, then paused, hand on knob, and licked his lips.

"Is—is anybody else in there?" At the odd looks of his children, he clarified, "Who stayed here with Will and Josie? Are they in there?"

"They're with Mrs. Waters, at her house," Lottie reassured him. "We can fetch them in the morning."

He stepped into the front hallway and stopped by the rack, marveling.

"My hat. Just hanging there like it was waiting for me." He quickly raised an arm, dabbed his eyes on his sleeve. Ralph wondered what Father'd done with the handkerchief he'd lent him in the courtroom. "Do you know, I didn't realize how much a man's hat becomes a part of him until I didn't have it at, at the place. I used to think, sometimes, that they took our hats away so we wouldn't go thinking we were still men."

Ralph looked away, embarrassed.

"Foolish, I know, but a man takes all kinds of notions, sometimes."

He hung the hat back up, strode across the parlor and through the other door. They heard his steps down the hallway, up the stairs, dying away down the hall above them. A door closed.

Henry looked at the items atop the bureau. A saucer with some collar buttons, a hairbrush, Anna's old New Testament that she'd rarely used but liked to keep handy. A hand mirror, lightly powdered with dust; Lottie rarely dusted or even came into this room, though sometimes Josie and Will's games brought them through it.

He looked at himself in the mirror, then looked away. Mirrors were scarce in prison, and it now seemed rude to stare. He half expected his reflection to scowl and snarl, "Here! What're you lookin' at?" He turned and looked at the bed. It leered back at him, long empty, with dusty coverlet.

His suits hung in the wardrobe; slowly he divested himself of the ill-fitting sack suit he'd worn all the days of the trial. The shirt smelled; he wrinkled his nose, then wadded it up and scrubbed beneath his arms with it. Slowly at first, then more quickly, he dressed in his own clothes. They hung loosely, but were a better fit than the outfit he had come home in. He sat down and pulled on a pair of shoes. His feet immediately identified them as his own.

Lottie had brewed tea. "There's no cream, I'm afraid. Mr. Rideout's been seeing to the stock, and we told him to take whatever he wanted."

"This is fine." He took a grateful sip, enjoying the steam on his face, the smooth feel of the teacup handle in his hands, the spicy aroma of the tea, the fresh smell of the summer air through the window. Even the chicken yard's acrid tang smelled clean, free, and open to him. Foolish, he knew, but he had spent months smelling those other smells that had soaked his membranes, permeated his being. Old, stale, dirty, closed in, and nasty.

He lay in bed, eyes on his open window. It was hot. The mattress was too soft and too large. It stretched for miles in all directions. And quiet! No, noisy! It was both. The night was empty of the sounds of hard-shod feet pacing, fists occasionally whacking bars with a heavy wooden billy, moans, sighs, curses, and sounds of too many men breaking wind noisily from eating the rotten prison food. The velvet brown night was filled with the sounds of creatures, the "brrrrrzzzeeep!" of cicadas, the "ch-ch-zee, ch-ch-zee" of katydids. A distant owl, a closer dog. He began to drowse but was jerked wide awake by a shriek. He froze, mind darting down the corridor to identify the victim. He'd heard this sound before. After a moment he relaxed, laughing softly. An unwary rabbit, taken by a cat.

Missionary to the End

MANISTEE, MICHIGAN, AUGUST 12, 1896

CHARLOTTE TOOK A DEEP BREATH and stepped into the dining room at Mrs. Porter's boardinghouse. She had moved there nearly two years ago. It seemed best, in view of the circumstances. Though she knew that she'd done the same thing any decent person would have in testifying against Henry, still she felt hostility directed toward her from various quarters of Benzonia. Mrs. Bailey, for example, had remained outwardly civil, and yet Charlotte felt a distance, a subtle chill in her manner after the trial. And Mrs. Waters, that dear friend of their childhood, seemed to have cooled toward her as well.

Her nieces and nephews of course were lost to her. As kind and loving as she'd always been to them, as many gifts as she'd sent them from Turkey (remember those Turkish slippers, so cunningly embroidered, the pointed toes so quaintly turned up?), they now persisted in snubbing her quite rudely when she encountered them in public. The children had never bothered to visit since the time she had spoken truthfully on the witness stand about their father's many sins and crimes. She knew they were in the wrong, and yet it stung.

Too, there was the disrespect from common idlers as she passed them on the street or in the drugstore or the dry goods store. Men and boys standing in groups, wasting time they might have turned to better use, would whisper together and snigger. Often they didn't bother lowering their voices; "old maid sister" was the most common epithet. Of course she held her head high and affected not to notice; they were beneath the notice of decent women, and yet their jeering hisses stung as well.

Yes, sadly she realized that what had been her home since early childhood now pinched like a pair of outgrown boots. Times had changed, and not for the better. Fortuitously, she had attended the Congregationalist Church at Manistee following a joint missionary society gathering, and found the membership there most congenial. With a certain bitter satisfaction ("She'll miss that five dollars a month," she thought of her landlady), she gave her notice to Mrs. Bailey.

She attended a small farewell reception held by the ladies of the Benzonia Congregationalist Church, packed her trunk, and a few days later she had settled comfortably into a first-floor room at Mrs. Porter's, overlooking the town common.

The ladies seemed eager to hear about the trials and triumphs of the Turkish mission; recently there had been talk of sending another local person to eastern Turkey, to help in the struggle against the heathen Turk.

And now, Jesus help her, more disgrace had struck, like an ill-timed flash of lightning. Henry, that lying adulterer, had slandered her from the witness stand during his second trial. Not content to murder her sister, he had now, with the encouragement, no doubt, of the loose woman he'd whored around with four years ago, murdered the reputation of his own sister-in-law.

"Henry, I find that I am growing to think too much of you . . ." The hideous words in the *Benzie Banner* had seared her eyes, screamed in her ears. She knew only too well the sensation those lying words must have made among her acquaintances in Benzonia. She could picture Dr. Dean and Mary Bailey smirking at one another knowingly. She shuddered again. Had the slander reached Manistee? How many people had read this, heard about it from their neighbors?

She stepped through the doorway. Betty Jean, Mrs. Porter's hired girl, paused in setting the table. "Oh, is it six o'clock already? My land! Sit down, Miss Spencer, the dumplings won't take but a few minutes more. Isn't Mr. Calvin on his way down yet?" Chattering, Betty Jean bustled back toward the kitchen. Charlotte heaved a gentle sigh and sank into her chair. There had been no outward sign in Betty Jean's face that she knew. For a few more minutes, anyway, her secret was safe.

Orphans No More

LOTTIE AWOKE EARLY, feeling unaccountably joyous. Oh! Papa was home! Home for good! She slid out of bed, quickly changed nightgown for undergarments and a light cotton dress, and went downstairs, barefoot. She was getting too old to run barefoot in the summer, but for to-day, anyway, she would be a child again, a girl whose father now stirred in the room down the hall. She sighed happily and skipped down the stairs, went silently through the kitchen, out the back door, and went to look for eggs.

Henry was downstairs early as well. It made Ralph itchy to watch him meander from house to barn, yard to hen yard, back to the barn, back to the house, roaming from room to room, looking out windows, fingering curtains, picking up dishes and setting them back down. Now he sat, running his hands across the tabletop and watching as Lottie wordlessly washed the dishes.

"Ralph, did you say that Star's still working?"

"Just barely, I'm afraid, Father. He's really showing his age. I've been working with Esmeralda—she's steadying down, though still inclined to be skittish at times."

"Esmeralda? The filly?"

"Esmeralda, the mare, yes."

"But Star can still be worked?"

"If not too hard. He needs to rest every now and then." Ralph was shocked to realize how annoyed he was becoming. This was not a stranger, riffling the waters of their smooth daily schedule and bother-ing the livestock—this was Father, the rightful owner of all they had.

Still he worried about poor old Star, old and wheezy, but still willing, if not able, to do a day's work. What would be expected of him now? But when Henry stood up he went out the front door, not the back.

Mrs. Tennor gasped. "I declare, wasn't that Henry Thacker? That or his ghost, anyway; it looked just like him!"

"Do you suppose he's gotten out?" The two women peered out of the big grocery store window.

"Why, it must be! Look there, he's shaking hands with Mr. Dodge!"

"I don't know as I'd want to shake hands with him."

"Look! There he goes down toward the lake!" They craned after him, but Henry had disappeared from sight.

With the ten-dollar bill that Mr. Covell had discreetly slipped to him, he purchased a train ticket to Arcadia.

"YES?" Mrs. Jesse Bunker stared at the man on the doorstep for a mo-ment; then as recognition bloomed she tried to close the door. "Go away! We have nothing to say to you."

"Mrs. Bunker, please!" said Henry, his foot wedged in the opening.

"Remove your foot, please, or I shall have to call for help. No, don't—Jesse!" This last was shouted to her husband, who was nowhere in sight.

"Mother! What's—" Orah stopped, hand on the newel post, and stared at the sight of Henry's red face, framed by the narrow gap in the door.

"Get upstairs!" stormed Mrs. Bunker. "Close and lock your door, Orah! No! Wait! Go out back and fetch your father! Oh!"

This last, as Henry shoved the door open and squeezed in past her. Orah stood, rooted to the spot.

"Orah, would you ask your father to come in here, please?" Orah turned and left the room.

"I won't ask you to sit down," Mrs. Bunker said stiffly. "Mr. Bunker will set you on your way soon enough, and Torrence will be glad to assist him."

"I hope they don't," said Henry, and stood patiently until Jesse entered.

"Why are you here, Thacker?" he demanded. "Orah tells me you pushed your way in here and refused to leave. You'll leave now, by God, or I'll . . ."

"Please, Mr. Bunker, let me speak first. I've come to . . ."

As her father boomed threats and Henry expostulated, Orah slid further into the room and sat in the easy chair behind her mother, who saw the motion and whirled around.

"What are you doing in here, Missy? Get upstairs this instant!"

Orah gave her head a little shake, barely perceptible; it was the gesture of a horse annoyed by a gnat. Her lips thinned slightly in a smile; one eye half closed, she looked directly at Henry, who noticed her regard and reddened.

"When did you get out?"

His voice was barely a whisper. "Last evening. I came home on the night train, and came straight here this morning."

Virginia turned triumphantly to Orah. "The man has hardly paused to greet his children, and here he is on our doorstep. That's the kind of man he is!"

"A man needs good things to think about when he's in prison, else he'll go crazy. I'd think about the sun coming up over the lake, all those diamonds dancing in the ripples, or else I'd think about the children, what they were doing, and yes, I thought about you."

Pleased, Orah looked down at her hands, then back up.

"What do you want of me?" she asked simply.

Virginia snorted. "A man like that only wants one thing."

"I'm asking you to marry me. If you'll have me, that is. I know that I'm a little old for you . . ."

Virginia inflated with rage. "That's disgusting! Get out of this house, this minute!"

Jesse barked a hard incredulous bark of laughter. "Marry her? Do you have any notion the trouble you've brought to our family? Why in the world would my daughter marry a man like you?"

Henry looked at Orah, who smiled. It was a wry, noncommittal sort of smile, but Henry smiled back with his own timid tentative one. "Will you marry me, Orah?"

"You might as well," remarked Torrence, who'd stepped in behind Orah. "Nobody else is going to have you."

Orah glared at him, but Jesse's shoulders sagged, as he realized the truth of Torrence's words.

After some initial sputtering, Virginia acquiesced. Orah rode to the Manistee County justice of the peace, bracketed by her parents, Henry in the carriage behind them. At 3:45 P.M., they boarded the train for Benzonia, as Mr. and Mrs. Henry Thacker.

Another Shock for Benzonia

FRED BRANSON, Benzonia station's porter, pursed his lips and squinted his eyes. There was that Henry Thacker again, fresh out of prison, gone away and come back on the same day, and wasn't that Orah Bunker, his fancy piece, stepping down behind him, bold as brass, taking his hand? It was! Thunderstruck, he stared at her as she stepped up to him and nodded regally.

"Mr. Branson, I'm sure you don't remember me . . ."

"Indeed, I do remember you, Orah Bunker. I sh'd think you'd be ashamed to come back here, and with him, at that!"

"Fred, I'd like you meet my wife. We were married just this afternoon."

"Well, I'll be . . ."

"Mrs. Thacker will have a trunk arriving on the later train. We'd appreciate it if you'd store it overnight, and I'll have one of my boys come and pick it up in the morning." Arm in arm they left the platform, blissfully unaware of the scorching regard that followed them.

"THINGS WILL BE a little tight for a while, Orah. The trial expenses took quite a toll on us all. I might have to back off from farming for a little while and focus on the farm equipment business. Capital won't be a problem, though I'll have to borrow to get started. Tom Bates will help me out, he's been a good friend and we've done little favors for one another from time to time. I might need to mortgage some of the property."

Orah's arm tucked into his, he chattered artlessly as they made their way homeward, pausing occasionally to greet this neighbor or that.

"Orah, my dear, you remember Cornelius Snider, don't you? Cornelius, may I introduce my wife, Mrs. Thacker? . . . Good evening, Mr. Reed. Orah, do you remember Mr. Reed, the postmaster? Like you to meet my wife . . . Lovely evening, Mrs. Doty. I'd like to introduce . . ."

Given the condition of the townspeople left in the wake of her progress through the town, Orah might well have been Medusa. Serenely unaware, they dropped their bombshells as they wended their way homeward.

"THERE YOU ARE, PAPA! We didn't know where you'd gone. Dinner's nearly ready, and Will and Josie were very disappointed that you couldn't come with me to fetch them home." Lottie tried to keep the reproach from her voice, and then started. "Oh! Hello, Orah."

Will and Josie had rushed to the kitchen door and stopped, suddenly shy. Lottie gave Will a nudge and whispered, "Come in, silly boy, it's only Papa and Orah. You remember Orah."

"Well, Will, you're getting to be a big boy, aren't you?" Henry shook the limp hand shyly offered to him, and turned to Josie, who'd been firmly propelled in front of him. He reached a hand down toward her, and she cringed, clinging to Lottie. "He smells funny," she whispered to Lottie.

"Josie, you bad girl, go upstairs to your room and don't come down until you're ready to greet your poor papa properly!" Sniffling, Josie sidled out, followed gratefully by Will. A silence fell, lengthened.

"Lottie, I have some news for you. Well, for all of you. Where are the boys?"

"Ralph's down the road helping the Rideouts build a shed, and Roy's finishing up the milking. They should be in any minute. Orah, won't you sit down? We're out of tea, I'm afraid, but there's some milk . . ."

"Lottie, I have some wonderful news. This afternoon, Orah did me the honor of becoming my wife."

Lottie, dazed, stared at them both. "Why?"

"Lottie!"

She shook her head. "I'm sorry. I don't mean to be rude. Excuse me a moment, please." A rustle of fabric, and Lottie was gone. They heard her light footsteps run up the stairs, a door slam shut.

Henry's ears glowed red. "She's just surprised, that's all."

"I expect she is. I expect a lot of people will be," said Orah calmly, and stepped to the stove, where a large pot of water bubbled. Quickly she picked up the pieces of the broken dinner preparations and began to weave them back together again.

ROY FOLLOWED RALPH onto the back porch and froze, staring at the backs of his father and the new bride. Henry turned, smiling.

"Boys! Come on in . . ."

"What's she doing here?"

"Now, son, mind your manners. Orah's come to be your stepmother."

Roy's face paled under its dark summer tan. The pale white strip at the top of his forehead that was covered outdoors by his hat looked the color of old cheese.

"You—I—what? No, she isn't! Oh, no, not my stepmother."

He stepped back, reached behind himself for the door handle, pulled it open again. He stepped out, and was gone, the door clicking quietly into its latch. It sounded to Lottie, just entering the kitchen, like a mousetrap without the squeal.

Nobody spoke for a moment. Ralph, seeing his father's hurt and disappointment, wondered what he could say to make up for Roy. He couldn't think of anything. Father might have warned them!

"I think I'll go up to—to my room," he managed, and stepped around Lottie, and disappeared. Lottie felt a pain in her lower lip, realized her teeth had clamped down on it, and took a deep breath.

"Dinner's nearly ready. It's not much of a—a wedding supper, I'm afraid . . ." She tried to control a blush.

"Whatever you have here will be fine, vegetable stew, isn't it?" said Orah. "I'll help serve it up, shall I?"

"SOMETHING I CAN HELP you with?" The eyes of the clerk might have been staring over a rifle barrel for all the warmth in them, Orah thought. She pulled a short list out of her reticule and began, "Fifteen pounds of flour, please, and some cake sugar; five pounds should be enough."

"We're out of those things." The words were flat; the clerk's eyes looked past her now, out the window and into the distant sky. Orah heard a woman's whisper behind her, quickly shushed in the silence.

Orah looked pointedly at the sacks of flour behind the counter and back to the clerk. "Some of that flour behind you will suit me just fine," she told the blank face.

"Those are already spoken for—big order just came in."

A snicker sounded behind her.

"What is the matter with you? Must I help myself to the things I need?"

"I shouldn't, if I were you. In fact, I think you had better leave. We don't do business with . . ." he paused, "women of your sort."

He might have drenched her with a bucket of ice water. "Of my . . . sort?"

Silence.

"Very well. I'll take my business elsewhere." She hesitated, then turned and walked out. Whispers followed her.

Half an hour later, Lottie entered the store, carrying Orah's list.

"Good morning," she greeted the clerk. "I'd like some sugar, please, and some washing soda . . ."

"I'm sorry, Lottie, I just can't. I'm not allowed to do business with any of you Thackers now."

"Why not? We've paid our bill every month! If you check the ledger, you'll see that."

"It's not your bill, Lot—Miss Thacker."

"Did I do something wrong?"

The stony expression of Mr. Frist thawed slightly. "It's not you. It's what your father and his—it's because of—well, we just can't tolerate—it's a shame, for you youngsters, but there it is."

"I'm sorry," whispered Lottie, and backed toward the door, wondering why she had said that, and how she was to make the biscuits for the shortcake.

"It's Impossible"

MEANWHILE, Henry and Ralph stared helplessly at one another across the table.

"Father, it's impossible. Even if Mr. Bates were to help with a loan, they'd want collateral."

"Well, we'd just have to mortgage the southeast field, or the other town lot."

"Father, we sold the town lot, remember? That went two years ago. The southeast field's already mortgaged, and so's the house."

Henry paused, taken aback. "I'd forgotten. Well, we'll have to sell some of the stock."

"We have two cows, the chickens, and the horses. One wagon, and some machinery, none of it worth very much."

"The sheep?"

"Gone."

"The other forty acres?"

"Long gone." In exasperation, "Didn't Mr. Covell tell you any of this? Didn't you read my letters?"

"I'm sure he did, Ralph. I'm sorry, it just didn't seem real, I'm afraid. When you're facing a life in prison, your life outside becomes far and away, like a dream you once had. I am sorry, Ralph, I just didn't think. Never mind, I'll talk with Mr. Bates and see what he suggests."

THOMAS BATES ROSE stiffly and did not extend a hand. "I didn't expect to see you again, Mr. Thacker."

"Very pleased to see you again, Mr. Bates. I expect a few people will be surprised, pleasantly, I hope." He began to sit down, then realized that Mr. Bates remained at attention behind his desk.

"A number of them already have been quite surprised, I understand. Seems you didn't come to town alone."

"Oh, yes. I hope you'll congratulate me, sir. Orah Bunker has done me the honor of becoming my wife, and we hope to begin life anew in Benzonia. That's what I've come to see you about, to see about a loan to get me started again."

"I'm afraid that will be quite impossible. Perhaps it's as well that you came in today, after all. You see, there are some irregularities concerning the notes against your property in Benzonia. As you are no doubt aware, the First Bank of Traverse City holds notes against twenty improved acres and one lot with house on it. We helped your son sell forty other acres and miscellaneous mechanical implements last year."

"But surely . . ."

"The bank has authorized me to notify you that it intends to call those notes at the beginning of September."

"But why? Ralph tells me he's made the payments on the interest, and it's just a matter of time before we . . ."

"You'd do well to sell your remaining property outright, Mr. Thacker, and leave the area. I think you'll find that respectable people no longer wish to have anything to do with you."

"Because I was in prison? They found me innocent! I spent two years paying for something I didn't do! Are you saying they'll hold that against me?"

"Not because you were in prison, Mr. Thacker. I think most people, after emotions cooled, were willing to concede you the benefit of the doubt. A few will always be dubious, but for the most part, I think they've dealt fairly with your family and would have accepted you back. No, it's your . . ." He distastefully turned over some adjectives in his mind, settling for the tamest he could muster: ". . . your unfortunate choice in marriage companions that they will find unacceptable. That they do find unacceptable."

"Are you saying that Miss Bunker, that my wife is an unacceptable person?"

"Not she, as such. Had she married a young man of good character I daresay she'd have eventually redeemed her reputation. When you married her, it confirmed what the prosecution so strongly suggested, that your relations with her were not proper. The good people of Benzonia were willing to forgive and forget. You have made fools of them all, of us all, and you will not be forgiven for that."

"But surely . . ."

"Take my advice. Take your family as far as you can afford to go, and try to start over again."

LOTTIE STARTED at the knock on the front door. She rose and went reluctantly to answer it. Her slow footsteps slowed further when she recognized Sheriff Chandler's profile in the frosted glass. This made her sad; it hadn't been this way before "their trouble," as they'd taken to calling it.

Sheriff Chandler used to come to the kitchen door—he didn't knock, but opened the door a bit, just enough to stick his head through and shout, "Yoo hoo!" Sometimes that woke the baby, and Mother would get angry. But Lottie always ran to greet him. He'd look down at her, one eye squinted, and say, "I know you! You're that girl of Henry's! Let's see, is it Dottie?"

She'd shake her head and giggle.

"Tottie?"

"No!"

"Oh, I know, it must be Nottie!" She'd giggle harder. The sound of the word was close enough to "naughty" that she could then shout, "No, I'm not naughty, I'm Lottie and I'm good!"

"Why, so you are!" he'd crow, and try to rumple her hair. She didn't like that part so much. Her hair was braided neatly, which meant the pigtails were tight. His big hand moved her scalp briskly to and fro, pulling at the tight hairs in the tender places around her ears and low on her scalp in back. It hurt, but she always tried not to say "Ouch!" He was so nice, she hadn't wanted to hurt his feelings.

Then he'd be ⸱itting at the kitchen table, eating a slice of pie from whate~~　　　　ᴉson, rhubarb in early spring, strawberry and then 　　　　ᴉerry in summer, apple or pumpkin in fall into the 　　　　with a huge dollop of whipped cream. Lottie 　　　　ᴉe, secretly considered the pie as merely a base for

　　　　ᴉd when Mother died. First he had come to the 　　　　se red, Mrs. Chandler at his side carrying a pie 　　　　ttie remembered) and stammering his regrets 　　　　ᴉome had been to arrest Father, and the time 　　　　ᴉer home to make his final goodbyes to them. 　　　　ᴉer mind from that memory. It would live in a locked room of her memory alongside Mother's little puppy yelps when she was so dreadfully sick.

Then, he'd come to take Roy away for the holidays. None of these things were his fault. Still, she couldn't feel the same warmth for him anymore. Nothing to be done about it. She answered the door.

"Is your father in?" he asked formally. Oh! He'd come to arrest Father again, this time for marrying Orah! She had to run and warn him, he must, they must run away from this place! Lottie swayed; her ears rang slightly, black dots swarmed before her eyes, and a black fog rose from the floor. She knew it would envelop her; she bit her sore lip, hard, and the dots subsided. She hoped she wouldn't vomit.

"Sit down," she managed. "I'll go and find him." On trembling legs she left the room.

She found him in the barn, forking hay. "Father! Sheriff Chandler's come to arrest you again! Run away! You can write us and we'll join you . . ."

"Whoa! Stop! What's this?"

"Because you married Orah! He's in the parlor; he came asking for you again!"

"Did he say he's come to arrest me?"

"No, but he came in the front door!"

"Why don't you go back and ask him . . . Never mind, I'll go myself."

Lottie followed him up to the house, her footsteps lagging. She stood in the passageway and shamelessly eavesdropped.

"CHANDLER, you've scared my daughter half to death. She thinks you're here to arrest me again. Is it true? Did I break some law by getting married?"

"I'm not here to arrest you, Henry. What's that noise?"

Lottie, who'd slumped against the doorframe, straightened up and tiptoed away. She sat down at the kitchen table and breathed hard, once, before dissolving into tears. When Orah came downstairs, Lottie was fast asleep, her head cushioned on her arm on the table. "Henry, I'm sorry to have to be the bearer of more bad news. You're not under arrest, but it's pretty bad. Mr. Bates stopped by and gave me this to deliver to you."

Paper rustled. He read it, mumbled something under his breath, and read it again.

"That dirty son of a . . ."

"Now, Henry, the bank has a right to call its note whenever it deems it proper. That was in the contract your boy signed when he mortgaged the properties."

"He was underage when he signed that contract! It's not legal!"

"Yes, 'tis legal. You and your lawyers agreed to it. That's why you're on this side of the bars right now, remember; that second trial cost nearly everything your family owned. The list is right there, so it shouldn't surprise you. My advice is to take your losses and move somewhere else. You're still quite a young man, with grown children. You can start over, with Roy and Ralph's help."

"Not Roy. He's leaving. Says he's going out west." Henry tried to keep the sadness from his voice.

"Well, Ralph anyway, he's a good worker. So's Lottie, for that matter. You'll do fine."

"What if I don't choose to leave?"

"Your children will suffer. Nobody in Benzonia will do business with you. Not many folks, anyway. They won't let you join the church."

"Oh, the church. I'd nearly forgotten. Good Christians, all of my loving neighbors."

A bitter silence filled the room.

"Henry, have you been to the cemetery yet?"

"Cemetery? Why? What do you mean?"

"Did your children tell you about the headstone?" Henry shook his head, bewildered by this non sequitur.

"Perhaps you should pay a visit to your wife's grave, then, if you haven't. Anna grew up in this town, and memories are long. Take my advice; leave town."

"Faithful Unto Death"

"RALPH, what's this about your mother's grave? Chandler wouldn't tell me."

"We should have written to you, but couldn't think how to tell you. Someone put a stone on Mother's grave, and it wasn't us."

"A stone? What kind of stone?"

Ralph was patient, as with a slow child. "A headstone, Father. It must have been Uncle Brainard or Aunt Charlotte. Shall I go with you to see it, or would you rather go alone?"

Henry walked down the hill and climbed the low rise to Anna's grave. All around him were the stones of his neighbors and his neighbors' wives. There was a pattern to all of the stones for women who'd been married: "Mary Ann Yoder, honored mother and wife to Joseph." "Allison James, beloved wife and mother."

Anna's stone was modest, a light gray granite, and read simply, "Anna A. Thacker, dau. of D. B. Spencer. 1850–1894, Faithful Unto Death."

Henry's shoulders sagged. He turned and walked down the hill.

RALPH HADN'T REALIZED how hard it would be to uproot himself from Benzonia. He remembered reading a story in school about a lifesaver. As a boat sank offshore the lifesaver could only rescue one more person. As he'd tried to save the only woman passenger, she had thrust her blanket-wrapped infant into the lifesaver's arms. Even as the waters had closed over her, her eyes had remained locked on the child. Ralph had thought the story rather silly at the time; one baby looked pretty much like another, and women had plenty of them. In his twelve-year-old superiority he'd thought, why didn't she save herself and just have another one?

He looked down the hill, past the hole he'd so laboriously filled in after the elm had fallen in the big storm, across the fruit trees so carefully pruned and trained, across the valley below the house where their sheep had grazed, where the children had sledded in the winter, across the thickets where they'd picked berries, and now he understood that fictional woman.

He had no doubt they'd soon find new land, build or buy another house, plant trees and crops, make a new home. But a much younger Ralph inside him stamped its feet and wailed, "But I don't want another home! I want this one!"

Then there was the sheer belly-wrenching business of preparing for the sale, determining what was actually theirs to keep and what belonged to the bank. The baby Ralph kept whispering that they should remove the things they most wanted and hide them, before the bank's deputy wrote it into the inventory. After all, it reasoned, there were already two criminals in the Thacker family, or at least two who'd been in jail. Somewhere in the family was a murderer, so why shouldn't they cheat and save a few treasures from the bank sale? The adult Ralph squelched these thoughts determinedly, for the most part, anyway.

The remaining livestock could not be hidden, of course. Lottie's chickens, the cows, and the two good working horses, Esmeralda now worth much more than they could afford to buy new. Star worried him most of all. Star, he could fool himself no longer, was indeed getting old. Hollows showed above Star's eyes, his hipbones were more evident, and his muzzle was graying.

Ralph had seen what often happened to horses that were no longer useful. They were sold cheaply to common fellows, hitched to delivery wagons, fed bad food, whipped when they stumbled, and finally, when no more work could be beaten from them, away to the knackers. If they were fortunate, the first blow (or rifle shot) between the eyes killed them. Ralph shuddered, seeing poor old Star down, blood streaming from a misplaced blow, his honest, gentle eyes puzzled and frightened. He'd rather take Star out to the woods and, after feeding him all the carrots he desired, shoot him himself.

"Oh, I know it's likely criminal to do that," he confided to Thomas Rideout, "but I'm not sure I care, just now. You know how a body gets attached to an animal, sometimes."

He was only mildly surprised that Rideout seemed to understand. "What if I offered to buy him? From the bank sale, I mean?"

"Whatever for? You know how old he is. That old nag has five more years in him at best, and only three of them worth the oats he's fed."

"Oh, let's just say that you've been a good help to me many times when I needed an extra pair of hands, and you've been a good friend to us. I feel like I owe you a favor or two. Besides, I can use old Star for light work around the place, and he can finish his old age out in the pasture."

Ralph wiped his nose on his handkerchief. "I won't forget this," he managed.

Once Star was off his mind, he resolutely turned his mind from his own problems. Lottie's face was now a picture of woe.

"The bank can't take Grandma Spencer's dishes, surely?"

"We don't know what they'll take."

"Then we should tell them they aren't worth anything except to us!"

He'd patiently tried to explain how they needed to make as much money as possible for each item sold, so the bank's note would be covered.

Roy had already taken his own store of possessions, leaving much more than he took. "You can have 'em, I won't need 'em out west," he'd said, waving a dismissive hand at a pile of odds and ends topped by his old band uniform, schoolbooks, and other trappings of childhood. Roy was gone; he'd said his goodbyes to his brothers and sisters, shouldered his baggage, and without a backward glance at his father, left them all.

"RALPH, what did you say we have that isn't mortgaged?" Henry didn't seem to understand much more about the bank sale than Lottie did. Ralph tried to be as patient as he could.

"Not much. The horses aren't, anyway."

"But didn't Mr. Bates say that we'd have to put everything in the bank sale?"

"He did, but there's nothing that says we can't buy them back."

"With what?"

"With the one hundred dollars that we've managed to put away." He strove to keep the pride from his own voice; he didn't want to damage his father's pride any more than it already was.

"Can you get them for that?"

"Probably not."

But Ralph wasn't really sure. Sheriff Chandler had warned him that auctions were tricky; things that should have gone cheaply sometimes caught the eyes of competing bidders who would drive the price up, and things nearly new sometimes went for a song.

The Auctioneer

"MY NAME'S DRISCOLL, auctioneer. I'll be presiding over this little shindy on Saturday." He stuck out a large and hairy hand.

Chandler had taken a dislike to the man the moment he laid eyes (and ears) on him. It wasn't just that he talked too loudly, which he did, but an auctioneer would naturally talk loudly, wouldn't he? It was that he was loud, in the worst ways a man could be. He dressed in wide-bottomed pants with large checks on them, in a garish combination of orange and green, and a brocaded waistcoat that would have looked fancy if it had been clean. Clownish yellow shoes and a bright green derby completed the getup, and when the auctioneer removed his hat, his black hair dripped with some sort of pomade that made the yellow jackets cluster around.

Driscoll smelled terrible. Some of it came from his mouth; his breath was just nasty. Overlaying the rankness of his breath was a miasma. It wasn't the stink of honest sweat, exactly, but that sweat closed up in cheap rooms, soaked into linens never properly washed for weeks on end. Chandler kept trying to edge away, but Driscoll kept closing the distance.

He couldn't keep his hands to himself, either. He joked along, crude jokes they were, too; he slapped Chandler on the shoulder several times, and he elbowed him once, chortling at his own witticisms and displaying great yellow teeth like an old horse's.

The man's face was red; Chandler suspected, from the medicinal fetor of his breath, that he drank, and his gross habit of chewing and spitting was frankly revolting. "You'll have to refrain from chewing that stuff if you're going to work in Benzonia," warned Chandler. "It's something that our people despise, and if they catch you spitting they'll get in their wagons and leave. At least the married men will, their wives'll make them."

"Henpecked lot, are they?" chuckled Driscoll, and poked Chandler again for punctuation. "I'll do my best, but can't make any guarantees, a man's got to have his chew once in a while."

"There's one more thing." Chandler was irritated to realize that he now had trouble meeting Driscoll's eyes. "There's a team of horses in the sale. Nothing flashy but good solid working beasts. Well-trained, no bad habits. I want you to let 'em go for one hundred dollars. There'll be a young man bidding, I'll point him out to you on Saturday." He stopped, angry and mortified, feeling his face burn.

"Making a little something for yourself, hey?" Chandler, in all his years as a sheriff, had never seen a man actually leer before. He itched to wipe that leer off the auctioneer's face, and that wish showed in his own. Driscoll, a big man, flushed and stepped back.

"Why, Sheriff, a fellow could get in some trouble doing a thing like that. That's defrauding the bank, that is. I've got my scruples, you know."

Chandler swallowed. "Never mind. Forget I mentioned it."

But Driscoll blandly continued, "If a man was to forget his scruples for a little while, it'd sure need to be worth it to him."

Understanding dawned; the sheriff pulled his pocketbook out and opened it. He placed a five-dollar bill on the outstretched palm. The palm remained open; Driscoll's eyes remained fixed on Chandler's. He grimly pulled out another five dollars, then, when the hand remained open, added one more. They stared at one another, and finally Driscoll's eyes dropped to his hand, which closed around the money and made it disappear.

"It's sure been nice doing business with you, Sheriff," said Driscoll as he began to climb into his unthrifty buggy.

"There's a wagon as well," added Chandler, who no longer tried to meet the inquiring gaze. "It's not worth anything anyway. Throw it in with the horses."

Driscoll prepared to negotiate this new deal, but Chandler snapped,

"Just do it. Keep your piehole shut and just do it. Or I'll ask Mr. Bates to find us another auctioneer, if I have to bring the fellow here from Lansing."

"Just as you say, Sheriff." Driscoll drove away, leaving, Chandler thought, a yellow cloud of stench in his wake.

SHERIFF CHANDLER PACED and fumed; Driscoll was late, and people were growing edgy. He finally arrived, pulled in his buggy by a different pair of mismatched, dirty horses.

The day was clear for the sale, bringing folks in by the wagonload from the entire county. Henry and Ralph had stayed for the sale, but Lottie had taken the younger children down the road for the day.

Had it been anybody else's sale, Ralph might have enjoyed it. There was a musical rhythm to the auctioneer's chant that made, he noticed, all but the oldest and deafest of the bidders sway as if about to break into dance. The individual competitions for certain items, the auctioneer's interesting and entertaining comments about those items, the screams of the running children, and the ebb and flow of the crowd made for an exciting, festive atmosphere.

But it wasn't anybody else's sale. It was their own possessions, their own family's history laid out to be fingered, turned over, and speculated about. He supposed it was selfish of him to wish this misery onto anyone else, but it was so.

Orah kept herself well indoors and out of sight, and Father kept a discreet distance from the proceedings. The sight of him would annoy the bidders, but Orah seemed to particularly inflame them. Ralph, they tolerated.

He'd been the one who'd sternly enjoined Lottie to take the children out to the orchard to play, and now he was glad he had. It was hard enough for an adult to watch his life being sold away, piecemeal. A child, he thought, would be devastated. They were all to keep their clothing and personal articles, and the children their small toys. But larger articles couldn't be easily carried, especially since the family would probably need to hire transport out of their limited finances. Besides, the larger items might be worth something.

Lottie's dollhouse now stood before the crowd. Ralph remembered how they'd all worked on that house, the week before her seventh birthday. He, Father, and Roy had done the woodworking, and Mother had sat up every night but Sunday when Lottie was abed, cunningly stitching tiny curtains and cushions, bed linens and towels. He had made a rocking chair from a section of spool. How Lottie's face had glowed when she first saw it! She and her friends (he could never sort out their names, Nancy, Beth, Kathleen or Nora; they were all pigtails and giggles) had played "house" by the hour, their already high voices raised in falsetto to impersonate the doll-voices of their miniature homemakers. Later, Josie had joined and then supplanted Lottie, and even Will had used the house as a stockade for his lead soldiers.

Now it sat naked in the sun, paint faded, its furniture worn and smudged by grubby hands; it was part of a "lot" made up of Will's old rocking horse, Mother's kitchen chair, some tableware, and other odds and ends. The lot sold for seventeen dollars.

Ralph endured these stings for the next hour, until finally, at a signal from Sheriff Chandler, he went to the barn and led out Esmeralda and Duchess. With a curious mixture of pride and anguish he heard the appreciative comments as they passed the bidders.

"Fine-looking team." "Look how that young mare carries herself— pretty showy for a workhorse." "Yes, but sweet manners, look how she leads." "I've seen them work, they're a good team."

He'd stayed out late in the barn the evening before, grooming them both. It was against their own best interests for him to show the team at its best, he was aware of that. As well as he knew some of the tricks men used to make a bad horse look better, he knew how to do the reverse— but he couldn't do it. "You've been a fine and useful span, might's well show it," he mumbled to them, embarrassed, and he set to work with currycomb and brush, sponge and hoof pick, rag and oil. Father had joined him as he finished oiling Duchess's off fore hoof.

"If we're to win the bid, better make 'em look worse, not better," Henry opined.

"I know, but somehow I just can't bring myself to. There's no sense pretending we don't know what people say about the Thackers right now," and seeing Henry wince, he swallowed but went on, "But I've never heard anyone say we don't do an honest day's work or that we don't care for our stock. I'm damned if I let 'em say that!"

He was shocked at himself for this last epithet, but Henry only looked thoughtful. He kicked at a clod, and then squared his own shoulders.

"You're right, son. Where's that—oh, here, just where it always was." Picking up the block of saddle-soap and a scrap of sponge, he began to work on the harness. Absorbed in his task, he suddenly looked better, Ralph thought, than he had since getting out. More like himself. Ralph returned to Duchess's feet.

At last they stepped back and admired their handiwork. The harness, old and worn, shone mellowly with soap and oil. The plain brasses and the buckles had been polished. The horse's coats gleamed softly in the setting sun which came in through the door. Ralph had braided a bit of Josie's old hair ribbon into Esmeralda's mane, just behind her ears. Eyes bright, ears pricked, the horses tossed their heads, seeming to appreciate their own beauty.

Now Ralph groaned at his own foolish vanity as he led the horses to their places in front of the crowd and heard the interest they generated. He moved to a place in front of the crowd, as Sheriff Chandler had advised. The bidding had begun at twenty-five dollars, and swiftly climbed to forty-five dollars, then sixty, seventy, eighty, and now the auctioneer chanted, more softly, Ralph thought, "I have ninety, ninety, who'll gimme ninety-fi' dollahs, ninety-fi', ninety-fi . . ."

Ralph raised his hand and said clearly, "One hundred dollars." He waited, breath in, for the next bid.

"One hundred, going once, going twice, sold! For one hundred dollars to the young man right here in front!" Ralph stood, stunned. Driscoll stared at him impatiently. "What's the matter, Sonny? Step right over there to the cashier if you want to pay for them horses."

A mutter rose up behind Ralph. "What? What do you mean? The bidding wan't done yet!"

"Hey, I had my hand up right over here! Whyn't you take my bid?"

"I wanted those horses!"

The rumbling grew. Driscoll laughingly raised his arms.

"Settle down, folks. Auctions are fast-moving things, you gotta speak up or you'll lose some mighty good opportunities. Besides," here he let his voice drop confidentially with a waggish glance toward Ralph, now floating toward the cashier in what felt like a pink fog, "you're well shut of those animals. One of 'em's ailing for something, maybe the swaggers, it's as plain as day."

Ralph turned incredulously and stared at his team. Swaggers? What in the world were "swaggers"? Neither horse was ailing in the least! But it finally sank in. His team! He had them! He didn't know how, but he had them!

The auctioneer was still talking. "Settle down. I know it wasn't fair to saddle that young'un with a sickly team, so let's just throw in that old wagon as a consolation to him. It's not worth anything anyway, the load-spring's sprung and the ratchet-lever's about to go. Now, ladies . . ." He smoothly turned to the table that had been in the dining room this morning.

"If you'll feast your eyes on this lovely table, solid oak, big enough to sit the whole fambly around it without the twins being able to kick each other underneath it! Who'll gimme ten, ten dollahs, I've got ten dollahs, who'll gimme fifteen . . ."

"What in Tophet?" demanded a farmer to his neighbor. "What's a load-spring? And what's he mean by a ratchet-lever? Is that man crazy? He just gave that wagon to Ralph Thacker without so much as a by-your-leave!"

"I'll bet the sheriff has something to say about that," commented the other.

"Shush, William, and pay attention," demanded his wife. "I've got my eyes on that sofa and I mean to have it!" William rolled his eyes and fell silent.

Ralph gently removed the bridle from Duchess, then did the same for Esmeralda. He willed his hands to stop shaking; rather than burying his face in the horses' necks and bawling like a baby, he contented himself with giving each a hearty slap on the rump as he turned her into her stall.

By the time he had enough command of himself to return to the auction, the rest of the farm equipment had sold and few bits and pieces remained. The item currently before them was the lounge that Mother had lain on during her last days, and had died on. No stains showed on its surface, invisible testimony to their efforts to keep her clean and comfortable as her dwindling fluids had leaked from her. The sheets she'd lain on, however, had been soaked with substances that would not wash out.

Ralph saw clearly in memory now that Monday after Mother's funeral, when he'd come upon Lottie stooped over the wash cauldron, tears leaking down her cheeks and falling into the wash water. "They'll never come clean, Ralph. I can't use them on anyone else's bed, oh, poor Mother!" He'd shushed her, told her they had plenty of sheets, and those sheets had gone into the rag bag.

The lounge had sat on the lawn all through today, a sort of inanimate version of the proverbial senile relative. The townspeople, Ralph noticed, had carefully avoided seeing it. They knew the lounge's history, and in whispers had shared that information with the country folk. Less genteel, the farmers, and more especially their wives, had circled around it avidly.

Driscoll, it was obvious, had held that piece until late in the auction. "Now, folks, here's a chase lounge that has lots of family history behind it, and most of you know what I mean. We're selling it by itself and we're going to start the bidding at, oh, at thirty-five dollars . . ."

Ralph gritted his teeth and tried not to hear the buzz of comments around him.

"Is that the one where she died?"

"Hanged if I'd have that in my house."

"'Chase' lounge? Wherever did that auctioneer go to school?"

"The wife'd never let me bring it in the door."

"Look at that spot! D'you suppose that's blood?"

"That's not a spot, it's just the shadow of those maple leaves."

"I hear that—hush! That's one of the sons standing right up there. How d'you s'pose he feels, seeing that up there with the bloodstain on it?"

Ralph edged deeper into a group of townspeople. Unlike the farmers from outlying areas, these neighbors lacked that avid, almost obscene fascination with Mother's penultimate earthly resting place.

Ralph had been touched by the kindness of some of their neighbors in these days of preparing to move. Mr. Bates from the bank had agreed to waive some of the foreclosure fees so that there might be some money left from the sale. "You be sure to notify us as soon as you're settled, with your location."

Mrs. Bailey, whom they were sure hated the very sight of any Thacker, had bought Lottie's entire flock of hens for a good price, and had even sent one of her boarders to round them up and move them.

"If you aren't here to sell me my eggs," she'd explained, "I might as well go into the business for myself and eliminate the middle man." Lottie had proudly added this fifteen dollars to Father's dwindling reserves.

Even Mrs. Shaw, the minister's wife, had stopped him in the yard this morning and thrust a large new loaf of white bread into his hands. "For the children's breakfast tomorrow," she had explained and, waving off his thanks, had bustled away.

"Seventy-fi', seventy-fi', do I hear eighty? Eighty, eighty, going once at eighty dollahs, this is your last chance, folks, to acquire this historical artifact, going twice, sold! For eighty dollahs! To this gentleman in the overalls, yes, you sir, step over there to the clerk and put your money down."

Ralph shook his head in disgust and wandered over to his father, who'd been deep in conversation with a portly farmer.

"Ralph, you remember Mr. Smith, lives at the county road toward Manistee? We sold him that cultivator back in eighty-three, wasn't it, Smith?"

"Spring of eighty-three, that's right, Sheriff. Fine cultivator, still use it."

Ralph stared for a moment, before belatedly putting out his hand in greeting.

Henry shook his head ruefully. "Thank you kindly, sir, but my sheriff days are over for good, I fear. It's just plain Henry from now on."

"Maybe that's so, but these folks are making a mistake, for my money; you were the hardest-working man this town had."

Henry ducked his head in appreciation, then changed the subject. "Ralph, Mr. Smith here has kindly offered us his hospitality for a couple of nights."

"That is kind of you, sir," agreed Ralph. "Are you sure it won't be an imposition? There are six of us, you know."

"The more the merrier. You just let me get along home now with this new bed, to sweeten up my missus. She's been at me for months, saying Jody's outgrown his cradle and needs a real boy's bed. I hope you don't mind that I bought it," he added, suddenly embarrassed.

"No, that's fine, Jody's welcome to it. We can't carry a lot of furniture in a single wagon, you see. We'll live like real pioneers for a while, until we get settled."

They spent a final night in the house. Ralph gave up trying to relax into sleep on his makeshift pallet and moved out to the barn where the hay cushioned him and the comfortable sound of horses munching their oats lulled him, finally, into sleep.

The departure was anticlimactic. Their few goodbyes had been said the day before, and now everyone else was at church. They dressed in their everyday clothes and loaded their remaining belongings into the wagon. Lottie helped Josie into the back, despite her stormy protestations of "I can do it my own self!"

Henry and Orah on the wagon's front seat, they rattled out of the

245

yard. Nearly one hundred years later, a booklet titled "Historic Struc-
tures in the Benzonia-Beulah Area" said of the house, "There were
many changes in ownership before Herbert B. Woodard purchased it."
No mention was made of the Spencers or the Thackers.

They rode down the hill without looking back. The road south
passed the cemetery. Neither Henry nor Orah looked toward it. "Goodbye, Mother," whispered Lottie, softly, so the others couldn't hear her.
Ralph's eyes, too, looked up the rise to where the stone sat, keeping its
counsel among its granite neighbors.

The Road South and East

THE WAGON TRAVELED south with its load of refugees, following the
road that meanders along the woods bordering Lake Michigan, to
Manistee.

"I can't thank you enough, Lyman. I don't know where we would
have put up for the night if you hadn't invited us to stay."

Bessie, Lyman Smith's young wife, was all a-flutter at having such
notorious company. Before the infamous goings-on in Benzonia, her
husband had often spoken of Sheriff Thacker, a pillar of his community.
The headline-making news only added to the cachet of hosting such a
distinguished family. As she cleared away the table, she studied every
detail of the family's apparel and manners so as to regale her neighbors
the next day. She lingered in the doorway to the kitchen, listening.

"I was wondering if you know of any land for sale nearby, where we
can get another start?"

"What, around Manistee, you mean? Why, Sheriff, uh, Mr. Thacker,
you shouldn't even think of that! Folks around here, well, they're still
pretty upset about it all."

Silence fell around the table. Henry tried again, "Well, that's all
right, we'll head on eastward and see how things look around there. I
had just thought, well, Orah's family is right nearby in Arcadia, you
know, which would have made visiting convenient."

Orah looked at Henry strangely. Hadn't he even noticed the reception her family had given him when he came to propose? She rose and
began to help Bessie clear the table.

Ralph, embarrassed, went out to check the horses. He lingered in the barn, fussing over them both, until the lateness of the hour allowed him to retire courteously.

THE FAMILY TURNED INLAND from the broad and shining freshwater ocean. The road east was one lane of compacted dirt and gravel; it wound through cleared lands and large sections of woods already showing gold on the paper birches, red on the maples, and oxblood on the lobes of the oaks.

"Will, look! It's a hippopotamus!"

Five heads jerked to the right where Josie's finger pointed. Sure enough, the enormous gray boulder in the adjoining cow pasture was exactly the shape and size of a hippo. Shadows from the overhanging poplar danced across it, giving the impression of movement.

The glaciers that formed Michigan's lakes had left a number of "accidental" rocks of a rich variety of sizes, shapes and colors in this area. The Thackers had arrived at the web between the little and the ring fingers inside the Michigan Lower Peninsula's "mitten," and these "accidentals" spotted the area thickly. A misery for plowing, but a boon for house and barn foundations. Plus, Ralph thought privately, they were pretty.

Ralph found himself smiling; it felt good to be smiling again, out here away from sidelong looks and sneering whispers. Maybe it did a body good to get transplanted once in a while.

"Ralph, what's the nearest town? Are we near Cadillac?"

"I think that's north of us. We're somewhere between there and Big Rapids, I think."

"What do you think, son? Should we stop at the next town?"

Orah nodded. Lottie and Ralph followed suit. The "hippopotamus" seemed as good an omen as any.

They stopped at the town of Tustin, far enough from home to have outrun the outrage if not the gossip; Henry had furnished lower Michigan with enough flavorful meat to be chewed for many a year, and no place in Michigan would be far enough to remain anonymous for quite some time.

Henry paid five dollars to hold a parcel of land outside Tustin, taking out a mortgage to pay for it, and the family settled down to a winter of hard work and scant rations, no novelty for any of them.

Ralph, powerful for his diminutive size, and agile, left home for the winter to earn his living in the lumbering camps in the north woods. He was to do this work for many winters, returning south to work the family land or work "out" when jobs for pay offered themselves.

New Neighbors

LEROY, MICHIGAN, NOVEMBER 1896

HARRIET MADOLE, hearing her father's step on the back stoop, quietly closed *The Natural History of Man* and pushed it behind the serving bowls. She supposed he was right when he said there was a time for study and a time for work, and to do either properly, they shouldn't be mixed.

But paring turnips was one of those repetitive jobs you could do with your mind miles away, on the other side of the Pacific Ocean, with the Melanesians to be precise. You only needed to glance down now and then to be sure you got all the really green part off the top, feel around the sides for any holes from borers, and then it was just a matter of cutting it into pieces of a certain size. At age thirteen she could do it in her sleep, and still learn about the Melanesians and their distant neighbors, the Fijians.

The book was not hers, of course, but her teacher, impressed by the girl's enthusiasm for the subject, had let her borrow it during the summer vacation. "I know you'll treat it with respect and return it in its pristine condition," he'd cautioned her.

When her father came in, he smiled approvingly at the sight of the dutiful young girl at the kitchen table applying herself single-mindedly to her task.

"Turnips, eh? Mash 'em up good with lots of butter, you know I like 'em that way. Where's your mother, Hattie?"

"She's upstairs."

Footsteps tapped down the steep staircase (more of a ladder with broad rungs, really), and Mr. Madole stepped into the other room to greet his wife.

As their voices sank to a quiet murmur, quick as a flash Hattie wiped her hands on her apron and recovered her book, finding her place quickly. She propped it open with the edge of the white ceramic turnip bowl and continued reading: "For the more domestic avocations stone axes, three and four-pronged fish spears, and well-made nets of cocoa fibres are employed. Canoes are hollowed out from the trunks . . ."

So engrossed was she that she failed to hear her father say, "I heard some interesting news today. Hoover stopped by. Says he met the family who's working shares on Brewer's place. It's that sheriff that murdered his wife over Traverse City way."

"Oh, no! Surely not!"

"Hoover says he seems like a perfectly nice fellow."

"We can't allow him to stay, surely?"

"I guess it's not certain that he's the one that did it. He's out walking around, anyway."

"Oh, he's probably friends with the judge. How terrible, that he's come here!"

"He's got a new wife, Hoover says, a real looker, too. She's not worried, apparently."

"That's just the sort of thing Mr. Hoover would notice . . ."

Hattie dreamed along with the New Hebrideans, unaware that in the next room her parents were discussing the father of the young man whom she was, eight years hence, to marry.

Death in Hadjin

HADJIN, TURKEY, FEBRUARY 1904

THE ROOM SHIMMERED and danced before Charlotte's half-open eyes. Insects buzzed in her ears, burrowed into her skin; worms chewed through her joints, or so it seemed. Her fever raged, as it had every day for nearly two weeks.

She longed for a drink of cool water, but the ceramic bottle by the bed was empty. She didn't call out; Miss Sullivan had plenty to worry her just now, without having to drop everything and tend to her. Just a few minutes ago (unless it was a few hours, or maybe it was yesterday?) the main door to the compound had rattled and crashed again under the butts of Turkish rifles. It was a good solid door, built of cedar to withstand hard use, but they didn't dare to leave the door closed under the imperious summons of "the sultan's troops," dirty ragged fellows who would have spent their days in prison under ordinary circumstances.

The sultan was no fool, of course. Bands of men like these local hoodlums, armed with German guns and trained by Turkish-speaking "experts," terrorized the Armenian communities and the American missionaries with impunity. When the U.S. government protested, Abdul Hamid denied any involvement. "Bandits, Kurdish revolutionaries, not Turkish soldiers," his representatives insisted.

The soldiers came to the compound regularly, searching for "insurgents" and often dragging away this or that one of the faithful Christian Armenians who lived and worked with the missionaries. None ever returned. It was rumored that the men were tortured and shot. The girls and women, if they were young and pretty, ended up immured in the homes of this soldier or that, condemned to a life of concubinage.

Charlotte wasn't sure exactly when she'd decided to return to Turkey. Her mortification at Henry Thacker's "revelation" didn't really last for long. The citizens of Manistee were fairly uninterested in the doings of Benzonians, and as far as she could tell, nobody snickered at her behind her back. In fact, her life was fairly pleasant at Mrs. Porter's boardinghouse. It seemed she could have spent her remaining years there.

Then the news made its way to her that Henry Thacker had actually married the Bunker girl, and the family had moved away, nobody knew where. It shouldn't have mattered to her, but suddenly she felt terribly lonely. "I have no family left, nobody at all to care for me," she realized, and wept, dry, hiccupping sobs that left her feeling no more comforted.

When, since childhood, for that matter, had she felt a sense of welcome and belonging? Why, as a missionary in Turkey, that's when. She thought of her time in Biltis. The work was hard, conditions primitive and dirty, yet they were nonetheless happy, knowing they worked for the common purpose of bringing civilization and the word of God to people who craved it so much they were willing to die for their beliefs.

She thought of the evenings with Miss Jacobson in the small room they shared. Every evening they had tea together, and often took turns reading to one another from the missionary paper or from letters they'd received, commenting over the news, laughing or lamenting together. They had been so close, just like sisters.

She could remember, clear as the waters of Crystal Lake, the day she had first arrived in Constantinople. The ship docked; half-naked men in turbans had scurried around it, catching ropes and securing them to posts embedded into the ground, rushing up with a gangplank, securing it to the dock as the sailors secured it to the ship, loosely, so that passengers had to quickly hop to board the sliding walkway.

This journey had seemed such a grand adventure when she first wrote to the Missionary Board, but as the ship wallowed its way across the rough Atlantic waters and into the smoother Mediterranean Sea, her trepidation grew into panic. She clung to the railing, trying to think how she would explain to the American Missionary Board why she'd felt it necessary to turn right around on the same ship and return to America.

A young woman strode confidently up the gangway followed by a Native in Western attire, and approached Charlotte.

"Are you Charlotte Spencer?"

At Charlotte's mute nod she thrust out her hand, took Charlotte's, and gave it a hearty shake.

"I'm Betsy Jacobson. We're to room together when we get to Biltis. Is this your trunk?"

Another mute nod.

"Don't worry a thing about it; Mamet will take care of it. Just bring your reticule and come along."

Tucking Charlotte's arm in hers, she marched to the gangplank, hopped nimbly back onto it, and escorted Charlotte down it, chatting all the while in a frank and hearty manner that emboldened Charlotte to relax and almost to enjoy the walk through the exotic (though foul-smelling) streets. To her amazement Charlotte soon found herself chattering artlessly along, telling all about her sea voyage and the train to New York City from Lansing.

She stopped, charmed by a sudden song, or was it a chant? that floated through the air, high-pitched and singsong. "How fey and lovely!" she began to say, then froze at the look of mingled distaste and alarm on Miss Jacobson's face.

"Quickly! Into this doorway! Look down, and don't make a sound!" She added hastily, "Whatever you do, don't smile or laugh," with a meaningful glance at the amusing sight before them.

A tiny donkey, led by a skinny brown urchin and burdened with an enormously fat man, sagged to a halt almost directly before them. Were it not for the high saddle, the man's slippered feet would have dragged the ground as he rode. With the boy's help, he stepped from the donkey's back.

The song wailed to a finish. The boy had briskly removed a rug from behind the saddle, unrolled it with a snap, and laid it on the ground before the man. He helped the man to kneel on it, and then he himself knelt in the dust to the left and slightly behind the rug. Both leaned forward, touching hands and then foreheads to the ground.

Charlotte had been drinking in the scene with discreet little glances, like a thirsty lady sips lemonade when there is company. The now-Charlotte lying fevered in her bed groaned involuntarily, wishing she'd not thought about lemonade. Her dry tongue scraped her lips with a rasp that echoed in her head, and then her mind rambled back to the past.

The donkey had reached out his muzzle and nibbled at some weeds that protruded from the foundation of the house they took refuge against.

The man looked so funny, his great buttocks, clad in baggy trousers, quivering in the air as he rocked back and forth, in contrast to the skinny shanks of his servant. Charlotte had a hard time suppressing a smile, but Miss Jacobson's strong fingers dug into her forearm.

They waited, scarcely breathing, until the man and boy arose and the rug was once more rolled up and stowed behind the saddle. The man was helped onto the donkey's poor little back. Only then did the man notice Charlotte and Miss Jacobson, whose gaze remained averted. His eyes, dark and not amusing at all, stared into Charlotte's. Another hard clutch to her arm reminded her to cast her own eyes down.

With a grunt that even she could translate as "That's better," he nudged the boy with his foot, and the procession meandered down the street. Miss Jacobson slumped in relief.

"What was that about?" whispered Charlotte.

"I'll explain when we're safely inside." And, subdued, they proceeded to their lodgings.

"The chant you heard was the Mohammedan call to prayer," and Miss Jacobson then elaborated on current conditions, the religious hostility toward Christians, and the political climate that Charlotte's hasty indoctrination had touched upon before she arrived.

It hadn't occurred to Charlotte that heathens prayed, or took their prayers seriously if they did. "They dislike Jews, but they dislike Christians, all Christians, even more."

For the next several days, as they traveled across the countryside, winding through mountain passes and up the sides of sheer hills that made Charlotte gasp, Miss Jacobson continued to tell her all about the hatred of Mohammedans for all Christians, be they Protestant, Roman, or "Oriental."

"You'll learn that, despite our differences, we're all Christians. What hurts one of us, hurts us all," she had said, and Charlotte learned, over the years, the truth of this. Her mind wandered back over the good times and the awful ones with her dear family of missionaries.

Oh, that terrifying time they had heard the soldiers at the doors and had hidden two of the young Armenian men, one under an end table with a floor-length table covering and the other under some bedding in Miss Jacobson's trunk. The soldiers, laughing cruelly, had slammed through their rooms, tearing pillows and sofas with their swords, peering behind curtains, but had somehow missed those particular places where Aram and . . . (what was his name? she couldn't recall) cowered.

After the soldiers had departed, muttering, the missionaries had clung together in relief. She and Miss Jacobson, in near hysteria, had hugged weakly, shaking, giddy with foolish laughter. Yes, the missionaries had been a family, and she had belonged to it.

Miss Jacobson was back in America, she knew, having married a young man studying for the ministry. But she, Charlotte, was free of ties and strong enough now to return to the work and community that needed her. It would be a good penance for all of her sins, an offering to the Lord. It was a short step from this realization to the act of going to the local missionary board and offering her services once again.

Now here she lay in her bed, unable to help herself or anyone else, a burden to the community. This, she was sure, was how her sister had felt near the end. Weak tears trickled down her face; she lacked the strength to wipe them away, so she let them drip.

A Humble and Christlike Life

MANISTEE DAILY NEWS, MARCH 3, 1904

"WORD WAS RECEIVED today of the death at Hadjin, Asiatic Turkey, of Miss Charlotte D. Spencer. Miss Spencer left Manistee nearly four years ago as a missionary under the American Board. Her maintenance was provided for by members of the Congregational Church of Manistee among whom she has been known as 'our missionary.'

"It has been known here for some time that Miss Spencer was critically ill, and announcement of this fact was made from the pulpit last Sunday.

"Full particulars of her death have not been received yet.

"Miss Spencer's work has been among the girls at Hadjin, where a school was maintained. As a teacher she seemed to achieve great success."

A letter from the Near East Mission of the United Church Board in what is now Istanbul, Turkey, spoke much more warmly of Charlotte Spencer.

"She had endeared herself greatly, not only to her American associates, but also to the people among whom she lived and worked. Her only wish seemed to be to spend and be spent for the Master. Her humble, gentle, devoted, and Christlike life produced, according to the testimony of Mr. Martin, an influence that would abide and bear fruit increasingly as time went on. During her sickness of several weeks, she had a rare peace of mind and even joy amidst her pain and sufferings. Her strength was unequal to the strain, and she passed away February 11, 1904, at the age of fifty-three.

"According to other information, Miss Charlotte Spencer was buried along with Miss Alice C. Martin, who died in 1896, in the Protestant Cemetery at Hadjin (a mountain town in the area of Adana)."

Ralph's News

TUSTIN, MICHIGAN, FALL 1904

RALPH STIRRED his fried potatoes around on his plate, not looking up. He wished Father weren't so cheerful just now, planning next spring's activities for them all as though he expected everything to stay the same, forever and ever amen. It made it that much harder for Ralph to share his news.

He didn't know why he felt so shy and shamefaced about it. Other young men announced their engagements joyously, as self-satisfied as if they'd just brought in a bumper crop of oats all by themselves. He supposed there was something about having your father's unsavory personal affairs and scandalous doings with the "fairer sex" broadcast to the world for several years, to make you a mite skittish about such matters. He was twenty-seven now, much older than most men marrying for the first time. For that matter, Lottie didn't seem to be rushing to the altar either, though she had kept company with one or two young men in the area.

"Ralph? What's the matter with you? I've asked you twice if you're finished with your dinner. Look at your plate! Goodness!"

He looked up to meet the stares from the family, Henry's quizzical, Orah's annoyed, Will's amused, Josie's curious. Forrest, his half brother, grinned. Unlike Orah, he was a happy-go-lucky fellow. Ralph thought that Forrest was most like Roy on a good day. They didn't talk about Roy very much these days.

Lottie stood at his elbow, a stack of dirty dishes in her hands.

He plunged in. "Father, I didn't like to interrupt you, but the fact is, I won't be able to help you clear that north section."

"Sure you will. I know we'll be busy with the planting, but if we . . ."

"No, I mean, I'm going to be working elsewhere." He held up a hand to forestall Henry's interruption. "I've put an option down on the old Whitticomb place over in Leroy."

"Whitticomb? The furniture fellow in Grand Rapids?"

"That's the one. I asked around about that farm off the Tustin road, the one with the little logging cabin up the road. It has a shed barn . . ."

"Son, we can't handle the acreage we have now . . ."

"I'm sorry, I'm putting the cart before the horse here." Ralph's ears felt hot—in fact, his entire face did.

"What I mean to say is, I've asked Harriet Madole for her hand . . ." This sounded foolish and affected to him, but he hurried on, "And she's accepted. We're getting married."

"Ralph, you're never!" Dishes rattled at his ear. Startled, he looked up into Lottie's face, but she was beaming with pleasure for him.

"Why, son, that's wonderful!" Henry rose and came around the table to pound Ralph on the back.

"Lottie! We can be bridesmaids!" Josie's braids quivered at the prospect.

"Oh, silly, the bride chooses her own bridesmaids," reproved Lottie.

Ralph smiled shyly, wondering why he'd been so hangdog about admitting his engagement to the pretty Leroy schoolteacher.

Hattie and Ralph Get a Parcel

LEROY, MICHIGAN, SUMMER 1905

RALPH ARMED SWEAT from his forehead, leaving a black smudge on his faded blue work shirt; he'd been burning out some stumps on the north field. Several cords of firewood lay seasoning under a lean-to against the barn, a testament to his industry in this field.

He could have used the services of Harley, Hattie's old rawboned gelding, but Harriet had driven Harley to town to barter eggs for groceries they needed. Ralph knew that Hattie sometimes used her own money from her meager schoolteaching account in addition to the eggs and garden produce to support the household. This bothered him only slightly; he knew that they each provided whatever they could to the partnership, and together they would make, if not wealth, then at least a living.

He exchanged the mattock for the shovel, to further loosen the stump's roots beneath the hole's surface. Time floated away, followed by his thoughts, as so often happened when he labored hard. He knew that he thought as he worked, but sometimes he couldn't have told you afterward what he'd been thinking about, nor how much time had passed. He worked, he thought, time passed, that was all.

The day was calm and sounds carried across the silent fields. Ralph returned to the present when he heard the "tlot-tlot" of Harley's ground-eating trot.

"Homely as a hedge fence," Hattie would say of the horse that she'd ridden and driven for the past eighteen years, and it was true. Harley was leggy and had a long neck that seemed insufficient to support his huge head with its outsized ears and small eyes. His tail was stringy, his back long "like one of those German sausage-dogs," as Hattie's father had said more than once. But my, how Harley's long legs could eat up the miles! "Pretty is as pretty does," Hattie would reply amiably to her father.

Ralph leaned his tools against the stump (now leaning quite a bit itself; another while and he'd be able to start on the next stump). He straightened his back with a "crii-ck!" and started home; his stomach told him it was nearly lunchtime anyway.

Harriet greeted him with her peaceful smile. Her smile, that clear indicator of her calm and easygoing nature, was what had first drawn him to her. Whenever he saw that quiet smile he was glad afresh that he'd overcome his shyness enough to "walk out" with her.

None of the other women in his life seemed to have that same capacity for calmness and patience, certainly not his mother, ever stern and pious. Nor Lottie, dear and kind as she was; she had a nervousness about her as though she always feared to do the wrong thing. Nor Josie, always busy, always entertained by the world around her, nor Orah, quirky and clever, though given to "moods" now and then. He supposed Hattie had come by it from her years of teaching rooms full of children of all ages. You'd have to be pretty calm and patient, he thought wryly, or you'd burn the place down around your own ears in desperation.

Behind her smile now, however, she seemed uncharacteristically anxious, even fidgety. She'd already taken her groceries in and stored them, and had begun to unhitch Harley. Ralph stepped to the off side and began to help.

"I stopped at the post office and picked up the mail."

"Anything interesting?" It wasn't quite time for the summer Sears and Roebuck catalog, but maybe it had come early; perhaps that accounted for her seeming tenseness, the impatience with which she fumbled with the harness straps and buckles.

"Well, yes. There's a packet, looked like it had been all around the world. When I looked at the address, I saw that it had!"

"What!"

"It's from a Mr. Martin, in Adana, Turkey."

"Charlotte Spencer!"

"I should think so." She gave Harley's bridle a cursory wipe and hung it unceremoniously on the three-nail hanger inside the shed door. Ralph led the animal to the gate and gave him a friendly pat to send him out to pasture.

They hurried to the house, Hattie to begin preparing noon dinner, Ralph to carefully slit open the Adana package with his clasp knife, keeping the string intact and giving especial care to preserving the stamps with their cancellation marks and the return address.

The wrapping was of an almost parchment-like paper, yellowed and with a grainy finish; coarse fibers threaded through it. The writing was water stained and faded; clearly the parcel had passed through many hands, some of them none too clean.

It was addressed to "Thacker, General Delivery, Bensonia, Michigan, United States of America." It had traveled, the cancellation marks indicated, to Bedford, Michigan, thence to Benzonia, then, inexplicably, to Traverse City, before finding its way to Tustin. That the postmaster had delivered the package to Ralph and Hattie rather than to Henry and Orah spoke volumes about community feeling.

Inside were a letter and a worn, leather-bound book. It was the sort of book one kept accounts in; the beaten cover, held to the light at just the right angle, still showed "Ledger" faintly stamped into the leather. He set the bundle aside and unfolded the letter. Standing beside the kitchen table, one hand resting on its oilcloth cover, he read the letter to Hattie, who was digging the eye out of a potato:

"Dear Mr. Thacker,

"Pray forgive my obvious haste in writing to you and preparing this parcel, and forgive me that I do not remember your Christian name. We have experienced two incursions recently of Kurdish irregulars of his majesty Abdul Hamid, laboring under the misapprehension that we harbored 'Young Turk' spies against the government.

"We are all at sixes and sevens, and many of our records have been lost. Among them were the addresses of your late sister-in-law's relatives. I know that Miss Spencer had a brother who lives somewhere in the state of Illinois, but I do not know what town. She had also made mention, on occasion, that her deceased sister Anna is survived by you and several nephews and nieces, in the town of Bensonia."

Ralph grinned, thinking of how Auntie Charlotte must have spoken about her sister's husband and children. Hattie stood patiently, paring knife in one hand, half-peeled potato in the other, and he hastened on.

"As you no doubt know by now, Miss Spencer left the disposition of her material possessions to my wife and me, and we have distributed all of her clothing and personal items among our Armenian students and their families, many of whom suffer great privation.

"In the cleaning of Miss Spencer's quarters, however, one of these young students, Dorya by name, discovered the book which I enclose in this package. Dorya tells us that it had been tucked beneath Miss Spencer's mattress, and that it tumbled into view as the mattress was removed for airing.

"I have not opened it except to determine that it appears to be Miss Spencer's diary or journal; I assure you that as soon as I ascertained its personal nature, I did not show it to a single soul nor did I read any of its contents."

Ralph raised an eyebrow skeptically, but Hattie shook her head. "If he says he didn't read it, I believe him. He's a missionary; he'd sooner steal your aunt's purse than lie so directly about anything."

"You're probably right. My mother wouldn't have, either. Well, I'm not a missionary."

Hattie turned back to the sink and picked up another potato. "You needn't be, for me," was all she said.

Ralph continued reading:

"I send this book to you in the assumption that you will see to its proper disposition.

"I have no doubt you are aware of the high regard in which we hold your sister-in-law, Charlotte Spencer. We trust that she lies in the bosom of her Lord and Savior whom she so strove to emulate. You'll be comforted in the knowledge that although her physical sufferings were great, she bore them with great courage and fortitude and died peacefully.

"Rest assured that we did all that we could to aid and comfort your sister-in-law in her last days, and she died with the praises of her savior upon her lips. We buried her in hallowed ground, beside the remains of our own beloved daughter, Alice.

"Your brother in Christ,

"John Martin"

"She must not have told the Martins very much about us," said Ralph as he slowly refolded the letter and closed it inside the faded cover of the ledger. He and Hattie sat down to their noon meal, and it was late evening before Ralph had a chance to open the ledger.

Charlotte Spencer's Journal

RALPH IMMERSED HIMSELF in the book all evening, fascinated by the various vignettes of life for a group of American missionaries isolated in the eastern Turkish mountains. Charlotte had not made entries every day; he flipped through several pages, noting that days and sometimes weeks and even months might elapse between entries. Occasionally a page would be illustrated in the margins with a sketch of a bird, a flower or tree, and in one case a surprisingly lifelike cartoon of a young woman in Western dress.

He read the entry on that page: "Betsy Jacobson and I packed a small luncheon today and went up the southern slopes of the yayla, where the women drive their goats for the summer grazing. We had seen those slopes in the distance so many times as we traveled to the villages, and indeed the surrounding peaks resemble pictures of the Alps of Switzerland. Betsy's charm and good nature rendered the rather arduous journey a delightful adventure. We lingered for three hours at the highest vantage, her shoulder warm against mine until our elongated shadows warned us that part of our travel home would be in the dark. The light in those eastern mountains is different from any light at home. It seems almost *thinner*, if light may be described as having a density . . ."

Fascinated, he browsed through descriptions of the animals and the countryside, bemused by the affection and admiration that his aunt had for this missionary roommate. Betsy Jacobson, he learned, had returned to the United States in 1883, not long before Aunt Charlotte had left Turkey to rejoin the family to "help take care of Grandpa," as it had been explained to him at the time.

He flipped back until he found an entry in 1884. He had been quite young when Aunt Charlotte arrived. Five? Seven? He thought he had just begun school, his mind all engrossed with the joys of Morning Break with the other boys his age, with the glories of science and history books wrapped together with a strap, and learning to play ball on the large field when the college boys weren't using it. The arrival of a stern and disapproving aunt hadn't impressed him as much as it obviously had the adults around him.

"The house is Bedlam Cottage today. I do believe the children grow more like a herd of western buffalo every week. Henry spoils them unbearably, and then goes his way and leaves poor Sister the task of training their unruly spirits to the right way. I admit to disappointment in young Lottie; I believe she has no affection for me at all, but obeys me from a sense of duty when her mother forces her to. The boys are simply young ruffians, who go their ways and seem completely unaware of my existence at all. I am so lonely, sometimes, but I only weep in private. Sister is so good to me that it makes up for all the others . . ."

His heart smote him briefly. Auntie hadn't been easy to live with, but then he supposed he hadn't either. Sometimes Father would call Roy and him "you little hellions," though he would say it with a twinkle in his eye.

He flipped forward a year, to August in 1885.

"Elvira has finally gone to Glory. She is with Father, at least everyone at the service said so, but then if that is so, where is our mother? I hope I am not unkind when I suggest, only to myself, that Mother had first claim to our father, and once again she may find her place usurped by a woman who only happened along later and served as a sort of governess for us. I know that Anna would never agree that this is a fact; Elvira always favored her. I always felt that Elvira behaved as an older sister to Anna, and a disapproving stepmother to Brainard and me. Of course, everyone in Benzonia has always liked Anna better than me. I wish I felt better, and could return to my true home with the Mission . . ."

"Poor old Auntie," remarked Ralph. Hattie looked at him inquiringly.

"We thought she was a tiresome old imposition, always wanting to be waited on and fussed over, and then a malicious old busybody, trying to cause trouble for Father. Now, I just don't know, seems as though she was more pitiful than anything. I don't suppose anyone but my mother ever showed any real affection for her."

He saw that Hattie had closed her own book, a finger between the pages, and had given him her attention. (He promised himself to try to do better when she wanted to talk and he was immersed in something.)

"I remember one time when Roy and I came racing into the house, whooping and pretending to be Red Indians. We'd been studying about the tribes who'd lived in the Grand Traverse area before the settlers came, and Roy was trying to tomahawk me, or something. Auntie came out and gave us the dickens, and Mother made us go to our rooms and keep quiet until dinner or she'd wear us both out."

"That seems a little harsh, certainly. 'Quiet down' should have been sufficient, used in the right tone of voice. You hadn't broken anything, had you?"

"No, but we should have thought. Our grandmother'd been shot, we think by a Dakota Indian or maybe a Chippewa, and Auntie was kind of sensitive about it."

"I suppose she might be. That was her mother, was it?"

"It was, and I think she was in the room when it happened. I guess if my own mother'd been shot . . ." He stopped, not wanting to think too much about how his own mother had died.

"Well, you were young. I suppose you hadn't any understanding of how an older woman would feel."

"We hadn't, true enough. We thought Auntie was the crossest patch in the whole state of Michigan."

He added anxiously, "Do you mind, Hattie, if I finish reading this all through before giving you a turn at it? I do mean for you to read it as well, that is, if you want to?"

"I wouldn't mind. You go ahead. My, look at the time! I'm going up. You stay and read some more if you like." She put her own book aside.

Reluctantly, Ralph set the ledger on the side table. Mornings came early, and it would still be there the next day.

As he resumed reading the next evening he had to chuckle at himself. He always looked forward to the few minutes he allowed himself, after dinner and evening chores were complete, before preparing for bed, to read a few pages of something. History and natural history intrigued him, but sometimes he dipped into a collection of stories or novellas; he loved the escape into other places and times, other people's minds and hearts.

He read about Auntie's helpful assistance in delivering Will and Josie in their turns; to hear her tell about it, she was the faithful old family retainer who saw to everything. His own recollection was of Mrs. Waters coming to help them for a spell, and clucking her tongue at Aunt Charlotte's imperious summons when Auntie required something at an inopportune time.

Several more entries lingered, almost lovingly, on Auntie's hatred of the girl who had come to Help Out. If Ralph and his siblings had considered Charlotte Spencer a termagant, he imagined what Orah must have thought. He remembered a distinct chill between those two during the two or three years Orah had been with them, and at the time he couldn't understand it; the rest of the family had breathed a sigh of relief when Mother was allowed to sit and rest once in a while. She'd been less handy with the switch once she was allowed some occasional peace and quiet, he knew that.

Of course there was, after Father's remarriage, ever a polite distance between Orah and her stepchildren. Some of that was natural, but he could also feel that Orah had never forgiven any of them for the reception she'd received from them on her wedding day.

He wasn't sure she'd ever forgiven his father, though she'd never shown it outwardly in front of them. He'd heard rumors that her buggy excursions with Ada, who was Hattie's stepmother, weren't entirely innocent. The rumors questioned the paternity of Orah's baby daughter, who died before she was a week old and had never been given a name. Orah had doted on young Forrest, named for her favorite brother, but hadn't been seen to cry at the baby girl's burial. Ralph had been working in a lumber camp in the Upper Peninsula during that time, but Lottie whispered the sad story to him when he'd returned home.

He shook his head at this and reopened the ledger to the place he'd marked, with a scrap of the paper from its parcel wrapping. Hattie had carefully snipped John Martin's return address and tucked it into her address book. She would, he knew, write a letter of acknowledgment to

Mr. Martin. He smiled; it would cause a sensation at the post office when she purchased the stamps to mail it to Turkey.

An entry from fall of 1891 read, "If That Woman comes into this room again today, I swear to Goshen I'll throw my dish of stew right into her face. I cannot understand why Sister allows her to run roughshod over the household as though she were the one who 'held the keys.' I'm sure she goes through my possessions in my absence. Brother Henry makes sheep's eyes at her when he thinks nobody's watching. It's disgusting!"

Bemused, Ralph flipped through more pages. "That Woman" was the kindest reference. "Harlot," "strumpet," and "trollop" made their appearance with a certain regularity as well. He wouldn't have thought Auntie had it in her to use words like that.

Thunderstruck, he stared at a paragraph on the left leaf of the page. Absently, he noticed that the handwriting had grown more cramped and difficult to decipher, but the word blazed redly up at him: "Whoremaster"!

"My Lord," he murmured. He'd heard the word before, of course, but certainly not from any respectable source. Once when he was thirteen, he and Charlie had giggled over the "Whore of Babylon" reference in the book of Revelation, but "whoremaster"? From the pen of his own prim spinster aunt?

He returned to the top of the page and read the paragraphs leading up to that shocking word: "I cannot tolerate the situation another day. Sister continues blind and obdurate. No, not blind. She understands perfectly well what is going on, I can see the pain in her poor, worn face. She *will not* take control of the situation as she ought, and I, a frail and delicate woman, have not felt up to the task."

A smudge was on the page here, and Ralph couldn't tell just what it was. Something greenish . . .

"And now, after all I've tried to do for her, Sister speaks of sending me away! I see that I must intervene, and what I do, though harsh, is for the good of all of us. Drastic measures are required if we are to summon the involvement of a more firm hand. (I believe that Mary Bailey would be just the ticket.)

"I have suffered with illness for a good long period of time myself, oh yes, and I know how much a body can endure and still go on. Well, let us see how much affection the Whoremaster and his strumpet retain for one another as they vomit helplessly for hours at a time. . . ."

The next paragraph must have been written later, though Charlotte's earlier habit of dating entries, more erratic as the journal continued, had quite gone by the wayside by this part of the ledger.

"Practical considerations render it impossible to administer the medicine to That Man and That Woman only. And I find that I could not do that to the children, much as they dislike me and I, I must admit, care less and less for them as the months go by. I cannot help comparing them to our blessed Armenian orphans, so full of humility and gratitude for every help we give them, so patient and earnest. Dear little children! It is on their behalf that I withhold my hand from giving us *all* a good strong dose of the medicine."

And how long had Aunt Charlotte (impossible, now, to think of her as "Auntie"!) brooded before the next entry?

"I see now that it must be Anna, who is ever in this room with me, whose food and drink often passes through my hands (as mine passes through hers). My heart reproaches me for the misery this must cause her, though it will be only misery of the body, a peccadillo compared to the misery of the heart that she and I have both felt these past few years. The Lord will forgive me because I mean this for the best. When That Woman is gone from the house and perhaps from the town entirely, there will be no need for me to hide the truth about the step I am taking. Sister, most likely, will approve of my little stratagem."

It Is Finished

RALPH TOOK A deep breath. He felt Hattie's eyes on him, so he stretched ostentatiously before continuing. "Dear Lord, I pray that I haven't given her too much of the medicine! I have had to estimate the dosage, and Anna isn't a large woman. Of course the symptoms are extreme. They must be extreme, to attract the notice of Mary Bailey, Dr. Dean, and others. But oh, kindly Savior who leads us through life's daily toils and snares, why must she vomit and purge so violently that she bleeds from every orifice? Surely, if her body expels the toxic substances with this much vigor it will begin to heal itself immediately after the final dose.

"I fear that my sister's strength isn't up to this trial. What if, oh dearest heaven forbid, she should die of this medicine? How can I live in this benighted village without my dearest relation? And what if, oh horrors, the responsibility of her death, however accidental, is laid at my door? Have I the strength to live with the public disgrace? While the Thacker name is already soiled beyond redemption, the Spencers are still held in utmost regard by all who remember Father.

"They believe me! It is a wonder, how simple it is to decoy the suspicions of the gullible. May God forgive me that this mendacity comes to me so easily. Truly, Satan's wiles and traps are easy to fall into, and difficult to extricate oneself from! How I will pray and do penance when this ordeal is over. Sister, forgive me. Jesus, in your infinite mercy, forgive me.

"How pathetic that I once felt the stirrings of regard and even affection for my foolish brother-in-law. I would even now prefer to point the finger of suspicion at the Harlot, but alas, now that public opinion has (at last!) driven her far from our door, nobody would believe it possible.

"So it shall be Henry Thacker. So obvious, when one considers it. (And in truth, he has poisoned the very air of this household!) Mary Bailey, ah, dear, strong Mary Bailey, is only too happy to believe anything of him, and of course Dr. Dean . . .

"It is finished. God, have mercy. Christ, have mercy, have mercy upon me, a miserable sinner, in my manifold sins and wickedness. The final dose, indeed. I am a wicked, foolish woman. A murderess? No, not that, never that. I loved my sister, even as she persisted in her blindness and fondness for her ne'er-do-well husband. I loved her dearly, and now she is gone.

"Her children, whom I wished to love, despise me. Why do they not despise the true cause of Anna's pain and death? They consort with the Whore and her paramour, and cast cold and contemptuous looks at their mother's dearest relative. Truly, I'm well away from that house. Lord, I abase myself before thee. In pain I shall approach thee, and I shall live in penance and humility all the days of my life . . ."

HE SAT BACK in his chair, realizing his neck was slightly stiff. The tension with which he'd been reading must have been immense; chopping stump roots never caused this much stiffness!

He had long believed that Mother hadn't written the "suicide" note. She would never do such a thing, and she would never have written so childishly, no matter how feeble she'd grown toward the end. He considered this again, reaching the same conclusion as he had before. Lottie, of course; she knew how to spell "feels," certainly, just as she knew, at fourteen, how to be the woman of the house. But at fourteen, she was still a child in her moods, and none of them were at their best during those dreadful days.

Hattie was no longer in her chair; she'd gone up without his even noticing. He closed the book and set it on the side table, and went up to bed too. Harriet lay asleep already; early mornings and long days of work did that for a person. But he lay awake for a long time, considering.

RALPH LATCHED the outhouse door. The new house was to have modern indoor plumbing, but Mr. Whitticomb's loan had only gone so far. The plumbing would have to wait for another year or two, or maybe longer. He sat on the edge between the two seats, and pulled the ledger from inside his shirt. He took his clasp-knife from his pocket and opened it. Opening the book, he smoothed it on his knee. He removed the slab of pasteboard that he'd tucked into the book this morning, and slid it behind several pages. He sliced through those pages and removed them; he could drop them into the stove later on.

"I see you've finished with her journal."

"Yes, indeed," he was pleased with how casual his voice was. "Aunt Charlotte was quite a character, all right. I'll let you read it for yourself if you like, and you can tell me what you think."

HATTIE CLOSED the book and set it aside. "It's surely interesting. Did you notice, Ralph, that some of the pages were missing?"

"I noticed. Those were about the time that Mother took sick and died. Things got pretty terrible. I wouldn't be a bit surprised if Aunt Charlotte wasn't ashamed of some of the things she said about us, later on, and took those out."

"A sensible thing to do. Shall your father want to read this, do you think, or would he find it too painful?"

He thought about his father, a mostly good, kindly, hardworking man, prosperous in his time. He'd be honored wherever he went, had he not been led by his weakness. Orah, now, he could never really understand his father's fatuousness in regard to Orah. She was nice-looking, Ralph supposed, and clever and even witty at times. But something had been left out of her. She never quite seemed to realize where the border lay between rectitude and, well, whatever she felt like doing or saying.

Ralph still squirmed inwardly when he recalled Henry's visit, that summer day last year when Orah and Ada had dressed to the nines and gone stepping out, wide-brimmed hats flapping in the breeze as they drove down the road to town.

"I know she's being unfaithful to me," Henry had confessed, tears brimming his eyes, his nose reddening unbecomingly. Ralph noticed with some surprise that his once-handsome father was becoming an old man, and not a very distinguished-looking one at that.

"But what can I do? I love her, always have. She's still my Girlie."

Ralph poured his father a cup of tea and gave him a consoling pat on the shoulder, yet what could he say, really?

It hadn't escaped Ralph's notice that long marriages could mellow into something kindly, pleasant, a friendship and business partnership that made life nicer for everyone around. Or they could deteriorate into mutual despite, the unwilling partners yoked to a hateful course, and everyone suffered.

When he married Harriet Madole he had felt some stirrings of a determination. Now, as his father cried into his teacup, it took a more concrete form. He would work hard, like his father had, but he would also live in friendship with his wife, no matter what the future brought. He wanted his children to never need feel pity for their own parents.

Ralph felt bad about his prevarication regarding Charlotte Spencer's ledger, yet how could he bind his wife to a secret against the rest of her in-laws? Or should he turn the book over to his father, or to the authorities? No. Enough was enough. The sad story had crept, like the rot from one potato in a barrel in the cellar, into too many lives already.

It was enough to have already involved Hattie, however distantly, in the public part of the story. Whenever he went to Benzonia to visit the Rideouts, Harriet, too, would meet the bland, empty stares of other townspeople who remembered, would always remember, the cuckoos in their nest.

"I expect Father doesn't need to know about it. What's past is past. Interesting as the stories about Turkey are, I was thinking of putting it into the stove."

"You do what you think best," was all Hattie said to this. Ralph, relieved, began to serve himself squash, running with melted butter. They had recently purchased a young Holstein; she was a lot of work, but paid for herself every day in milk, butter, and sour cream. The young Thackers were among the first in the area to experiment with sour cream on their baked potatoes; this was an invention of Hattie's, and Ralph enjoyed it very much.

He felt, rather than heard, the long silence, and looked up. Harriet smiled at him, a little sadly.

"Oh, I know, she wasn't my aunt. I didn't know her, and I needn't know what secrets she may have had."

Their eyes met. Slowly, Ralph nodded.

Hattie began to stand up, to fetch one thing or another that women feel a meal requires, but Ralph laid a hand on her arm to stop her.

"Tell me what you need, and I'll get it."

Hattie sat back down.

"Not a thing. We really don't need another thing."

The Next Generation

LEROY, MICHIGAN, SUMMER 1917

CHARLOTTE LIMPED ACROSS the dooryard, trying to control the trembling of her lower lip. The ache in her foot was sickening; she imagined she could still feel the point of the nail as it punched into the bottom of her bare foot, into that place between ball and arch, where the tendons flex and slide with every step.

Almost worse than the ache was the terror. People who stepped on nails sometimes got lockjaw, a terrible sickness that you never got better from, and you died in frightful agonies, so all the women put on their black Sunday clothes and hats and came to church and whispered and looked at each other meaningfully. Lockjaw was probably worse than scarlet fever or even cholera, Charlotte thought.

In addition to the pain and terror, Charlotte was ashamed of herself. Here she was, seven going on eight, old enough to take care of baby Francis who was just beginning to walk. Gale, only a year older, was able to help with the haying, the milking, and the potato harvest.

She had been named for her aunt Lottie, Papa's younger sister. "You're much prettier than your aunt," her mother had told her privately, "but you'll have your work cut out for you to turn out as brave and true as she."

Now here she was, she repeated in disgust to herself, a great big girl, stepping on nails like an ignorant baby and nearly crying about it. This thought, rather than steadying her, made her eyes fill. Furiously she dashed her forearm across her eyes, took a tremulous breath, and walked right into Grandpa Henry.

"Here, here," he chided gently, catching her by the shoulders. "You're not crying, are you? A big girl like you?"

"No," she gulped, "I'm just . . ." she floundered, not really knowing just what she was going to do. "Grandpa, I just stepped on a nail like a stupid baby and what if I get lockjaw and we don't have any money for a doctor, and if I die I'll miss the spelling bee!" Her worries became jumbled in her own mind, and she wasn't sure whether her foot felt better or worse.

Grandpa Henry patted her on the back, his brow furrowed in thought about how he might comfort her. He brightened and turned Charlotte so that she faced the barn. "Do you see that weathervane up there? On the west end of the barn?"

Charlotte nodded, somewhat put out by the foolishness of the question. Of course she saw it; she saw it every day of her life. It saw her out of sight nine months of the year as she set off down the dirt road with Gale on the walk to school. It welcomed her back in the afternoons, glinting, in the winter, in the sideways light of the setting sun. It had a bit of glass embedded in it that sometimes shown like it had a tiny lantern inside. Charlotte had secretly thought of this homely object as a benign presence in her life, something that watched over her like God but didn't demand that she be good in return.

"I got that weathervane at the state fair oh, maybe ten years ago. We got the prize for new potatoes; it was just a ribbon and a couple of dollars, but a fellow had a booth there with brass weathervanes and boot jacks. Well, we already had a boot jack, don't you know." He chuckled in that annoying way that adults often had when they said something that wasn't, in Charlotte's opinion, the least bit funny.

Charlotte didn't understand the point to Grandpa Henry's ramblings, but his voice was comforting nonetheless. She noticed with some surprise that her foot didn't ache as deeply as it had.

Grandpa went on, "I've always been partial to that weathervane, but you know, nobody lives forever, so I think I'll give it to you now. It'll be your own personal weathervane, yours especially."

Charlotte considered this. She owned a few things: a doll, her clothes, some books, but she had never before thought of owning a real part of the family farm. The lands, the buildings, the tools, were just there, just part of the world, like air and food. The idea that part of it could be hers was a new and somewhat unnerving thought.

She looked at the weathervane with new eyes, lockjaw and ache in foot momentarily forgotten. She looked gravely up at Grandpa Henry and nodded her thanks. He nodded gravely back at her. Charlotte went on into the kitchen and began to pour hot water from the kettle into a basin. "Wind's turning around to the west," she informed her mother importantly, and sat down to soak her foot.

The End

Afterword

AS MOST AMERICAN CHILDREN enter their teens, a typical rite of passage is marked by their elders' deeming they are old enough to know "the facts of life." It was the same in our family. One day in our teens we heard the timeworn phrase "I think you're old enough to hear . . ." followed by ". . . the story of your great-grandmother's murder."

Some of my best memories of my father's family center around the lively debates at the dining room table at the farm. The dining table debates among my father, Thomas, my uncles Gale and Francis, and my aunt Charlotte (named after Lottie, Ralph's sister), with occasional corrections from my grandfather Ralph and his sister Aunt Jo ("Josie" from the story) concerned the murder (or could it have been suicide?) of our ancestor Anna.

On the surface, the facts are these:

Anna Spencer, her sister, Charlotte, and her brother, David Brainard, were the children of missionary parents. In their early childhood their mother, Cornelia, was shot by an unknown person, probably an Indian, while sitting up with young Charlotte, who was ailing.

David Spencer Sr. remarried soon after, and the family moved to Benzonia, the site of a Congregationalist college. Years later, William Henry Thacker, a young student at the college, boarded with the Spencers. Eventually he married the older, less attractive of the Spencer girls.

Anna died, in 1894, of a mysterious ailment. Her sister, Charlotte, became suspicious and demanded an autopsy. The body was dug up, and arsenic was found in the tissues in such an amount as to have been the probable cause of her death.

Henry was accused of her murder primarily because he'd been "carrying on" with the young and pretty housekeeper, Orah. He was convicted and served two years in prison before a suicide note was found under mysterious circumstances. This prompted a retrial, resulting in a different verdict.

As soon as he was released, he immediately married Orah. In a fit of righteous indignation the townspeople of Benzonia drove the family out. Sister Charlotte removed herself to Eastern Turkey and died ten years later, shortly before the massacre of the Armenians by the Turks began.

Henry and Orah eventually sold their farm at the start of the Depression and moved to Detroit, where Henry worked as a road mender until he died of a stroke. Orah supported herself by keeping a boardinghouse after that.

Ralph married Harriet Madole, and they raised four children, all of whom lived long and well. Their second son, Francis, still lives on the farm Ralph and Harriet purchased. In the year 2005, the family farm became a Centennial Farm.

Interestingly, among all of Ralph and Harriet's married descendents there is only one divorce, even to the present day.

To this day, questions abound. Was Henry, known by most of the town of Benzonia (and by his own children and grandchildren) to be the most gentle and amiable of men, capable of murdering, with malice aforethought, his wife, the mother of his five children? Could Orah, who also had motive, have been the perpetrator? Or was someone else guilty? Or did Anna, pious daughter and sister of missionaries, indeed commit suicide? If not, who did write the conveniently discovered suicide note?

Charlotte Spencer remains an enigma. Why did Henry marry the older, plainer Anna instead of prettier Charlotte? Did Charlotte become a missionary to nurse a broken heart or from religious fervor, or for some other reason? Why, then, had Charlotte returned from Turkey?

Her nieces and nephews remember her as a tedious and fretful invalid, constantly demanding attention, while the missionaries with whom she served apparently admired her greatly, describing her as devout and almost saintly. Her testimony, taken directly from the trial transcripts, was rambling, broken, and filled with non sequiturs, sometimes almost incoherent.

Why was she living with Anna and Henry? Was she actually the invalid she seemed to be, and if so, how did she find the strength to undertake the rigors of a trip back to Turkey in the 1890s, only to die within the decade at a relatively young age?

Who placed the stone on Anna's grave that proclaimed, somewhat gratuitously, "Faithful Unto Death"? Not the least strange, to my mind, is: what was a common Michigan farming family doing with a house-keeper anyway?

My search for some of the answers took me on a search through a number of sources, starting, of course, with those relatives then living who remembered Henry and Orah and remembered some of the stories and anecdotes from Ralph, Lottie, and Josephine, who had lived through Anna's death and their father's two murder trials.

A visit to Benzonia provided newspaper reports of the events and some photos, including of Anna's mysterious headstone and of the Thacker house, which still stands, though fire damaged and abandoned. The newspaper stories guided us to the Benzie County courthouse, where we were able to obtain copies of transcripts from the first trial.

While some of these documents are used in the novel, I have made some alterations to make them more readable and consistent with the story.

Newspaper accounts provided the detail about the second trial. The Historical Society of Benzonia possessed surprisingly little information about the events in their town; it was as if nobody, even one hundred years later, wanted to discuss the case at all.